Conveni ound

Three royal ki ge—
or love?

When the kingdoms of the Three Isles—Aidara,
Mattan and Kirtida—are threatened, for their
young royal leaders duty becomes paramount.
But in putting their countries first, they discover
that their strategic marriages in name only run
the risk of opening their guarded hearts to love…
for real!

Find out more in:

United by Their Royal Baby

Childhood sweethearts Queen Leyna of Aidara
and King Xavier of Mattan bear the emotional
scars of ruling alone. But they now have nine
months to find their way back to each other
again…

Available now!

Falling for His Convenient Queen

King Zacchaeus of Kirtida and Princess Nalini
of Mattan must unite their families in a marriage
of convenience to secure their two kingdoms. But
Nalini wants more than the cold marriage
Zacchaeus has to offer. And it's up to her to
rescue his heart.

Available February 2018!

UNITED BY THEIR ROYAL BABY

BY
THERESE BEHARRIE

First Published in Great Britain 2018
By Mills & Boon, an imprint of HarperCollins*Publishers*
1 London Bridge Street, London, SE1 9GF

© 2018 Therese Beharrie

ISBN: 978-0-263-93636-0

23-0118

MIX
Paper from
responsible sources
FSC™ C007454

This book is produced from independently certified FSC™ paper to ensure responsible forest management.

For more information visit: www.harpercollins.co.uk/green

Printed and bound in Spain
by CPI, Barcelona

Therese Beharrie has always been thrilled by romance. Her love of reading established this, and now she gets to write happily-ever-afters for a living and about all things romance in her blog at www.theresebeharrie.com. She married a man who constantly exceeds her romantic expectations and is an infinite source of inspiration for her romantic heroes. She lives in Cape Town, South Africa, and is still amazed that her dream of being a romance author is a reality.

For Grant, the light who helps me face my fears.
Thank you for always treating me like a queen.

And Luke and Leah,
I hope when you grow up, reading books where
characters look like you is the norm.
For now, this is for you.

I love you.

PROLOGUE

PRINCESS LEYNA OF AIDARA thought she'd never been more content than right at that moment. She had the sun shining on her, the ocean in front of her and the sandy beach around her.

And, of course, she had the future King of Mattan lying next to her.

'We should do this more often,' she said, and dug her back a little deeper into the sand.

'We do this at least once a week, Leyna.'

She could hear the amusement in Xavier's tone and her lips curved.

'We *visit* the beach at least once a week. Doing this—' she lifted a hand into the air and gestured to the towels that lay side by side '—is a rarity that we should definitely make more time for.'

'You're only saying that because you want to escape your royal duties,' Xavier teased.

'And you don't?' she shot back, turning her head to offer him a grin.

And ignoring the inner voice that sounded dangerously like her grandmother telling her that Xavier was an excuse to do just that.

'I'm the future King of Mattan, Princess,' he said, sarcasm dripping from his voice. 'I'm aware of my duties. Even though there are things expected of me that I can't possibly *begin* to imagine.'

Hearing the fatigue, the annoyance just beneath his words, she turned her body to face him, resting her head on her hand. 'Are your mother and grandmother at it again?'

He mirrored her position. Before she could stop herself, her eyes took in his muscular body, the dark brown hair that was a mess from their swim earlier and the kindness that was clear in every feature of his face. Her heart began to race. And then she told herself to stop it, and notice how that kindness was now eclipsed by sadness—tinged with the slightest bit of anger—that she knew came from his hopelessness about his family.

'When are they *not* at it?' He shook his head. 'Every time I think I do something right, they counter with something I should have done instead.' He paused. 'Maybe I'm just not doing anything right.'

'Oh, that's rubbish and you know it.' She sat up now, curling her legs under her. 'I've never seen someone put more effort into their crown than you have.'

'Besides you, you mean,' he said with a smile.

'Of course.' She smiled back, though the voice in her head had returned, this time telling her she would put in even more if she didn't have Xavier in her life. 'But what I meant was that that dedication already means you're doing something right, Xavier. Trust it.'

She reached over to squeeze the back of his hand, but he turned his over so quickly she didn't know it until his fingers threaded through hers. Her heart jumped, and she opened her mouth to cut off what she knew was coming.

'No,' he said before she could. 'You're not going to put me off this time, Leyna.'

'What…what do you mean?'

'I'd like you to marry me.'

Her chest tightened. 'I don't think that—'

'Both our families want this, Leyna,' he interrupted.

'They want Aidara and Mattan bonded, yes. This— you and I?' She shook her head. 'They aren't *quite* as invested in that.' When he didn't answer her, she frowned. 'You know this. You know what they think about our friendship.'

'But I know what *we* think about our friendship, too. Don't you think that's more important?'

She didn't know what to say. But she *did* know that she was glad they were on Aidara's private beach, where there would be no prying eyes witnessing their conversation.

'Leyna.' He sat up now. 'There is no choice for me. I *have* to marry you or my heart won't ever forgive me.' The seriousness in his eyes upped her heart rate even more. 'I know you feel the same way, too.'

'Why are you doing this?'

'Because it's time,' he said simply. He stood, and held out a hand to help her do the same. She took it, but when she was on her feet she snatched her hand back.

'It's time to ruin something that means more to me than anything else?'

'No. It's time to finally make this—*us*—into what we were always supposed to be, Leyna. A family.'

'I *have* family. I have parents who are King and Queen of a kingdom that needs them.'

So they don't have time for me to need them.

'And a grandmother whose heart is still broken from losing her husband almost ten years ago.'

And who's so focused on the crown she can't support the person who'll one day wear it.

'I have family, Xavier,' she repeated. 'What I *don't* have are friends. I need us to be friends.'

'You don't think we'd be friends if we were married?' His sombre tone told her things would probably change between them now, regardless of what she chose.

The panic inside her told her to make the right choice.

'We're best as friends. *Just* friends.'

'Is that you speaking, or your family?'

'It's me.' But a part of her wondered. 'I haven't listened to what they've said about us before. I don't care about that.'

'Then why are you so scared of what's between us, Leyna?' He closed the space between them with one step.

'Because…' She cleared her throat when her words came out more breathily than she wanted. 'Our lives aren't easy. The thing that's helped me through it is our friendship. We've been friends for almost twenty years.' Her voice broke. 'Don't take that away from me.'

He lifted her chin. 'I'm not taking anything away from you. I want to add to that friendship.' The left side of his mouth curved into a half-smile. 'Yes, we've been friends for twenty years. But you know I've been in love with you for most of that time.' She opened her mouth to dispute his words, but he shook his head. 'You know it's true.'

'No,' she said firmly.

'Really?' he drawled. 'Why have you been trying to stop me from saying it to you for all these years then?' His eyebrows lifted when she didn't reply, and then he nodded. 'Because you *do* know it. We both have from the moment I gave you that rose when we were five.'

When her heart melted at even the memory of it, she finally acknowledged the truth of his words. But he was right. She *was* scared. Scared of the change, and of what that change would mean for her life. One day she would be Queen of Aidara and she knew what that would demand from her.

And it wasn't because her grandmother had warned her of the demands of the role. Or the way she constantly referred to Xavier as a distraction, and their friendship as 'childish'. After years of defending what they had, Leyna had learnt to brush it off, knowing that Kathleen had a limited idea of what real relationships were.

No, Leyna's fears had nothing to do with Xavier, and everything to do with what she knew those demands would cost her. Because she'd seen exactly how they had affected her father.

King Clive had gone from exuberant Prince to reserved King. She had memories of her father being happy, chasing her around the royal gardens as her mother watched on, laughing. But in the ten years since he'd become King, that man had slowly faded away. Wrinkles of stress had replaced those of laughter. Every smile he gave her seemed like the hardest thing in the world.

The only remnant of the man her father used to be was the love he clearly still had for her mother. It made her ask, 'Will you still love me when I become Queen, when you become King, and we both have the hardest jobs in the world?'

'Of course I will.' His hand moved from her chin to brush away a stray curl. 'Who better to love and support you than someone who knows *exactly* what you're going through?'

'It's going to be harder than anything we've had to do so far, Xavier,' she said, to remind herself just as much as to remind him. 'You've seen what it's done to my father,' she whispered.

'We'll get through it,' Xavier said softly.

'What if we got through it better as just friends?'

'We've never been just friends, Leyna.'

'So why bring it all up now?'

'Because it's your birthday in two days. You'll be twenty-one and you'll be expected to marry. Just as I've been expected to marry for the last year.'

She pulled a lip between her teeth at the reminder of their one-year age difference.

'You know I've been waiting for you. It's the only reason I've managed to put my family off. I love you, Leyna. I want to be married to you. And I know that we'll be stronger together than we'll ever be apart. Apart here meaning *just* being friends.'

She smiled at that and felt the punishing pulse of fear ease. 'It's not as charming as you think, you know. Having all the answers.'

She saw the relief in his features, and he grinned. 'And yet you're still in love with me.'

'Full of yourself, too.'

'But you love me,' he insisted.

She studied him and felt a smile claim her lips. 'Since you seem so sure, I suppose I don't have to say it.'

'If you don't say it, I'll be forced to carry you back into that water.'

'And *I'll* be forced to decline your proposal.'

His eyes widened in mock fear. 'You *wouldn't*.'

'You have no idea what I'm capable of.'

'Show me.'

The teasing tone of his voice disappeared in a flash, and the light that had been in his eyes heated.

'Are you *propositioning*—'

She was silenced by his lips on hers.

It wasn't their first kiss—that had happened when they were thirteen and fourteen, beneath the very palm tree they stood under now. But it might as well have been their first. When they were barely teenagers, the kiss had been out of curiosity. It had been exploratory. As had the other kisses they'd shared since.

None of them compared to this.

It had the heat of a summer's day in Aidara. And the promise of passion that had been restrained for years. Leyna's arms were around Xavier's waist before she fully knew it, their bodies so close together she could feel every part of him. Her body responded and, for the first time in her life, Leyna felt like a woman. Not a daughter or a granddaughter. Certainly not like the heir to a throne.

No, she felt like a *woman*.

One who could make a man moan just as Xavier did now. One who had the power to make a man lift her from the ground and press her against the trunk of a tree so he could press even closer to her. She was lost in the sensation of his lips against hers, of his tongue in her mouth.

She was suddenly grateful they were at the beach, wearing the attire required by their location. It meant she didn't have to battle with clothing to feel the muscular planes of Xavier's body. It meant she could enjoy the way his hands touched—*claimed*—the curves of hers.

When his hand lifted a thigh so he could angle himself against her, Leyna heard a sound come from her throat. She felt Xavier still, and then he pulled his head away, just far enough so he could look into her eyes.

'What's wrong?'

'Nothing,' she breathed, and put a hand on the back of his neck, urging him closer.

'Leyna,' Xavier said. 'I've known you all my life. Tell me.'

'I just…' She felt her face burn. 'I've just never…'

'You know I haven't either.'

'I know,' she echoed, knowing that if Xavier had had another woman, she would have known about it. 'But… are we doing this now? Against a tree on a beach, with our bodyguards a short distance away?'

'I… I didn't think about that.'

Xavier took a deep breath, and then took a step back. Leyna immediately missed the contact.

'I didn't mean that we can't do it at all. I just… Well, I just pictured it on our wedding night. In a bed surrounded by candles and rose petals. With champagne cooling.'

She sounded like a fool. More so when silence followed her words. But then Xavier smiled.

'You *pictured* it?'

Her cheeks went hot, but she laughed. 'Maybe.'

'On our wedding night?'

Her heart softened at the emotion she heard in his voice. 'Yes.'

'So you always knew there was more, too?'

'Of course I did. Did you think I was resisting something I knew wasn't true?' She frowned. 'You were so sure…?'

'I was betting with the most important thing in my life, Leyna. I had to be.'

She stared at him, and then shook her head. 'If I didn't already love you, Xavier, I think I might have fallen for you right now.'

'But you do. Love me.'

'I do.' And, realising that he needed to hear the words, she said, 'I love you, Xavier.'

He pulled her into his arms and rested his forehead on hers. 'And you're going to marry me.'

'I am,' she answered, though it wasn't a question. 'As soon as I possibly can.'

'I think this might be—'

It happened so quickly that Leyna barely registered what had cut Xavier off. All she knew was that her royal aide, Carlos, was now standing in front of her and Xavier. Their bodyguards hovered just beyond him; their expressions were twisted with an emotion she couldn't read, but it had her heart pounding with fear.

'What is it?' she asked, stepping out of Xavier's embrace.

'I'm sorry to interrupt—' there was the briefest moment of hesitation before Carlos said '—Your Majesty.'

CHAPTER ONE

Ten years later

'Is he here, Carlos?'

'I'm afraid not, Your Majesty.'

For the second time in Leyna's life, Carlos had brought her news of the last thing she wanted to hear. Now, of course, he was bringing it to her as her private secretary and not as a royal aide.

But then, her father's death had changed more than just Carlos' title. She'd become Queen immediately, and had lost the only man she'd loved. And now the news that King Zacchaeus of Kirtida had not arrived for the State Banquet intended to affirm the Alliance of the Three Isles threatened to be just as life-changing.

She closed her eyes for the briefest moment and then nodded. Released a breath.

'Please find His Majesty, King Xavier, and ask him to join me in the library.'

'Of course, Your Majesty.'

When Carlos left, Leyna took another deep breath. And a moment to deal with the feelings tumbling through her stomach. She opened the doors to the balcony of her library and greedily inhaled the fresh air.

It felt like the only thing keeping her alive.

The panic came now. Not dull as it had been when she'd first heard that King Jaydon of Kirtida had been overthrown by his son, Zacchaeus. And nowhere near how it had felt when he'd consistently refused her and Xavier's attempts to discuss the future of the alliance binding their islands together, though she'd believed it sharp then.

No, the feeling cutting through her lungs now, tightening her throat and making her hands shake, was much worse.

But she only had a few moments before Carlos returned with Xavier. She forced herself to focus on her breathing, something she'd learnt to do when she'd taken over the crown after her father's death.

When her heart, broken from her breakup with Xavier and from her mother fleeing, had beat so hard she thought it would explode from her chest.

She straightened her spine when she heard the knock on the door, turning in time to see Xavier stride past Carlos into the library. As it always did when she saw Xavier—despite the fact that their relationship now was only a political courtesy—her chest tightened.

She told her memories to stay where they belonged, but couldn't help the relief that washed through her at his presence.

'He's not here,' Xavier said immediately, and she tried not to wince at the tone.

'He's not. Which means—'

'That he is renouncing Kirtida's place in the Alliance of the Three Isles.'

'I'd like to think that isn't true. That Kirtida is still a part of our alliance.' She saw a glint in his blue—almost grey—eyes, and tilted her head. 'But his actions since he overthrew Jaydon speak volumes.'

'Refusing our calls to set up meetings *and* refusing to see us when we resorted to just arriving at Kirtida in hopes of a meeting?' Xavier asked gravely. 'Tonight was the last hope we had that he's willing to work with us, Leyna. So yes, I think his actions tell us exactly where we stand with him.'

'If we assume he'll withdraw—' panic rippled through her chest again '—what do we do?'

'We respond accordingly.'

'How?'

'We ensure that Zacchaeus knows the alliance between Aidara and Mattan is still intact. We ensure that our people know it, too.'

'I'm sure there isn't any doubt about that,' Leyna said. 'You *are* here at the dinner intended to do that very thing after all.'

'It isn't enough.'

She saw the determination in his eyes—in each of the once kind, now intimidating angles of his handsome face—and the relief she'd felt steadily ebbed. Her body tensed, and she saw that tension reflected in his tall, muscular frame, too.

'What do you have in mind?' she asked carefully.

'Something that will leave Zacchaeus and our people without any doubt about the strength of our alliance. Something that will reassure our people that Kirtida's absence from the Alliance of the Three Isles doesn't mean they are unprotected.'

Silence pulsed in the room, and then Leyna said, 'Tell me what you'd like us to do, Xavier.'

'We should get married.'

Leyna's thoughts immediately went back to that day on the beach when Xavier had proposed to her.

Her knees nearly buckled and she turned away from

him and walked straight onto the balcony. She gripped the railing and fought for breath. And then she fought to be free of the memories.

They were vicious, she thought, and crept up on her when she least wanted them to. She'd only been fooling herself with her hope that they'd stay in the past. But she'd been desperate. Perhaps because she knew every moment she spent with Xavier would threaten to draw her back into what could have been.

She couldn't afford for that to happen. She couldn't afford to think about the hope, the love, that she'd felt on the day he'd proposed to her. If she did, she would inevitably think of the cold feeling that had come over her when Carlos had first called her 'Your Majesty'.

She would think about the days she'd spent in a daze of heartbreak, worsened by her mother leaving Aidara the moment they'd buried her father. She would remember the fear she'd felt about ruling alone. How all the warnings her grandmother had given her about Xavier had haunted her dreams.

And the utter devastation when she'd realised that she couldn't be the Queen Aidara needed with Xavier by her side.

She took a minute to compose herself. When she was sure the emotion and memories were as far away as she could push them, she walked back into the library. Xavier's face was stony, but just above his lip was a twitch Leyna recognised as anger.

'How would that work exactly? Us, married?'

'If we got married,' Xavier spoke in a careful tone, 'it would be clear—not only to Kirtida, but to the world—that Aidara and Mattan are united. And with our collective military, our resources, our people, we would be powerful enough to defend against anything Kirtida attempts.'

'Marriages end, Xavier,' she said in the same tone, and saw the heat of anger flare in his eyes.

Good.

'Royal marriages don't just *end*.'

'No,' she agreed. 'But you and I both know we can't anticipate what might happen in the future.'

Maybe bitterness spurred on her words, but she didn't give it much thought. Whatever motivated them didn't change that what she'd said was the truth. She'd seen it with her parents. Her father's death had made her mother forget her responsibilities to the crown. To Aidara. To her daughter.

Granted, Helene *had* married into the royal family of Aidara, and hadn't been Aidaraen herself. When Leyna was feeling sympathetic towards her mother, she thought it must have been hard for Helene to stay in the place where her heart had been broken.

But those times were rare, and quickly followed by the reminder that Helene had left her daughter to fend for herself in the hardest job in the world. Without any support.

'What does *that* mean?'

'It means exactly what I said. Marriages don't last for ever. You know that better than anyone.'

'Leave Erika out of this,' Xavier nearly growled, and Leyna's bitterness meshed with jealousy.

'You're the one bringing her into this,' she said lightly. Carefully. 'I wasn't talking about your marriage—I meant the institution, not your spouse.'

She gave him time to process—though, if she were honest with herself, it was more for *her* to find her own control again.

'What are you suggesting, Leyna?'

'Only that marriage is not enough to secure an alliance. Especially a precarious one.'

'So what do you want then? A child?' he asked sarcastically.

She'd had a nippy reply on the tip of her tongue that disappeared the moment her mind processed his words. There was something in that, she thought. But, for the life of her, she couldn't wade through the flood of emotions his suggestion had released to identify what that something was.

But, because she had to, she struggled through it. Through the hope that came from a dream she'd given up on a long time ago. Of being a family with Xavier. Of having children with him.

Through the sadness that had come with the realisation that that would never happen. Through the resentment that she would still have to carry a child—with some man who would be her husband though she would never love him—for the sake of the crown.

And again, through the resentment that she'd given up her dreams for the crown.

And then again, through the hope that maybe duty would make that dream come true after all.

'It's not a real option,' Xavier interrupted her thoughts. Her gaze moved to his and held, sparks she would never admit aloud still flying between them.

'Unless it is.'

'How would that possibly improve the situation with Zacchaeus?'

'For the reasons you outlined. Except now we don't only have the marriage backing our alliance, but a child as well. Which would mean that even if something happens to one of us, Aidara and Mattan would still be protected by the other.'

'Mattan would take care of Aidara if anything happened to you,' Xavier answered stiffly.

'Even if that's true, whoever I marry would need to give me a child. An heir to the Aidaraen throne. You know that,' she told him, and saw the confirmation of it in his eyes. 'The same goes for you. There'll need to be a child for the Mattanian throne, too. And you can't deny the political power in having one child as an heir to both kingdoms' thrones.'

Xavier ran a hand through his dark hair, giving her a glimpse of the lighter streaks that she knew showed when it wasn't styled so precisely. It made the colour of his skin, which spoke of the mixed African and European heritage they both had, look like a tan. As though he had lazily picked one up on holiday instead of from the work he did amongst his citizens.

But anyone who knew Xavier couldn't deny he was a king. Leyna had always thought he looked exactly as a king should—authoritative, uncompromising, powerful. Only she had been privy to the other side of him when they'd been growing up. The easy, laidback man who'd relaxed on the beach with her and would casually hold her hand as they walked through the gardens.

It felt like a punishment that she no longer saw that Xavier. No, now she, too, experienced only that authoritative, uncompromising and powerful side of *King* Xavier.

Just as everyone else did.

But could she blame him?

'Let me see if I understand this,' Xavier said. 'You think that if we marry it won't be enough to strengthen the alliance between Aidara and Mattan on the off-chance something might happen to one of us. So you want to have a child to make sure that *if* something happens, our kingdoms will still be protected because there is a single heir to both our thrones?'

'Yes,' she answered. 'And don't be so dismissive of the possibility of something happening to one of us. We've both seen people we love die younger than they should have. It *is* a possibility.' She gave him a chance to process before continuing. 'A child gives us assurances in both cases. If something happens and if it doesn't, because there's no way Kirtida can misinterpret marriage and an heir. There's also no better way to strengthen the alliance.'

'That might be true, except for one little thing.'

'What?'

'I can't give you a child.'

CHAPTER TWO

XAVIER WATCHED THE shock in her eyes disappear behind the curtain that hid all her emotions. The emotions he'd once been able to read as easily as he did his favourite books.

'What does that mean?' Leyna asked softly. He wanted to tell her—would have, had it been ten years before—but he couldn't bring himself to say that he was infertile. The fact that he'd alluded to it at all told him how much she shook him.

And how much he wanted to shake *her*.

How much he wanted to crack that perfectly logical, reasonable veneer she wore like a shield.

'It means there are cracks in that perfect plan of yours. And it's all a little…desperate.'

'*You* were the one who brought it up,' she shot back, reminding him of yet another of his slips. 'And yes, a child is desperate, but aren't we in a desperate situation?'

'So, you're saying desperate times call for desperate measures?'

'If you'd like to use that cliché to help you understand it, then yes.'

'And how would we conceive this child?' He knew he wasn't asking it because of his fertility problems but, again, because he found himself wanting to pierce through that cold facade. 'Should I stay after the banquet for us to get…reacquainted?'

He hated how bitter he sounded—worse still, how the bitterness had made him more vulgar than he'd intended. He watched her honey-coloured skin go pale, and felt the satisfaction of it just as acutely as he felt the shame.

Her lack of colour made the golden-brown of her hair—the green of her eyes—all the more striking. And if he added the gold dress she wore, which clung to her curves in a way that made him forget she was a queen…

She wasn't the delicate Princess from their youth any more, he thought. Though her face still had its slight angles and there were still freckles lightly spread over her nose, the woman who had laughed with him in the waters that separated their islands—the woman who'd once agreed to marry him—was gone.

The woman who stood in front of him now had a realism in her eyes that sent an ache through his body. The light that had always been there had been dimmed by whatever she'd gone through in the ten years since they'd been close. There was power, more authority, too. She'd changed, he knew.

But then, so had he.

'It won't work,' she told him, colour flooding her skin again. 'I know you're trying to shake me, but it won't work.'

'Won't it?' he asked, taking a step towards her. Her eyes widened, and awareness sizzled through his body. He'd loved those eyes once. They'd told him everything he needed to know. And though there were many less disturbing memories to choose from, his mind offered him the day Leyna had agreed to marry him.

Her eyes had shone with a love he hadn't thought capable of hurting him the way it—the way *she*—had. And then there had been the desire in her eyes a few moments later. When he'd had her against a tree. She'd wanted him as much as he'd wanted her, but there had been fear, uncertainty, too.

He saw those emotions in her eyes again now. And it made him wonder whether they were caused by the same reason. That she'd never been with a man before. The thought stirred a mess of emotions in his chest that he didn't want to think about. Though there *was* one thing he couldn't ignore, and that was the fact that he still wanted her, regardless of what the answer to that question was.

It shocked him into stepping back.

'No, it won't,' she said, and he heard the breathiness she tried to mask. 'Because we both have kingdoms to think about. Unless you've forgotten that's the real reason for all of this?'

She was right, he thought. He needed to think about his kingdom. And that meant he couldn't deny her suggestion had merit. If he pushed all his feelings about it aside, he could recognise the strength and subsequent protection a marriage and child would offer Mattan.

He was also sure his family would approve. Sure, they'd treated his relationship with Leyna as an indulgence in the past. Mostly because they couldn't deny how beneficial a union between him and Leyna— between Mattan and Aidara—would have been. But the moment they'd realised that wouldn't be happening, they'd told him to snap out of it. To think of his kingdom.

Since that was what drove him now, too, he knew they would approve. And since the man he and Leyna had grown up with no longer seemed to exist in Zacchaeus, Xavier was forced to face that this might be their only option.

Which meant he needed to tell her the truth of his fertility problems.

The thought had him heading straight to the alcohol decanter next to her desk. He flipped over two glasses, and poured a splash of the brown liquid into each. He offered her one and, when she took it, downed his own. He would have liked another, but that wouldn't have been wise considering what he was in Aidara to do. Or what he was about to say.

'I can't have children.'

He set the glass back in its tray. It gave him a reason to avoid the emotion on her face.

'You…' Her voice faded. 'I'm so sorry, Xavier.'

'I've accepted it.'

'How…how do you know?'

'I was married, Leyna,' he reminded her, and saw hurt pass over her face so quickly he didn't know what to think about it. So he continued. 'Erika and I tried to have children before she died. We could never conceive.'

'That must have been terrible for you…and Erika. I'm sorry.'

Emotion churned inside him. Erika had been devastated by their battle to have children. And when they'd found out that there was no medical reason why they couldn't, she'd turned angry.

By then, she'd learnt that the allure of marrying a king had only been in her imagination. That the reality of it was far more demanding—and sometimes more demeaning—than she'd wanted.

Would she still have felt the same if she'd become a mother?

He never gave himself the permission to consider it. All he knew was that the only thing that had kept Erika committed to being Queen had been the prospect of a child. And when that hadn't happened she had become more and more withdrawn. And he'd felt more and more guilty. Because though there'd been no proof that it was him, it *had* to be.

'Why not? Why can't you have children?' Leyna's soft voice interrupted his thoughts.

'We tried and we didn't conceive.'

'Yes, you said that.' She frowned. 'That doesn't mean *you* were the reason you couldn't conceive.'

'It wasn't Erika's fault,' he said sharply.

'I wasn't saying that it was. But there *is* such a thing as unexplained infertility.'

It was what the doctor had told them, too. But, as someone who'd needed answers, Xavier hadn't been happy with that. Neither had Erika. So he'd accepted the blame for it.

'So there's no medical reason that you can't conceive?'

He clenched his jaw. 'No.'

'Then we still have a chance.'

'I must have missed this unfeeling side of you when we were friends.'

He saw her flinch, but her voice was steady. 'The reality of our lives—of our *duty*—doesn't always allow us to feel, Xavier.'

'Is that how we'll conceive this child then? Without feeling?'

'Why not?'

'You have to have *some* kind of feeling to conceive a child, Leyna.'

'Perhaps, if you want to do it naturally.' She raised

an eyebrow—taunting him, he knew, with the insinuation. 'But, since this is going to be a contract, I think we should consider other options. To keep things…official.'

Relief and disappointment mingled in his chest. 'You mean artificial insemination?'

'Or IVF.'

'It would take time we might not have.'

'Which is why we should do it as soon as possible.'

With each word, his heart grew heavier. It weighed down his response so that, although he knew she was right, he couldn't bring himself to agree. Agreeing would mean that the distance he'd sought from her for ten years would be destroyed. It would bring back all the feelings he'd avoided thinking about since Erika had died. Feelings of failure, of heartbreak.

And if he agreed to marry Leyna he knew he would feel as though he was being disloyal to Erika. Worse still, if it worked and Leyna fell pregnant, he would feel as though he'd *betrayed* Erika. He'd be living the life she'd once accused him of always wanting.

He wasn't sure he could live with that guilt.

'Do you agree, Xavier?'

'Does it matter? You seem to have everything neatly planned anyway.'

'Neatly?' she repeated, disbelief in her voice. 'This is probably the least neat thing I've ever planned, Xavier. Do you think I want to be married to you, to carry your *child*?'

'Well, if it's such a burden then—'

'Stop it,' she snapped, anger turning her cheeks red. 'Our lives are filled with burdens. They're called responsibilities. They're a part of our duty.' He saw her chest heave, revealing the passion with which she spoke her words. 'Duty comes first, Xavier. It always has and it always will. This plan I've so *neatly* outlined is going to require sacrifices from the both of us, and it won't be pleasant. In fact, I'm pretty sure it might destroy me.'

Her eyes widened and she turned away from him. It had been her first real show of emotion—proper, spontaneous emotion that told him the veneer of aloofness had been cracked. It had surprised her and, though he'd wanted to crack that shield, it had surprised *him*, too.

He didn't know what to make of her words. *What* would destroy her? Working with him? Being married to him? Carrying his child? Was she just as affected as he was by the prospect that this decision would make them share their lives in the way they'd always imagined? Or was it because the circumstances of this life together were nothing like they'd imagined, ensuring that this decision would make their lives infinitely more complicated?

'Perhaps there's a simpler solution,' he said suddenly, his thoughts turning him desperate.

'There is no simple solution for us. For this,' she said, turning back to him. Her eyes were bright, troubled, and he wanted to reach out and comfort her. But he didn't. Of course he didn't. He didn't know her any more. Comforting her wasn't his job.

'Duty is never simple,' he said mockingly. But she responded seriously.

'No, it isn't. It will never be simple for us, nor will it ever be simple between us.'

It was the first time she'd made any kind of mention of their past, and he wasn't sure how he felt about it. So he didn't respond, instead letting the silence stretch. He felt it build, felt the tension pulse from both of them.

It made him want to ask her why she'd done it. Why she'd broken his heart. Why she'd broken *them*. It made him want to tell her how long he'd been broken. How he'd still had to pick up the pieces in the first years of his marriage to Erika. How that had started the cracks that had eventually broken him and Erika, too.

'We can try to set up a meeting with Zacchaeus one more time,' she said, breaking the silence.

'You know that won't work.'

'Then we move onto Plan B.'

'Marriage and a child?'

'Marriage and a child,' she confirmed.

'We don't have the luxury of time here,' Xavier said quietly. 'If Zacchaeus decides to attack either of us, our kingdoms will be helpless to stop him.'

'One more attempt at diplomacy, and then we move onto Plan B, Xavier,' Leyna said again. 'Now, we should get back before they realise we're gone.'

She set the glass down, its contents untouched, and walked out of the room before he could reply.

CHAPTER THREE

LEYNA HAD HAD to leave the room—to escape Xavier's company before she said something she regretted.

She already regretted too much of that conversation. That burst of emotion had reminded her of the woman she'd once been. The woman who'd died long ago. She needed to remind herself that the Leyna who'd let emotion guide her was gone. She *had* to be led by logic and reason. By the needs of her kingdom.

Because she was terrified of what would happen to her—*inside* of her—if she didn't.

Her steps faltered. Her heart stuttered. Hurt pushed at the wall she'd hidden it behind. She closed her eyes, gave herself a moment. And then she straightened her shoulders and pushed ahead, forcing it all out of her mind as she walked into the hall.

Her royal duties required her attention.

Each year one of the islands in the Alliance of the Three Isles hosted the State Banquet to affirm their ties with other countries. There were thirty dignitaries there that evening and, considering the Isles' geographical location, many of them were from Africa. The others were European, who, in honour of the three British men who'd found the islands with their African wives at the end of the eighteenth century, kept their ties with the Isles.

Leyna mingled, moving from the King of Spain to the King of Swaziland, and then to the delegation from South Africa. Before she knew it, dinner had been announced. She walked to the head of the table, her stomach turning when she saw Xavier. It wasn't a surprise—it was custom that the monarchs of the Isles sit there—so she forced her feelings at seeing his blank expression aside and thought again of her duty.

She touched Xavier's arm before he could take his seat.

'We can't have an empty seat at the head of the table. It would make Zacchaeus' absence more conspicuous, and I won't be able to field questions as easily if it's staring our guests in the face. Someone has to sit in Kirtida's place.'

He frowned down at her, but nodded. 'Aidaraen?'

She shook her head. 'My grandmother is the only one from Aidara who would be appropriate, and she—' *She no longer seems to think she needs to support her kingdom when she doesn't approve of its queen.* 'She isn't here. Can you ask someone from your family?'

'My grandmother,' he said immediately, but she could sense his reluctance. So things hadn't got better in the ten years they'd grown apart, she thought. 'She'd be the best option, considering my mother couldn't be here tonight.' His mother was ill, Leyna remembered. 'Please excuse me.'

Formality—distance—lined his words. But it was for the best, she told herself, and hated the ache in her chest that said otherwise.

A few minutes later, Xavier returned with a graceful older woman at his side. Envy slithered its way through her before she shook it off. It was natural to envy the grace and poise the former Queen Consort of Mattan carried effortlessly with her. But envy was not a trait Leyna wanted to have as a queen, nor as a woman.

'Your Majesty,' Leyna said and curtsied.

'Let's not waste time with the formalities, Leyna.' Xavier's grandmother brushed kisses on both Leyna's cheeks, and Leyna found her lips curving.

'It's lovely to see you, ma'am.'

The older woman sighed. 'I recall you using that term years ago. But perhaps now we've reached the point where we can both use each other's first names. Paulina will do. And don't you dare refuse.'

Paulina lifted a hand to wave off Leyna's response, and Leyna nodded.

'As you wish...Paulina.'

Though she got an approving smile from Paulina, the name felt wrong on Leyna's lips. To deal with it, Leyna made a point of avoiding addressing Paulina by name. She received a few looks that told her Paulina knew what she was doing, but Leyna just smiled in return and moved onto the next topic. Conversations were easy for her. Except when they were with former best friends—*fiancés*—Leyna considered, her eyes flitting over Xavier.

'I'd hoped to see the new King of Kirtida here with us tonight,' Paulina said when things were loud enough at the table that no one would overhear.

Though she could hardly manage to forget it, Leyna winced at the reminder. 'I had, too.'

'We should have anticipated this mess,' Paulina continued. 'There was always something in that boy's eyes.'

Leyna didn't respond, and Paulina turned her attention to the conversation beside her. Leyna was grateful.

Her thoughts had clamoured at Paulina's words, and she told herself, very deliberately, that it didn't make her any less of a queen that she *hadn't* anticipated their current situation.

It didn't mean she'd failed her people.

She lived with the constant fear that she wasn't doing enough. It didn't matter how hard she worked, that fear remained. And she'd worked *hard*. She'd had to rebuild the morale of a kingdom that had lost its King and Queen in a matter of weeks. She'd had to earn their trust and make them believe that, though she was only twenty-one, she *could* be their Queen.

It had required all her time and all her attention. It had reminded her of her grandmother's warnings. Was it any wonder she hadn't had time for Xavier any more? She'd broken things off the minute she'd realised— *really* realised—how much work she had ahead of her.

It had hurt her to do so—more still when the demands of *his* crown hadn't kept him from having a life. From having a relationship.

With someone who wasn't her.

She closed her eyes against the anger, the jealousy, the resentment and *pain,* and fought off the loneliness that threatened to creep in. As it did almost every day.

'Stop frowning,' Xavier said under his breath. 'People will think there's something wrong with the food.'

'Not the food, just the alliance they're all here to celebrate.'

'Don't,' he warned. 'We'll talk about it later.'

'Yes, sir.'

She looked over in surprise when she heard his fork scrape against the plate. He was holding his utensils so tightly that his knuckles were white. It had her heart racing, especially since she wasn't sure what had upset him.

'Relax,' she said lightly. 'We have to keep the illusion of peace between the two of us.'

'Are we at war then?'

'No,' she answered truthfully. 'But our lives might end up being the collateral to stave one off.'

He didn't respond to that, and somehow they made it through the rest of the dinner without saying another word to each other. Leyna led her guests to the more casual State Hall where the speeches would take place and gifts would be exchanged. She stood at the front next to the royal family of Mattan—Paulina, Xavier, his sister, Alika, with her husband, and his other sister, Nalini—accepting gifts with a smile even though she knew she was being watched.

No, she thought when her spine went rigid. She wasn't being watched so much as *judged*. She knew her guests were wondering where the other member of Aidara's royal family was. They'd always wanted that show of unity, especially after her mother had left Aidara. It seemed to reassure her people and their allies that Aidara was still as strong as it had been when Leyna's grandfather, her grandmother Kathleen's husband, had ruled.

But the last time Leyna had refused a suitor Kathleen had brought before her, her grandmother had declared that Leyna was a lost cause and had left Aidara for a diplomatic trip to South Africa.

It spoke volumes to Leyna that that was the least of her problems now. Because she also knew her guests were speculating more about the absence of the royal family of Kirtida than they were about Kathleen.

Murmurs had spread through the room as they'd

gone through the formalities of the gift exchanges. No doubt discussing what the implications of Kirtida's absence would be. She'd soothed many of the concerns when she'd done her rounds earlier, but that wouldn't stop the rumours.

And there was nothing she could do about that.

She felt the room snap to attention before she saw why, and then felt her own body straighten in anticipation of the speech Xavier would be giving on behalf of the Isles. He'd stepped in front of the small podium that had been designed for the occasion. It was his presence, she thought. It commanded attention. She admired it.

He carried it with him so effortlessly—the authority, the confidence—that no one would have suspected he'd once begged Leyna not to leave him.

'You'd never know how broken he is, would you?'

Leyna frowned, wondering how someone had read her thoughts. She shook it off and glanced over to see Xavier's sister Nalini now standing beside her.

'What do you mean?'

'What do you see when you look at my brother?'

Leyna's eyes shifted to Xavier. His muscular body wore the uniform representing his kingdom with ease, his handsome features set in an expression that was both commanding and open. Her heart fluttered, and she blushed when she saw Nalini watching her.

'I see a king.'

Nalini took a few seconds to respond. 'I think that's who he sees, too. I think that's the *only* thing he sees. He lost the man somewhere. I think maybe it was when he lost the woman he loved.'

'I can only imagine what he must have gone through when Erika died. Losing someone you love is difficult.'

'That *was* hard, of course,' Nalini agreed. 'But I was actually talking about you.'

Shock seized her tongue, and there was a long pause before Leyna replied.

'No. I mean, he didn't... I don't think that's true.'

'Oh, it's true,' Nalini assured her, uncharacteristically serious. 'Things became worse after Erika. But it started with you.'

Leyna had no response to that.

'Xavier's marriage wasn't...easy, Leyna. And then they struggled to have a baby, and... Well, it was a heavy burden on Xavier. Worse because Erika didn't know how to carry her part of that burden—of being Queen *and* of not conceiving naturally.'

Leyna felt as if she were being sucked into quicksand. She drew on her breathing techniques, knowing that she had to control the panic building in her chest.

'He loved her and he was devastated when she passed on. But it's been three years now and...' Nalini's voice faded and Leyna could see the Princess's concern for her brother.

'Why are you telling me this?'

'Not to upset you,' Nalini said quickly. 'I'm sorry if I have.' Leyna nodded, but didn't speak. 'I think... I'd *hoped* that you'd help him. I know that's probably out of line, but you're the only person...' She trailed off and then took a breath. 'I'm telling you this because I thought you'd be able to remind him of the person he used to be. The man who'd *lived* and didn't just rule.'

Leyna barely noticed that Xavier had finished his speech, but her heart raced when she caught him walking towards them.

'Please,' Nalini whispered, and Leyna didn't get the chance to respond when Xavier joined them.

'That wasn't incredibly boring,' Nalini said brightly. Perhaps *too* brightly, Leyna thought.

'Thank you, I think?' But he frowned, looking at Nalini and then Leyna. It took Leyna a second to realise that she should say something to him, too, and she cleared her throat.

'It was wonderful, thank you. I hope my speech next year is just as elegant when Mattan hosts the banquet.'

'Are you okay?'

'Yes,' she answered quickly, and avoided Nalini's eyes. 'Please excuse me. I think Carlos is looking for me.'

He wasn't doing anything to indicate that he was, but Leyna strode towards him with enough purpose that anyone watching would think he *had* called for her. When he saw her coming, his eyes widened and he stood at attention.

'Your Majesty.'

'You can relax, Carlos. I just need an excuse to get some air.'

She gave him a shaky smile and saw some of the tension seep from his stance.

'Would you buy me some time? Tell anyone who's looking for me I'm speaking with someone else privately. You can do that until I return. I won't be long.'

Though she read confusion in his eyes, Carlos nodded and Leyna made her way through the secret tunnels that led to Aidara's private beach. She kicked off her shoes at the edge of the sand and lifted the hem of her dress. It was practical—she wanted to be able to walk more easily—but she also didn't want to ruin the beautiful dress. Then she stopped just before the water reached her feet and took a long steadying breath.

This beach held so many memories for her. Despite

the fact that those memories were tainted with sadness now, it was still the place she came to for calm. For balance. She needed both now as the information Nalini had told her swirled in her head.

Xavier had had a difficult marriage. The knowledge grieved her. Even though she'd felt betrayed when he'd moved on so quickly from her, Leyna hadn't wanted him to be unhappy. She'd wanted him to find contentment. To live a full life without her.

No, she corrected herself. What she'd wanted was for him to live a happy, full life *with* her. It was a contradiction that Nalini's words had alerted Leyna to. She had never wanted Xavier to be unhappy but, if she was honest with herself, she didn't want him to be happy without her.

She was a selfish, *selfish* person.

And now she was planning a marriage with him. And a *child*.

Hadn't she *jumped* on that? She hadn't wasted time thinking about what being married to him, what carrying his child would cost her. Not until she'd admitted to him that it might just destroy her.

She hadn't *wanted* to admit it, but she couldn't deny the truth of it now. She'd worked even harder rebuilding *herself* than she had on rebuilding her kingdom ten years ago. Turning away from Xavier had been absolutely soul-destroying. The only way she'd been able to survive the decision since was to focus on her duty. To focus on what she'd turned away from Xavier for.

She'd refused her grandmother's suitors, had refused to date since. Hell, she'd refused to make time for *any* emotion that wasn't necessary to run her kingdom. And now, with the possibility of a future with Xavier looming… It was enough for all the emotions she'd been ignoring to come flooding back in.

Leyna could see herself carrying a baby that was part her, part Xavier. She could already feel it move inside her, and see herself holding it for the first time. It would have Xavier's almost grey eyes and her brown curly hair. It would have his laugh…

'You can't keep abandoning your guests like this, Leyna.'

She whirled around at Xavier's voice, wondering for the briefest of moments if she'd imagined it. But he was there, walking towards her, his bare feet a stark contrast to the full-dress uniform he wore.

'I just needed a break to think.'

'About?'

She let out a strangled laugh. 'What do you think?'

'I think you need to put duty first. Doing that means marriage. And, apparently, a child,' he added, and her heart thudded.

'Easier said than done,' she told him, and turned back just in time to see the water splash millimetres from her feet.

'The conundrum of duty.'

'You say that like it's affected your life somehow.'

'That's a joke, right?'

'I don't mean in the usual sense.' Her eyes followed the waves as they pulled back before crashing at the shore again. 'I mean, how has it changed your life? How has it *dictated* your life?'

'You really want to know?' he asked, his voice low, tinged with something that had her turning towards him. A poor decision, she thought immediately, when she saw the look on his face—when she saw the seriousness, the fire, in his eyes.

Her belly stirred with a desire long-forgotten, her heart reminding her that they were in *their* place. That the reason he'd been able to find her when no one else would have was because he knew this was where she'd come to think. Where he'd found her countless times before.

Suddenly, the sound of the waves provided an alluring backing track. The night-time sky with its moonlight and stars offered more romance than she wanted.

She took a step back. 'Tell me.'

'Why don't you go first?'

'What is this? I show you mine, you show me yours?'

'No.' He took a step towards her now, and her heart pounded even harder as her body tightened. 'But something tells me that your experiences are the reason for mine.'

CHAPTER FOUR

'THERE YOU GO AGAIN,' Leyna said hoarsely. 'Thinking you have all the answers.'

'Not all of them,' he replied, his hand lifting before he could stop it to brush at a curl that had escaped from her bun. 'Just this one.'

He knew he was playing with fire. The beach, that dress, the magnetism she exuded without even trying… It was bound to get him burned, and he still had the scars from the last time he'd played with the fire.

Yet he couldn't move away.

'I've made too many decisions for duty,' she said softly. 'I can't possibly begin to name them all.'

'How about the night you told me you couldn't be with me? When you said that you'd mistaken the love you felt for me *as a friend* for more?' Forgotten anger stirred and his hand moved to the small of her back, pressing her closer to him. 'I *begged* you to tell me what was happening, to help you get through whatever it was.'

'I told you the truth then.' Her voice shook. 'There was never more. There *couldn't* be more.'

'You're saying there isn't more, Leyna?' He dipped his head so their mouths were a breath apart. 'What royal duty had you deciding you couldn't be with me?'

'Stop it,' she said, and tried to put distance between them. But he kept his hand on her back, refusing to allow her to pull away from him again. 'Xavier, let me go.'

Her voice had gone cold. The shield was back up, he realised. His hand loosened its grip on her and he slipped it into his pocket and took a step back. His fingers curled into a fist when he realised his hand was now shaking, and he took another step away from her.

She was making him lose his mind. His bearings. And if he didn't have them, what would stop him from continuing where they'd left off ten years ago?

It was the talk of marriage and children—as though it were as easy as it had been then—that had made him forget about the life he'd lived in those ten years since. He could almost hear Erika's voice mocking him, asking him whether she was really so easy to forget. Taunting him that things were turning out exactly as he'd wanted them to all along.

It had been a constant argument between them. No matter how much Xavier had told her he was committed to *them*, that Leyna had no part in *their* relationship, the argument had remained. And no matter how hard he had fought to keep Leyna separate from his life with Erika, she was always there. In the simplest things, and the most complicated emotions.

Erika had deserved more. She hadn't deserved to be compared to another woman. Didn't he know what it was like to be compared to someone who'd come before? To be held to an unfair standard? It didn't matter who that person was, the feeling was terrible. And his wife had deserved more than that. She'd deserved more than a sudden death when she was barely thirty, too.

He hadn't been able to give her all that she'd deserved

when she was alive, but he could try to make up for that now. And what she deserved now—what her memory deserved—was that he keep things between him and Leyna strictly professional.

His kingdom deserved it, too. He could still hear the words his father had said to him after Leyna had broken up with him. Xavier had been so heartbroken he hadn't been able to keep up with his responsibilities. His father had taken him aside, and had given him the tough love he'd needed.

Always put the kingdom first.

He might not have a choice about what they had to do to protect their kingdoms, but he could choose to remember that. To honour his kingdom and his wife. To set boundaries where Leyna was concerned. Yes, he could do *that*.

'We'll have to make the people believe it,' he said. If she was confused—or relieved—by the shift in topic, she didn't show it.

'I don't think it matters whether they believe it. They'll appreciate our attempts to protect them.'

'They probably will. But they'd know why, and it might have them panicking. If we do this, it will speak to their desire to believe that everything is fine.'

'I suppose that's true,' she said, and shifted the hem of her dress from her left hand to her right. It drew his attention to her long, shapely legs, and he looked away before they tempted his already tenuous control. 'We should head back.'

He walked with her but said, 'We should talk about this more.'

'I agree. Tomorrow? We can meet here again, if that suits you, and talk through the details. Xavier?' she said when they reached the pathway leading back to the castle. 'Are we really doing this? Getting married and having a child?'

'We have to.'

She nodded. 'I suppose there's a wedding and a baby in our future then.'

'For the sake of our kingdoms.'

He said it as a reminder to both of them of what was at stake. They had to put their feelings aside and focus on protecting their kingdoms.

She straightened her shoulders, an expression fierce with determination on her face, and repeated, 'For the sake of our kingdoms.'

Xavier made his way to the roof of the Aidaraen castle, more than a little annoyed that Leyna was there when she should have been in her library, preparing for their meeting together. They'd agreed the previous evening to hash out the details of their arrangement there. And, since it was something neither of them really wanted to do, the least Leyna could have done was to make sure she kept to their plan.

As he climbed the stairs, though, he realised that he should be glad she wasn't at the beach. He'd struggled with the memories when they'd been there together the night before. In the clear light of day—after the sleepless hours he'd spent thinking about it—he knew that seeing her in the place that had always been theirs had been partly responsible for the spell that had taken over him.

The other parts he didn't care to think about. But, since he'd made a pact with himself the night before, it didn't matter anyway.

The more he thought about it, the more he realised the roof of the castle was the perfect venue for the type of conversation they needed to have. Private, secure. But his thoughts stalled when he walked through the door.

The usually empty space now held a round table in the middle of it. The table was set for an intimate date, with red and pink flowers in the centre and an ice-bucket with champagne cooling just beside it. Each corner of the rooftop held a potted tree and colourful plants, green and bright, as though they'd been there since the beginning of time.

His eyes then moved to the woman who stood beside the table, and his gut tightened.

Leyna wore a simple white dress that was cut in a V at her neck and flowed gracefully down to her ankles. It was perfectly respectable. Or it would have been, he thought, if it had been on anyone else.

On her, the demure dress looked as if it was designed to be torn off. Thrown aside by hands—*his* hands—in order to roam over the slim curves of her body as his lips took hers, his tongue tasting whether she was still as innocent as she'd been when he'd first kissed her at fourteen, or as alluring—as *seductive*—as she'd been the day she'd said yes to his proposal.

He clenched his fists and though he knew he ought to make his way to her, he moved back. It was a futile attempt to distance himself from the memories. From the attraction. From the consuming need his body ached with when he saw her, tempting him to suggest they try for a child the natural way.

Why was it so difficult to ignore? He had the best reasons not to want her. She'd broken his heart, damn it, and trampled on its pieces when she'd walked out of his life. He'd even promised *himself* that he would try harder. For his kingdom. For Erika.

He had the best reasons, he thought again, and still

they didn't seem to be enough. Not when he had a compelling reason for them not to be.

He took in the classically beautiful features of her face, framed by tendrils of golden-brown curls. The rest of her hair was tied at the top of her head, almost making a crown, he thought. The casual style seemed no less royal than the elegant, swept back one she'd worn the night before.

She was still as captivating, as *breathtaking* as she'd been when he'd first fallen in love with her. And damn her for it.

'What's all this?' Xavier said, refusing to wince when he heard the sharpness in his voice.

'Well, you said we need to make our kingdoms believe this,' she said mildly. 'There'll be a helicopter flying over the castle in about thirty minutes. They'll take pictures, which will accompany an article suggesting we've been seeing each other in secret for the past month.'

It was clever, he thought, but didn't say so. 'You think one month will be enough?'

'They've always shipped us together, even when we weren't.' She lifted a shoulder and then dropped it gracefully. 'It'll say a month but they'll believe it to be longer. I think it will work.'

He nodded, and looked at the table in front of them. 'I assume there'll be some sort of meal involved with this.'

'Yes.' She nodded at a man who had somehow known to appear behind him at the appropriate moment. 'We can take a seat in the meantime.'

They were alone on the roof—a rarity for both of them, he knew. It indicated the privacy they had there, especially as he was sure their guards had every possible entry covered. He pulled her seat out for her and then took his own. And wondered how their solitude would affect the lascivious thoughts he'd been having about her.

'There have to be rules with this,' Leyna started.

'Well, first, we have to decide what *this* is.'

'I thought we already had. We're getting married. Having a child.'

They were words that had been repeated so often in the last twenty-four hours he thought he'd remember them for the rest of his life. Just as he would the determination covering the hesitance in her tone.

'Yes. But *when* will we get married? *When* will we have the child? Will it be a big, flashy wedding? Will we use IVF or IUI? And when we announce all of this, what will we do about Zacchaeus?'

'I get your point,' she said. 'So let's get to the details then. First, though, I want to say that I reached out to Zacchaeus again this morning.'

'So did I.'

Her lips curved slightly. 'Great minds. I'm assuming you got the same response I did?'

'You mean no response?'

She nodded. 'We've tried to resolve this diplomatically. Now we move on.'

'Let's talk about the wedding first. When?'

'We'll need at least a month to plan a proper wedding. Two or three if we'd like to have our international allies attend.'

'That might be too long,' he said. 'The situation with Zacchaeus is a ticking bomb that could go off at any moment.'

'I agree, but I don't think we'd get away with a rushed wedding. Not if we want to assure everyone that the alliance is intact and will thrive because of our marriage.'

'We can't just wait around for Zacchaeus to decide to make a move.'

'I know.' Her fingers tapped lightly on a champagne glass. 'What happened to him? Zacchaeus, I mean. He was quiet, yes, and perhaps even a little one-sided and angry. But he was never malicious. Not like this.'

'I thought the same thing when I heard about the coup. I heard…' He trailed off, shook his head. 'It's all speculation. Not worth mentioning.'

'Well, you've mentioned it now. You might as well tell me.'

He almost smiled. 'I heard that Jaydon had fallen ill, and Zacchaeus overthrowing him had been a way to save face.'

'That can't possibly be true. Why would either of them have to save face because of an illness?'

'Which is exactly why I didn't think it would be worth mentioning. There's another possible explanation for all of this, so we have to act.' He waited for the food to be served, and when they were alone again continued. 'What if we announced our wedding at the end of this week?'

'It *would* send a clear message about our intentions,' she considered. 'But the end of this week might be too soon if—' She broke off and her cheeks went pink.

'If what?'

She straightened her spine. 'I saw my doctor this morning. After our discussion, I wanted to be proactive so—' the pink darkened '—I spoke to him about what it would mean for us to do IVF or IUI.'

His heart beat faster but he only raised his eyebrows. 'Busy morning for you.'

'You just said we didn't have the luxury of time with this situation,' she said defensively. 'And I knew the process could include medication and…' She sighed. 'Why am I defending this? It's something we have to do. So, would you like to hear what he said or not?'

'I already know what he said,' Xavier replied. He thought about all the doctor's appointments he and Erika had had. How, after each of them, he'd felt her shrink into herself. How, after several rounds of IUI which had failed, when they'd finally decided on IVF, she'd had an aneurism before they could do the embryo transfer.

'Our options are IUI or IVF,' he said almost mechanically. 'IUI might be our best option considering our time constraints, depending on where you are in your cycle.'

'Yes,' she answered, looking taken aback. 'How…' Her eyes lit with realisation. 'Erika. Oh, Xavier, I'm so sorry.'

'Don't be,' he said gruffly. 'It's been over three years. Long done.'

'It might have happened a while ago, but those emotions—regret, disappointment, hurt—tend to linger.' She fell silent and he watched her face with a frown, wondering what she was talking about. But she cleared her throat and continued before he could spend any more time thinking about it. 'But yes, you're right. The doctor seems to think the time is right for us to try IUI by the end of this week. We'd have to monitor it to find the best day, but…if we want to do this, it'll be the right time.'

He held his breath, ignoring the food that was going cold in front of him, and then released it unsteadily. 'This is all happening so fast.'

'I know. But there's no guarantee it'll work.'

He nodded, knowing the truth of that all too well. 'And if it does work?'

'Then we have our protection against Zacchaeus. We announce our wedding after the insemination, and we can tell our people it was a honeymoon baby when she or he comes. Which would mean we would have to push to have the wedding in two months at the most.'

'I didn't mean about that,' Xavier said softly. 'I want to know what happens with *us* if this works.'

'We'll be married and become parents,' she replied stiffly. 'We'll rule our kingdoms together. We'll protect them. That's all.'

'And you think it'll be that simple?'

'It has to be,' she said through clenched teeth now.

'Just because it has to be doesn't mean it will be.'

'Stop pushing, Xavier.'

'Or what?' he asked, doing exactly what she'd told him not to. He shifted the plate in front of him and leaned forward. 'What will happen if I keep pushing?'

Her eyes flashed. 'You might not like what you find.'

CHAPTER FIVE

'I THINK I *will* keep pushing,' Xavier replied. 'I might finally find the answers to questions I've had for years.'

Fired up, she sat back. 'Fine. Let's get it out of the way so you can get over it. Ask me what it is you want to know.'

'Why did you really break up with me?'

'Because I realised how much the crown would require of me, and I couldn't have given Aidara what it deserved if we'd been together.'

'What does that mean?'

'You know what it means.' When he shook his head, she clenched her teeth. 'Have you suddenly forgotten all the things our families told us?'

'Refresh my memory.'

'You know what I'm talking about,' she said impatiently. 'You know they had their doubts about our relationship.'

'I remember us deciding that their doubts had no foundation.'

'Yes. Until I actually became Queen and started asking myself whether I *was* using our relationship to run away from my responsibilities. And whether you *were* distracting me.'

'And your answer to that was that you were? And that I was?'

'I… Yes,' she faltered.

She remembered how much she'd wanted him by her side after her coronation. How much she'd rather have spent time with him than deal with her new life. How much she'd longed to go back to that day on the beach with him. Happy. Peaceful. Without the weight of the world on her shoulders.

She'd spent too long dwelling on it when she should have been thinking about her new responsibilities. About how she would be Queen to a grieving nation. How she would grieve herself. For her father and her King. For her mother, and the woman she'd thought her mother had been.

She should have spent her time trying to come to terms with all the duties her life would now revolve around. Duties which hadn't included Xavier.

When she'd realised that he'd become more important to her than her responsibilities as Queen, she'd panicked. She couldn't have allowed that. She couldn't have allowed her grandmother's predictions about their relationship to become a reality. She couldn't have allowed the fears that some day they *would* distract her, keep her from giving her kingdom her all.

'My people needed my attention. My full attention. And dedication. Me being with you… It didn't allow for that. It wouldn't have.'

'So none of it was because you didn't love me?'

She pushed out of her seat, needing distance between them. But as soon as she did, he followed. 'What does it matter, Xavier? We moved on. *You* moved on. Wasn't it three months after we ended things that you started dating Erika?'

'Was I supposed to wait for you, Leyna?' he snapped. 'You told me you didn't love me, and that you wouldn't marry me. Was I supposed to wait for you after that?'

'You were supposed to mourn me like I mourned *you*,' she shot back, angry tears forming in her eyes. She waited for them to go away—she *would not* cry in front of him—and then said, 'I didn't expect you to wait, but the least you could have done was give it more than three months.'

'You mourned?' he asked softly then.

'Of course I mourned. I'd lost my best friend.'

'But not the man you loved?'

'Oh, for heaven's sake.' She turned to him. 'I loved you, Xavier. I only told you I didn't because I knew you wouldn't let me go otherwise.' Her eyes started to fill again, and she allowed herself a moment of weakness when she said, 'You were an idiot who insulted everything we had for believing I didn't.'

He moved quickly—so quickly that her mind hadn't had the chance to process it before his lips were on hers. The rational part of her mind told her that she should stop him—that she would regret it if she didn't. But in that moment she allowed herself to be carried away by finally—*finally*—kissing him again.

His lips were soft. They moved gently against hers, as though kissing her was completely normal. As though it was something he was used to doing. Warmth went through her body, settling low in her belly. It demanded she move closer, so she did. Her hands settled on his waist, and when she felt the slight tremble beneath them she pressed even closer, sliding her arms around his body.

Her body shivered as it felt the muscle, the strength, the *maleness* of him.

And then she felt her body dissolve when his hands ran over it, sending frissons she had no control over juddering through her. She gave a small moan when his tongue touched hers. Groaned when it moved inside her mouth. Every nerve in her body felt raw, every bone as though it were melting. She couldn't remember wanting—*needing*—anything more than she did Xavier right in that moment.

The whirring of a helicopter flying above them brought her back to reality. She'd forgotten about the pictures, she realised, and moved to step away from him. But he put a hand on her back, his eyes telling her that she couldn't leave their embrace without ruining the photo op.

So Leyna stood there, her body still touching his, her lips still pulsing from their kiss. The fire that had consumed her only a few seconds earlier turned to ice as she realised what they'd just done. As she realised what it would mean for her now that she knew what it was like to kiss him again. Now that she could no longer ignore the emotions she'd shunned for the last decade.

Worse still, she could feel him pull away from her. It was confirmed when the helicopter finally flew off and he let go of her and strode back to their table.

'I suppose this isn't needed any more,' he said in a tone that told her he had no intention of talking about what had just happened.

Too bad.

'Why did you kiss me?'

'I saw the helicopter. Thought it would make a great picture.'

She stared at him, wondering if it was true. And thought that if it was there'd be another crack added to her already broken heart.

'We can discuss the rest of this now, or we can choose to do so later,' she said, making sure her voice gave away none of her hurt.

'Now. But let's make it quick.'

She nearly laughed. But then she took a moment to process, and walked back to the table and sat down. She picked up her knife and fork and started eating the meal that had gone cold, not tasting a thing. She heard his chair scrape against the floor when he followed her lead, and they ate the food in utter silence.

She knew it was stubbornness—from both of them— but they didn't speak until the food had been cleared. Then she sat back and said, 'Rules for this marriage. There can't be anyone else.'

'Why would there be?'

'I don't know, Xavier,' she said dryly. 'Why *would* there be?'

She saw that he'd got her implication when his eyes flashed. 'If there's any kind of *commitment* between us—marriage or a child—you have my word that there won't be anyone else for me. How about you?'

Now she did laugh. 'There won't be anyone else.'

'You sound sure.'

'I am sure. Not only because of the common sense of it, but because I'm not interested in there being anyone else.' She immediately realised it sounded as though she was talking about there not being anyone besides *him*, and quickly added, 'I'd rather focus on my duty. As you well know.'

'You won't regret that?' he asked, ignoring her slip. 'You've never been married. You haven't even dated, really.'

'Keeping tabs?'

'It's not keeping tabs when your life is national news.'

She tilted her head but didn't press. 'I won't regret it. I haven't, these past years.'

'Why haven't you?'

Her eyes didn't leave his. 'I already told you.'

'Fine, then tell me this. Does you not dating mean you haven't...*been* with anyone?'

'How is that any of your business?' she snapped, her heart racing. It wasn't something she was ashamed of—and she sure as hell didn't think that it defined her. But she didn't want *him* to know that she was still a virgin. That the closest she'd come to making love to anyone had been with him, on the day he'd proposed. That the memory had been so treasured that she hadn't wanted to spoil it by sleeping with anyone else.

That in the deepest, stupidest part of her heart she was still holding out for him...

'It's not,' he answered, but the glint in his eye told her he'd got the answer he wanted.

It had her grinding her teeth, but she told herself to return to the purpose of their discussion. The sooner they did, the sooner they would finish and the sooner she'd be able to deal with the emotions whirling inside her stomach, making her feel ill.

'There has to be a big engagement,' she heard herself say. 'And a ball after, celebrating.'

'I don't think that's necessary.'

'That would happen if we were marrying under normal circumstances, Xavier. You were the one who wanted us to make this believable,' she reminded him when he lifted his eyebrows.

'And this would be our engagement announcement, I assume?'

'Yes.'

'You already have something in mind, don't you?'

She felt her cheeks heat, but she straightened her spine. 'The Aidaraen Tropical Fruit Festival is next week. I thought announcing our engagement in the orchard would work nicely.'

'And there will already be a ball to celebrate the winner, so it won't require too much extra effort. Which will save time,' he added, and then nodded. 'I'm fine with that.'

'Good.' There was more, she knew. But there were too many details to anticipate, so she told herself that they would have to discuss them as they came up. Which brought them to the baby. Her heart thudded, and that sick feeling in her stomach grew more urgent.

'The baby,' she started, but stopped when she saw the shake of his head.

'Let's simplify this part. You can let me know when I'm needed for the IUI.'

'You're happy with that? The IUI, I mean. With it happening so quickly, too.'

'I'm not happy about any of this, Leyna. But, as you said, duty comes first.' He stood. 'I'll see you for the procedure.'

He didn't give her a chance to respond before walking away, and it took her a few minutes before she'd fully realised he was gone. She pushed out of her chair and went to the edge of the rooftop, standing in one of the grooves that allowed her to see the Aidaraen orchard at the top of a green hill and the beaches just beyond it.

She should do this more often, she thought. She should come and take a look at the beautiful land, at the people carrying out their daily tasks. At the place she had to take care of and the people she had to protect. It reminded her that the pain throbbing with each beat of her heart was worth it. That working with the man she'd once loved—that marrying him—despite how much it threw her off balance, was worth it.

And that living the life she'd always dreamed of despite circumstances from hell was worth it.

It *was* worth it, she thought again, but it was threatening to break her, not just throw her off balance. She could almost feel the progress she'd made in the past ten years being eroded. Again, her responsibility to her kingdom was requiring her to forget about Leyna the woman. To sacrifice *everything* that woman had done to protect herself from unimaginable hurt and focus on what Leyna the Queen had to do.

Which, up until the State Banquet, she'd been fine with.

Though not *entirely*, she thought, as she remembered all the times her stomach would jump at seeing Xavier over the last ten years, every time they'd had a political meeting. Or the hope her heart would beat with in that very first moment, before she'd remembered the reality of her decision meant that there *was* no hope.

It would be worse now. Now, she would have the reminder of that decision every time she looked at Xavier, her *husband*. Every time she looked at *their child*.

Her heart felt as though it had caught fire. She turned, leaning her back against the wall and closing her eyes in a desperate attempt to control the pain. *This* was why she should have thought more about this plan. *This* was why she should have given herself the chance to grieve—again—for the life she'd wanted but would never have before going through with this plan.

The prospect of having that life without the love she'd thought would accompany it was heartbreaking. And in the next week that prospect would become reality, and that reality would include the *pretence* of love. It would include kisses that made her want and need as a woman, and threaten every part of her that was Queen.

She gave herself a moment to dread it, and then fortified the shield around her heart. She *would* survive this. And surviving meant that she needed to put her personal feelings aside and focus on her duty.

Again.

Leyna glanced back at the kingdom she was serving, felt it remind her of her purpose. She squared her shoulders. She'd served with a broken heart before, so she knew that she could do it again. Satisfied, she strode back to her library.

She had a kingdom to run.

CHAPTER SIX

IT HAD BEEN a mistake.

Safely back on Mattan, it was all Xavier could think about—that kissing Leyna had been a mistake. It had also been an involuntary reaction to hearing that she'd loved him. That she hadn't broken up with him because she hadn't loved him, and that she'd wanted him to wait for her.

It was night now, the sea breeze cooling his heated body where he stood on the balcony of his bedroom. It helped him breathe, that familiar smell of salt and water. And breathing had become difficult the moment he'd touched his lips to Leyna's and had experienced the feel—the taste—of her mouth again.

It had been better than the memories. Better than the dreams he'd had about it even though he'd fought so hard to suppress them. But now that he'd done it, he didn't know how to deal with the emotions it had awoken in him. How *could* he deal with the hurt, the anger, the guilt that kiss had awoken?

He felt the hurt of the words with which she'd ended things between them as sharply as the day she'd said them. And he felt the anger that she'd lied to him about her feelings then. Now that anger was compounded by the fact that she actually *had* loved him. As was the hurt that she'd told him the thing that would hurt him most to make him leave.

And then there was the guilt. *He'd* kissed *her* before he'd even seen that damn helicopter. He thanked the heavens for it now, that he could blame that for his moment of insanity. Because if he'd been in his sane mind he would have never kissed Leyna. No, he wanted to keep things between him and Leyna as professional as possible.

For Erika.

The reminder—and the wave of guilt that came with it—had him gripping the railing of his balcony. He should be thinking of his wife, and all he owed her. He shouldn't be thinking about what would have happened if he hadn't succumbed to his family's urges that he marry. If he hadn't been reminded of *his* duty. If he'd just waited a few more months for Leyna…

The thought was a punch in the gut and he slammed a hand down against the railing, ignoring—no, *welcoming*—the pain that came with it. Erika had sacrificed her dreams to be married to him. And they had been happy in the beginning.

But that was because she'd actually tried in the beginning.

He hated the thought, but he couldn't deny its truth. Erika had been an exemplary queen at first. She'd joined him on all his duties, and had done so with poise and dignity. Even when it was clear that his people didn't quite like the idea of her as much as they had Leyna. Even when the media turned against her.

They'd been relentless in their judgement, in their comparisons to Leyna. They'd called Erika the consolation prize, had printed headlines screaming that she would always be second place in their King's heart.

It had been tough—on both of them. Especially as Xavier had still been trying to convince himself that being in a relationship with Erika—that marrying her—was best for his kingdom. He'd tried to push it away when Erika had asked him about it. When she'd accused him of exactly what those headlines had said.

He'd told her not to worry, that he was committed to her and only her. And he'd done his utmost to convince her—and maybe even himself—of that. But then Erika had started to recoil from doing public events. He'd had to cajole, convince and eventually beg her to join him. And when she had, she'd done so from behind a shield even he couldn't penetrate.

Then there'd been their struggle to have a child, which would have tested any marriage. In a royal marriage it had been amplified. More so when that marriage had already been on shaky ground.

If he'd had the chance to do it all over again, he would have done it so differently. He would have worked harder to make sure Erika knew he was committed to *her*. That, despite the way they'd come together and the troubles they'd inevitably faced during their relationship, he loved her no matter what.

Those were the what-ifs he needed to think about. Not the ones with Leyna. If he was going to dwell on the past, it should be on his relationship with Erika and how he could do better for her now.

He didn't have to think too hard about that. He knew how he could do it. He had to stop fantasising about a life with Leyna that he would never have. It didn't matter that they were going through the formality of marriage and a child—their responsibility to their kingdoms was the reason for that. There was no emotion behind the decision, and absolutely no cause for him to ever have to kiss her again. Unless it was for show.

He could do that. He *would* do that. For Erika.

'Your Majesty...the Queen is on the telephone for you.'

Of course she is, Leyna thought, and waved a hand to indicate that she would take her grandmother's call. Her grandmother *would* call the morning the doctor had given Leyna the go-ahead for the insemination. Xavier was on his way, which had already knotted her stomach, and now she had to deal with her grandmother.

She sighed and picked up the phone.

'Hello, Granny.' Leyna forced cheer into her voice. 'It's lovely to hear from you. Are you enjoying South Africa?'

'I haven't called to exchange pleasantries, Leyna.' Kathleen's sharp voice would have made Leyna wince if she hadn't expected it. 'I've heard about Kirtida. I should have heard about it from you. A month ago.'

'You would have known about it if you'd returned for the State Banquet as I requested.'

'So you've kept me uninformed about what's happening in my home as punishment?'

'Of course not.' *But didn't you leave your home?* 'I just didn't want to worry you when we didn't have any cause for concern.'

'There was cause for concern the moment Zacchaeus overthrew his father. Surely you know that?'

'Yes, I do. Which is why Xavier and I have done everything we possibly can to get in touch with Zacchaeus to talk it all through.'

'Have you succeeded?'

Leyna closed her eyes. 'Unfortunately not. But it's

allowed us insight into where we stand, and we have a plan.'

'I'm listening.'

She'll find out soon enough anyway. 'Xavier and I will be getting married.'

A stony silence followed her words, and then her grandmother spoke again. 'Are you marrying the King of Mattan, or the man you're still in love with?'

'I'm not—' She broke off, sucked in a breath. 'Does it matter?'

'Yes, it does.' Kathleen's voice had softened, and it was so unexpected that her next words sliced through the shield Leyna always wore with her grandmother. 'Love is a wonderful thing, but when you lose it you lose sight of what's important. Just look at your mother.'

Her words pierced the wound Leyna had always tried to protect.

'Your duty is most important.'

'Yes, Granny,' Leyna said in a hoarse voice. 'I know.'

'So are you marrying for duty or for love?'

'For duty. To protect Aidara.'

There was relief in her grandmother's voice when she replied. 'Good.'

'I must say goodbye now. I have an urgent appointment. Keep well, Granny.'

She put down the phone before her grandmother could reply, and stood.

And then sat back down when her legs started to shake.

She clenched her fists when she saw that her hands were shaking, too, and told herself to breathe when the familiar throb of pressure grew in her chest. And while she fought to keep herself from having a panic attack, she reminded herself that her grandmother's advice was based on her own experiences.

Just as she had when her grandmother had handed out her warnings about Xavier.

Leyna knew how much Kathleen had hurt after her husband had died. And then she'd lost her son, too, and her purpose in life along with him. She hadn't seen supporting Leyna as a purpose. And when she'd grieved for her son, she'd channelled her energy into the sense of purpose that had been kindled after her husband's death. The crown. And when Leyna's father had died, the only remaining link to Kathleen's husband and child.

But it was only the crown that she cared about, and not the granddaughter who wore it. Duty had become an obsession, and Leyna was subject to her grandmother's opinions on her ruling, marrying and bearing an heir. It had made a tough job even tougher, and Leyna had to keep reminding herself of why Kathleen was like that.

She reminded herself of it on the days when she felt alone, when her grandmother's sharp tongue spoke of responsibility and not family. It made her miss her mother even more, as Helene had never allowed her mother-in-law to dictate to Leyna as she had to Leyna's father.

But thinking about her mother would send her into a panic, and Leyna had erected a shield to protect her from distressing interactions with her grandmother. It was just that on days like today, when Leyna already felt vulnerable, she let her shield down.

She didn't have any more time to give in to it when Carlos knocked on her door. She laid a hand on her chest—still tight, but she was past the possibility of an attack now—and then she straightened her shoulders and followed him to the room that had been prepared for the insemination.

Xavier was already there, his face set in a grim expression that had her stomach tumbling.

'Is everything okay?'

'Yes.'

'No, it's not.'

'Of course it's not,' he hissed and strode to the door, shutting it with a bang. 'This is a terrible idea.'

She kept her voice calm. 'Have you changed your mind?'

'No,' he snapped, running a hand over his forehead. 'I just... I don't think this...' He blew out a breath. 'What if this doesn't work?'

'Then we try again next month.'

'And what if *that* doesn't work?'

'We try IVF.'

'That might not work either.'

'There's no reason it shouldn't.' But his words had their intended effect, and she swallowed the bile that rose to her throat.

'Leyna,' he said, his voice sounding like a plea. 'I told you how long Erika and I tried. We tried IUI. We failed.'

'We won't fail,' she insisted.

'How are you so calm about this?'

'Because I have to be. This is our future. The future of our kingdoms.'

But she wasn't calm. In fact, Leyna could only remember feeling *less* calm ten years ago. Right before she'd told Xavier she didn't love him. The panic in her chest was back in full force now and made its way higher, clutching at her throat. She went over to the side of the bed where a jug of water stood, and drank as though her life depended on it.

She closed her eyes and when she had control of herself again turned back to Xavier. He still had a troubled expression on his face, and perhaps that was the reason he just nodded and said, 'Let's get it over with then.'

She watched him open the door and call for the doctor. And then, before she knew it, she was on the bed with her legs open, watching the doctor prepare the catheter that would place Xavier's sperm into her uterus.

'Stop!' she said when he settled at her feet, no longer able to ignore the panic.

'What's wrong?' Xavier asked at her side.

'You were right,' she said as her chest started to heave. 'This is a terrible idea.'

'Are *you* changing your mind now?'

'Yes, I am.'

'Your Majesty?' her doctor queried.

'Give us a moment, please,' Xavier instructed.

When they were alone he turned back to her. 'What's going on, Leyna?'

'I told you. I don't want to do this.' She put a hand on her chest, hoping it would somehow help her to breathe easier.

'I thought you were fine with all this. For our kingdoms.'

'I *had* to say that. You were panicking.' She squeezed her eyes shut. 'But everything you said makes sense. This might not work. And if it doesn't, what do we have to protect our kingdoms?'

'Our marriage.' His voice was sure, the earlier hesitation in his tone gone.

'And what if...what if something happens to me?'

He took her hand. 'Is that what you're scared of?'

'My kingdom needs me.' She turned her head to him now, the fears she didn't want to reveal spilling out of her mouth. 'If something happens to me, who will look out for my people? And what if I can't be a mother? What if I can't do *this*? What if I can't be a wife?'

'Breathe,' he said sharply, but his grip on her hand squeezed reassuringly, softening his words. Helplessly she obeyed, and forced air into her lungs. And then did it again and again, until she felt calmer. Or at least until embarrassment set in.

She swallowed. 'I'm sorry—'

'Don't apologise.' He shook his head. 'This is an... extreme situation. Neither of us could have anticipated the way we've reacted.' Though she appreciated the words she didn't reply, and he continued quietly. 'Nothing's going to happen to you. And if it does—' he cleared his throat '—I'll make sure Aidara is taken care of. As for the rest of it... Leyna, you're the strongest woman I know. And the bravest. You can do this. You can be a mother, and a wife, *and* a queen. And you can get through this procedure.'

She bit her lip. 'Thank you.'

'It's true. You can do this.' He paused. 'Unless you don't want to because you no longer believe it's the best thing for our kingdoms.'

It was a reminder of why they were doing it. And when she looked at his face she saw that he'd meant it to be. She pulled herself together and then nodded.

'Call the doctor.'

'Are you sure?'

'No,' she said, but gave him a small smile. 'Call him.'

He did, and the doctor came back. His face was clear of expression, though he hesitated when he sat down at her feet again. She nodded at him, but turned away from the screen he was using when he began to guide the catheter into her uterus.

She closed her eyes and bit her lip, praying that she wouldn't start crying. She felt a warm, strong hand grip hers, and then she heard Xavier's voice in her ear.

'It's going to be fine, Leyna. Whatever happens, we'll handle it together.'

She bit down on her lip even harder, her only response tightening her hold on his hand. She held her breath and a few minutes later the procedure was done.

'As I explained earlier, I'd like you to rest for a while,' Leyna's doctor told her. 'I'd even advise that you take it easy for the rest of the day, too. After that, you can go ahead as normal.'

'Thank you, Doctor,' she murmured, and pulled the covers over her. When the doctor left, she cleared her throat.

'I'm sorry about all of that.'

'I told you, you don't have to apologise.'

She nodded and then said, 'You don't have to stay. You've done your part.'

'I'd like to,' he said very quietly. 'If you don't mind.'

She shook her head in answer, and just closed her eyes. They sat like that for a while, and Leyna used the time to make sure that her emotions were in check. It was the enormity of the procedure that had made her feel so emotional, so uncertain, she told herself. Though she knew there was more to it than that, she forced herself not to dwell on it.

But the longer the silence stretched, the more she found herself wanting to know what that *more* was. And, since it sat heavy in her throat, she worried she might not be able to control herself if she thought about it any more. So she sighed in relief when Xavier finally spoke.

'Are you okay?'

'Fine.'

'Leyna.'

The tone of his voice had her opening her eyes, and she turned to look at him. Her heart ached at the expression on his face. It was kind and compassionate, and looked so much like *her* Xavier that she wanted to sob.

'This was a huge step today,' Leyna forced herself to say in a calm voice. 'I just need some…time.'

'Of course,' he replied. 'But I just want you to know that if you want to talk…well, I'm a good listener.'

She squeezed her eyes shut again, but it was no use. She felt the tears trailing down her cheeks, and was horrified when he brushed them away. More so when she felt the bed dip and his arms go around her.

Her eyes flew open. 'What…what are you doing?'

'I'm holding you.'

'You don't—'

'I know I don't have to,' he replied mildly, and then drew her in tighter to him. It didn't send that spark of electricity through her as touching him normally did, though there was a slight buzz of heat that reminded her of her attraction to him.

But no, this was purely comfort and, before she could help herself, she snuggled closer.

There were no more tears, she realised, and told herself to inform him he didn't have to hold her any more. But her heart asked for a few more moments—just long enough for it to memorise being in Xavier's arms again. As she gave in to it, she felt herself drifting off.

In the arms of the man she'd once loved.

CHAPTER SEVEN

XAVIER WASN'T SURE whether he could explain the emotion that had him climbing onto that bed. He'd felt fear and panic just before the procedure, and had almost given in to it. Now that he had time to think about it, he knew that was partly because he and Erika had gone through the same thing so many times with the prospect of failure looming over them, almost punishingly.

With him and Leyna now, the stakes were even higher. And the prospect of failure more menacing. When Leyna had told him to snap out of it, he'd been annoyed. Angry. And then she'd broken down, and he'd realised her reaction revealed her own fear.

Perhaps that was why he'd got onto that bed. The fact that the unfeeling Queen of Aidara wasn't so unfeeling after all. Or perhaps it had been everything that she'd said. And the emotion that had hit him in the gut when she'd said it.

He knew she was right. Especially as she'd voiced his own fears. The IUI was a desperate attempt to save their kingdoms, and if it didn't work… He took a shaky breath, his arms tightening around Leyna. He didn't want to let her down as he had Erika. No, he corrected himself. He didn't want to let his *kingdom* down in the same way he had before. With Erika.

But he also knew that what she'd said before the panic had gripped her had been right. If this round didn't work, they would do another. And then they would try IVF. And they would keep trying.

He ignored the pain in his chest at the prospect of going through the struggle of infertility again. And told himself the pain wasn't worse now because he was putting Leyna through it, too. No, time had just faded the memory of the pain, and now that he was feeling it again, made it *seem* worse than it had been before. He had to convince himself extra hard of that since he was lying on Leyna's bed, holding her. Since he hadn't felt more complete in years. He closed his eyes, memorising the sweet floral smell of her and the way she fitted into his arms so perfectly. As he rested his head on hers, he smiled, thinking her curls provided enough support and softness that it could be a pillow.

It was the last thought he had before he heard her gasp.

He sat up just as she did, and then shifted off the bed when she put her arms out, indicating that she wanted space. Helpless, he watched as she set a shaky hand on her heaving chest, and felt his heart twist as she calmed herself. When she did, she looked at him, her eyes a little wild, though embarrassment obscured it.

'I'm sorry,' she said with a forced smile. 'Bad dream.'

He nodded and returned to the chair where he'd sat during the procedure. 'About what?'

'I don't remember.'

'You're lying.'

'I'm not,' she denied. 'But I *am* hungry. I think I'll call down for something. Would you like anything?'

'No.' He waited for her to call the kitchen and then asked, 'How often do you have these dreams?'

'On and off.'

'About the same thing?'

'I told you—I don't remember what it was about,' she said, and he saw a muscle jump in her brow. Knowing that she needed to avoid stress, he didn't push.

'How are you feeling?'

'Fine.'

'Really?'

'Yes, really. You can leave now, if you want.'

'Do *you* want me to leave?'

Her eyes told him that she didn't, and he felt warmth creep into his heart. But she only said, 'It's completely up to you, Xavier.'

'Then I think I'll stay.'

He wasn't sure why he wanted to, especially after his resolution the night before. Especially after what had transpired that afternoon. But the arrival of her food distracted him from pondering it. His mouth watered, reminding him that he hadn't eaten since that morning.

'Would you like me to call down for something for you, too?' Leyna asked, her eyes lit with dull amusement. 'Before you drool all over my food?'

'No, thank you. I'm fine.'

'When was the last time you ate anything?'

'This morning. But I'm not hungry.'

A tight ache in his stomach cursed him for lying, and a moment later Leyna leaned over to the phone beside the bed and called the kitchen for something to be sent up for him as well.

'You didn't have to do that.'

'I know, but you were lying. And being the proud man that you are, you wouldn't have said anything even though your eyes have already eaten my meal in the minutes we've been discussing this.'

He refused the smile that threatened. 'Thank you.'

She nodded, and then intertwined her fingers.

He frowned. 'You should start eating. Before your soup gets cold.'

'It's a bit too hot at the moment, so it needs to get cold.'

'You're waiting for me, though, aren't you?'

When she lifted her shoulders—exactly *how* did she manage to make the action look graceful?—he shook his head.

'You're a stubborn woman, Leyna.'

'We always used to have that in common,' she replied.

Silence followed her words, and he wondered if this was how their future together was going to be. Stilted small talk, never about anything personal, only dealing with necessities. But sometimes—like when she'd panicked about the procedure, like when she'd been so emotional it had led her to tears—things were *so* personal between them that both of them had to ignore it.

It complicated matters that she might be carrying his child. His heart beat so hard in his chest at that thought—one he hadn't allowed himself right until that moment. Why did the prospect make him so happy? Was it because this was Leyna? Or was it because he was getting another chance at having the child he'd always wanted?

Both options made him feel ill, because it felt like betraying Erika. But he'd always known he must have a child. He had to have an heir. There was no other option. But he'd wanted a child with his wife. And he felt as if he'd failed her because that hadn't happened for them.

He *still* felt as if he'd failed her, because now it was a possibility for him and Leyna.

He told himself that it was for the good of his kingdom. And reminded himself that with marriage and a baby on the way, his mother and grandmother would finally stop nagging him to marry again. He'd listened to them the first time and, because his father had added weight to it, he'd married Erika.

But the heartbreak following her death had given him a reason to resist the next relationship his mother and grandmother had attempted to push him into. And now, with marriage and a possible child in his future, he would finally be free of the pressure from his family—to produce an heir for the sake of the crown. To prevent him from falling short of the legacy of the men in his family.

He hadn't thought about any of it until that moment, sitting across from Leyna, waiting for his food to arrive.

A sigh of relief released from his lungs when it did, and he busied himself with the meal, ignoring the look Leyna had given him at the sound. They ate in silence but it was woefully short and, before he knew it, Leyna was arranging for their food to be taken away.

'Thank you,' she said when they were alone.

'For what?'

'For allowing this to happen on Aidara.'

'Were you afraid I would insist that this intensely personal procedure be done on Mattan?'

'Maybe,' she said with a small smile. 'Perhaps irrationally. In my fear about all of this.' She paused. 'It helped, to have it done here in my home.' When she looked at him there was something so vulnerable in her expression that it had the feelings he'd tried to banish the night before stirring again. 'After dealing with something like this... It's nice to be somewhere familiar.'

'Of course,' he said softly. 'Is that what you felt earlier? Fear?'

'The dream?' He shook his head. 'Oh, you mean the panic. And the tears.' She looked down at her hands. 'I suppose so. Yes.' Seconds passed in silence but he didn't reply, knowing she wasn't done. 'This is scary.'

'I know it is.'

'Are you scared?'

He wanted to take her hand again but he only said, 'You know I am.'

'So you feel like a coward, too?' Now he heard the anguish in her voice. 'Like we shouldn't be questioning this because it's something we're doing for our people. To protect them.'

He took a moment before he replied. 'We're still human, Leyna. We both have fears, and anxieties. Especially about this.' He fell silent when he thought about his own fears, his own anxieties, but then pushed on. 'But we can't let them keep us from doing what we need to do for our people. To protect them.'

She nodded, and there was a long pause before she spoke again. 'Do you know how long it's been since I last cried? Years,' she said, answering his silent headshake.

'What did you cry about?'

'My life falling apart.' She bit her lip as though she'd said too much, and then she turned her head to face him. 'It was after I found out my mother had left, after...after I'd ended things with you.' She looked away at that. 'I'd lost everyone I cared about. All I had left was an uninterested grandmother and responsibility for the lives of millions of people.'

'So you told yourself you couldn't waste time grieving and focused instead on running your kingdom.'

'Exactly.' Her lips curved. 'We're still so alike, aren't we?'

'More than either of us want, I'm guessing.'

She laughed. 'You wouldn't be wrong.'

There was silence again and then she asked, 'Is that how you felt after Erika died?'

He felt something tighten inside him, but he answered, 'Yes.'

'And you feel guilty about it.'

It wasn't a question, and it made him snap his next words. 'Do you?'

She didn't seem upset by his reaction, only shaking her head. 'I *did* grieve for my father. But I was allowed to. Expected to. But the others… Well, one of them was because I'd chosen it, and so I kept those feelings to myself and never let them influence the way I ran the kingdom. The other…' She trailed off and took a breath. 'My mother left me with only a note saying goodbye. I didn't think she deserved me mourning her.'

Again, he found himself wanting to reach out and take her hand. To comfort her, to ask how she'd coped with the loss of both her parents so close together. There was a part of him that felt as though he should have been there for her. That accused him of abandoning her when she'd needed him the most.

But a bigger part reminded him that he *couldn't* have been there for her. It would have killed him to go back to being just friends with her. It didn't ease the guilt or the regret, though it did make him wonder, again, whether things would have been different if he'd just given it some time. If he'd just ignored his father's reminder of the need to do his duty.

'Erika's death was so unexpected,' he said suddenly. It took him a moment to realise he'd said it to remind himself of the pact he'd made the night before. 'I woke up early that morning to do something—I can't even remember what it was now—and when I got back to the room she was gone.'

She reached for his hand immediately, squeezing. 'I'm so sorry, Xavier.'

He nodded. 'It was some time after her funeral that I realised I couldn't go on in that state. So I told myself that living would be my way of celebrating her, and her life.'

'It's an honourable way of looking at it,' she said quietly, her hand lifting from his. 'Beautiful, too. Though I'm not surprised. You both always had so much light together.'

His heart stalled. 'You thought that?'

'Yes. I thought it the moment I saw you look at each other on your wedding day.'

His world swirled, and then straightened almost abruptly.

'You weren't at the wedding. You were meeting with the South African president about the trade deals between their country and the Isles.'

'I came back. Just to see the ceremony.' She paused. 'You didn't think I would miss my best friend's wedding, did you?'

There was a teasing glint in her eyes, but he saw a lot more there.

Regret. Longing.

A ball of tension began bouncing in his chest.

'We weren't best friends then, though. We weren't anything.'

'Maybe,' she allowed. 'But I still cared about you. You can't just switch off twenty years of caring,' she added, as though he didn't know that himself. 'I wanted to share one of the most important days in your life, even if it was just in the form of an obscured view from the crowd. But because I wasn't supposed to be there, I made sure no one saw me. Of course, Jacob helped with that.'

Xavier sifted through his memories of that day, trying to recall whether he'd seen her bodyguard there. He knew he hadn't seen her. He'd never forgotten the relief he'd felt because of it. But it wasn't a surprise that he didn't remember seeing Jacob. He'd taken care to ensure his eyes were only on his bride that day. He hadn't wanted to give any grounds to the speculation in the media. He was marrying Erika because he wanted to. Not because he couldn't have Leyna.

But that wasn't quite true, was it?

He closed his eyes.

'I've upset you. I'm sorry, I didn't mean to.'

'You haven't upset me.' He opened his eyes again, his heart trembling at the angst he saw in hers. 'I suppose it was just that I didn't think you cared enough to attend.'

'I know that's my fault. And I completely accept that it is. But I told you I mistook my love for you as a friend for romantic love.' She lifted a shoulder. 'Even in that I was still telling you I loved you.'

He didn't have an answer to that. To him, her words had meant she'd felt nothing for him. Her actions had supported that, too. Was he now supposed to believe she'd loved him as a friend all along, even when she'd treated him so poorly? Caring about someone meant caring about their feelings, too. It had been clear to him then that she hadn't cared about his feelings, or else she'd never have done what she did.

'So, we'll try again if we don't fall pregnant this

time,' he said, focusing instead on the future. On parts of the future that he *could* control.

'Yes,' she replied. 'But there's no reason for us not to.' She held up a hand when he opened his mouth to protest. 'I know what I said earlier. As I told you, I was scared. I still am. But we *have* to focus on the positives if we want to get through this. And the positive here is that there's no medical reason for us not to fall pregnant. We have to trust in that. If not... Well, like you said, we'll deal with it then.'

He wasn't as prepared for this response as he'd been for her first one. Not when suddenly he was thinking about how differently Erika had approached things. Even *after* she'd had the chance to process.

It made his next words come out more harshly than he'd intended. 'And if we never fall pregnant? What then?'

He watched her struggle for words, and then she said, 'We'll adopt. One child from your kingdom, one from mine. We'll be open about our struggle. We'll be human. And our children will fill the same role.'

'That's unprecedented.'

'And not something we have to think about yet,' she told him. 'But we have options.'

He watched her. Wondered at her. 'Are children really that important to you?'

'Yes,' she said simply. 'I need to make sure Aidara is taken care of. You have your sisters, Xavier, and a nephew to take over from you should anything happen. You'll have even more assurances once Nalini marries. I, on the other hand, only have distant cousins who live in the luxury of being royal but would never survive serving their kingdom. Not the way it deserves. So, I have to make sure that my people are taken care of. The only way I can do that is if I raise their future ruler myself.' She took a breath. 'If it means changing the law—if it means breaking tradition—I will.'

Respect—fierce and solid—erupted in him. 'Your people are lucky to have you, Leyna.'

Her face changed into a charming expression of surprise, and her cheeks coloured slightly. 'As are yours. For a king, I mean.'

He smiled but shook his head. 'I don't think we're on the same level.' Before he could stop himself, his deepest fear spilled out. 'Sometimes I think they deserve more.'

'Why?'

And now that he'd started, he couldn't seem to stop. 'Because they've had more. The kings before me…they were *better*. They didn't make mistakes.'

'What mistakes have you made?'

He let out a short bark of laughter 'What mistakes *haven't* I made?'

'Fine then. Tell me why you think they were better.'

'Because…' He frowned, wondering why he couldn't come up with one specific reason for that belief.

'Because that's what you've been told for the whole of your life.' His gaze caught hers and he felt as if she could see right through him.

'No, there are reasons.'

'Because you believe you've made mistakes they wouldn't have made?'

'Yes!' he exclaimed, almost grateful she'd given him a reason.

'But you can't name one mistake you've made.'

'Leyna, all of this is beside the point.'

'What *is* the point, Xavier?' she asked. 'Because I'd really like to know how you could convince yourself that your people deserve more than a king who'd sacrifice his entire personal life to make sure they were protected.'

Again, he couldn't find the words to speak.

'I know exactly how you feel, Xavier,' she said softly, her hand finding his again. This time, he found his own hand turning over and his fingers sliding through hers. 'That uncertainty? It's part of what we are, of *who* we are. And, yes, it's worse because we have families who constantly point out what they believe are our failures. But we can't give in to that, or to that little voice that tells us they're right.'

She offered him a small smile now that went straight to his heart. 'And now we have each other to remind us of that.'

This was why he'd fallen so hard, he realised. He'd spent his entire youth seeking the light she brought into his life, which had been filled with condemnation *but* for her. Her positivity, her strength, her spirit—they were things he'd tried to forget.

But they were exactly the things that had made that task almost impossible.

When he leaned in for the kiss this time, he watched her eyes widen and then spark with pleasure. And then they closed, as did his, and he sank into the kiss.

It was slow and sweet, filled with an emotion he knew they'd never speak of. The warmth of it rippled through him, unsettling the walls and guards behind which he'd hidden his feelings for her. His free hand lifted to cup her cheek, and then lowered over the curve of her breast—pausing briefly there—and then settled on her waist. He knew that if he'd let himself explore how her body had changed—if he let himself explore the full softness of her breast—the tone of the kiss would change.

And if the tone of the kiss changed, he might not be able to stop himself from making love to her.

The prospect had him edging away, but she moaned in protest and pulled him towards her. He climbed onto the bed, his body mirroring hers, and let himself take more. Desire stirred from where he'd tried to hide it after their first kiss those few days ago, and he heard its demands in the pounding of his blood in his ears.

'Leyna,' he whispered hoarsely, drawing back. 'We can't do this.'

'Why not?'

He couldn't think of a single reason. He sucked in air and then shook his head. 'You didn't want it to happen like this.'

'I also didn't want it to happen when I was thirty. But it is what it is.' She inched closer.

'Can you honestly tell me you won't regret it?' he asked desperately now. 'It happening like this?'

She hesitated briefly and then said, 'It's just sex.'

'It's *not* just sex.' He pushed up from the bed now, set his feet on the ground. 'It'll never be just sex. Not for us.'

'Maybe not when we were younger. But we might have just made a baby together, for heaven's sake. Why *not* try it like this, too?'

'This is not the way you want it to happen for the first time.'

He stood, unable to be so close to her now. It only succeeded in testing his control. He was desperately trying not to take her up on her offer.

'That's irrelevant, Xavier—'

'No, Leyna, it's not,' he said sharply. 'I know you well enough to believe that you know that, too.'

He got up and strode out of the room before she could reply.

CHAPTER EIGHT

IF THERE WAS anything more embarrassing than offering herself to a man—only to be rejected—Leyna wasn't sure she'd experienced it. It made things only marginally worse that that man was going to become her husband and the father to her child.

Was it any wonder the air was so tense between her and Xavier as they made their way to the Aidaraen Tropical Fruit Festival?

They were silent as the car travelled the short distance from Aidara's castle to the orchard where the festival was being held. Leyna knew the tension was compounded by the fact that they would be announcing their engagement just after announcing the winner.

And they had no idea how their people would respond.

'Do you think they'll believe I'm only here to judge the contest with you?' Xavier asked, breaking the silence.

'It doesn't matter,' she said demurely. 'Because you're *not* only here to judge the contest with me, and they'll find that out soon enough.'

She heard his impatient sigh but ignored it, and turned her head to look out of the window. There were people lining their path to the orchard, waving the Aidaraen flag and smiling brightly at them.

Another reminder of why she was putting herself through this, she thought, and turned back to Xavier.

'But it is believable,' she said, offering him a soft smile for the sake of the pictures. 'We have guest judges every year. You've been one of them.'

'But not since I married Erika.'

She fixed a smile on her face. 'They'll believe it if we make it convincing. So, try to pretend you can stand the sight of me today.'

'Leyna, you know that's—' He cut off and sighed again. 'If we're going for pretence, you should probably wear this.'

Her eyes fluttered down to find a ring in the palm of his hand. An emerald-cut diamond in a band of rose gold sparkled up at her and she quickly rested her hand over it, her heart thumping in her chest.

'Don't just hand that to me like it's a mint,' she hissed. 'People are taking pictures. If one of them saw it, the festival will be overshadowed by the news.'

'I think the festival will be overshadowed regardless, Leyna,' he said dryly, but slipped the ring back into his jacket pocket.

'Where did you get it anyway?'

'I had it made.'

'For our fake engagement?'

'Yes,' he answered, but something flashed in his eyes that made her doubt the truth of his words.

She didn't want to dwell on it. Not when she was still a little raw from what had happened at the insemination a few days ago. She'd already spent too much time thinking about that day. About how she'd let her panic overcome her. About how she'd started crying when it had been the last thing she'd wanted to do. *And* about how she'd woken up from a dream where Xavier had told her their plan had been a mistake and he'd walked out of her life for ever, her heart hammering in fear.

She'd tried not to think about the fact that he'd witnessed that. Or about their conversation after she'd woken up. *Or* that sweet, passionate kiss that had her melting and wanting at the same time. That had her offering something she hadn't wanted for ten years.

No, she couldn't think about why Xavier was lying to her about that ring. There was too much else to focus on. Or, she thought more accurately, to *avoid* focusing on.

'This is beautiful,' Xavier said when the car slowed as it reached the road leading to the orchard. She followed his gaze and took in the bright, colourful trees that stood tall and impressive, even though they were still some distance away.

The Royal Aidaraen orchard was the most prominent in the kingdom—where most of their exports came from—and being able to plant on its land was an immense honour for any citizen of Aidara.

There were several contests throughout spring and summer leading up to this one, which ranged from the smallest orchard to the Royal Aidaraen orchard. Winners were allowed to plant on a more prominent piece of land the following year. It took years to reach the Best Fruit of the Kingdom contest in the Fruit Festival, and the winner's fruit was automatically included in Aidara's exports for that year.

The event was prestigious, by invitation only, and that meant every prominent member of society would be there. And that they would witness everything she and Xavier did that day.

'It *is* beautiful,' she answered Xavier. 'And you will

say the same to every contestant we speak to today. It is an honour for them to have made it this far, and they will be honoured should they win.'

'You say that as though I've never been to the festival—or been a judge—before.'

'As you so kindly reminded me, that was such a long time ago.' She paused and then added, 'I wasn't sure you'd remember.'

'Of course I remember. I remember all of the festivals I attended. Especially the night of one almost seventeen years ago when we ran away to—'

'Oh, yes,' she interrupted him, feeling her cheeks flush. 'I remember that, too.'

'I don't think you do,' he said. There was no indication on his face that he was teasing her, but the tone of his voice—the unexpected warmth in it—told her he was. 'You told me there was something urgent you needed to tell me. I didn't think you would be so devious as to lie to me, so I followed you down to the beach. And then you told me you'd seen a movie—I don't recall what that movie was—but the girl had been thirteen years old when she'd had her first kiss and since you were thirteen, you thought it was time you had yours, too.'

'Please stop,' Leyna almost groaned. If they weren't visible to the people in her kingdom she would have covered her face with her hands so he wouldn't be able to see how much he was embarrassing her.

'You pulled me under the palm tree because no one would see us there, and closed your eyes, puckered your lips and waited for me to kiss you.'

Going with it now, she let out a croak of laughter. 'But you didn't know what I expected from you, so you poked me in my stomach and had me opening my eyes again.'

'And I told you that I wasn't going to kiss you because kissing was disgusting.' He smiled now. 'I was lying, by the way. I was too old to think that, but too young to acknowledge that I wanted to kiss you.'

'I didn't know that,' she said, smiling back at him.

'It didn't matter. You gave the biggest sigh I had ever heard in my life and told me that one day I would be grateful you'd been the first girl I'd kiss because no one would know how gross it was.'

'You're welcome,' she said cheekily, and got a grin in return. 'And then I told you to stop talking, to close your eyes, and I kissed you.'

'It was a peck, really, so I'm not sure whether we could call it a kiss.'

'It *was* a kiss,' she answered. 'And you liked it, or you wouldn't have convinced me to try it again.'

'And then again a year later, but this time with tongues.'

'*That* one was gross.'

He chuckled. 'Only because neither of us knew what we were doing. The one after that was fine.'

'I suppose it was.' She was silent, lost in the happiness of the past for a moment. 'How did it end up being so good six years after that?'

'Because we were adults then and had realised there was a little more to kissing than just experimentation.'

She bit her lip. Happiness had quickly turned into regret.

'Being an adult is overrated,' she said, and felt her face heat when she turned back to him and saw he was watching her.

'I'm not sure that's true.'

'Because you're no longer thinking logically,' she said automatically, and nearly gave in to the urge to lean over and show him she wasn't thinking rationally either. It was a great relief when her bodyguard opened the door and the slight breeze floated into the car, bringing her back to reality.

They made their way down the short path to where a beautiful bronze arch covered with vines indicated the official entrance to the orchard. There was no time to talk about anything then. They spent hours greeting contestants and their families, tasting fruits and posing for photos.

Leyna had been tense at first, fully expecting questions about the state of the alliance to be thrown at her and Xavier. But there was none of that. Instead, the atmosphere was festive and easy.

Leyna felt herself relaxing slowly, though she stiffened whenever Xavier would whisper something in her ear or touch the small of her back. It was for show, she reminded herself. And it was working, too, she thought, as she saw sparks of interest on the faces of those they spoke to.

There was no surprise in those expressions of interest, just a simple acceptance. Some gave her a knowing look, as though they'd expected it. Some nodded to her in approval. It should have alarmed her.

It didn't.

In fact, she was quite comfortable with the looks and smiled in return. As if there was a part of her that mirrored those feelings. She'd only remember that it wasn't reality when she looked at Xavier and saw the carefulness in his eyes.

There hadn't been any of that the day of the insemination. When they'd opened up to each other like they had once before. The hours she'd spent trying not to think about it had, of course, led her to do just that. And every time she came to the same conclusion about why he hadn't wanted to spend the night with her.

He was still in love with his wife.

Though the realisation hurt as much as it had when she'd first read the headline about Xavier and Erika ten years ago, it gave her a reason to keep her distance, too. Especially when he touched her, like he did now, taking her hand to lead her to the privacy of the vineyard at the edge of the orchard so they could decide on the winners, and her stomach flip-flopped.

'How are we possibly supposed to decide?' he asked, dropping her hand as soon as they got there. The lack of contact made her feel a little cold.

'We pretend to be discussing this very carefully, seriously, and we choose someone who needs to win.'

'We don't choose honestly?'

'They were all delicious, weren't they?' she asked, and continued when he nodded. 'Was there one that stood out for you?'

'I'm… Actually, I'm not sure.'

'Exactly, so there were no stand-outs regarding taste, which happens occasionally. When it does, we choose the person who this would mean the most to.' She paused. 'This contest is rarely about the fruit. It's about hope and opportunity. So we choose someone who needs that the most.'

'How would you know that?'

'Because I know *them*. The blonde woman we saw first? Her husband just got diagnosed with cancer. They have two little boys. Winning this could mean they'd get the opportunity to supply some of the local businesses with fruit as well. That would help pay for his chemotherapy. And the brown-haired man we saw last has just opened his own organic wholefoods store. His parents don't support him, and they've told him they'd give him a year before they kicked him out. Winning this could mean a successful business for him and perhaps the pride of his parents.'

'How on earth do you know all this?'

'I do some research on them, and invite them over to the castle for a celebratory dinner before the contest.'

'And they haven't picked up yet that the most down-on-their-luck contestant wins?'

'Oh, it's never clear. Not when everyone has such delicious fruits and I have very careful, serious discussions with my co-judges.' She smiled at him, and then sobered when she saw the look on his face. 'What?'

'I'm just…amazed.' He shook his head and then looked out to the vines in front of them. 'You put so much…*thought* into running your kingdom. Into your people.'

'It's part of the job,' she said, uncomfortable with the praise.

'It should be,' he agreed. 'But it isn't always.' He was silent for a moment. 'And you've sacrificed so much for them.'

'No more than you have.'

It was tempting, so very tempting, to tell him that he—*they*—had been a part of what she'd sacrificed. And that some days she regretted it more than anything else in her life. That sometimes, like their situation now, she resented it for turning her life into something she hadn't anticipated and was very sure she didn't want.

'No, *definitely* more than I have.' He looked at her. 'I've spent most of my time as a king trying to live up to my father's name. To my grandfather's legacy. And here you are, creating your own legacy.'

'You're making me sound much better than I actually am,' she told him. 'I've done the things I've had to, Xavier. That doesn't mean I wanted to do them, or that I was okay with doing them.'

'Like what?'

'Like this.' She gestured between them. 'Do you think I enjoy sacrificing my own sanity to protect my kingdom?'

'Are you saying I make you insane?'

'I'm saying that this entire situation is enough to make the world's sanest person insane. Don't tell me you don't feel it, too.'

'No, I do,' he answered quietly. 'But I'm glad for it. For this opportunity to make up for the mistakes I've made, and to create my own legacy.' He paused. 'I hope some day my people will see that I did this for them, and they'll remember me for it.'

'What are these mistakes you're talking about, Xavier? You keep referring to them, but you can't tell me what they are.'

'I don't *want* to tell you what they are,' he corrected, and she felt her eyes widen.

'No, of course not.' It stung, but she wouldn't let him see that. 'So, we decide on the winner now. I'll put the ring on before we go back, and then we announce the winner, offer our congratulations, and then make the special announcement of our engagement.'

'I moved on, Leyna,' he said instead of answering her. 'We both did. We're not the people who confided in each other as teenagers. Not any more.'

'You say that as though I'm not reminded of it every moment I spend with you.' The words came out less angry than she'd thought they would, tinged with a sadness she saw he'd heard, too.

'Why did you do it?' he asked, and she saw the Xavier she'd hurt that day so long ago. 'The real reason, not the lie you told me.'

'It wasn't—' She broke off when she saw his face. Sighed. 'It wasn't entirely a lie.'

'Okay.' His eyes were deadly serious. 'So tell me why you did it.'

'You told me you weren't able to function properly after Erika died.' It pained her to bring it up, but it was the only way to make him understand. 'Well, that's why. I couldn't *not* function, for Aidara's sake.'

'And you couldn't function with me by your side?'

'No, I couldn't,' she said. 'All those things my grandmother told me? The things your parents told you? I realised they were true. Our friendship—and then more than just a friendship—*was* a distraction. I thought about you constantly, and I kept thinking about…about how they were right. About how I was spending more time thinking about you than I was about my kingdom.'

She paused, her heart pounding at what she'd just said. But she couldn't seem to stop.

'I kept waiting for that to be the reason I failed at my duties. And I thought if I kept thinking that, some day I *would* fail and I would blame you.' She took a breath. 'It was better that I broke up with you. That I didn't blame you for any of it. And that way I could stop anticipating that I would lose you, too. And I could finally let go of that debilitating fear.'

CHAPTER NINE

'WE HAVE TO decide a winner soon,' Leyna said immediately after sending his thoughts into disarray with her words. She was no longer looking at him, but he couldn't bring himself to stop looking at her. Not if there was a chance her face would give away any more clues to her thinking.

'Is that true? Are those the real reasons?'

'Xavier, please,' she whispered, the plea piercing straight through his heart. 'I'm trying to…focus on what we need to do.'

'No, you're avoiding a conversation we should have had a long time ago.' Despite the effect her pleading had on him, he couldn't just let it go. Perhaps because of the stirring of anger he felt building in his chest.

'And maybe we would have had that conversation, Xavier, if you hadn't just given up on us so completely.'

'You're blaming *me* for this?'

'Yes, I think I am.' Anger had splashed her cheeks with colour. 'Do you know what that time in my life was like for me?' She didn't wait for an answer. 'From the moment Carlos called me 'Your Majesty' my life started unravelling. I lost my father and then my mother, and I kept expecting you to leave me, too. I kept waiting for the warnings my grandmother had given me to play out. I kept waiting to fail. The fear of it stayed with me in every single thing I did, and I couldn't think, I couldn't *breathe* without it choking me.'

Her chest heaved and he wanted to take a step forward and tell her to take it easy. To calm down. But her words paralysed him.

'I thought I would get ahead of it and break it off with you. I wanted to be free of that sickening anticipation. I told you I didn't love you but, damn it, I never expected you to believe it.'

'But you knew it was exactly the thing to say to get me to.'

'Maybe. Or maybe I was waiting for the man who was so insistent—so *sure*—on the beach when he proposed to me to make an appearance. To tell me he didn't believe me. Maybe I was hoping for that man to fight so I knew he wouldn't leave, too. Maybe it was even a test.' She lifted a hand to her mouth and he saw it trembling.

But still he couldn't move.

'But that man never showed up, and you failed that test miserably. And still I waited. I *waited* for you to come back to me, Xavier, and tell me that my fears weren't real.' Her gaze was steady on his now. 'I waited three months until I saw the picture of you and Erika on your first date, and then I stopped waiting and realised you weren't that man after all. And that maybe our relationship *had* been childish, and this was the proof I needed to squash my knee-jerk reaction to defend us and claim that it wasn't. So I focused on my kingdom. On what was real and stable. Just like I've been doing for the past few weeks.'

He wanted to tell her it wasn't fair—that pushing him away, expecting him not to accept it, *testing* him, wasn't fair—but his voice wouldn't work.

'You wanted to know, Xavier,' she said, her voice shaking slightly. 'Now you do. I'll head back up and you can follow.' She slid her hand into the pocket he'd put the ring in, and then slid it onto her finger. 'Don't take too long.'

She left him speechless. He knew he didn't have time to process what she'd just told him. Especially not if he considered everything that was swirling around in his head. And now he had to go back up and pretend they were happy together—that all the blame he'd placed on her for ending their relationship hadn't suddenly been shifted to him and hadn't just rocked his entire world.

He relaxed the jaw he'd only just realised he'd clenched and made his way back to the festival. Leyna waited for him just a few metres away from where the guests were gathered, out of their sight, and started walking when he reached her side. They slipped into their royal personas as soon as they were visible, Leyna particularly bubbly as she made her way through the crowds.

He knew she was putting on a show, but he wasn't sure if it was in anticipation of the announcement that needed to be made. She *was* supposed to be a blushing bride after all. The other option was that she, like him, desperately wanted things to go back to the way they'd been before he'd rocked the boat.

When they made their way to where a little stage had been set up to announce the winner, he realised he didn't even know who would win. Not that it mattered, he thought, and clapped along with the crowd at the announcement of the young blonde with the sick husband as the winner.

As the congratulations were made and the photos were taken, he felt nerves skitter through him. He held his breath when the time came for their engagement to be announced, and watched Leyna do it with poise and just the right amount of enthusiasm.

His eyes fluttered over the crowd. He wasn't sure what he'd expected, but the cheers that came a beat after Leyna announced their engagement was definitely not it.

Again, he didn't have time to ponder it. He received the congratulations, posed for the pictures and welcomed everyone to the celebratory ball that evening. It was his only part in the announcement but it exhausted him and by the time they headed back to Aidara's castle Xavier was longing for some privacy.

'Did Carlos speak to you about the arrangements for this evening?' Leyna asked halfway to the castle.

'Yes, he did. They've arranged for me to change in one of the rooms in the east wing.'

'Good.'

Silence followed her words again, and then he heard himself asking, 'Are we going to talk about what happened back there?'

'The engagement?' she asked, her eyes telling him she knew what he was really asking and that the answer was *no*. 'I didn't expect them to react that way,' she continued. 'Did you?'

'I'm not in the mood to play games, Leyna,' he answered tersely.

'I'm not playing a game, Xavier. I'm trying to stay focused on our task. If you'd let me do that from the beginning, we wouldn't have needed this conversation in the first place.'

'How are you so calm about this?' he demanded. 'You just told me something that brings into question everything about the last decade of our lives.'

'No, it doesn't. We've made our choices and now we live with the consequences.' Her face was clear of any emotion. 'We focus on the present. That means we have to convince everyone at tonight's ball that we're happy enough to marry. Can you do that?' she asked very deliberately.

'Yes,' he said through a clenched jaw.

She nodded her head. 'Great.'

The car pulled up in front of the castle then and when Jacob opened her door she moved to get out.

'I'll see you this evening,' she said over her shoulder before leaving the car.

Xavier took a moment to realise he needed to get out, too, and then went directly to the room Carlos had shown him to earlier that morning. He would have liked to go to the gym—*his* gym, to use the punchbag he'd grown used to taking his frustrations out on. But, since that wasn't an option, he poured himself a drink and pushed open the doors to the balcony instead.

He settled in the chair there, resting his legs on the railing as he thought about the mess his life had become over the past weeks. It had started with Zacchaeus, but the convoluted path Xavier and Leyna had taken to deal with that situation hadn't brought them any closer to finding out what Zacchaeus had planned.

It was insurance, yes, but he couldn't help but wonder if they should have tried harder to speak with the King of Kirtida. Perhaps a simple conversation would have clarified things and his life wouldn't have got so complicated.

That was cowardice talking, Xavier told himself. But was it any wonder he wanted to be a coward when being brave had brought him knowledge he should have never pressed for?

Leyna had told him she'd wanted him to fight for her, and he'd *wanted* to. He'd desperately wanted to. But his broken heart had kept him from that in the beginning, and then his family had insisted it was time he moved on and, before he knew it, he was dating and then marrying Erika.

He had to face that part of the reason he'd given in was because he'd been tired of being told what to do. He'd thought that if he gave in to this one thing— this one, massive thing—they would stop. He'd even told himself it wouldn't matter—the only person he'd wanted to marry was Leyna, and since that wasn't happening he might as well give in.

But he'd been a fool. Their judgements about what he did and their opinions about what he should do… It never stopped. In fact, giving in had made them think they had more power. It exhausted him. He'd had to fight to keep Erika happy, he'd had to rule his kingdom *and* he'd had to deal with his mother and grandmother constantly peeking over his shoulder.

No wonder he'd missed the light Leyna had brought to his life.

And perhaps that had been another reason he'd given up on her. His feelings for Leyna had been all-consuming at times, too. His craving for that light had become more and more pressing the older he'd become. In fact, on the day he'd proposed to her, when he'd told her she wanted to escape her royal duties to spend time with him, he had been doing that very thing with *her*.

When she'd broken his heart she'd broken it completely. And so, with his father's reminder about his responsibilities, perhaps it had been easier to accept what they'd wanted him to do. Perhaps he hadn't wanted to fight for her so hard after all…

He downed the drink and set the glass back on the ground. He'd so badly hoped Leyna hadn't been right. Especially since her words made his heart ache. But paying attention to that pain would mean so much more than facing the fact that he hadn't wanted to fight for her. No, admitting it also forced him to accept what he hadn't wanted to in the last ten years—that he hadn't given his marriage all of himself.

It crushed him. He set his feet back down and rested his head in his hands. His family's expectations of him might have been unrealistic at times, but perhaps in disappointing them it had been a bad omen for the future.

He'd disappointed Leyna by not coming back and, though it might not have been fair of her to expect him to, he agreed that their years together meant she might have expected him to try. He'd disappointed Erika by not being the husband she deserved—not only in what he'd offered her of himself, but by being unable to give her a child, too.

He didn't think that feeling could be topped until he realised that he was disappointed in himself, too. And *that* was perhaps the worst of them all.

She'd fallen back into the honesty that had once come so naturally between them.

That was the only reason Leyna could think of to explain why she'd told him something she'd only just discovered herself. Perhaps it was because of all the not thinking—and then the inevitable thinking—she'd been doing over the last days. And when she'd finally allowed it to come to her consciousness, the realisations had come spilling out of her mouth.

The reason they had spilled out to Xavier could only be because she'd been lulled into a false sense of security by remembering what they'd once shared. There wasn't any other reason—none that would make her feel confident in her decision to marry him and carry his child, that was.

So, instead, she thought about what she'd told Xavier. It was so clear to her now that she'd been afraid of losing him. It made sense to her, too. More than any other reason she'd given herself for making that decision. In the years following it, she couldn't think of one reason why she'd done it. She'd regretted it, had felt a knife twist in her heart every time she'd seen Xavier and Erika together—a reminder that *she'd* been the one to push him away.

But now she knew that she'd needed time. More importantly, she'd needed him to tell her that he wouldn't leave. That they could rule together without losing sight of who—and why—they were ruling. She'd been young, she'd had her entire life thrown on its head with her father's death.

She reminded herself of that when she felt accusation claw at her. When her thoughts filled with how much she'd hurt him.

If she didn't remind herself of it, she'd spend her life struggling to forgive herself. And she didn't want to live like that.

Would she struggle to forgive him, too? she wondered, starting the ritual of getting ready for the ball. She'd always told herself she'd been hurt because he'd moved on so quickly to Erika. Now she knew she'd really been hurt that he'd moved on at all.

She smiled at the ladies who'd helped her get ready for events all her life, but her mind wandered as she let them do their work. She felt…lighter at the realisation.

It settled something that had been brooding inside her for so long.

The feeling made her think that she *would* forgive Xavier. That maybe she already had. And that the tightness in her chest as she made her way to the ballroom was because she needed to ask him for his forgiveness, too.

Maybe it would finally help them both to move on. To build their future without hurt being part of their foundation.

And then she forgot about all of it as she stood at the top of the stairs and saw Xavier waiting for her at the bottom.

She'd thought it the night of the banquet, too, but then she hadn't really allowed herself to enjoy seeing Xavier in his uniform that night. Though she wasn't sure what had changed, she was glad it had. He was strikingly handsome, his hair combed back in a style that made it all the more obvious. The uniform fitted him perfectly—suited him, too—and, though it didn't reveal much of his body, knowing the muscular shape of it sent a slow thrill through her.

Their eyes met and lit a fire across the staircase. Her body heated from it—from the fire she saw reflecting in his eyes as she made her way down—and she was afraid that she would go up in flames when she finally stopped in front of him.

'People might suspect that our child isn't a honeymoon baby if you keep looking at me like that,' she said huskily as she slid her arm into the one he offered.

'You shouldn't have worn that dress then, Your Majesty.'

She looked down at the off-the-shoulder burgundy

dress that only really revealed her shoulders. 'This dress is perfectly acceptable.'

'Sure it is,' he said softly as they approached the ball-room. 'For one purpose.' He glanced down at her and his eyes told her exactly what he thought that purpose was. She blushed and then put on a smile as they were announced in the hall.

If she had to judge how her people felt about her engagement based on the ball that evening she had nothing to worry about. And though she received comments that told her some guessed the real motivation for their marriage, they were all supportive. And usually accompanied with some form of 'It's about time' remark.

They gave the proper honour to the winner of the festival, too, and before she knew it dinner had come and gone and she and Xavier were opening the party on the dance floor. Her body braced as he placed his hand on her waist, and as she placed hers on his shoulder while the other took his hand she felt his body tighten, too.

'Relax,' she whispered when the music started, and she forced herself to take heed of the instruction just as she felt Xavier did. It helped, but didn't lessen the tension between them. She relaxed slightly when the other couples joined them, and forced herself to release an unsteady breath.

'I take it you'll be returning to Mattan this evening,' she said to focus her mind on something else.

'That would probably be for the best.'

'You're welcome to stay, though.' She smiled as the festival winner and her husband—who looked healthier than Leyna had seen him in a while—passed them in a twirl, and then directed her gaze at Xavier. 'You're always welcome here.'

Something softened in his eyes, but he shook his

head. 'It wouldn't be a good idea for me to stay here. But thank you for the offer.'

She nodded, and told herself it was for the best. She was preparing herself to return to mingle when the next song came on, and felt her breath catch when Xavier pulled her in until their bodies were moulded to one another.

'I don't think people will mind thinking our child was conceived out of wedlock,' Xavier told her a few moments later.

'Of course you don't,' she replied, fighting to keep her tone light. 'If you did, you wouldn't be looking at me like we will be conceiving the baby as soon as we leave the room.'

He gave a small laugh. 'I could probably turn it down a notch.'

'You should,' she agreed. 'You're good at that, too.'

She felt his body stiffen, and shifted her gaze so she didn't have to look into the eyes that saw too much. 'You know why I did that, Leyna. It wasn't because I didn't want you.'

'Wasn't it?' she asked, keeping her tone light. 'You don't have to explain it. I know you were married and that—' she struggled with her next words '—you and I aren't on the same page any more.'

'And that, to you, means that I don't want you?'

'Wanting someone physically and wanting them emotionally isn't the same thing, Xavier.'

'I know that,' he said, his voice strangled. 'And somehow you've got it into your head that I only want you in one of those ways?'

'You loved Erika. I don't blame you for not wanting to—' she cleared her throat '—tarnish that by…by making love with me.'

'That's what you think?' Something in his tone had her looking up at him, and she nodded. He didn't reply and they swayed together, a weight she'd never expected settling between them. When the song was done she put distance between them, looking up in surprise when Xavier didn't let go of her hand.

'Come with me,' he said, half-plea, half-command. She nodded and followed him to the door where Carlos stood. Xavier whispered something into her secretary's ear and, without expression, Carlos nodded and bowed to them both.

Leyna followed Xavier helplessly then, holding her breath when she realised he was leading her through the secret tunnels that went to the beach.

To their place.

She shook her head, cautioning herself not to go there. She watched him grab the blanket that was always at the door and went outside with him, only stopping before they hit the sand.

'I'm not going down to the beach in a *ballgown*,' she said, exasperated. 'Especially not if we're going back to the ball.'

'We're not,' he answered, taking his jacket off. Her eyes greedily took in the muscles that were clear in the white T-shirt he'd worn under his uniform jacket, and then she forced them back to his face.

'What do you mean, *we're not*?'

'I mean I told Carlos we wouldn't be returning.' He dropped to take off his shoes, and then started on hers. She gasped when she felt her feet leave the shoes as he scooped her into his arms, the blanket now over his shoulders.

'Wh...what are you doing?'

'I'm saving you the time it would have taken to tell

me you couldn't ruin a dress made with such effort and expertise by walking through the sand.'

'So you thought you'd treat me like a caveman would?'

'When's the last time you saw a movie or read a book? This is romantic.'

'I beg to differ,' she said, though, in all honesty, she *did* think it was a little romantic. Not because of the action, but because of the motivation behind it. He was being thoughtful as she *would* have worried about ruining her beautiful dress, and *that* was pretty romantic.

Being alone on the beach under the stars didn't hurt, either.

But then he stopped, and she could almost see the smoke coming from his ears as he tried to figure out how he would get the blanket from his shoulders to the ground.

She laughed. 'How about I help with that, Mr Romance?'

'Thanks,' he said with a sheepish smile and, though awkwardly, somehow they managed to spread the blanket on the ground and she sat down without touching the sand. He joined her then, settling on his back with his arms behind his head. She caught a glimpse of toned flesh as his T-shirt crept up, and she quickly lay on her back beside him, carefully placing her hands on her belly to ensure one of them didn't somehow land on the skin she'd just seen.

'I doubt this is going to go down very well. The hosts of an engagement party leaving before their guests do.'

'They'll get over it,' Xavier said easily. She turned her head and saw him take a deep breath. 'I needed this.'

'To escape?' she asked softly, and he smiled.

'I'm not sure we can ever escape. Not really. Our

guards probably had us surrounded the moment we came down here.'

'So this is as good as it's ever going to get,' she replied and took a deep breath of her own. 'From where I am, I don't think it gets better.'

'You're just saying that because this is your favourite place. Or was,' he added quickly.

'It still is.'

'I should have known when I found you here after the State Banquet.'

'I have only good memories here,' she told him and then shook her head. 'Mostly.'

Silence followed her words, though, for some reason, Leyna didn't find it tense. She kept her eyes on the stars twinkling down on her, reminding her of the beauty in the world.

And, though she would probably regret thinking it later, she enjoyed being there with him. It felt a little like that day when both the best and worst thing had happened to her. But now she was here and she'd survived them both.

'Do you regret it?' he asked suddenly. 'Saying yes to me?'

Her heart gave an uncomfortable thud in her chest. 'No.'

'Not even now, knowing what you know?'

'No,' she said again, and took a deep breath to prepare herself for what she knew she had to say next. 'I do regret the way I ended it, though. I regret hurting you as much as I did.' She inhaled and used the breath to say the words she should have said that afternoon. 'I'm sorry, Xavier. I truly am sorry for hurting you.'

'And I'm sorry for not fighting for you,' he replied

softly. She turned her head to look at him. 'You were right. I should have.'

'But it was unfair of me to expect it from you.' Emotion, thick and heavy, sat in her throat. 'I didn't know that I had expected it, not until I told you so this afternoon. But I was young, and afraid, and—'

'Fear doesn't always make us think rationally.'

'No, it doesn't.'

She looked away, afraid the emotion of the moment would make her cry again. It was ridiculous, even having the urge, but she supposed that was only to be expected. She'd kept everything about that time in a box, shut tight, refusing to let it make her any less of a queen.

And maybe she'd managed to keep it locked for so long because she hadn't had anyone to share it with. Until now, it seemed.

'My family wanted me to marry Erika.'

The unexpected words had her head whipping to look at him again. 'What?'

'They realised that whatever had happened between us hadn't been a simple tiff and insisted I move on. So I did.'

She opened her mouth, and then closed it again. When she was sure she could speak without giving away her emotions, she asked, 'So, you only dated her because they told you to?'

'That's what I thought, yes. Until this afternoon. And then I realised maybe it had been easier to listen to them than to face possible rejection from you again. I don't think my heart would have been able to take it a second time.'

Her mind spun with the information, and she heard herself asking him about his marriage. 'So how did you decide that you would date Erika?'

'She was the daughter of one of my father's advisers. She'd been doing humanitarian work, had a good reputation in the influential circles of Mattan, and my mother and grandmother thought she was a suitable match. My father did, too.'

'Was it…arranged?'

'Not in the way you mean.' He shifted his body so he was on his side, looking at her. 'It was a *suggested* marriage. And I'd already wasted the year after my twenty-first birthday—in their opinion—waiting for you.' He fell silent.

'I don't think any of them believed in love. My grandmother had chosen my mother for my father to marry, and they'd grown to care about each other over the years. I don't think they knew how it felt to love someone like…' His voice faded, and she saw the hesitation in his eyes before he continued. 'I don't think they knew what it was to feel what I felt for you.'

Her heart broke and not for the first time she found herself wishing she could go back. That she could stop herself throwing away the love Xavier had had for her. That she could stop herself hurting him as badly as she clearly had, denying herself the chance to be loved.

'Did you try to tell them?'

'What was the use?' He shook his head. 'I didn't think you loved me, and that would have been the only motivation. Besides, I was devastated. And I can see now that moving on with Erika… It was an expectation. A command, even, from my King. I couldn't disobey him. I had no reason to.'

She understood it, even if it broke her heart even more.

'So I listened to them and I married, because that's

what a king has to do.' He shrugged in a way that told her his family had reminded him of that fact as well.

'And Erika was fine with that?'

'She didn't entirely have the option not to be. She had a father who wanted her to marry into the royal family, and a king who expected her to marry his son. How could she refuse?'

'So you *both* didn't want to be in the relationship?'

'I didn't say that.'

'I thought…' She faltered. 'I'm sorry, I just can't imagine being in a relationship because that's what people told me I should do.'

'Is that why you haven't dated since us?'

She gave a soft laugh. 'Walked straight into that one, didn't I?' But, because he'd been honest with her, she would give him the same courtesy. 'Yes, I think so. I've always known that I would have to marry one day. But I was postponing it for as long as I could. Despite the urges of my grandmother.'

'She wanted you to marry?'

'In the same way your family wanted you to move on. She concocted the most outlandish ways to get men she thought appropriate in front of me without saying that she wanted me to meet them. At first,' Leyna added, thinking about recent years. 'But then she gave up and started telling me outright that I couldn't be a spinster queen. That I needed to give Aidara a future ruler.'

'And even that didn't sway you?'

'It should have, but…' She trailed off, her mind spinning a bit at the prospect. 'It *has* now, though, hasn't it?' she said, instead of what she really thought.

That perhaps duty hadn't dictated *every* decision of

her personal life. And what did it mean that she'd let it do so now? With Xavier?

'See, I told you that you were stronger—better—than I was.'

'Because I didn't marry when my grandmother told me to?' she scoffed. 'That's hardly something to be proud of.'

'I disagree,' he said softly. 'Maybe if I'd done the same, she wouldn't have—' He broke off.

'She wouldn't have what?'

He shook his head, rolling onto his back again. 'It's nothing.'

She pushed up onto her forearms. 'It isn't nothing, Xavier, or you wouldn't have brought it up. What did you want to say?'

'It's nothing,' he repeated stubbornly.

'Is it nothing?' she asked, trying a different tactic. 'Or is it just something that you don't want to share with me?'

'Don't make this about you, Leyna.'

'But it is, though, isn't it? What else could it possibly be about?'

'Erika,' he snapped. 'My wife. The woman I should have protected.'

CHAPTER TEN

XAVIER'S CHEST WAS heaving and he closed his eyes, fighting for calm. Leyna's hand closed over his and it helped steady his breath. But he couldn't keep the contact when he was talking about Erika and he pulled his hand away, settling it on his chest.

When he opened his eyes again, he pretended not to see the hurt on her face or how she sat up, the ease that had her lying on her back gone.

'What should you have protected her from?' Leyna asked quietly, turning away from him. He sat up now, too, and felt the guilt at hurting her throb in his chest.

'I shouldn't have brought it up.'

'But you did, so clearly some part of you wanted to talk about it.'

'Or you pushed so hard that I had no choice.'

She gave a soft bark of laughter. 'If it helps you to blame me, then by all means go ahead.' She pushed up to her knees and Xavier got to his feet to help her up. She let him, but let go of his hand the moment she was standing.

He couldn't blame her, and shouldn't have let it bother him. Yet he felt the same hurt that she'd had in her eyes when he'd let go of her hand minutes ago.

'Can you take me back?' she asked, not looking at him.

'Leyna—'

'Can you just take me back, please?' she asked sharply now.

He sighed and lifted her into his arms, thinking about how different things had been just a few moments ago. He was responsible for that, he thought. He needed to face the truth of that—that he so easily blamed her without taking responsibility himself.

Something he was beginning to realise happened more and more.

So when they reached the path to the castle and he set her back on her feet he opened his mouth to apologise, but was silenced when she spoke.

'We need boundaries,' she said, slipping her feet back into the heels she'd worn. 'Things we shouldn't talk about because it would undermine the cordiality we'd like to maintain in our relationship.' She straightened. 'I think I already know what's on your list and, since we've cleared the air about what happened ten years ago, I'd like to add our past to that, too.'

'You think we can avoid talking about our past?' he asked in disbelief.

'We must if we want to keep this marriage as civil as possible.'

'And that's essential, isn't it?' he said, hiding his anger. But he should have known that she'd see through it.

'You don't get to be angry with me when you're the one who put up walls. Perhaps you didn't say it—' she cut off his protest '—but not wanting to talk about it, snapping at me when I ask you to, that's a wall. And I refuse to feel…' Her voice faded and he saw a flash of hurt on her face. 'I don't want us to take our anger out on each other any more. So—' she straightened her shoulders '—can I count on you for that?'

'Yes,' he replied a little helplessly.

'Then I'll say goodnight. I'll have Carlos let you know when the results of the pregnancy test are in.'

She walked away from him then, leaving him speechless. It occurred to him that it wasn't the first time she'd done it that day, and he was beginning to wonder whether that was how she dealt with difficult situations.

But then, he knew that wasn't true. She'd faced *their* situation—which in optimistic terms could be described as difficult—head-on, with the strength and grace he'd come to expect from her as Queen. Perhaps then it was Leyna the woman, not Leyna the Queen, who walked away from difficult situations. And perhaps it wasn't so much the situation as it was the person.

Him.

He couldn't blame her, he thought. He'd lashed out and let his emotions get the better of him. But it felt wrong talking to Leyna about Erika. About what he should have done for Erika.

Because if he told her why he'd needed to protect Erika, what was there to stop him from telling her that he'd needed to love his wife more, too? That he'd needed to give up the hope that he'd somehow still carried for him and Leyna—even though he'd been *married*—and put his wife first?

He'd been avoiding telling Leyna what his mistakes were because his biggest one had partly been because of her. And how could he tell her that? How could he admit that out loud? He had enough trouble facing it himself, let alone validating its existence by telling her about it.

His dilemma was that she was the only one he'd ever

been comfortable talking about it with. He sighed, wondering, not for the first time, how his life had become such a mess.

The next morning he found out.

He'd got the news that Zacchaeus had positioned a fleet of ships off Kirtida's shores as soon as it happened. Less than an hour later, Xavier was alone with Leyna in his library after being briefed on the latest developments.

'So, one of the ships from that fleet is on its way here,' Xavier said. 'I can only imagine it's Zacchaeus.'

'Who else could it be?' she agreed. 'And if it is, his timing is interesting.'

'Right after our engagement announcement.' Xavier nodded. 'I think our plan might be working.'

'Or it could be backfiring,' Leyna said. 'We were told his ships could be in position to either attack or defend. At this point, we don't know which is more likely.'

'I suppose you're right.' Xavier thought about it and then said, 'He's on his way to Mattan, though. Why?'

'Because he doesn't know that I'm here and he wants to offer *you* a proposition.'

'Whatever it is, I'm not interested.'

'Of course you aren't,' she said dryly. 'Or else this—' she wiggled the fingers on her left hand, making the engagement ring glint at him '—would have been moot.'

'I couldn't exactly go to Zacchaeus and ask *him* for his hand in marriage as part of an alliance,' Xavier replied sarcastically, and felt some of the tension that had settled at the pit of his belly dissolve when she laughed.

'You're right,' she said in mock seriousness.

'That's the only thing keeping me on your side, Your Majesty,' he said with a smile of his own. They stayed like that for a moment, smiling at each other as though the threat to their kingdoms wasn't on his way to see them.

Leyna was the first to snap out of it. 'We're going to have to make an announcement to our people after this. They've been waiting for it, and I don't think we'll be able to delay any longer. Especially considering that our fleet will have to respond.'

'You're right.' Xavier sat opposite her. 'What will we say?'

'That our diplomatic attempts with Kirtida have failed, and that Zacchaeus is no longer interested in being a part of the Alliance of the Three Isles.'

'They might not be in the mood for a wedding after that.'

'Perhaps,' she considered. 'Or perhaps they'll be thrilled because we'll tell them that the wedding will assure the alliance of our two kingdoms and therefore keep them safe.'

His thoughts once again went to how strong, how graceful a queen she was, but he kept them to himself. Considering her words, he said, 'What does it say about me that I'm hoping we can resolve all of this right now with Zacchaeus?'

'It says you'd like to avoid the disaster of a possible war for the sake of your people.' Her expression went from serious to soft. 'It's not a weakness to want to solve this without violence, Xavier.'

'It feels like it.'

'Then we're both weak.' Her gaze stayed on his, and he wasn't sure what he saw there that had her nodding. 'You know, we have a trump card in this discussion.'

'Which is?' She laid a hand on her belly and his

chest suddenly tightened. 'You want to tell him about the *baby*?'

'Don't make it sound like an unreasonable suggestion.'

'But…we don't even know if it's a reality yet.'

'We don't have to know. All we have to do is convince *him* of it, which might have him thinking twice about going into war.'

'Why?' Xavier asked, the emotion he couldn't identify that was churning in him making the words fierce. Bitter. 'Because an unborn child is going to tap into his compassionate side?'

'No.' Her eyes flashed with annoyance. 'Because it means that Aidara and Mattan are unequivocally and irrevocably linked.'

'Is there nothing sacred to you?' he snapped. 'Or is everything just leverage? In the name of duty?'

He read the emotions that sped across her face like a book he hated but couldn't put down. Shock. Indignation. Hurt. He braced himself when anger finally settled, but there was no chance for her to tell him how he'd made her feel. Not when Xavier got the call telling him Zacchaeus had arrived and was on his way up.

He could see that Leyna knew what the phone call had been about and she walked onto his balcony, the summer breeze tousling her hair. He ran a hand through his own and contemplated going out to her to apologise. But he wasn't sure what he would be apologising for, and thought that the anger still sizzling in his stomach might actually be useful for the conversation they were about to have.

A knock at the door edged that anger with nerves. He heard Leyna enter the room again and straightened his shoulders as he called for their guest to come in.

'King Zacchaeus is here, Your Majesty,' his private secretary announced and quickly closed the door behind her.

'Zacchaeus,' Xavier said when he saw the dark-haired man he'd once considered an ally. 'We weren't expecting you.'

'And I hadn't expected a "we",' Zacchaeus answered, his brown eyes settling on Leyna.

Xavier felt jealousy coil inside him when he saw the appreciation in Zacchaeus' eyes, and forced himself to ignore it. Zacchaeus was baiting him, the logical side of him knew. And it was smart, he thought, when Zacchaeus' eyes settled on him again with a glint that told Xavier it was strategy.

'There's always a "we", Zacchaeus,' Leyna said. 'That "we" used to include you and your kingdom. Are you here to clarify whether that's still the case?'

'I'm here to offer my congratulations,' Zacchaeus said easily. 'I must say I feel partially responsible for you two finally getting together.'

'Oh, you're entirely responsible,' Xavier answered in the same tone. 'But, if we're all being honest here, you already knew that.'

'Yes.' The answer was curt, Zacchaeus' bantering tone gone. 'And it's disheartening to see Kirtida's allies act as a duet as opposed to a trio.'

'That tends to happen when a member of a three-way alliance removes themselves from the alliance,' Leyna said.

'That's not entirely true, though,' Zacchaeus answered, and something behind his guarded expression had Xavier wondering what was happening with the new King of Kirtida.

'What would you call refusing to answer our requests

for a meeting then?' Xavier asked, keeping his eyes steady on Zacchaeus' face. 'What would you call refusing to *see* us when we arrived at Kirtida to talk about the future of our alliance?'

'Complicated,' Zacchaeus answered.

'If this is some kind of game to you, Zacchaeus, we're not interested,' Leyna said. 'All we'd like to know is whether you're formally withdrawing from the alliance. If you aren't, then we can use this opportunity to discuss the agreement, since you seem unfamiliar with its terms.'

Zacchaeus' expression darkened at her words but Leyna continued. 'And if you are, then we should discuss the legalities of that, too. Either way, this meeting will be productive.'

'You know I've always liked you, Leyna,' Zacchaeus told her, his eyes lit with admiration. Although he wasn't sure, Xavier thought it was genuine. 'Respected you, too. And, in honour of that, I'll be as honest with you as you are with me.'

Xavier doubted that, but he kept silent and watched as Zacchaeus shoved his hands into his pockets. For a moment, Xavier caught a glimpse of the man he'd known growing up. But when he looked at them again, Zacchaeus' eyes were harder, darker, and Xavier knew not to make the mistake of thinking he was the man he'd once appeared to be.

'Contrary to your belief, Leyna, I *am* aware of the terms of the alliance. I might not have ruled for as long as either of you have, but that doesn't mean I'm a novice,' Zacchaeus said grimly. 'I knew what it would mean when I chose not to attend the Banquet.'

'You intended it,' Leyna said, and something flashed

across his face—could it have been uncertainty?—
before he replied.

'Now you both understand how serious I am about
what I'm here to discuss.'

'What *are* you here to discuss, Zacchaeus?' Xavier
interjected.

Zacchaeus' face went blank, except for the seriousness in his eyes. 'We need to renegotiate the terms of
the alliance. Or there will be no alliance at all.'

CHAPTER ELEVEN

THOUGH SHE'D EXPECTED the words the moment she'd heard about Zacchaeus' fleet, Leyna's chest constricted at the confirmation. She felt the insidious pulse of panic throb with each heartbeat and fought to keep it from showing on her face.

Instead, she focused on the fact that she wasn't supposed to have been there at all, and the indignation that came with that realisation.

'You intended on renegotiating the terms of the alliance without me?' she forced herself to say lightly. 'I'm not sure if you meant for me to be insulted, Zacchaeus, but you've certainly achieved it.'

'When I heard about your engagement, Leyna, I assumed Xavier would tell you everything that I told him.'

'But there's more.'

'Yes,' Zacchaeus allowed. 'If he had agreed to renegotiating the terms when it had been only the two of us, I would have wanted assurances that Kirtida's part of the alliance would be just as strong as Mattan's and Aidara's. Unfortunately, you can't help with that.'

Her mind quickly pieced it together, but Xavier started to ask what Zacchaeus meant and then stopped when realisation dawned on him. Horror, lined with a fear she'd never seen him show before, passed across his face, but was quickly replaced by a carefully blank expression.

'Is that why your ships have been readied?' Xavier asked, his voice dangerously low. 'To intimidate us into negotiating with you? To intimidate me into offering you *my sister*?'

'They were readied for the same reason yours will be as soon as I leave here, I imagine,' Zacchaeus responded. 'That is why this discussion is so important.'

'Which terms do you want to renegotiate?' Leyna asked quickly. She wasn't sure Xavier would able to speak without provoking Zacchaeus.

'The Protection of the Alliance of the Three Isles.'

'What about it?'

'I need assurance that should Kirtida be involved in a...disagreement, its allies would step in and support the action.'

'That's what the agreement currently states,' Leyna replied, and then she frowned. 'But since you're here, specifically mentioning this, there's clearly a loophole that doesn't cover your particular kind of disagreement.'

'We need protection from every country, Leyna.' Zacchaeus' eyes were more sombre than she'd ever seen them.

'Again, that *is* the purpose of the Protection of the Alliance...' Leyna trailed off. 'You mean with one of our allies? With the alliance's allies?'

'Yes.'

It suddenly made sense, she thought. He hadn't come to the banquet because he might have had to face the ally he was requesting protection from.

The pulse of panic slipped into her blood, coursing through her veins, becoming harder to ignore. She swallowed, and begged her body to give her more time.

'We can't agree to that,' Xavier said, his eyes moving from Leyna—where it flashed with concern—to Zacchaeus. He seemed to have put his feelings about Zacchaeus' implication aside. 'It could undermine *all* of our international relationships.'

'Perhaps it's time to forge new ones.'

'Zacchaeus, this isn't something you can just decide on the spur of the moment,' Leyna said, finding her voice again. 'It takes thought, reasoning, negotiation. You've been King for a month and you already want to jump into this?'

'Does this sound like something I *want* to jump into, Leyna?' Zacchaeus snapped. 'There are factors at play here that—' He cut himself off, clenching his jaw. 'Regardless of how long I've been King, I *am* responsible for Kirtida. And this is what is necessary to ensure that my kingdom is protected.'

'What have you done, Zacchaeus?' Xavier asked. 'Tell us what's happened to make this such a necessity.'

Leyna saw the conflict in Zacchaeus' eyes before he cleared them of emotion. 'That's not possible. Not now. I understand you might need some time to think this through, but I'd like you to consider this. We're stronger as three than as one. If I withdraw from the alliance—'

'There'll be two of us and one of you?' Xavier asked, and Leyna saw Zacchaeus' jaw tighten once more.

'There'll be conflict,' Zacchaeus replied. 'It would be better for that conflict not to be within an alliance that spans centuries.'

He was out of the door as soon as the words had left his mouth, leaving a stunned silence behind.

Leyna lowered herself onto the couch, forcing air into her lungs as she closed her eyes. She prayed that Xavier would give her a moment to regain control, but she didn't check to see whether that was the case. She was painfully aware of her stomach, her heart, her chest—and she just wanted them to relax again.

She gave herself a few minutes and then opened her eyes when she felt steadier. Xavier sat across from her, his face carefully blank.

'Are you okay?'

'I'm fine,' she replied, feeling her cheeks heat. 'I just needed a moment.'

He nodded and got up to pour her a glass of water. 'Is it possible that this is a side-effect—'

'Of pregnancy?' She took the water from him and watched him sit down again as she took a sip. 'No. There should still be some time before the symptoms show up. *If* I'm pregnant. Besides, it's happened before.'

'And what exactly is *it*?'

'Anxiety.'

Now, she felt the colour seep from her cheeks. She didn't want Xavier to know about the panic attacks she'd started having after her mother had left. They'd been much, much worse in the past but each episode—regardless of its intensity—left her feeling so incredibly vulnerable and fragile.

She'd put those days behind her, developed strategies to cope. She hadn't had one—the kind that had had her bodyguards develop a protocol for them anyway—in years. The dreams, like the one she'd had the other day, came and went, but not the panic attacks. It felt awful that she'd come so close in recent weeks.

Just as she had before, she would cope.

But she didn't want to share that with him.

'You shouldn't have to deal with it alone,' Xavier said, interrupting her thoughts.

'With my anxiety?' she asked, shaking her head.

'It's not exactly the kind of thing you can share with other people.'

'Sometimes it is.'

'Not in our position.'

'But now we have each other.'

Her heart stalled at the words, but she accepted them, telling herself this was all part of the cordiality they'd agreed to the night before. She nodded. 'Yes, we do. So let's talk about what we're going to do about Zacchaeus.'

It felt good to finally discuss the situation in the light of new information. Not that it was positive, Leyna thought, telling Xavier as much. They didn't have many options. On the one hand, they could refuse to negotiate with Zacchaeus. But they didn't know what trouble he was in, or how it would impact Mattan and Aidara.

On the other hand, they *could* negotiate with him, and be impacted by that trouble willingly. But that might also entail a marriage between Nalini and Zacchaeus, which neither of them were willing to decide on.

'You could talk to her,' Leyna said. 'Leave it completely up to her.'

'And tell her what? That the future of Mattan is in her hands?'

'Of course not. The future of Mattan is in *our* hands. But how are we going to make a decision about *either* of our kingdoms without knowing what *all* of our options are?'

'If Nalini *did* agree to marry Zacchaeus, how would that help us decide on what to do?'

'I know this is hard, Xavier.' Leyna resisted the urge to lean forward, to grip his hand with hers. *Boundaries.* 'But we have to make some kind of decision. And, based on Zacchaeus' reaction, we won't have very long to make it.'

'If we don't negotiate with him, we have war between the Isles *and* a possible external threat. We'll break a centuries-long alliance and threaten the trust of our people, putting their lives at risk.' He got up and poured himself a drink now. 'If we do, we have *no* war between the Isles, face a *possible* external threat, and my sister has to marry the man who's put us in this situation in the first place.'

'Those are our options,' Leyna confirmed, her gaze staying on him. She waited for what she knew—what she'd feared—would come next.

'If we'd just waited before doing all of this, we might not have been in this situation.'

'We *did* wait, Xavier,' Leyna said, forcing coolness into her tone. 'And you know our actions are the reason Zacchaeus was here in the first place. Why he was willing to talk about this at all.'

And because it was easier to pre-empt, she said, 'In my view, our best option is to talk to Zacchaeus about the protection clause in the alliance agreement. But we'll ask him for a week to consider it before we tell him that we've made a decision.'

'Why?'

'Because we'll find out whether I'm pregnant in a week.' She went on, needing to accept the finality of her words, 'If I'm not, we go to Zacchaeus as equals— all three of us. Nalini won't have to marry Zacchaeus and—'

'You mean break off our engagement?' She nodded. 'So you get to break up with me all over again.'

'There's nothing to break up, Xavier,' she said, ignoring the emotion inside her that screamed the contrary. 'And you can't deny that you were looking for a way out. I'm offering you one. So, if I'm not pregnant, you'll protect your sister and we'll protect our kingdoms.'

She didn't wait for a reply, leaving the room—leaving his company—so she could catch her breath again. The panic wouldn't be as easily abated this time, she thought, which had the tension in her chest increasing.

She escaped as far as she could away from the library, hoping no one would see her. But with each step the pressure grew, eventually causing her to stop and press her back against the nearest wall.

She didn't know how long she stood there, nor did she care. All she knew was that her head suddenly felt as if it were on a roundabout and her lungs felt as if they were burning.

'Leyna.'

She nearly groaned when she heard Xavier's voice, but instead opened her eyes. 'I just need a few moments.'

'And you can have them,' Xavier answered softly. 'In private.'

'Okay,' she replied, but couldn't bring herself to move. After a few seconds, Xavier sighed and scooped her into his arms just as easily as he had the night before.

'You don't have to do this,' she said automatically.

'No, apparently, I do,' he said in strained annoyance.

She didn't see where he took her and only realised she was in his bedroom when he laid her on the bed. She rested her head against the pillows and watched him open the windows. The sea air immediately filled the room, stilling some of the spinning in her head.

'Why do you insist on doing this to yourself?'

'It's not a choice.'

He started to pace. 'Fine, but I thought you were going to let me help you.'

'How can I let you help when you're the one making me feel this way?'

He stopped. 'I make you anxious?'

'Yes. No.' She sighed. 'I don't know if it's you or the situation.'

'Both, probably,' he said, and lowered himself next to her on the bed. 'How can I make it better?'

'You can't. Not unless you can go back to the past and change everything I did to ruin us.' She was tired, she thought, and blamed that for the slip. 'I'm sorry, I shouldn't have...' She shook her head. 'Boundaries.'

'I didn't agree with that idea then and I don't agree with it now.'

'Really? So you want to keep going back over the past like a broken record? Because that's what it feels like, Xavier. And I can't stop listening to the stupid record because every time I see you it plays on repeat.'

'Then let it,' he said, and turned towards her. 'Let it play.'

'And what would that achieve? What would replaying that hurt, those mistakes, possibly achieve?'

'It'll remind us of what we need to stay away from in the future.'

'Why, Xavier? There is no future for us. There can't be. Not when so much has happened.'

He didn't reply immediately, and she could hear emotion in his voice when he spoke, though she couldn't identify it. 'Is that why you have the dreams, the anxiety attacks?'

'No, those come from ruling a kingdom by myself with no support.'

'But having no support is because of the choices, the *mistakes* you've made, isn't it?'

Realising what he was doing, she moved to the opposite end of the bed from where he sat and set her feet on the ground. '*This* was a mistake. I shouldn't have said anything.'

'It wasn't a mistake, Leyna.' He got off the bed, turned to face her. 'It was you finally being honest with yourself.'

She let out a bitter laugh. 'I *am* being honest with myself. I'm facing the fact that this marriage isn't something you want, let alone this child. Or maybe it is, but just not with me. You moved on, remember?' she said before he could protest. 'And you were so reluctant to go ahead with this plan.'

'This was *my* plan, Leyna. Getting married was *my* suggestion.'

'Because your kingdom was in danger!' Leyna knew she should leave but something wouldn't let her. 'You had years to salvage our relationship.'

'So did you!'

'And how would I do that? Come to see you and *your wife* and tell you that I'd made a terrible mistake and that I still loved you?'

CHAPTER TWELVE

'*LOVED*,' LEYNA SAID in a voice just as stunned as the expression on her face. 'I said loved. Past tense.'

'When did you stop loving me?' Xavier asked, ignoring the voice that warned him not to.

'When you got married to someone else.'

'But you said that you would have had to tell me *and* Erika that you still loved me. Which would mean you still loved me when I was married.'

'I was talking about when you two were dating,' Leyna said, though he heard the desperation in her tone. 'Why does it matter?' She didn't wait for an answer. 'We have enough to deal with in our present, Xavier. And in our future. We don't have to keep going back to the past.' She gave him a beseeching look. 'Okay?'

He wanted to say no. He wanted to get to the bottom of what she'd just admitted to him. But his eyes fluttered to the bedside table near where she stood. A picture of Erika smiled back at him, and he felt emotion seize his vocal cords.

He saw her eyes follow his and when she looked back at him they told him she knew he wouldn't argue with her.

'I'll call you in a week, once I get the test results,' Leyna said, none of the angst they'd shared in the last minutes evident in her voice. 'We can decide what to do then.' She walked to the door. 'I'll tell Zacchaeus we need the time. I don't think he'll be a real threat until we've made a decision, but I'll get his assurances. You can talk to Nalini. It'll be best if we know where she stands when the time comes.'

And then she was gone, and Xavier could no longer ignore the feelings tumbling through him. He walked to the picture of Erika and picked it up, wondering how she still had so much control over him three years after her death.

Perhaps it was because he hadn't given her what she'd deserved when she was alive. And perhaps he was just using *that* as an excuse to ignore that he'd started feeling something for Leyna again. He *needed* an excuse to face that. To somehow mute the voice that told him he was making a mistake.

Fool me once, shame on you. Fool me twice...

But he'd felt a real, visceral fear when she'd given him the option to back out. And he'd known why she'd done it. Just like ten years before, she was making a decision *for* him. To protect herself from anticipating it in the future. And though that made him wonder why she thought she needed to protect herself—especially if, as she claimed, there were no feelings involved— that fear remained.

But he couldn't deny that her offer had been tempting—which was probably why he hadn't called her out on what she was doing. His life would go back to what it had been. Yes, there would be the complication of Zacchaeus, and whatever had prompted this entire situation. But he wouldn't have to marry Leyna and be reminded of a life he shouldn't have. And Nalini wouldn't have to marry Zacchaeus...

Then he realised his life hadn't been all that wonderful before this had happened. He'd been racked with guilt about his wife, and he'd felt so terribly alone. And though the guilt was still there now—more pressing, perhaps—at least he no longer felt alone.

Because he had Leyna.

The realisation had him shaking his head. To keep himself from thinking of it, he went back down to his library. He checked that Leyna had left Mattan safely and, when that was confirmed, called for Nalini. He used the minutes before she arrived to prepare his words, but nothing he came up with made *Would you like to get married to our enemy to protect the alliance?* sound good.

Nerves settled heavily in his stomach, even when Nalini bounced into the room with her usual energy.

'You look like hell,' she said cheerfully, flopping down onto the couch.

Xavier gave her a sour look. 'It's called running a kingdom.'

'*And* you're in a bad mood. This is fantastic.' She grinned at him and he couldn't help his smile. 'How are things with Leyna?'

His lips straightened. 'Fine.'

'Really?' Nalini's eyebrows rose. 'Things are *fine* between you and the woman who broke your heart— excuse me, your fiancée?'

He was suddenly grateful he'd kept the possible pregnancy to himself. 'You're making it sound—'

'Complicated?' She grinned. 'It is complicated, though, isn't it?'

'You have no idea.' But she would. Soon. He just needed to find a way to tell her about it. But, before he could, she straightened and her expression lost its amusement.

'I was actually glad you called. I wanted to know how you were handling all of this. And truthfully. Not the rubbish answers you give us all at breakfast.'

'As well as can be expected, I guess,' he answered truthfully, and ran a hand through his hair. 'How *should* you handle a threat against your kingdom forcing you to come face-to-face with everything you've struggled with in your past?'

'You've been through worse,' she reminded him softly, and he nodded.

'Yes, I have.'

'But that doesn't mean things aren't bad now. Especially if you still feel something for Leyna.' When he didn't say anything, Nalini's eyes widened. 'You *do* still feel something for her. I knew it!'

'I loved my wife, Nalini.'

'Your wife's dead, Xavier,' she said gently, though the words still sent a ripple of unhappiness through him. 'You can't keep living your life as though she isn't.'

'I can't just move on either. Especially not with the woman everyone accused her of replacing.' He shook his head. 'Especially not with the woman *she* always accused me of wanting. I won't do that to her. I *can't* do that to her.'

'I know you don't want to hear this, but love is stronger than duty.' Nalini's voice was firmer now. 'Leyna was love. Erika was duty.'

'I loved Erika, too.'

'I know you did. But it wasn't the same, was it?' She waited but he didn't answer. 'Being with Leyna now. How does that feel?' Again, he didn't say anything. What could he say? That she was right? 'I don't care if you won't tell me, Xavier, but you should at least be honest with yourself.'

He blew out a breath. 'Things *are* complicated,' he said, and she smiled.

'You can tell me I'm right when we're on the other side, talking about how glad we are that we're through it.'

It reminded him of what he'd called her there for. He cleared his throat. 'You must have heard that Zacchaeus paid us a visit today.'

Her smile sobered. 'Yes, I did. And I saw him. Briefly, in the castle. He looked like he'd just left a storm behind.'

'I'm afraid he wants to bring you into the storm with us.'

Xavier explained, as briefly and as clearly as he could, what the meeting had been about. He felt her entire demeanour become serious—an obvious change since she was always so full of happiness—and told her that the decision was completely hers.

'I'd like to talk to him.'

'About what?'

'I want to know how serious he is about this.'

Sensing her reluctance to talk to him about it, he nodded. 'Sure. If we decide to do this, you can talk to him.'

'When will that decision be made?'

His mind raced. 'Leyna and I have to first talk through the implications of both options.'

She nodded. 'Would you let me know as soon as you've made your decision?'

'Your feelings about this will affect that decision, Nalini.'

'I'll do it,' Nalini said softly. 'I want to talk to him about it first, but I'll do it.'

'Are you sure?'

'It's my duty, Xavier, and you're my King.'

'You know that's not—'

'Relevant here?' She smiled. 'I know. But, like it or not, this *is* my duty. Especially if it protects Mattan.'

He walked to her and pressed a kiss on her forehead. 'We're lucky to have you as our Princess.'

She gave a soft laugh. 'We're lucky to have you as our King.' There was a beat of silence, and then she said, 'And, as one of your people, Xavier, I want you to be happy.'

He sighed. 'Nalini—'

'Erika would have wanted you to be happy, too, Xav.' Nalini stood now. 'I know your relationship wasn't traditional, and that things were harder because of your fertility problems, but she loved you.' She patted his cheek. 'She would have wanted you to be happy. Even if it was with Leyna.'

Nalini left him wondering whether that was really true.

CHAPTER THIRTEEN

IT WAS A strange thing, waiting for the results of a pregnancy test. Leyna's doctor had taken the blood sample a few hours ago, and he'd told her to expect the results in the next hour. The nerves sat in her chest, reminding her that when the news came it would change her life.

Once upon a time, a long time ago, she'd wanted a child. She'd wanted a family and she'd wanted to rule. But then she'd realised that ruling had been more important than her desire for a family. Yes, she'd got there because she'd been afraid of losing Xavier—of disappointing her kingdom—and had pushed him and those dreams away. But when she'd thought about it, she'd realised she wouldn't have had the time to be a queen *and* a mother. Not the mother she wanted to be anyway.

Not a mother like hers had been.

Leyna poured herself a glass of water and raised it shakily to her lips. She'd had to face all her issues in the last few weeks. All of the emotions and memories she'd hidden in the crevices of her mind had burst out, demanding her attention. It had only been a matter of time before she thought about her mother, really.

And, considering the news she was waiting to receive, it wasn't a surprise that that particular issue had come up now. But it didn't mean that she wanted it to.

Not when it had her wondering, a little out of the blue, whether abandoning a child could be a genetic trait. Whether putting her own needs above her child's was something she'd learnt without her knowing it.

Whether she could serve her kingdom and be the mother that her child deserved.

'Leyna.'

The glass almost fell out of her hand, but she corrected quickly and only a little water splashed out onto her fingers.

'I'm sorry, I thought you were expecting me.'

'I was,' Leyna replied and set the glass down on a piece of paper, wiping her hand on the side of her dress. 'Just a little lost in thought.'

'I could see that.' Xavier stopped in front of her. 'Everything okay?'

'Perfect,' she said brightly. 'Just waiting to hear whether we're about to become parents.'

Nerves flashed in his eyes, and it made her feel better about her own. 'When will we know?'

'Any time now.'

She'd just finished speaking when the phone rang. It took a beat for her to move, but then she walked back around her desk and answered.

Then slammed the phone down after her doctor told her the results.

'Was that your doctor?' She nodded numbly. 'What did he say?'

She walked through her balcony doors then, desperately needing air. And, when she heard him behind her, she spoke without turning around.

'I'm pregnant.'

Before she knew what was happening, he'd pulled her into his arms. She could feel his body shaking—

or was that hers?—and allowed herself to take comfort from him for one short moment. She wrapped her arms around him, letting her face rest on his chest. She closed her eyes and again felt dangerously close to tears.

Except this time she knew she could blame it on her hormones. Which, apparently, were in full swing despite her being only two weeks pregnant.

The reminder had her moving out of his arms and heading back into the library.

'You don't seem happy about this,' Xavier noted quietly when he joined her.

'That I'm pregnant and trapped in what will be a marriage of convenience?' She closed her eyes and then shook her head. 'I didn't mean that.' She took a breath, and then another, and forced herself to think rationally. 'I only meant that it's still early. This might not work out.'

'You mean you might miscarry our child? Is that what you want?' he asked, his voice low, though she could still hear the pain.

'Of course not! I'm just… I'm just in shock.' She offered him what she was sure was an unconvincing smile. 'I'm allowed to process.'

'Yes, you are.' He paused. 'But even if you are processing… It doesn't mean what you just said wasn't what you felt.'

'*Of course* I don't want to have a miscarriage, Xavier—'

'I was talking about you being trapped. Is that how you feel? Is that why you made that offer a week ago?' He walked closer to her, but stopped a metre away. 'You made it seem as though you were giving *me* an out, but maybe you were giving yourself one. And now you don't have it. Now,' he continued, gaining steam, 'you have to continue the charade of this marriage. You can't push me away now, afraid that I would walk away first—'

'That's *not* what I was doing.'

'No?' he asked. 'So you're telling me that you weren't scared I would suggest backing out of our alliance?'

Trapped, she found herself floundering. 'You didn't want Nalini to—'

'No, I didn't,' he interrupted. 'But that didn't mean I was just going to abandon you, or the promise we made to each other. To our kingdoms.'

'It wasn't a promise,' she said now. 'It was a *plan*. Plans change.' She closed her eyes, and turned away, but whirled back at him. 'Do you think this was how I *planned* to have a child? To be married?'

'Do you think this is how *I* planned to have a child and marry?' He took a step towards her now. 'You told me our responsibilities come first. That what's happening now.'

'But it *shouldn't*. It shouldn't come first.' The words were ripped from her. Ashamed, she sat down, giving her shaky legs some reprieve. 'I didn't mean that.'

'No, you did.' He took the seat opposite her. 'And it's fine.'

'It's not fine,' she nearly sobbed. 'I know my duty comes first. I believe it does.' But she was trying to convince herself of it, not him. There was a long stretch of silence after she'd said it, giving the guilt time to do its work. She lifted a shaky hand to her face and felt the guilt mingle with shame.

'Why is duty so important to you, Leyna?' Xavier asked quietly. 'And I'm not talking about you serving your kingdom or being responsible for your people's lives. I'm talking about *you*.'

'I… I don't know what you mean.'

'That's part of the problem.'

'Why is duty so important to *you* then?'

He threaded his fingers together and didn't meet her eyes, but answered. 'I think because it was a way to prove myself. To prove that I could be as good as my father. Or maybe to try and show them—my mother and grandmother—that we shouldn't be compared.'

Compassion poured into her. 'You shouldn't have been. Your father was a good man, and a great king. And so are you, but in a completely different way.'

'Except there was only one way in their eyes, and that wasn't the way I was.' His gaze lifted to hers. 'You know what they used to say to me. How they treated me. None of that changed when we stopped being friends.'

'I know.'

'In fact, it probably got worse.' She could see the struggle on his face, and only realised why it was there when he continued. 'When I married Erika, her expectations of me were added to the ones I already had no hope of living up to.'

'What do you mean?'

'For most of our marriage Erika was miserable. She didn't want this life. Our life.' Emotion—hurt, regret—flashed across his face. 'I shouldn't have agreed to marry her.'

The years that they hadn't been friends faded away so that when she reached out to take his hand it was as his best friend, not as the woman who'd agreed to marry him. 'You feel like you should have protected her from what being royal meant.'

'Yes.' The admission was said in a hoarse voice.

'Could you have?' she asked, knowing that he wouldn't have asked it of himself. 'Because you told me that neither of you had a choice. Not really. So could

you have said no to your King and your family and refused to marry her?'

'That's not what I meant—'

'No, but that's what protecting her would have en-
tailed, Xavier.' She let that sink in and then continued
softly, 'And if she really wanted to, she could have protected herself, too. She was an adult, and she was a part
of your circle. She must have known what she was getting herself into when she said yes.'

'No one from the outside can know what they're getting themselves into, Leyna.'

'Maybe not entirely, but she saw what was required
of you. She must have known it would be required of
her, too.'

'It wasn't that simple.'

'I know that. We've spoken before about how that
term doesn't apply to us. But I think you're making it
more complicated than it has to be.'

'You don't understand.' He pushed up from his seat,
and she saw she'd made him angry.

'Did she make you happy?' she asked instead of
pushing, because she needed to know, as much as she
wanted to distract him.

'We got along well. Really well,' he said with a
frown.

'And that was basically the same as being happy.'
It wasn't a question. 'For the kind of relationship you
had, with all the factors influencing it, it was enough.'

He would need to think about that, she knew. And so
would she. She hadn't allowed herself to feel hope when
Nalini had first told her about Xavier's unhappy marriage. And she'd reminded herself of that after Xavier
had told her his marriage had essentially been arranged.
It had been easy to do when it was clear he was still so

consumed by whatever had transpired in his relationship with his wife.

But now she let the idea soothe some of the hurt she
still carried about him moving on from her. Not because
Xavier and Erika hadn't been happy together—Leyna
believed, as she'd told him, that happiness for people
like them wasn't black and white. But because he hadn't
got over *her* as easily as she'd thought he had.

She felt shame at that, but it still alleviated some of
her own pain. But *that* realisation had the emotions that
had been hidden behind her hurt become more pressing, and the relief was short-lived. Especially when she
realised one of those emotions was the very hope she'd
suppressed when he'd first told her about the circumstances of his marriage.

It worried her. And made a different kind of panic
than the one she was used to throb along with her heartbeat.

'What you had with Erika,' she forced herself to say,
making sure her voice was calm and matter-of-fact.
'That's more than most people get, Xavier.'

'Maybe for us, Leyna. But not for people like Erika.
She was *normal* before she married me. And normal
people should have a chance at real happiness.'

'She *was* happy, Xavier. That light I saw between the
two of you on your wedding day? That was happiness.
That was someone who was happy with the choice she'd
made. Why don't you want to believe that?'

'Because she didn't die happy, Leyna,' he choked
out. 'And that was my fault.'

CHAPTER FOURTEEN

'I FAILED HER.' Now that he knew he wasn't infertile, he felt the truth of those words even more. 'I should have given her a child, Leyna.'

'Or she should have given *you* a child.' Leyna's expression was impassive. 'It was more important to you. You needed an heir. Mattan needed an heir. In fact, it was her civil responsibility.'

'That isn't fair.'

'No, it isn't, is it?' she told him mildly. 'I agree. And yet that's exactly what you're telling yourself.'

He was too stunned to feel betrayed by the trap. But it felt…strange to accept what she was saying. For so long he'd blamed himself for their struggle to conceive. It hadn't mattered that there hadn't been a medical reason indicating that either of them had been responsible. It had been almost…simple, *easy*, to accept the blame. Just as he had taken the blame for her unhappiness, for her struggle with being Queen.

It was the first time he'd considered either, and he didn't know what that meant. All he knew was that Leyna telling him she was pregnant had changed something. First, it had added to the guilt. But now, along with her telling him he was being unfair to himself… it had changed things. And because he didn't want to face what that meant right at that moment, he suddenly remembered how they'd reached this conversation in the first place.

'If I admit to being unfair to myself, would you admit that you're doing the same?'

She frowned, and he knew it was because of the question as much as the change in the direction of their conversation. 'What are you talking about?'

'This obsession you have with duty.'

She gave him a look. 'Really? We're engaged and about to become parents for the sake of our kingdoms and I'm the only one who has an obsession with duty?'

'At least I know *why* I'm obsessed. Why are you obsessed?'

'I'm not obsessed,' she said dismissively. 'I don't have a choice. It's different.'

'But you did have a choice.' He kept his eyes on her face. 'You had a choice long ago, and you chose duty.'

'I told you why I did that.'

'Yes, and you were afraid then. But there's something more, Leyna, because you're afraid now, too.'

'Xavier, we don't have time for this.' She stood, and he saw the annoyance in her face and the set of her shoulders. But he also saw that it wasn't *only* annoyance. No, her face held the same expression that she'd had when she'd told him she was pregnant. And since he knew that news had terrified her, he wanted to know what was scaring her now.

'We have time,' he said in a serious voice. 'Tell me why duty is so much more important than love for you. Even though you admitted that it shouldn't be.'

'Duty is the most important.'

'Love is stronger than duty,' he replied, repeating Nalini's words.

'Is it, Xavier? Is it really? Because you chose duty over love when you married Erika. How was love stronger there?'

'Since I've already told you that, we both know you're deflecting.'

'So you're allowed to bring up things we've already spoken about, but I can't?'

'Still deflecting.'

'I'm *not* deflecting,' she snapped. 'I just don't want to talk about this right now. I've just found out I'm pregnant, for heaven's sake. I've listened to you speaking about the woman you replaced me with—'

'She was *not* a replacement,' he hissed, and saw her wince.

'No, of course she wasn't.' She closed her eyes. 'I'm sorry, Xavier, I shouldn't have said that.'

'But you did,' he replied in a hard voice. 'Because keeping this secret is so much more important to you than speaking about it.' He shook his head, the desire to get her to admit what was really going on disappearing. 'I'm trying, Leyna. I *have* tried since this entire situation began. But no more. I'm not putting myself through this any more.'

'Through what? Through trying to figure out the past? I *told* you there was no point in it. You can't be angry with me for that.'

'I'm not,' he answered, his anger seeping away, leaving only a bone-deep tiredness. 'But you're fooling yourself if you think that all of this is because of the past. Not ours, at least.'

When he saw she didn't understand what he meant, he told himself he would try one more time and then move on. This was for his child, he thought, and ignored the voice in his head telling him it was for him, too.

'You're carrying something around with you, Leyna. I don't know what it is, but it's there and you're using your responsibilities as Queen to coat it so you don't have to deal with it.' He gave her a moment to process his words before he continued. 'Of course, duty is important. But you were right when you said it earlier. It *shouldn't* be the most important thing. Not if we want to lead our people properly.'

'You think putting our happiness before our duties will make us better leaders?' she scoffed.

'No, but doing it the other way around doesn't either.' He realised the truth of his words as he spoke them, and felt something free inside him. 'I've done it the other way, Leyna. I know how that ends. And for a little while *that* made me a bad king. So yes, maybe I *do* think being happy will make us better leaders.' Again, he thought of the conversation he'd had with Nalini. 'And you know? I think our people would want us to be happy, too.'

She didn't respond, and silence grew between them for several minutes before he realised he was no longer needed—or wanted—there. He walked to the door, ready to leave, but before he did he said, 'You've always put duty first, Leyna. Do you think doing that has made you the kind of queen you always wanted to be? If so, then fine, we'll go on to be dutiful spouses and parents. But if not...'

He left with the possibility his words had suggested hanging in the air.

Damn him, she thought furiously. Damn him for bringing up something she'd told him in confidence when he'd been her best friend.

For pushing when she'd told him not to.

For seeing right through her.

Leyna's hand itched for something to throw, but instead she walked to the balcony and breathed in the sea air. She'd seen her father do the same thing so many times. She didn't think he'd ever noticed, but she'd watched him all the time. Even as a young girl she'd known that she would one day take on his role, and it had made her perceptive.

And what she'd perceived had scared her.

The crown had taken her father away from her. He'd changed so drastically after his coronation that Leyna had known it had been because of the crown and what it meant. She'd told Xavier once that she hadn't wanted to turn out that way. She'd repeated it the day he'd proposed. And now Xavier was telling her she'd become exactly what she'd feared.

Oh, he hadn't said it so explicitly. He wouldn't. But she knew that was what he'd meant. And now she was worried that she had inherited the ugly sides of both her father *and* mother.

She pressed a hand on her belly at the thought, squeezing her eyes closed against the tears she had no power to stop. She desperately hoped that wasn't true. What would she be leaving her child with then? It had suddenly become incredibly important that she give her child more. He or she didn't deserve what Leyna had received. Her child deserved what she'd had at the beginning—supportive, caring parents who'd put their child first. Not what she'd ended up with.

She stilled, realising for the first time that there was something more important to her than duty. It shook her. So much that she barely made it back to the couch before her legs gave way. She took a breath, steadied herself and ignored the inner voice that screamed at her to ignore the realisation. She'd done that so often in the past that it had become her default, but she needed to think this through.

Her first thought was that Xavier was right. Clearly there was something in her focus—she refused to call it an obsession—on her duty that wasn't purely about duty. She saw now that it was partly because she hadn't wanted to turn out like her father. And she'd thought that zeroing in on her duty was how she was going to prevent that.

Her father had been a good king, but he'd not been the best father once he became King. So, she'd reasoned, if she didn't have a family to let down, she could focus on being Queen. It made sense in a cruel, ironic sort of way. Because, though she'd succeeded in being Queen and doing it well, it had turned her into the miserable person that her father had been.

And yes, she wasn't disappointing her family. But she was disappointing *herself*, because that wasn't the kind of queen she'd wanted to be. Or the kind of person.

Then there was her mother. Even the thought made her nauseous, so she knew how much it affected her. She shut her eyes against it, and brushed impatiently at the tears that kept on coming. She couldn't stop them. Not when she'd just realised why she'd placed so much emphasis on her responsibilities. Leyna hadn't wanted to be like her mother either. Not as a mother, and not as a woman.

Responsibilities meant something. But because Leyna hadn't had responsibilities other than the crown, she'd channelled her passion for that belief into ruling. Now she had more. She had a child to think of. She had someone who deserved her love and respect—she wouldn't abandon them when they needed her the most. Or when the demands of the crown became difficult.

Love is a wonderful thing, but when you lose it you lose sight of what's important.

Her grandmother had been right. When Leyna had lost Xavier, she *had* lost sight of what was important. But that hadn't been duty. One day Leyna would forgive herself for thinking that. Because how could she not? Her grandmother, the closest family member she'd had left, had drilled it into her. She'd focused on duty so absolutely herself that Leyna had had no choice but to follow.

But no, what was most important was *love*. She'd convinced herself it wasn't and that she hadn't needed it when she'd pushed Xavier away. When she'd let her fears overwhelm her and overshadow her feelings. And then she'd forgotten how to love herself, and her dreams for her future.

Those dreams had been a balance between family and her royal duties. Those dreams had been filled with a family with Xavier. With them balancing their royal duties *together*.

Losing him had been the worst thing that had happened to her. Losing his friendship *and* his love. It had made her into a version of herself she hadn't wanted to be. And now, with their child on the way, she wanted to be better. She wanted to show her child what was important.

And since she'd just realised love was important, and that love included Xavier, she had a lot to think about.

For herself, and for her child's sake.

CHAPTER FIFTEEN

XAVIER WAITED TWO days before he contacted Leyna again. He knew they were on a deadline with Zacchaeus, but forty-eight hours wouldn't change anything. At least that was what he hoped, and he would have dealt with it if something had come up.

But he needed time to think, to process after his last conversation with Leyna. And he'd wanted to give Nalini one more chance to back out before she made a decision that would change her life for ever.

Had he known how much *his* life would change when he'd agreed to the marriage and pregnancy of convenience with Leyna? If he had, he'd muted the warnings. He'd done what he'd thought was required of him. And that was what Nalini was doing now, stubborn in her decision to go ahead with the arranged marriage with Zaccheus if that was what he and Leyna wanted.

He'd warned her. He'd told her all the things he wished he'd known before he'd made *his* decision. But she'd just given him a look and lightly told him that their experiences wouldn't be the same.

'You're getting married to your first love for the sake of the kingdom,' she'd told him. 'I'm getting married to a man I barely know. Obviously, I have the harder job here, so while I appreciate that our situations are similar, they're hardly comparable.'

And that had been the end of the conversation.

But the moment he'd found out Leyna was pregnant, he'd known their options were limited with Zacchaeus. Aidara and Mattan would have to negotiate with Kirtida, and face whatever the consequences would be. They'd find out the details in the negotiation, but that conversation would only happen once they told Zacchaeus of their decision.

Which would entail speaking with Leyna.

The thought of it had his heart racing, but he forced himself to make the call and was now waiting for Leyna to arrive. So, naturally, everything he'd wanted to avoid thinking about when it came to the woman who was carrying his child was now traipsing through his mind as casually as teens in a mall.

There was the happiness—the pure, unadulterated happiness—he felt about being a father. And, of course, the guilt that came along with it. He'd thought once that he would never become a father. He'd felt Erika's devastation—and his own—thinking they would never have a child. And with Leyna pregnant, so easily, too, he knew there would be guilt.

But it wasn't as consuming as it had been before. Perhaps because he'd realised that there were some things outside of his control. And, yes, also because Leyna had shown him that blaming himself or Erika for something that neither of them could logically take responsibility for was unfair.

But it had him thinking that struggling with the fact that there *was* a child was just as difficult for him as the fact that *Leyna* was carrying the child. He wasn't sure if *that* guilt would ever entirely go away either. For that to be a possibility, he would have to accept that Erika had loved him as much as Nalini said she had. And there was something inside him that just didn't quite believe that to be true.

He didn't like what that said about them or their marriage. Especially since he'd agreed with Leyna when she'd said he and Erika had been as happy as they could have been, given who they were and how they'd come to be together. Things had been complicated between them, and that was how he'd always remember it.

But that was why he was wary of getting involved in another complicated relationship. In another complicated marriage. More so now because there was a child involved. And, for the sake of his child, he would ignore the feelings he could now admit he had for Leyna. The feelings that had perhaps never really gone away. And maybe never would. But their marriage, their relationship, would be cordial and respectful for the sake of their duties—royal and parental.

He felt pretty confident in his convictions until Leyna walked through the door to his library in a beautiful blue dress with her hair falling freely around her face. It was as if his heart was mocking him for thinking he could be anything but in love with her.

That thought stole his breath, had him sucking in air like a dying man, and had her rushing to his side.

'Are you okay?' she asked, wrapping an arm around his shoulders.

'Yes,' he rasped and walked away, out of her embrace and away from that intoxicating floral scent she wore. And then he turned back to her.

'What upset you?' she asked, but he wasn't completely listening to her. No, he was listening to the voice in his head telling him to kiss her.

He wanted to see whether he was fooling himself by believing they could be in an amicable marriage. He wanted to know if the feelings he'd only just allowed himself to acknowledge were in fact love.

But when he strode towards her, snaked an arm around her waist and touched his lips to hers, he thought only that he really, really wanted to kiss her.

Though he knew it was, it didn't seem like a terrible idea when he could feel her melting against him. When her mouth opened to offer more and her tongue plunged, taking more.

He wanted to pull back and enjoy her. To enjoy the way she looked in the soft sunlight streaming through the open balcony windows directly onto them. To savour the look of her, needy and womanly, in that beautiful blue dress with her hair framing her face.

In his arms.

But he didn't, too afraid that if he pulled back he would come to his senses—that *she* would come to hers—and stop before he'd had his fill.

Take, a voice whispered in his head, and he listened. He let his hands roam over her body. Up the sides of her, revelling in the slight curves, the tempting softness, and stopping just beneath her breasts.

He could feel her heart beating and smiled against her mouth when he thought her heart rate matched his. One hand slid up to cup the base of her neck and then pulled gently at her hair, angling her head so that *he* could now take, now give, more.

His mind, already hazy from their contact, went completely blank when her hands pulled his shirt from his pants. His body, already heated and wanting, ached more as she undid the buttons of his shirt, exposing his skin and torturing him as she started her exploration.

His heart sprinted towards an unknown finish line as her hands ran over his skin, heating his body until he thought he would combust. Her lips moved from his to kiss his jaw, his neck, her tongue joining to tease him. To drive him crazy. She lifted her head, smiling up at him in a heady way that had the same effect as her kisses.

And then she froze, and he saw the transformation in her eyes.

Lust and desire turned to fear and embarrassment. The colour in her cheeks faded so quickly he worried she would faint. But she just took a step back, and then waved a hand at him and turned away. It took him a moment to realise she wanted him to button his shirt and he made quick work of it, his body's denied desires making him edgy.

Making him ignore what his experiment had confirmed.

'I'm done,' he said tersely, and went to the decanter next to his desk for a drink—just as much for thirst as for sanity—and then he set the glass down and squared his shoulders.

'I'm sorry. I should have…' Her voice faded, and she looked more vulnerable than he liked.

'It wasn't you,' he replied. 'It was me. I wanted to—'

'You wanted to what?'

'Nothing.' What was the point in telling her? It wouldn't take away the dread or fear at the realisation of the extent of his feelings for her. In fact, it only added to it. Because if he told her, she would feel the need to respond. And he didn't want her to respond. 'We need to make a decision about Zacchaeus.'

Accepting the shift in his focus, she gave him a quick nod. 'What did Nalini say?'

'She'll do it.'

'You told her she didn't have to, though, right?'

'Of course I did,' he snapped. 'I even warned her about all the delightful things she can come to expect.'

Her eyebrows lifted. 'Like moody men?'

'And women in denial,' he shot back, and then shook his head. Told himself to stay on topic. 'She's aware of what she's agreeing to. As much as she can be.'

'So we're negotiating,' she said. 'That's the best option we have, I suppose.'

'The safest one, too.'

She nodded, and then sank into the chair behind her. 'Does this mean the nightmare is over?'

He felt himself softening. 'I'm afraid not.'

'No, of course not.' She pursed her lips. 'Now we find out what trouble Zacchaeus has got himself—and us—into.'

'You know, when he told us that things were complicated on Kirtida, I believed him.'

'I did, too. He sounded sincere.'

'Like the Zacchaeus we knew.'

'Maybe,' she considered. 'But then, forcing your sister to marry him isn't entirely like the man we knew.'

'I don't blame him, though,' Xavier admitted. 'I hate that it's Nalini, but wouldn't you want to have the same guarantee as the other members of a three-way alliance?'

She was silent for a moment and then said, 'I think if this wasn't personal and we saw it completely from a business point of view, then yes, I'd agree. And I'd probably do worse if my kingdom was on the line.'

'And you did, didn't you?' It was a joke, but he'd felt his chest tighten at her words—at the reminder of her *duty*—and he didn't want to go there again. Perhaps to prove to himself that he could.

But then she settled a hand on her belly, a soft smile on her lips, and he felt as though someone had squeezed his heart in their hand.

It was such a simple gesture but it had all the pictures he'd fought off over the last two days reeling through his mind. Pictures of her with a rounded belly. Beautiful. Graceful. Strong. He imagined their first doctor's appointment, and hearing their baby's heartbeat for the first time. Touching her stomach to feel their child kick. Holding him or her for the first time.

He'd imagined it all so often when he'd been young, so in love with her that it had made him dream of a future that he suddenly felt incredibly lucky to have. Because of that, those pictures now felt like memories, not images of the future. And it told him that being in love with Leyna had never been a choice for him.

Knowing the effect of that on his marriage too was hard to accept. He'd tried to deny it, had thought he'd put the nail in its coffin when Erika had asked him about Leyna. How could he not? He'd been married and his wife had questioned his feelings for another woman. So he'd shunned them, painting what he'd felt for Leyna with shame and anger.

The light, the goodness his feelings now shone with, told him he'd turned a corner. But he wasn't entirely sure what to do about it.

'Is that all?' Leyna asked now, her eyes careful.

'No.' He took a breath. 'I want to talk about the kiss.'

She blinked. 'What?'

Since he'd been taken aback by it, too, he understood the reaction. But, now that he'd said it, he realised that his heart had prompted the words, showing him what he needed to do about those feelings. So he said it again.

'I want to talk about that kiss.'

'I… I don't think that's a good idea.'

'But I do.' He took a seat across from her. 'For a long time I thought I hated you.' He saw her wince, but told himself it would be worth it. 'I didn't, not really, but when you broke my heart I thought I did. I certainly blamed you for it, and the resentment that went along with that blame…' He released a shaky breath. 'It was intense—intensely negative.'

'Why…why are you telling me this?'

'I'm getting there,' he replied, and then continued before he lost his nerve. 'It was a…a shock, when you told me that you blamed me, too. And rightly so, I now realise. I should have seen how much you were suffering. How scared you were—'

'Xavier—'

'No, I'm not done. I should have been there for you, Leyna. I should have fought for you. I should have.'

'But I told you I didn't love you and gave you no reason not to believe me.'

'Except a twenty-year friendship that should have told me to at least try.'

'I shouldn't have blamed you,' she said softly. 'I was angry and—'

'Why are you giving me so much slack?'

'Why are you being so hard on yourself?' she shot back. 'Is it because you've finally realised how unfair you've been to yourself with Erika and now you're doing it with me?'

As soon as she'd said it, she regretted it.

'Oh, Xavier, I'm sorry. I shouldn't have—' She covered her face with a shaky hand and commanded herself to pull it together. But she felt so incredibly raw, so incredibly vulnerable after realising she loved him that she didn't want to delve any further into her emotions.

It might have been a cowardly thing to do, but she'd been brave enough already in facing her feelings that week. Perhaps even that year. She didn't need to think about the emotions swirling inside her after her realisation.

His face had lost some of its colour, but Xavier merely said, 'It was a fair assumption to make.'

She nearly laughed. 'No, it really wasn't.'

'Who's the one being too hard on themselves now?'

Leyna knew he was right, but she preferred being hard on herself than thinking about how long she'd ignored the fact that she wasn't over him. How long she'd pretended she didn't regret pushing him away. As though by creating a life for himself without her he'd only hurt her and not *broken* her.

She'd got over the rest—at least she would—but still having feelings for him, still being *in love* with him... *That* was a hard thing to accept.

It was also hard to ignore.

As was the fear pulsing inside her. She had no clue why it was still there after she'd realised—and admitted—that she'd pushed him away out of fear of losing him. But they were going to be married, for heaven's sake. She was *pregnant.* She wasn't going to lose him— at least not his presence, or his friendship, she thought, considering his current mood. So that sickening, alarming feeling in her chest made absolutely no sense.

'I think I should go,' she said, and shifted forward.

'I'm not done, Leyna.'

'You feel guilty for not accepting your part in the

way things ended between us. You want to apologise. You're forgiven.' She stood.

'Let me apologise,' he said through his teeth in a voice she'd never heard before, and she lowered back down to the couch.

'Fine. Apologise.'

'I was getting there,' he growled, and then took a breath. The entire scene would have amused her if not for that feeling in her chest. 'I said I should have fought for you. But you know why I didn't, and then I couldn't.' She nodded. 'I'm sorry for that. For not, at the very least, telling you about it in person.'

Stunned, she nodded again.

'But as much as I wanted to forget you and the awful things I felt about you, I couldn't. Because those awful things... Well, they went away pretty quickly, Leyna.' His eyes shone with sincerity. 'And all I was left with was a terrible hurt that told me I still cared.'

'I'm sorry,' she apologised again, as she had that night on the beach. This time she said it in a whisper. But he shook his head.

'I'm not telling you this because I want you to feel bad, Leyna.'

'Then why are you telling me?'

'Because that day, almost a month ago now, that Zacchaeus didn't attend the banquet—' She held her breath at the emotion in his tone. 'I wasn't as unhappy with our plan as I should have been—' he paused for a beat '—had there not been a part of me that really wanted to marry you.'

CHAPTER SIXTEEN

LEYNA FELT AS though the world had slowed. Why else would she hear her heart beating in her ears? Or feel the pulse of it carry the blood through her veins?

She needed water, she realised, and moved to stand. But when she was on her feet, the ground opened beneath her and she found herself falling. Strong arms caught her before she landed, helped her to sit, and then a hand pressed her head between her knees.

'Breathe.'

Xavier's voice spoke from a distance but she obeyed, opening her mouth to suck in the air she'd only just realised she had stopped inhaling. After repeating it for a few minutes, she straightened and felt the blood rushing through her body again.

But then she looked at the concern on Xavier's face and felt it nestle again in her cheeks.

'I'm calling the doctor,' he said, and stood.

'No, Xavier, I'm fine.' She nearly stood, too, to stop him, but then realised that if she did and her head wasn't as steady as she felt, it would definitely have him calling for a doctor. 'Really, I'm fine.'

'What happened then? Was it the pregnancy?'

'No.' It was ridiculous to admit, but she went on,

knowing it would be the only way to keep him calm. 'I stopped breathing.'

The look of disbelief on his face had a laugh tickling up her throat. 'I know, I know, it's not funny. But your face...' She bit her lip, thinking about what had caused her to stop breathing to sober herself.

'Was my admission such a surprise to you?'

'Yes. Yes, it was.' All amusement gone now, she frowned. 'There's no way you wanted to marry me, Xavier. You had years to redevelop a *friendship* with me and you didn't. You didn't want to marry me,' she repeated.

'I didn't admit it to myself, Leyna, but there was some subconscious part of me that did.'

'But the conscious part of you wanted to protect your kingdom. That's enough for me.'

It had to be.

'It's not enough for me.' He sat again, next to her this time. 'I thought this plan was a disaster at the beginning. A necessity, but a disaster nevertheless.' He paused. 'I told myself I'd get through it by making sure we had boundaries. By making sure that everything was strictly professional. Which is why I agreed to the artificial insemination.'

'But you kept pushing me,' she said, confused. '*You* were the one who kept going back to the past when we could have just kept things professional.'

'Because that plan didn't work. I kept wanting to fix the past so...so we could fix the future.'

'Because we were going to be married and become parents.'

'No, because my plans when it comes to you... Well, they never work.'

He couldn't deny that trying to have a child had put a strain on their marriage, but maybe it hadn't been because *he'd* failed *her*. Maybe it *had* been because she thought she'd failed him.

Regret filled him immediately. It must have been an incredible pressure to marry into a royal family and struggle to provide an heir. He realised then that it would have been worse in *his* family, and that Erika wouldn't have been immune to his family's unreasonable expectations.

It seemed glaringly obvious now that she must have felt those expectations directed at her, too. She'd spent a lot of time with his mother and his grandmother. Plus, Erika would have seen their ease at being royal even though they'd both married into it, and her own struggles must have been magnified.

Was it any wonder that things had become worse between them before she'd passed away? That pressure must have grown each day, with each negative pregnancy test. Her lashing out, allowing him to take the blame for the infertility… All of it could have been coping mechanisms to deal with a life that she just couldn't fit into.

Including when she'd asked him about Leyna. She could have been comparing *herself* to a woman who'd always been put on a pedestal…

He would never know for sure, but this explanation felt…right. He wished he could have spoken to her one last time to comfort her. To let her know that he didn't blame her. To apologise for his part in it all. He closed his eyes, hoping that if she could see him—hear him— she would know how sorry he was.

It didn't magically absolve him of his part in the way things had ended for them. It didn't mean that he didn't still feel guilty about the feelings he'd harboured for Leyna. But it *did* help him to think that he'd made an effort to set those feelings aside for his marriage. For Erika. He'd tried to ignore twenty years of friendship and love so his marriage could have a chance.

It made him feel better, and suddenly Nalini's words came to his mind. *She would have wanted you to be happy.* If he let himself believe that, he knew what would make him happy. Leyna. But there was so much history there, so much hurt, so much denial that he wasn't sure…

She wouldn't have wanted a child with you if she didn't love you.

Everything inside him froze, and then heated with the feel-good warmth he'd only felt once in his life before.

One day, ten years ago, when Leyna had said yes to his proposal.

'Thank you for helping me see that,' he told her gratefully, and prepared himself to make her admit that she loved him, too.

CHAPTER SEVENTEEN

'YOU'RE WELCOME,' LEYNA ANSWERED.

His expression told her he'd just realised something he never had before. That realisation had comforted him, she saw, and she told herself that was all she'd wanted. For *him*. And ignored the voice in her head telling her he needed closure to move on.

Why would that be important to her? She knew where she stood with Xavier. At least she had before he'd told her that maybe there'd been a part of him that had wanted to marry her all along and that their baby was a miracle. But if she ignored that—just as she was currently doing—she knew where they stood. Theirs would be a political marriage and they'd give their child as much love as he or she could stand.

She was fine with that. Happy, even. As she'd realised over the last few days, the standard of happiness for them was lower than for others. Than for normal people, as Xavier had said. So she would balance all of her duties going forward, and be careful not to let any one of them become an obsession.

She nearly smiled when she realised that she'd finally admitted exactly what Xavier had asked her to. She considered telling him, but knew that if she did she would be opening a can of worms. She didn't want to go back to that conversation. She didn't want to think about feelings she couldn't identify—about *that* feeling still lightly pumping with her heart—and she definitely didn't want to think about how much she loved him.

One way to do that would be to get out of his company.

'So, which one of us is going to tell Zacchaeus the news?'

'Does it matter?' he asked with a smile. 'You and I are essentially the same person from now on.'

That feeling began to pulse harder in her chest again with his words, but she forced herself to respond in the same light tone as him. 'Oh, I don't know about that. I think we're still very much our own people.'

'Oh, I know that. We both do. But you know how people are. They'll begin to group us together until there is no Leyna and Xavier, only Leyna-and-Xavier.'

'But we won't let that happen, will we?' she replied shortly, and stood. 'I think I'll head back to Aidara—'

'Why does it bother you so much?'

Xavier's voice had become serious, and he was studying her. Had he been doing that all along? she wondered. Surely not. If he had been, it would mean he suspected it bothered her. That he'd been taunting her. That somehow he knew about how tight her chest had suddenly become.

'It doesn't bother me, Xavier.'

'Then why are you running away?'

'Haven't you learnt your lesson about pushing yet?' she asked lightly, but meant it.

'Yes, I have. I've learnt that pushing gets you to tell me the truth. And, considering the honesty I've given you this evening, the least you could do is offer me the same.'

'The least…' she repeated. 'I don't know what's got into you, Xavier, but I'm not sure I like it.'

'I wasn't sure I did, either. Not until a few minutes ago when you helped me realise how important it was to talk to someone.' He stood with her, and took her hands in his. 'The only perspective you have is your own, and sometimes… Well, sometimes it's tainted by your own experiences, your own issues, ones you don't even know you have.'

'I don't know what you're talking about,' she said and pulled her hands from his. She needed to get out, she thought, and headed for the door. 'I'll talk to you in a few days—'

'I love you, Leyna.'

She froze. Her heart pumped uncontrollably in her chest and she lifted a hand, rested it there in hopes of getting it to slow. She didn't turn back when she heard him walk towards her, and took a deep breath when she felt him behind her.

'Leyna, I said—'

'I heard what you said.' She whirled around. 'I heard what you said, you selfish, *selfish* man.'

His face twisted in surprise. '*What?*'

'I said you're selfish. And you are.' She stepped around him and began to pace the room. 'Just because you've had some sort of…revelation doesn't mean you get to do this to me.'

'Leyna, I don't know what you're talking about.'

'I'm talking about putting me in this position. Telling me you love me and expecting me to believe you.'

'But—'

'Because I can't believe you, Xavier. I can't. I did once, and look where that got me.'

'That's not fair,' he said, and she could hear the anger.

'Neither is this.' She stopped. 'And so I'm not going to accept it. None of it. Not the fact that you think this marriage was meant to be, and not the fact that you're in love with me. Because you're not.'

'I am,' he shot back. 'Don't you dare say that I'm not.'

'Even when it's the truth? Because, like I told you about Erika, Xavier, people who love you don't leave.'

'So you're blaming me for leaving? Again?' He shook his head. 'I thought we were past this, Leyna. And if I can't blame you for pushing me away, you can't blame me for walking away.'

'Yes!' she sobbed. 'Yes, I can. Because I loved you with all my heart and it broke me, it *broke* me when you left. I can't do that to myself again. I won't.' She wiped impatiently at tears. 'I won't do that to our child either.'

He watched her in silence and she turned away from him, not wanting him to see any more of the tears that had come from nowhere. The anger inside her settled in the quiet, and she felt embarrassment take its place.

But she didn't have to deal with it in front of him and she walked to the door, only stopping when Xavier threw his body in front of it.

'Get out of my way.'

'No.'

'Xavier, I just want to… Please don't do this to me.'

'But this isn't me, Leyna,' he said seriously. 'This is you, and the fact that you think all of this is because of me leaving when in actual fact it's because of your mother.'

'No, it's not,' she said immediately. Automatically.

'Yes, it is,' he insisted. 'You keep saying that people who love you don't leave. And you know what happened with me—with our situation—was different, so this has to be about your mother.'

She shook her head, but didn't speak.

'Finding out you're going to be a mother, too, must have brought all these feelings back again, Leyna. And that's fine. Absolutely fine. But you have to deal with them.'

'There's nothing to deal with,' she whispered, and felt the tears roll down her cheeks.

'Oh, baby,' he said, and pulled her into his arms.

The sobs came then—heart-wrenching sobs that she couldn't believe were coming from her. It was as if something had loosened inside her and as she cried, as she felt Xavier's arms tighten around her, she realised it was the same thing that had been stuck in her heart, in her throat, since her last conversation with him.

She'd thought she'd dealt with it. She'd thought that it was just because she didn't want to be the same kind of mother her own mother had been. Because she wanted to give her child more. And, though that was true, the tears that wouldn't stop, the sobs that broke as much as they healed, told her there was more.

Since she was standing in Xavier's arms, refusing his love because of it, she knew it had something to do with him, too. But she only realised it when her sobs subsided, when the tears dried, what felt like hours later.

'I'm sorry,' she said, stepping back.

'You don't have to apologise,' he replied, and she saw his body tense, as though he wanted to move forward but couldn't.

She'd put up boundaries, she realised. Not intentionally. But by stepping away from him she was telling him she didn't want his comfort. And while that wasn't entirely true, it was probably for the best. Because until she got through what she had to say, she didn't want him distracting her with his touch.

She was about to excuse herself to find something to mop up the remainder of her tears when he offered her a handkerchief. It was so sweet, so gentlemanly, so *old-fashioned*, that she had to bite her lip to keep from smiling. She turned away from him, tidied up her face and took a deep, steadying breath before she turned back.

'I *do* have to apologise, Xavier. Because you're right, I have been taking this all out on you when it wasn't really about you.' She tilted her head, considered. 'No, that's not true. It was—*is*—about you, too. But only because I'm... I'm afraid. You make me afraid.' She took another breath. 'Just like you did ten years ago.'

He nodded. 'You were afraid you would lose me.'

'Yes, I was. But...' She bit her lip, closed her eyes, and then spoke before she lost the courage. 'I was also terrified you would destroy me.' She opened her eyes then, and saw him try to mask his surprise.

'Why?' was all he asked.

'Look what happened to my mother, Xavier.' She rubbed a hand under her neck and then fisted it there, grabbing the top of the dress she wore. 'She loved my father very much, and it destroyed her when he died. It made her forget her responsibilities to what had become her kingdom, her home, too.'

'And she ran from her biggest responsibility,' he said, and his eyes told her that he understood. 'You.'

She nodded slowly. 'Yes. I didn't see before, and perhaps never would have if you hadn't pushed. Don't get cocky about it,' she said with a small smile when she saw his lips curve.

'Never,' he promised, and her smile widened for a moment before sobering.

'I think it was more than running from her responsibilities. I think it was, plain and simple, that love destroyed who she was. It happened to my grandmother, too. She used to be happy,' Leyna said, suddenly remembering a time long ago when her grandmother had smiled. 'She never used to be the unsupportive, unkind person she is now. But she lost my grandfather, and then my father...' She lifted her shoulders. 'And she blamed love. And because I was afraid of so much—of the crown weighing as much on me as it had on my father, of loving you, of losing you, of having it all change me, *destroy* me, of failing—I think it was just easier for me to blame love, too.'

Leyna shrugged again. 'My grandmother was the closest thing I had to a family—to the family I once had, Xav—that I just accepted what she said. And I pushed you away and focused on my duty, because duty was constant, stable. And if it changed me, at least it wouldn't destroy me. At least that's what I thought.'

'You've changed your mind now?'

'Yes. Because it *did* destroy a part of me. The one that longed—dreamed—for a life where family and duty were equally important. A life where I could be married to you and have our children and rule together.'

'But then it brought you that life anyway,' he said, and it was hard to ignore the hope in his voice, on his face.

'It did.'

'And you're not afraid any more? Of any of it?'

She lifted her eyes to his. 'I know what my life looks like if I live it in fear. I know what it looks like without you. I don't want to live like that any more.'

He walked towards her, stopping only a few centimetres away. 'Is that a declaration of love?'

'Yes.'

Hesitantly, she slid her hands around his waist and felt the ripple of his muscles beneath them. Her heart thudded.

'Tell me again,' she whispered.

He lifted a hand and brushed the hair from her face. 'I love you.'

'And you mean it.'

'I don't think I've ever meant anything more in my life.' His eyes shone with sincerity. With hope. With *love*. 'I love you.'

'And you're not just saying that because of the baby?'

'I'm not just saying that because of the baby. Though that does make me love you more.' His arms went around her now. 'You're going to be an amazing mother, Leyna. Just like you're an amazing queen.' He smiled at her. 'Our child will grow up to see a strong, compassionate woman be a mother and queen, and do both with the courage and grace I see in you.'

His words soothed a decades-old hurt, and she felt light. She felt *happy*. Real, genuine happiness that made her feel normal. The first real bit of excitement about her future, about her child, crept up her spine, settling in her heart. And she realised that the menacing feeling had disappeared from her chest.

'*And* our child—our children—will grow up according to standards we help them set for themselves. Of course, we'll teach them about what their duties will mean for their lives, but we'll allow them to figure it out for themselves. We'll guide, not compare. They'll be their own version of great. Just like you are. And we won't ever have to tell them to live up to you. Though they might want to,' she teased, and gave him a smile she hoped told him she loved him just the way he was.

'I love you, Leyna.'

'How many times are you going to say that?' she whispered, and felt her smile softening.

'As many times as it takes for you to say it back to me.' He pulled her in closer, and put his mouth next to her ear. 'Say that you love me, Leyna. Let's finally be happy together.'

'You'll have to say it again.' When he pulled back, she grinned at him. 'You said you'll say it as many times as necessary. So…say it again.'

He narrowed his eyes. 'I love you.'

'Again.'

'I love you.'

'One more time.'

He grinned now, and rested his forehead on hers. 'I love you, Leyna, Queen of Aidara.'

She bit her lip, holding back tears. If he asked her about it, she would blame it on the hormones. 'I *want* to tell you how I feel, but if I don't you'll have to tell me you love me on my every whim for the rest of your life.'

'What if I tell you I'll do that anyway?'

'That'll work,' she said, and felt her lips curving as her heart finally, finally felt whole again. 'I love you, Xavier, King of—'

His lips were on hers before she could finish.

CHAPTER EIGHTEEN

'ARE YOU SURE you want to do this?' Leyna asked Nalini. 'I know we've asked you that a million times, and you must be so annoyed by it at this point, but we can make a plan if you don't.'

Xavier didn't bother voicing his opinion on the matter. He'd already told Nalini that she could back out whenever she wanted to. As Leyna had said, they would deal with the repercussions if she did. But his sister was still being stubborn, insisting on going through with the plan.

'You want me to disappoint my future husband when he's on his way here? Right now?' Nalini teased, but Xavier heard the nerves in her voice. 'Let me do my part for the kingdom. For the alliance. I serve our people, too, you know.'

'Of course I know,' Xavier answered her. But he couldn't keep himself from adding, 'You do still have a choice in this. Now that we've entered into discussions with Zacchaeus about the Protection clause, we know Kirtida is facing sanctions from Macoa. We could use that as leverage to get him—'

'No, Xavier,' Nalini said firmly. 'That's not the way we do things.'

His lips curved into a half-smile. 'You still think you know better than me, don't you?'

'I know the kind of king you are,' she corrected. 'That isn't it.'

When he looked over at Leyna, she lifted her shoulders. 'Nalini's right. Besides, if Kirtida faces sanctions from Macoa, it impacts Aidara and Mattan, too. The alliance dictates our trade deals.'

'What concerns me about it is that Macoa knows that,' Xavier said, not for the first time. But it made him feel better to say it out loud. 'So their threat to impose sanctions on Kirtida is essentially a threat against the alliance.'

'Which means that negotiating with Zacchaeus is the best option,' Leyna replied, not for the first time either. 'Not blackmail.' She winked at him, and he felt his heart contract in the way it always had with her.

He knew that Macoa threatening Kirtida with sanctions didn't make sense. They had been an ally and business partner to the Alliance of the Three Isles for decades, and Zacchaeus' explanation that their gripe with Kirtida was personal hadn't been enough for Xavier. Especially since Xavier suspected, after dealing with Zacchaeus over the last week, that it had something to do with the coup that had started it all.

But Nalini was right. He wasn't the kind of king who would betray those who trusted him. And, to all intents and purposes, it seemed that Zacchaeus did trust him. Not enough to give them the details of the personal issue Macoa had with Kirtida, but enough to reveal that there *was* a personal issue. And to negotiate with them on how best to protect their kingdoms in light of it.

It seemed that Xavier and Leyna could trust Zacchaeus, too. He *had* given them the time to discuss their decision—or, in reality, to wait for the pregnancy test results—including the two days Xavier and Leyna had taken to sort through their personal feelings. He'd also told them the threat from Macoa had only been made once, and that though there had been no actions since to indicate they would act on it, he believed they would.

Xavier had no choice but to trust him. And if he was honest with himself, he had no reason *not* to believe him. Zacchaeus had been upright in their dealings since he'd made contact, and Xavier believed the reason he hadn't done so earlier *was* complicated, as he'd told them.

But until he reaffirmed Kirtida's place in the Alliance of the Three Isles, as all new kings were required to do, Xavier would be wary. Especially as the man had insisted on marrying his sister first.

'We've already announced the engagement, Xavier,' Nalini reminded him.

'Engagements can be broken.'

'Yes, they can.' He saw something in her eyes that had him wondering what he didn't know, but it was gone so quickly he thought he'd imagined it. 'But our kingdoms— both of them—' she smiled at Leyna '—have responded positively to this. It's a sign of a renewed alliance and, along with your engagement, soothes concerns.'

'But he hasn't signed the documents yet,' Xavier told her.

'Which is why I'm going to live on Kirtida under the guise of planning this wedding.'

After they'd told her what they'd decided regarding Zacchaeus, Nalini had called the King of Kirtida just as she'd told Xavier she would. When she'd returned, she'd told Xavier of this plan. It had worried him even more, but he knew that that worry would probably never cease.

But, as she'd reminded him, she was a grown woman and she could make her own decisions. And she'd made this one.

'I'll find out whether his intention of signing the documents on our wedding day is true.'

'It will be after all the details of the Protection clause are hammered out, too,' Leyna added.

'But still before yours,' Nalini replied. 'Our marriage is slightly more urgent if we take politics into consideration.'

'Oh, definitely,' Leyna replied smoothly, though he could see the amusement in her eyes. They hadn't told anyone about their pregnancy, both agreeing that it would be better not to disrupt the peace that had settled in their kingdoms once their people had heard about Nalini's engagement. Besides, it felt good keeping that news to themselves as their little secret.

'It'll be exciting,' Nalini said now. 'My own little adventure.'

'I thought you'd learnt your lesson about adventures.'

Her eyes flashed and though he wasn't happy referring to the time she'd left the castle as a teenager on an 'adventure' and had had to be rescued by the castle's guards, he needed her to be careful.

'You're no fun, Xavier,' she replied lightly, not taking him on for bringing it up. Now he *knew* she was nervous. But he didn't have time to ask her about it when his private secretary knocked on the door and told them Zacchaeus was on his way up.

'Last chance,' Xavier told Nalini. Her eyes had gone serious again, and she offered him a small smile before shaking her head.

'It's for Mattan, Xavier. That's enough for me.'

She straightened her shoulders and faced the door. Pride surged in him, and he couldn't place whether it was as a brother or as a king. Nalini was strong, he thought. She *had* learnt her lesson, and it had made her even stronger. She would take care of herself. And though he would still worry, he clung to that.

Zacchaeus was wearing all black when he entered, and Xavier felt a flash of annoyance. Was he trying to intimidate them? Why would he need to? He should have made more of an effort to make Nalini feel comfortable, Xavier thought, frowning.

He felt a hand slip into his then, and looked down into Leyna's eyes. Immediately some of the tension seeped from him, and he squeezed her hand. Together, they faced Zacchaeus.

'I'm glad you've agreed to this,' Zacchaeus said, his eyes revealing none of his emotion. He'd been speaking to Leyna and Xavier, but Nalini answered him.

'Actually, *I* was the one who agreed to it. You're marrying me, remember?'

Xavier watched something spark in Zacchaeus' eyes, but he didn't know if it was appreciation or annoyance. Again, he reminded himself that his sister could handle herself. Hadn't she just proved she was more than capable in a few words? This had been her decision. And it would be her decision whether she wanted to see it through, too.

Nalini hugged Leyna and whispered something into her ear that made Leyna's eyes glisten. Then his sister pulled back and hugged him.

'Call me,' he told her in a low voice. 'Call me whenever you need me.'

'I will,' she responded, her voice thick with emotion. But when she pulled back, her face was clear.

'Let's go,' Nalini said to Zacchaeus, but he frowned.

'Don't you want to say goodbye to your mother and grandmother?'

'I already have,' she answered. 'So let's get to it.'

Zacchaeus seemed taken aback for a moment, but he nodded to Leyna and Xavier and then they were gone.

Silence covered the room for minutes after they left. Leyna moved from his side to face him, sliding her hands around his waist and resting her head on his chest. Despite the emotion of having his sister leave with a man he still didn't know if he could trust, Xavier couldn't help the warmth spreading through him.

He held the woman he loved in his arms. They would have a child—be a family—in just over eight months. Their kingdoms were safe, and his sister's actions would ensure that if the time came when that wouldn't be the case, the Alliance would face it together. And though his feelings about Erika were still complicated, he felt as though he'd got some closure. Though he would worry about Nalini, he had to trust that she could handle herself.

Taking all of it into consideration, Xavier couldn't deny that his life was better than it had been in years.

'She'll be okay,' Leyna said, breaking the silence.

'I know.'

'She has her bodyguards, too, so she'll be safe.'

'I know that, too.'

'She's putting her kingdom first, Xavier.' Leyna leaned back. 'It's the same decision we made weeks ago. Perhaps even nobler because she didn't have ulterior motives.'

'I know.' But she'd got him to smile. And then he sighed. 'I'll worry.'

'I know.' She mirrored the grave tone he'd uttered the words in.

His lips curved again. 'Are you mocking me?'

'Never,' she said solemnly, and then walked to take a seat on his couch and patted the seat next to her.

But he shook his head. 'What do you think you're doing?'

She frowned. 'Sitting down?'

'You can't sit down, Leyna.'

He walked to the couch and scooped her into his arms. He'd discovered he liked the feeling of carrying her. It was a tiny way of showing her that he could, and would—and not just physically. Even when she made sounds of annoyance, as she did now.

'What are you doing?'

'We have somewhere to be.'

'And you couldn't have let me walk there?'

'I could have,' he said, and carried her through the door. 'But it wouldn't have been nearly as fun.'

She gave him a look that had him smiling, but she asked, 'Where are we going?'

'I owe you something.'

'If you don't tell me, you're going to owe me a lot more—' She cut off when he walked outside into the castle's garden. Though he'd felt fairly confident when he'd made the arrangements, he held his breath, waiting to see her reaction.

He'd filled a gazebo with flowers. White roses and pink lilies—her favourite—spilled over the sides, creating an image he'd hoped would be romantic. He set her down on a path of white and pink petals, leading down to the front of the gazebo.

Too nervous to wait any longer, he pulled her in and began to sway with her though there was no music. He felt her heart thud against his chest—though it could have been his, he thought, considering what he was about to do.

'What...what is all this?'

'Don't you know?' he asked, and twirled her around before pulling her close again.

'It looks romantic.'

He laughed. 'It's supposed to be.'

'Are you trying to soften me up, Xavier?' she asked in a mock stern voice.

'Is it working?'

She rolled her eyes, and then laughed breathily. 'You know it is.'

'Good.'

They swayed a bit longer and he leaned back to see her eyes closed, a small smile on her face. It was time, he thought, and drew back, taking her hands in his.

'Do you remember what you said to me when I gave you this ring?' He lifted the hand that wore the engagement ring and brought it to her lips.

'That you shouldn't hand it to me like it was a mint?'

He chuckled. 'Yes, that. You also asked me whether I had it made for our fake engagement. I didn't,' he admitted. 'I had it made for the real one, ten years ago.'

He watched as she opened and closed her mouth a few times, and then she whispered, *'Before?'*

'Long before. It was actually after one of our days at the beach. I was complaining about my family, as usual, and you were comforting me about it. As usual,' they said together, and smiled at each other. His nerves disappeared. 'And I remember thinking that I'd have the ring made so that when you were ready—when you would finally let me tell you I loved you—I would be ready, too.'

She bit her lip and blinked a few times, quickly.

'Are you—'

'No, you will not ask me whether I'm crying,' she interrupted him. 'You don't get to make me pregnant and then question what happens when I am.'

'Technically, that's true, but—'

'Whose fault is that?' she asked wryly. 'I've told you—'

'And I've told you that I want to wait.' He interrupted

her this time. 'I want to give you rose petals and champagne. Non-alcoholic, of course. On our wedding night.'

'It isn't such a big deal.'

'It is, to me. And you know it is for you, too.' He tilted her chin up so she could look up at him. 'You waited for me, Leyna. I'm going to make sure we do it the way we were supposed to. The way you wanted us to.'

She shook her head, but he saw a tear roll down her face. 'I regret telling you that.'

'I don't,' he said, and kissed her forehead. 'I love knowing that you're mine. *Only* mine.'

'And now I *really* regret telling you that.'

He laughed, and wiggled the ring off her finger. 'The real reason we're here is because I owe you a proposal, Leyna.' He got down on one knee and offered the ring to her as he was supposed to have done ten years ago. 'I wouldn't recommend political turmoil to anyone, but I have to say it worked out *really* well for us.'

He smiled when she giggled. It was a happy sound that he knew he wanted to hear for the rest of his life. 'I'm glad we got this second chance at a life together. That our dreams of having a family, having each other and ruling have finally come true. So, to make it all official... Will you marry me, my Queen?'

There were no tears when she said yes, and he slid the ring onto her hand and kissed her, before pulling back and narrowing his eyes.

'Why aren't you crying?'

'Because I'm stronger than my hormones,' she teased, and then sobered. 'Because I want to remember this moment—that picture of you on your knee—for the rest of our lives together, and it wouldn't have been clear if I'd cried.'

He stared at her, and then laughed as he pulled her in. 'You're incredible, you know that?'

'Yes.' She smiled.

'And you're going to marry *me*.'

'Well, you *did* ask nicely…'

He smiled at her, and then shook his head. 'I won't take my second chance with you for granted, Leyna. I'm going to spend my life giving you everything you deserve.'

She rested her hand on his cheek. 'You've already given me more than I could imagine. I love you.'

'I love you, too,' he answered, and sealed the promise—their dream come true—with a kiss.

* * * * *

Look out for the next royal romance story in the CONVENIENTLY WED, ROYALLY BOUND *duet*

FALLING FOR HIS CONVENIENT QUEEN

Coming soon!

If you enjoyed this story check out these other great reads from Therese Beharrie

THE MILLIONAIRE'S REDEMPTION
A MARRIAGE WORTH SAVING
THE TYCOON'S RELUCTANT CINDERELLA

All available now!

Mya placed her hand over Giles's. "Are you living out your dream?"

A mysterious smile tilted the corners of his mouth. "I am. Before I met you, my sole focus was on work, and the harder I worked, the more I was able to convince myself that I didn't need or want anyone to share my life." He pressed his forehead to hers. "Meeting you has proven me wrong. Not only do I want you, but I need you."

Mya closed her eyes, too stunned to cry. Men had told her they needed her, but those were glibly spoken words they believed she wanted to hear. She felt his hand shake slightly under hers and in that instant she was aware of the power she wielded over Giles. That he'd shown her vulnerability for the first time.

"I need you, too." Her voice was barely a whisper.

* * *

American Heroes:
They're coming home—and finding love!

CLAIMING THE CAPTAIN'S BABY

BY
ROCHELLE ALERS

First Published in Great Britain 2018
By Mills & Boon, an imprint of HarperCollins*Publishers*
1 London Bridge Street, London, SE1 9GF

© 2017 Rochelle Alers

ISBN: 978-0-263-93636-0

23-0118

MIX
Paper from
responsible sources
FSC™ C007454

This book is produced from independently certified FSC™ paper to ensure responsible forest management.

For more information visit: www.harpercollins.co.uk/green

Printed and bound in Spain
by CPI, Barcelona

Since 1988, national bestselling author **Rochelle Alers** has written more than eighty books and short stories. She has earned numerous honors, including the Zora Neale Hurston Literary Award, the Vivian Stephens Award for Excellence in Romance Writing and a Career Achievement Award from *RT Book Reviews*. She is a member of Zeta Phi Beta Sorority, Inc., Iota Theta Zeta Chapter. A full-time writer, she lives in a charming hamlet on Long Island. Rochelle can be contacted through her website, www.rochellealers.org.

Chapter...

Chapter One

Mya Lawson sat staring out the window in her home office as she waited for the pages she had revised to fill the printer's tray. She was still amazed that she had come up with yet another plot for her fictional New England series. What had begun as a hobby for Mya was now a vocation since she gave up her position as college professor to become a stay-at-home mother.

The sound of the printer spitting out paper competed with the incessant tapping of rain against the windows. It had begun raining earlier that morning and had continued nonstop throughout the midafternoon. Mya knew it was an indoor play day for Lily once she woke from her nap. An unconscious smile parted her lips when her gaze lingered on the oak tree shading the backyard. Mya lost count of the number of times she and her sister hid behind the massive trunk or climbed the thick branches once they were older while playing hide-and-seek with their mother. Although aware of their hiding places, Veronica Lawson elected to play along much to the delight of her rambunctious daughters. But as they grew older the game stopped because Veronica claimed she did not have the energy to chase after them.

An expression of melancholy sweeping over Mya's features replaced her smile. She and seven-month-old Lily were the last of the Wickham Falls Lawsons. What she found ironic was that neither she nor Lily shared DNA with their namesake ancestors. Graham and Veronica Lawson, after more than twenty years of a childless marriage, had decided to adopt. They adopted Mya, and then two years later Samantha joined the family.

Mya exhaled an audible sigh. Her parents were gone, Samantha was gone, and now there was only she and her niece.

Her sister wanted Mya to raise Lily in Wickham Falls—a small town with a population of little more than four thousand residents—even though Samantha had complained about growing up in a small town and couldn't wait to grow up and leave to see the world. She got her wish once she began her career as a flight attendant and got to visit many of the cities and countries she had fantasized about.

Sammie, as Mya always called her, had died a month ago and Mya was still attempting to adjust to the loss and her life without her sister. Sammie had returned to Wickham Falls for a rare visit with the news that she was six weeks pregnant. She told Mya of her affair with a New York City businessman, and despite using protection, she'd gotten pregnant. Her sister refused to disclose the name of her lover or tell him about the baby because he had been adamant when he told her he wasn't ready for marriage or fatherhood.

The sudden ring of the telephone shattered her reverie. Unconsciously her brow furrowed when she recognized the name of the law firm that had handled Sammie's will. She picked up the receiver before the second ring.

"Hello."

"Ms. Mya Lawson?"

Mya nodded before she realized the person on the other end of the line could not see her. "Yes. This is she."

"Ms. Lawson, I'm Nicole Campos, Mr. McAvoy's assistant. He'd like you to keep your calendar open for next Thursday because he needs you to come into the office to discuss your daughter's future."

Her frown deepened. "Ms. Campos, can you give me an idea of what he wants to talk about?"

"I'm sorry, but I cannot reveal that information over the telephone."

Twin emotions of annoyance and panic gripped her. She did not want to relive the anxiety she had experienced before the court finalized her adopting her niece. "What time on Thursday?"

"Eleven o'clock. I'll call you the day before as a reminder and follow-up with an email."

Mya exhaled an inaudible sigh. "Thank you."

She hadn't realized her hand was shaking when she replaced the receiver in the console. Leaning back in the desk chair, she combed her fingers through a wealth of brown curly hair with natural gold highlights, holding it off her forehead.

There never had been a question that she would lose Lily to the foster care system because her sister had drawn up a will that included a clause naming Mya as legal guardian for her unborn baby.

A week after Sammie gave birth to a beautiful dark-haired infant, she handed Lily to Mya with the pronouncement that she wanted Mya to raise her daughter as her own. At first she thought Sammie was experiencing postpartum depression, but nothing could have prepared her for the reality that her younger sister was terminally ill.

Sammie had been diagnosed with an aggressive form of breast cancer. Mya put up a brave front for her sister because she needed to be strong for her, but whenever she was alone she could not stop crying. The young, beautiful, vivacious thirty-two-year-old woman who was in love with life was dying and there was nothing she could do to help her.

Gurgling sounds came from the baby monitor on a side table. Mya glanced at the screen where she could observe her daughter. It was after three and Lily was awake.

Pushing back her chair, she rose and walked out of the office and down the hall to the nursery. Lily was standing up in her crib. She'd sat up at five months, began crawling at six and now at seven was able to pull up and stand, but only holding onto something. It was as if her precocious daughter was in a hurry to walk before her first birthday.

Months before Lily's birth, Mya and Sammie spent hours selecting furniture and decorating the room that would become the nursey. The colors of sage green and pale pink were repeated in blankets, quilts and in the colorful border along the antique-white walls.

"Hey, doll baby. Did you have a good nap?"

A squeal of delight filled the space when the baby raised her chubby arms to be picked up. The instant she let go of the railing, Lily landed hard on her bottom but didn't cry. Mya reached over the rail of the crib and scooped her up while scrunching up her nose. She dropped a kiss on damp, inky-black curls. "Somebody needs changing."

Lily pushed out her lips in an attempt to mirror Mya's expression. Mya smiled at the beautiful girl with long dark lashes framing a pair of large sky blue eyes. Lily looked nothing like Sammie, so it was obvious she had inherited her father's hair and eye color.

She placed her on the changing table and took off the damp onesie and then the disposable diaper. At thirty-four, Mya had not planned on becoming a mother, yet learned quickly. She'd read countless books on feedings, teething, potty training and the average milestones for crawling, walking and talking. She had childproofed the house—all the outlets were covered, there were safety locks on the kitchen cabinets and drawers, wires secured off the floor, and all furniture with sharp edges were placed out of the way.

She gathered Lily in her arms and pressed a kiss to her forehead. "You're getting heavy."

Lily grabbed several strands of Mya's hair as she carried her down the staircase to the kitchen. "If you keep pulling my hair, I'll be forced to get extensions." She had made it a habit to either style her hair in a single braid or ponytail because her daughter appeared transfixed by the profusion of curls resembling a lion's mane.

She entered the kitchen and placed Lily in her high chair. Opening the refrigerator, she took out a bottle of milk and filled a sippy cup. Lily screamed in delight when handed the cup.

Mya felt a warm glow flow through her as she watched Lily drink. Her daughter's life would mirror her biological mother's and her aunt's. She would grow up not knowing her birth mother, but Mya had started a journal chronicling the baby's milestones, photographs of Sammie and a collection of postcards from the different cities and countries her sister had visited. Once Lily was old enough to understand that her aunt wasn't her biological mother, Mya would reveal the circumstances of her birth.

"Giles, Brandt is on line two."

The voice of Giles Wainwright's administrative assistant coming through the intercom garnered his attention. He had spent the past twenty minutes going over the architect's rendering and the floor plan of six three-bedroom, two-bath homes on an island in the Bahamas he had recently purchased for the international division of Wainwright Developers Group.

He tapped a button on the intercom. "Thank you, Jocelyn." He activated the speaker feature as he leaned back in the executive chair and rested his feet on the corner of the antique desk. "What's up, cousin?"

"I'm calling to let you know Ciara and I have finally set a date for our wedding."

Brandt "The Viking" Wainwright's professional football career was cut short when he broke both legs in an automobile accident. Sidelined for the season and confined to his penthouse suite, Brandt had had a revolving door of private duty nurses before no-nonsense Ciara Dennison refused to let him bully her. In the end, Brandt realized he had met his match *and* his soul mate.

"Finally," Giles teased. "When is it?"

"We've decided on February 21 at the family resort in the Bahamas. It's after the Super Bowl, and that week the schools are out for winter break. And if adults want to bring their kids, then the more the merrier."

Giles smiled. "I'm certain you won't find an argument from the kids who'd rather hang out on a tropical beach than ski upstate."

Brandt's deep chuckle came through the speaker. "You're probably right about that. Ciara's mailing out the Save the Week notice to everyone. If the family is amenable to spending the week in the tropics, then I'll make arrangements to reserve several villas to accommodate everyone."

Giles listened as Brandt talked about their relatives choosing either to fly down on the corporate jet that seated eighteen, or sail down on the *Mary Catherine*, the Wainwright family yacht. Giles preferred sailing as his mode of transportation, because two to three times a month he flew down to the Bahamas to meet with the broker overseeing the sale of two dozen private islands now owned by Wainwright Developers Group International, or WDG, Inc.

The conversation segued to the news that there would be another addition to the Wainwright clan when Jordan and his wife, Aziza, welcomed their first child in the coming weeks.

Giles lowered his feet and sat straight when Jocelyn Lewis knocked softly on the door and stuck her head through the opening. She held an envelope in one hand.

Giles beckoned her in. "Hold on, Brandt, I need to get something from my assistant."

"I know you're busy, Giles, so I'll talk to you later," Brandt said.

"Give Ciara my love."

"I'll tell her."

Giles ended the call, stood up and took the letter from Jocelyn's outstretched hand. He thought of the woman as a priceless diamond after he had gone through a number of assistants in the four years since he'd started up the overseas division. Within minutes of Giles interviewing her, he had known Jocelyn was the one. At forty-six, she had left her position as director of a childcare center because she wanted to experience the corporate world. What prompted Giles to hire her on the spot was her admission that she'd taken several courses to become proficient in different computer programs.

He met the eyes of the woman who only recently had begun wearing makeup after terminating her membership with a church that frowned on women wearing pants and makeup. The subtle shade of her lipstick complemented the yellow undertones in her flawless mahogany complexion. "Who delivered this?" he asked, when he noticed that the stamp and the postmark were missing. Personal and Confidential was stamped below the addressee, while the return address indicated a Wickham Falls, West Virginia, law firm.

Jocelyn's eyebrows lifted slightly behind a pair of

horn-rimmed glasses. "George brought it up. He said it came with this morning's FedEx delivery."

Giles nodded. "Thank you." All mail for the company was left at the front desk. The receptionist signed for documents requiring a signature, and then she alerted the mail room where George logged in and distributed letters and packages to their respective departments.

Jocelyn hesitated and met her boss's eyes. "I just want to remind you that I'll be in late tomorrow morning. I have to renew my driver's license."

He nodded. Jocelyn had saved his department thousands when she redesigned the website from ordinary to extraordinary with photos of Bahamian-Caribbean style homes on private islands with breathtaking views of the Atlantic Ocean and others with incredibly pristine Caribbean beaches.

Waiting until she walked out of the office and closed the door behind her, Giles sat down and slid a letter opener under the flap of the envelope. A slight frown settled into his features when he read and reread the single page of type. He was being summoned to the reading of a will. The letter did not indicate to whom the will belonged, but requested he call to confirm his attendance.

Picking up the telephone receiver, he tapped the area code and then the numbers. "This is Giles Wainwright," he said, introducing himself when the receptionist identified the name of the law firm. "I have a letter from your firm requesting my presence at the reading of a will this coming Thursday."

There came a pause. "Please hold on, Mr. Wainwright, while I connect you to Mr. McAvoy's office."

Giles drummed his fingers on the top of the mahogany desk with a parquetry inlay.

"Mr. Wainwright, I'm Nicole Campos, Mr. McAvoy's assistant. Are you calling to confirm your attendance?"

"I can't confirm until I know who named me in their will."

"I'm sorry, Mr. Wainwright, but I cannot disclose that at this time."

He went completely still. "You expect me to fly from New York to West Virginia on a whim?"

"It's not a whim, Mr. Wainwright. Someone from your past indicated your name in a codicil to their will. If you choose not to come, then we'll consider the matter settled."

Giles searched his memory for someone he'd met who had come from West Virginia. The only person that came to mind was a soldier under his command when they were deployed to Afghanistan.

Corporal John Foley had lost an eye when the Humvee in which he was riding was hit by shrapnel from a rocket-propelled grenade. The young marine was airlifted to a base hospital, awarded a purple heart and eventually medically discharged. Giles prayed that John, who had exhibited signs of PTSD, hadn't taken his life like too many combat veterans.

He stared at the framed pen and ink and charcoal drawings of iconic buildings in major US cities lining the opposite wall. A beat passed as he contemplated whether he owed it to John or his family to reconnect with their past.

"Okay, Ms. Campos. I'll be there."

He could almost imagine the woman smiling when she said, "Thank you, Mr. Wainwright."

Giles hung up and slumped down in the chair. He had just come back from the Bahamas two days ago, and he was looking forward to sleeping in his own bed for more than a week and hopefully catch up on what was going on with his parents and siblings.

Most days found him working in his office hours after other employees had gone home. It was when he spent time on the phone with his Bahamas-based broker negotiating the purchase of several more uninhabited islands. Other days were spent in weekly meetings with department heads and dinner meetings in the company's private dining room with the officers and managers—all of whom were Wainwrights by bloodline or had married into the family.

Wainwright Developers Group was the second largest real estate company in the northeast, and everyone associated with the company was committed to maintaining that position or bringing them to number one.

Swiveling on his chair, he sent Jocelyn an email, outlining his travel plans for the following Thursday. Giles had no idea where Wickham Falls, West Virginia, was, but in another week he would find out.

Giles deplaned after the jet touched down at the Charleston, West Virginia, airport. A town car awaited his arrival. Jocelyn had arranged for a driver to take him to Wickham Falls. She had also called a hotel to reserve a suite because he did not have a timetable as to when he would return to New York.

The trunk to the sedan opened, and seconds later the driver got out and approached him.

"Mr. Wainwright?"

Giles nodded. "Yes." He handed the man his suit-case and a leather case with his laptop.

When he'd boarded the jet, Giles had experienced a slight uneasiness because he still could not fathom what he would encounter once he arrived. He had racked his brain about possible scenarios and still couldn't dismiss the notion that something had happened to John Foley.

He removed his suit jacket, slipped into the rear of the car, stretched out his legs and willed his mind blank. When Jocelyn confirmed his travel plans, she informed him that Wickham Falls was an hour's drive from the state capital. Ten minutes into the ride, he closed his eyes and didn't open them again until the driver announced they were in Wickham Falls. Reaching for his jacket, he got out and slipped his arms into the sleeves.

"I'm not certain how long the meeting is going to take," he said to the lanky driver wearing a black suit that appeared to be a size too big.

"Not a problem, Mr. Wainwright. I'll wait here."

Giles took a quick glance at his watch. He was thirty minutes early. His gaze took in Wickham Falls's business district, and he smiled.

It was the epitome of small-town Americana. The streets were lined with mom-and-pop shops all sporting black-and-white awnings and flying American flags. Cars were parked diagonally in order to maximize space. It was as if Wickham Falls was arrested in time and that modernization had left it behind more than fifty years before. There was no fast-food restaurant or major drug store chain. To say the town was quaint was an understatement.

He noted a large red, white and blue wreath suspended from a stanchion in front of a granite monument at the end of the street. A large American flag was flanked by flags representing the armed forces. Giles knew it was a monument for military veterans.

He strolled along the sidewalk to see if John Foley's name was on the monument. There were names of servicemen who'd served in every war beginning with the Spanish–American War to the present. There was one star next to the names of those who were missing in action, and two stars for those who'd died in combat. Although he was relieved not to find the corporal's name on the marker, it did little to assuage his curiosity as to why he had been summoned to Wickham Falls.

As he retraced his steps, Giles wasn't certain whether he would be able to live in a small town. He was born, grew up and still lived in the Big Apple, and if he wanted or needed something within reason, all he had to do was pick up the telephone.

He opened the solid oak door to the law firm and walked into the reception area of the one-story, salmon-colored stucco building. He met the eyes of the middle-aged woman sporting a '60s beehive hairstyle, sitting at a desk behind a closed glass partition. She slid it open with his approach. His first impression was correct: the town and its inhabitants were stuck in time.

"May I help you, sir?"

Giles flashed a friendly smile. "I'm Giles Wainwright, and I have an appointment at eleven to meet with Mr. McAvoy."

She returned his smile. "Well, good morning, Mr. Wainwright. Please have a seat and I'll have someone escort you to the conference room."

He nodded. "Thank you."

Giles did not bother to sit on the leather sofa, but stood with both hands clasped behind his back. He had sat enough that morning. First it was in the car heading for the airport, then all through the flight and again during the drive from the airport to Wickham Falls. He had altered his normal morning routine of taking the elevator in his high-rise apartment building to the lower level to swim laps in the Olympic-size pool.

Swimming and working out helped him to relax, while maintaining peak physical conditioning from his time in the military. Going from active duty to spending most of his day sitting behind a desk had been akin to culture shock for Giles, and it had taken him more than a year to fully adjust to life as a civilian.

"Mr. Wainwright?"

He turned when he recognized the voice of the woman who'd called him. "Ms. Campos."

The petite, dark-haired woman with a short, pixie hairstyle extended her hand. "Yes."

Giles took her hand and was slightly taken aback when he noticed a small tattoo with USMC on the underside of her wrist. He successfully concealed a smile. It was apparent she had been in the Marine Corps. *"Semper fi,"* he said sotto voce.

Nicole Campos smiled. "Are you in the Corps?"

He shook his head. "I proudly served for ten years."

"I was active duty for fifteen years, and once I got out I decided to go to law school. I'd love to chat with you, Mr. Wainwright, but you're needed in the conference room."

Giles always looked forward to swapping stories with fellow marines, yet that was not a priority this morning. He followed her down a carpeted hallway to a room at the end of the hall.

His gaze was drawn to a woman holding a raven-haired baby girl. Light from wall sconces reflected off the tiny diamond studs in the infant's ears. The fretful child squirmed, whined and twisted backward as she struggled to escape her mother's arms.

He smiled, and much to his surprise, the baby went completely still and stared directly at him with a pair of large round blue eyes. She yawned and he was able to see the hint of two tiny rice-like teeth poking up through her gums. He couldn't pull his gaze away from the baby girl. There was something about her eyes that reminded him of someone.

His attention shifted from the baby to the man seated at the head of the conference table. His premature white hair was totally incongruent to his smooth, youthful-looking face.

Giles smiled and nodded. "Good morning."

"Good morning. I'm Preston McAvoy. Please excuse me for not getting up, Mr. Wainwright, but I'm still recovering from dislocating my knee playing football with my sons." He motioned to a chair opposite the woman with the baby. "Please sit down."

Giles complied, his eyes meeting those of the woman staring at him with a pair of incredibly beautiful hazel eyes in a tawny-gold complexion. He wondered if she knew she looked like a regal lioness with the mane of flowing brown curls with gold highlights framing her face and ending inches above her shoulders. A slight frown appeared between her eyes as she continued to stare at him. He wondered if she had seen him during his travels in the Bahamas, while Giles knew for certain he had never met her because she was someone he would never forget; she was breathtakingly beautiful.

Preston cleared his throat and opened the file folder on the table. He looked at Giles and then the baby's mother. "I'm sorry when my assistant called to ask you to come in that she was bound by law not to tell you why you'd been summoned." He removed an envelope from the folder and withdrew a single sheet of paper. His dark eyes studied each person at the table. "This is a codicil to Samantha Madison Lawson's last will and testament."

Giles went completely still. The name conjured up the image of a woman from his past who had disappeared without a trace. Now it was obvious he had not come to West Virginia for an update about a fellow soldier, but for a woman with whom he'd had an off-and-on liaison that went on for more than a year.

"Ms. Lawson, before she passed away," Preston continued, "made provisions for her unborn child, hence named Lily Hope Lawson, to become the legal ward of her sister, Mya Gabrielle Lawson. Ms. Lawson, being of sound mind and body, instructed me not to reveal the contents of her codicil until a month following her death." He paused and then continued to read from the single page of type.

Giles, a former marine captain who had led men under his command into battles where they faced the possibility of serious injury or even death, could not still his momentary panic. A tense silence swelled inside the room when Preston finished reading.

He was a father! The woman sitting across the table was holding his daughter. He had no legal claim to the child, but his daughter's mother sought fit to grant him visitation. That he could see Lily for school and holiday weekends, Thanksgiving, Christmas and one month during the summer, while all visitations would have to be approved by Mya Gabrielle Lawson.

Giles slowly shook his head. "That's not happening." The three words were dripping with venom.

"What's not happening?" Preston questioned.

"No one is going to tell me when and where I can see my daughter."

"You've just been told." The woman holding the child had spoken for the first time.

Chapter Two

Mya was certain the rapid pumping of her heart against her ribs could be heard by the others in the room. She hadn't been able to move or utter a sound when the tall, black-haired man with piercing blue eyes in a suntanned face walked into the conference room. It had only taken a single glance for her to ascertain that the man was Sammie's ex-lover and Lily's father. He continued to glare at her in what was certainly a stare down. However, she was beyond intimidation because legally he had no claim over her daughter.

"That's where you're wrong," Giles countered in a low and threatening tone. "As Lily's biological father, I can sue for joint custody."

"If you do, then you will surely lose," Mya countered.

Preston cleared his throat. "I'm afraid Ms. Lawson's

right, Mr. Wainwright. Legally, you have no right to the child. But look on the bright side, because it was the baby's mother's wish before she passed away that you could have a relationship with your daughter."

Giles's eyes burned like lasers when he turned to glare at Preston. "You fail to understand that a woman carried my child and neglected to notify me about it. Even though she's gone, you're allowing her to become the master puppeteer pulling strings and manipulating lives from the grave?"

Preston shrugged shoulders under a crisp white shirt. "Ms. Samantha Lawson must have had a reason for not informing you about the baby. I'm going to leave you and Mya alone, and I suggest you work out an arrangement that you both can agree on. Please keep in mind it's what's best for the baby." Reaching for a cane, Preston rose to his feet and limped out of the office.

Lily began squirming again, and Mya knew it was time to feed her and then put her to bed. "We're going to have to put off this meeting for another time because I have to get home and feed Lily."

"I don't have another time," Giles said. "The sooner we compromise, the better it will be for all of us."

A wry smile twisted Mya's mouth. Spoken like a true businessman. She wanted to tell him it wasn't about compromising. The terms in the codicil did not lend themselves to negotiating a compromise. "That's not possible now because I'm going home."

"Then I'll go with you."

Mya went completely still, and she stared at Giles as if he had taken leave of his senses. Did he actually expect her to welcome him, a stranger, into her home as if she had offered him an open invitation? "You want to come home with me?"

He cocked his head at an angle. "I don't hear an echo."

Her temper flared. "You cocky, arrogant—"

"I know I'm an SOB," he drawled, finishing her outburst. "Look, Ms. Lawson," he continued in a softer tone. "Up until a few minutes ago I had no idea that I was a father. But if Samantha had told me she was carrying my child, I would've made provisions for her and the child's future."

Mya scooped the diaper bag off the floor and looped the straps over her shoulder. "In other words, you wouldn't have married Sammie, because you weren't ready for marriage and fatherhood. She wouldn't tell me your name, but she did open up about your views on marriage and children." Mya knew she had struck a nerve with the impeccably dressed businessman when he lowered his eyes. Everything about him reeked of privilege and entitlement. His tailored suit and imported footwear probably cost more than some people earned in a month.

"What's the matter, Mr. Wainwright? You see a little girl with black hair and blue eyes and suddenly you're ready to be a father? What happened to you asking for a paternity test?"

Giles's eyes narrowed. "I don't need a paternity test because Lily looks like my sister."

"If that's case, then you can save some money," Mya mumbled under her breath. Suddenly she realized she wasn't as angry with Giles Wainwright as she was with her sister. Sammie had completely blindsided her with the codicil.

Giles rounded the table and took the large quilted bag off Mya's shoulder. "Please let me help you to your car."

Mya resisted the urge to narrow her eyes at him. At least he'd said please. She walked out of the room, Giles following as she cradled Lily to her chest. Fortunately for her, the baby had quieted. She had parked the Honda Odyssey in the lot behind the office building.

Pressing a button on the remote device, she opened the door to the minivan and placed Lily in the car seat behind the passenger seat. She removed the baby's hand-knitted sweater and buckled her in.

"We'll be home in a few minutes," she crooned softly as Lily yawned and kicked her legs. She closed the door and turned around to look for Giles. He was nowhere in sight. Where could he have gone with the diaper bag?

"Are you looking for this?"

She turned to find him standing on the other side of the vehicle, holding the bag aloft. Bright afternoon sun glinted off his neatly barbered inky-black hair. Closing the distance between them, she held out her hand. "Yes. I'll take it now."

Giles held it out of her reach. "I'll give it back to you when you get to your house."

She didn't want to believe he was going to hold the bag hostage. Mya bit her lip to keep from spewing the curses forming on tongue. She wanted the bag, but more than that she needed to get her daughter home so she could change and feed her and then into her crib for a nap.

She knew arguing with the arrogant man was just going to delay her. "Okay," she conceded. "Follow me."

She flung off Giles's hand when he attempted to assist her into the van. The man was insufferable. She couldn't understand how Sammie was able to put up with his dictatorial personality. It was as if he was used to giving orders and having them followed without question.

Mya hit the start-engine button harder than necessary. Lily's father was definitely working on her very last frayed nerve. She maneuvered out of the parking lot, not bothering to glance up at the rearview mirror to see if he was following her.

Mya's fingers tightened around the steering wheel at the same time she clenched her teeth. She knew the anger and frustration she'd unleashed at the man who'd just discovered he was Lily's father was the result of Sammie keeping her in the dark as to her child's paternity; repeated attempts for her to get her sister to disclose the identity of the man who'd gotten her pregnant had become an exercise in futility. It was a secret Sammie had taken to her grave.

And why now? Mya mused. What did Sammie hope to prove by waiting a month after her death to disrupt not only her life, but also Lily's and Giles Wainwright's? She decelerated and took a quick glance in the rearview mirror to see a black town car following her minivan.

Giles closed his eyes as he sat in the back of the sedan. Samantha was dead and he was a father! What he found incredulous was that they'd never made love without using protection. And to make certain he would not father a child, Giles had always used *his* condoms, because he did not trust a woman to claim she was using birth control when she wasn't. And while he had been forthcoming when he told women he'd slept with that he wasn't ready for marriage and fatherhood, he never said he did not want a wife or children. It was just that the timing wasn't right, because after serving his country for ten years as a captain in the Marine Corps, he found difficulty transitioning to life as a civilian.

Giles opened his eyes and stared out the side window. Towering trees growing close to one another nearly blotted out the sunlight, while a series of waterfalls washing over ancient rocks had probably given the town its name. The mountainous landscape appeared untamed, forbidding. It was a far cry from the skyscrapers, crowded streets, bumper-to-bumper traffic and the sights and sounds that made his hometown so hypnotically exciting. He sat straight when the driver turned off into a long driveway behind Mya's minivan.

He leaned forward. "Don't bother to get out," he ordered the driver. "I'm not certain how long I'm going to be inside."

"I'll wait here, Mr. Wainwright."

Giles reached for the colorful blue-and-white-patterned diaper bag. He was out of the town car at the same time Mya had removed Lily from her car seat. The baby's head rested on her shoulder.

Looping the straps of the bag over one shoulder, he gently gathered Lily from Mya's arms. "I'll carry her." He met Mya's brilliant catlike eyes, not seeing any of the hostility she had exhibited in the law office.

"Thank you."

He followed her up the porch steps to a house he recognized as a modified Louisiana low-country home.

As a developer, he had gotten a crash course in architectural styles and he favored any residential structure with broad porches welcoming the residents and callers with cool shade. Tall shuttered windows and French doors were representative of the French Colonial or plantation style.

Admiring the house with twin fans suspended from the ceiling of the veranda, the white furniture, and large planters overflowing with live plants did not hold as much appeal as the small, warm body pressed to his chest. He lowered his head and pressed a kiss on her silky curls. The distinctive scent associated with babies wafted to his nose, a pleasing fragrance that reminded him of the times he'd held his nephews.

His previous declaration that he wasn't ready for fatherhood no longer applied, because the child in his arms was a blatant reminder that he had to get ready. He and Samantha engaging in the most intimate act possible had unknowingly created another human being. Even before sleeping together, he and Samantha had talked about marriage and children and he was forthcoming and adamant that he wasn't ready for either.

And when he'd walked into the conference room and had seen the infant for the first time, there was something about her that reminded him of someone, and within minutes of the attorney reading the contents of the codicil, Giles knew that someone was his sister. Lily had inherited Skye's raven-black hair and blue eyes. Giles, his mother, his sister and his cousin Jordan were the dark-haired anomalies among several generations of blond Wainwrights.

He watched Mya as she unlocked the front door; she tapped several buttons on the wall to disengage the house's security system. He stared at her delicate profile, wondering what was going on behind her impassive expression. She and Samantha may have been sisters, but there was nothing physically similar that confirmed a familial connection. Samantha had been a petite, curvy, green-eyed blonde, while Mya was tall, very slender, with a complexion that was an exact match for the gold strands in her chestnut curls.

She held her arms out for the baby. "I'll take her now."

Giles handed her the sleeping infant and then the bag. "What are you going to do with her?"

"She needs to be changed, and then I'm going to give her a bottle before I put her to bed."

A slight frown appeared between Giles's eyes. "It's lunchtime. Aren't you going to give her food?" he asked. Mya had mentioned having to feed her.

Mya shook her head. "No. I'll give her a snack after she wakes up. The bottle will hold her until then. Make yourself comfortable in the family room. I'll be back and then we'll talk about what's best for Lily."

Giles felt as if he had been summarily dismissed as he stared at Mya's narrow hips in a pair of black tailored slacks. He walked over to a pale-pink-and-white-pinstriped sofa and folded his tall frame down.

Everything about the space was romantic and inviting, beckoning one to come and sit awhile. He admired the floor plan with its open rooms, high ceilings and columns that matched the porch posts. French doors and windows let in light and offered an unobstructed view of the outdoors. Wide mullions in the off-white kitchen cabinet doors were details repeated in the home's many windows. The tongue-and-groove plank ceiling, off-white walls, kitchen cabinets, cooking island and breakfast bar reflected comfortable family living.

Family. The single word reminded him that he now had a family of his own. A hint of a smile tilted the corners of his mouth when he thought of his daughter. Then within seconds his smile vanished when he realized he had no legal claim to her. The lawyer had indicated Samantha was of sound mind and body when she drew up her will and then added the codicil, but Giles wondered if she actually had been in her right mind. It was obvious Samantha had died, and he wondered if she had known she was dying?

Giles knew he could challenge the will and authenticate his paternity. He had the resources to hire the best lawyers in the country to sue for sole or joint custody with Mya. Lily may be a Lawson, but she was also a Wainwright. And Giles wasn't above using his family name and wealth to claim what belonged to him.

He rose to his feet when Mya reappeared. She had exchanged her slacks and man-tailored blouse for a pair of skinny jeans and an oversize University of Chicago T-shirt. Thick white socks covered her bare feet. She had brushed her hair off her face and secured it in a ponytail. Giles found that he couldn't pull his gaze away from the small, round face with delicate doll-like features. He retook his seat after Mya sat opposite him on a chair.

"How old is Lily?" he asked; he decided he would be the one controlling the conversation.

"Seven months." Her eyebrows lifted slightly. "How well did you know my sister?"

Giles was taken aback by Mya's question. "What do you mean by how *well*?"

Mya crossed her arms under her breasts at the same time she crossed her outstretched legs at the ankles. "I know you were sleeping with her, but what else did you know about her?"

"Apparently not enough," he countered flippantly. "Maybe I was mistaken, but I thought she told me she was from a small town in Virginia, not West Virginia."

"You were mistaken because we've never lived in Virginia. What else do you know about her? Did she ever talk to you about her parents or her family?"

Giles cursed under his breath. He wanted to be the one to interrogate Mya, yet unwittingly she had turned the tables on him. "She told me her parents were dead, but nothing beyond that. Most times we talked about the places she had visited as a flight attendant, while I wasn't very forthcoming about my time in the military because I did not want to relive some of what I'd seen or done."

Mya's expression softened as she angled her head. "Were you deployed?"

He nodded. "I managed to complete a couple of tours in Afghanistan."

"Thank you for your service."

Giles nodded again. Suddenly he was reflective. Now that he thought about it, there wasn't that much he had known about Samantha Lawson, except that he enjoyed whatever time they had spent together whenever she had a layover in New York, which wasn't that often.

"Samantha and I did not spend a lot of time together," he admitted. "She would call me whenever she had a layover in New York and there were occa-

sions when we'd just go out for dinner. She loved the
theater, so if she had a few days to spare, I'd purchase
tickets for whatever play she wanted to see."

"But you did sleep with her."

"Yes. And I always used protection."

Mya lowered her arms. "Sammie told me you did.
But we both know the only form of birth control that
is one hundred percent foolproof is abstinence."

A wry smile twisted Giles's mouth. "I'm fully aware
of that now." He sobered. "You claim that you and Samantha are sisters, yet you don't look anything like her."

"That's because we were both adopted. Our parents couldn't have children, so they decided to adopt.
They adopted me first, and then two years later they
adopted Sammie. My sister spent all of her adult life
searching for her birth mother and that's probably the
reason why she wanted me to adopt Lily, so I would
be able to tell her everything she would need to know
about her mother. When she found out she was having a girl, she selected the name Lily Hope, after her
favorite flower and Sammie's hope she would some-
day find her mother. My sister spent hours writing letters to her unborn baby and making recordings so Lily
could hear her voice."

Sadness swept through Giles as he attempted to deal
with all that his former lover had planned for their
daughter. "Please answer one question for me, Mya?"

"What is it?"

"Did Samantha know she was dying?"

Mya averted her head. "Yes. When she discovered
she was pregnant, she was also diagnosed with Stage
IV breast cancer. Chemotherapy couldn't be given
during throughout her pregnancy, so she had to wait

until after the baby was born for radiation and hormonal therapy. However, during her second trimester she did undergo a mastectomy, but by the time she delivered Lily the cancer had spread to her liver and lymph nodes. Even though she never complained, I knew she was in pain. In the end, I hired a private duty nurse to take care of her because she refused to go to hospice. The nurse made certain to keep her comfortable, and several days after Lily turned six months old, Sammie passed away. And when she's older, I'll show Lily where her mother and grandparents are buried."

Giles felt as if someone had reached into his chest and squeezed his heart, making it nearly impossible for him to draw a normal breath. He hadn't found himself in love with Samantha, yet if he had known she was sick, he would have been there for her even if she wasn't carrying his child. "I'm so sorry."

Mya exhaled an audible sigh. "She's at peace now."

He leaned forward, hands sandwiched between his knees. There was something he had to know before he decided his next move and he hoped Mya didn't construe it as heartless. "Was Samantha of sound mind and body when she drew up her will?"

"Are you thinking of challenging her will because you don't believe she was in her right mind?"

"That's not what I'm saying," he argued softly.

"That's exactly what you're saying," Mya said in rebuttal. "There was nothing remotely wrong with Sammie when she drew up her will. She refused to tell me who had fathered her child, and I didn't understand her reasoning until Mr. McAvoy mentioned your name. Sammie did reveal that she was sleeping with a wealthy New York businessman, and when I finally heard the name Wainwright I understood her reluctance to tell me, because you probably would've talked her into having an abortion so as not to besmirch your family name when the word got out that you had a baby mama."

Giles covered his face with his hand, unable to believe what Mya was saying. "Is that what you really think?" he asked through his fingers.

"It's not what I think, but how Sammie felt. I know she withheld the fact that she had your child, but in the end she did redeem herself with the codicil. She didn't want Lily to spend her life looking for her father as it had been with her and her birth mother."

"What about you, Mya? Do you intend to raise Lily as your daughter?"

With wide eyes, she stared at him. "I *will* raise her as my daughter. I'm not only her legal guardian, but also her adoptive mother. I'm the only link between Lily's past and her future, so if you're thinking about suing me for custody, then I'm prepared to fight you tooth and nail for *my daughter.*"

Giles went completely still. He had underestimated Mya. There definitely was fire under her cool demeanor. "There's no need to fight each other when we both want what's best for Lily."

"And that is?"

"For her to grow up loved and protected."

"And you don't think I'll be able to love and protect her, Giles?" Mya asked.

He smiled. "I don't doubt you will, but she needs to grow up knowing she has a father."

"She will, because Sammie has granted you visitation."

"How many times a year? And don't forget a month in the summer."

"Being facetious will definitely not endear you to me, Giles."

"I don't intend to be facetious. I'm just repeating the terms of the codicil."

Mya closed her eyes. The verbal interchange was beginning to wear on her nerves *and* give her a headache. Not only was Giles strong-willed but he was also relentless in his attempt to undermine her sister's decision to conceal her pregnancy from him. The Wainwright name was to real estate as Gates was to Microsoft, and Samantha, knowing this, had attempted to make provisions for Lily that would prevent her from becoming a legal football between the Lawsons and Wainwrights.

"I'm not your enemy, but if you keep pushing me then I'll become your worst nightmare. I'm willing to grant you more liberal visitation than what Sammie stated in her will. And that means I'm not opposed to you taking Lily to New York to meet your family, but not without me. Wherever she goes, I go along."

"I don't have a problem with that."

Mya was mildly shocked he would agree to her terms. "You'll have to let me know in advance because she has scheduled doctor's appointments."

"What about you, Mya? What about your work schedule?"

"My schedule is flexible, because I'm now a stay-at-home mother. I resigned my teaching position once Sammie moved back home."

"What and where did you teach?"

"Comparative literature at the University of Charleston."

He mentally filed away this disclosure. "Do you miss teaching?"

"A little, but I love being with Lily." Mya didn't tell Giles that working at home allowed her to pen her novels in her spare time. "When are you going back to New York?"

A beat passed. "Tomorrow morning. Once I get back I'll have to rearrange my work schedule before I return. I'm going to give you several numbers where you'll be able to reach me. Jocelyn Lewis is my administrative assistant. So if you call my office, make certain you identify yourself and she'll put you through to me."

Mya stood, Giles also rising with her. "I'm going to get my phone so you can program your numbers into it."

Reaching into his shirt pocket, Giles handed Mya his cell phone. "You do the same with your contact info."

Her thumbs moved quickly over the keys as she tapped in her name, address, cell and landline numbers, along with her email address. She retrieved her phone from where she had left it on the dining room table and gave it to Giles.

"How many numbers do you have?" she asked when he took an inordinate amount of time tapping keys.

"Three. I'm giving you my cell, the number at the office, and the one in my apartment." Glancing up, he winked at her. "You can always send me a text if you need me for anything. And I do mean anything."

Mya stared, momentarily speechless. The warmth in his voice and the tenderness in his expression made her fully aware of why her sister had been taken with him. Not only was he urbane, but also unquestionably charming when he chose to be.

She smiled. "I'll keep that in mind if I do *need* you for something."

Giles returned Mya's phone to her. "I'll call you once I make arrangements to return. You don't have to see me out," he said when she made a move to walk him to the door.

Mya met eyes that shimmered like polished blue topaz. "Safe travels."

He inclined his head. "Thank you."

Giles settled himself into the rear of the car. He had revised his plan to remain in Wickham Falls for more than one day. Scrolling through his phone directory, he tapped Jocelyn's number. She answered after the first ring.

"I need you to arrange for a flight back to New York for tomorrow morning out of the regional airport." The regional airport was a shorter distance from his hotel. "And please call my mother and let her know I would like to see her tomorrow night at seven. Be certain to let her know dinner will be at my place."

"Consider it done."

"Thank you, Jocelyn."

He had asked Jocelyn to contact Amanda because Giles did not get to see his mother as often as she would like. Unlike her other son, Giles's position took him out of the country, and he wanted to tell her in person that she had another grandchild—and this time it was a girl.

And while he wanted to wait for Lily to wake up from her nap to see her again, he knew Mya needed time to accept that she would now have to share her daughter with him. Putting distance between them would also help him to try to understand why Samantha had elected not to tell him about the baby.

Had she viewed him as someone who had used her for only for sex? Did she not trust him to take care of her and the baby? Or had she denied him his parental rights because she knew he had been adamant about not wanting to marry or father a child?

There was one more person he wanted to call, but he decided to wait until after he checked into the hotel.

If Samantha hadn't told him about the baby, then he wondered if there were other things she'd sought to conceal from him. Not only did he intend to have Samantha's background dissected but also her sister's. And if anything negative about either of them surfaced, then he was prepared to bring holy hell down on Mya to secure full custody of his daughter.

Chapter Three

Giles settled into a hotel suite less than an hour's drive from a regional airport. After checking in, he changed into a swimsuit and swam laps in the indoor pool. Once he had showered and changed into a pair of walking shorts and a rugby shirt, he ordered room service.

A ringtone on his phone indicated a text message from Jocelyn:

Return flight scheduled for departure at 1:00 PM tomorrow at Tri State Airport. Ground transportation confirmed. Confirmed dinner with your mother

Giles responded with: Thank you.

He could always count on Jocelyn to simplify his life. Once he had set up the company's international division, Giles couldn't convince his older brother to run the department with him. Patrick had declined because, as a husband and now a father of two young boys under the age of six, he claimed he didn't want to be away from his family even if it was only for a week.

Patrick also professed he preferred working with their father in the legal department to jetting off to exotic climes, leaving Giles to ponder how much longer he would be able to maintain a one-man operation. Several third-generation Wainwrights cousins were still undecided whether to come and work for the company. He had made them generous offers to come and work with him, yet they still were ambivalent about becoming involved in the real estate business.

He finished his lunch and left the tray on the floor outside the door. Walking across the room, he flopped down on the king-size bed and reached for the cell phone on the bedside table and dialed the number to Jordan's cell phone. It rang four times before going directly to voice mail. He decided not to leave a message. Either Jordan was in court or with a client. He made another call, this time to his cousin's office.

Jordan had always teased Giles, declaring they were the family outsiders. Jordan and his law school mentor had gone into partnership, setting up Chatham and Wainwright, PC, Attorneys at Law. The firm was housed in a brownstone in Harlem's Mount Morris Park Historic District. Despite his reputation as a brilliant corporate attorney, Jordan refused to work for the family business, while Giles had opted for the military rather than join the company once he'd graduated college.

"Good afternoon, Chatham and Wainwright. How may I direct your call?"

"I'd like to speak to Jordan Wainwright."

"May I ask who's calling?"

"Giles Wainwright."

"Hold on, Mr. Wainwright. I'll see if he's available to take your call."

"Thank you." He didn't have to wait long before he heard Jordan's familiar greeting.

"What's up, G?"

Giles smiled. Jordan was the only one in the family who referred to him by an initial. "I'd like to hire your firm to conduct a background check on a couple of people." A swollen silence followed his request.

"Why are you asking me when your legal department can do it?"

"I'm asking you because what I'm going to say to you should stay between us. Attorney-client privilege," he added.

"What's going on, Giles?"

He knew he had gotten Jordan's attention when he addressed him by name. Giles was completely truthful when he told Jordan everything—from sleeping with Samantha, the phone call asking him to come to Wickham Falls, West Virginia, and to the revelation that he was now the father of a seven-month-old little girl and the rights extended to him as her father.

"That's really a low blow," Jordan drawled.

Giles smiled in spite of the seriousness of the situation. "I agree. I need to know everything about Samantha Madison Lawson and Mya Gabrielle Lawson. Both were adopted, so I don't know how far back you'll be able to go."

"I'll have the investigators begin with their adoption records and go forward from there. Is there anything you've noticed about the aunt that would make her unfit to be your daughter's mother?"

"Not really. We spent less than an hour together. Her home is clean and tastefully furnished, and she claims to have taught college-level literature."

"Does she appear financially able to raise and educate the child until she is emancipated?" Jordan asked.

Giles stared up at the ceiling. "I don't know. That's what I need for your people to find out." Although Mya drove a late-model vehicle, it wasn't in the luxury category. He also had no idea if Samantha had life insurance, and if she did, if Mya had been her beneficiary. His concern was how she was supporting herself as a stay-at-home mother.

He had called Jordan because he knew he would never divulge what Giles had just told him. However, Giles knew he owed it to his parents—his mother in particular—to let her know that they had another grandchild.

"Are you prepared to accept the results if they come back clean?"

"I'll have to accept it, but that doesn't mean I'm going to stop fighting to claim my daughter."

"I wouldn't expect you to give up," Jordan continued, "because I would do the same if I were in a similar situation. What I wouldn't do is antagonize your daughter's mother. Try to remain civil with her and perhaps she'll come around and allow you more involvement in the baby's life."

"That's what I'm hoping will happen." Giles paused. "Do I have an alternative if the background checks yield nothing? What can I use to sue for at least joint custody?"

"Your only other option would be charging her with neglect. You'll have to be able to prove that the child has failed to thrive, that she doesn't get the medical care she needs, or if you've witnessed any verbal or physical abuse. I've never handled a child abuse or neglect case, but Aziza has. Although she's well versed in the family court system, I don't want to involve her in this because she's so close to her due date. Maybe after the baby's born and if she feels up to it, I'll ask her to look into this for you."

"When is she due again?"

"October 5. The doctor says the baby could come a week before or a week after that date."

"You still don't know if you're having a girl or a boy?"

"No. We want to be surprised."

"Have you narrowed it down to names?"

"We're leaning toward Maxwell if it's a boy and Layla if it's a girl."

"I like those names."

His cousin and his wife were given the privilege of selecting names for their unborn baby, while he'd had no say in naming his daughter. Every time he thought about Samantha's deception, it served to refuel his anger.

"Look, G, I'm going to hang up because I have a client waiting for me. And don't worry about the background checks. I'll have the investigators get on it ASAP."

"Thanks, Jordan."

"No need to thank me. Talk to you later."

Giles ended the call and rested his head on folded arms. He would take Jordan's advice and not do anything to antagonize Mya because she held all of the cards when it came to Lily's future. At least for now.

What she wasn't aware of was his intent to use any and everything short of breaking the law to claim his daughter.

The following evening Giles opened the door to his apartment and waited for his mother to emerge from the elevator.

Amanda Wainwright stepped out of the car, her smile indicating she was as pleased to see him as he was her. It was a rare occasion when Giles saw his mother without a fringe of hair sweeping over her ears and forehead. Tonight she had styled her chin-length, liberally gray-streaked black hair off her face. She was conservatively dressed in tailored taupe slacks she had paired with a white tailored blouse. She was hardly ever seen in public without her ubiquitous navy blazer, Gucci loafers and the magnificent strand of South Sea pearls and matching studs she had inherited from her grandmother.

There had been a time after graduating college and before he'd joined the marines when they had rarely spoke to each other. However, that changed when Giles called to inform his mother he was being deployed to Afghanistan. After all, he'd owed it to her to let her know he would be going into combat.

That single call changed him forever. It had taken days before he could forget the sound of her heart-breaking sobs. He apologized for severing all communication with her, while she apologized for interfering in his life and attempting to control his future. He returned to the United States after his first tour, shocking his parents when they opened the door to find him in uniform grinning ear to ear. The homecoming signaled a change in their relationship. He was still their son, but he had also become a decorated war veteran.

"Hello, gorgeous."

An attractive blush suffused Amanda's fair complexion with the compliment. Giles had been truthful. His mother's stunning beauty hadn't faded at sixty-four. It was her tall, slender figure, delicate features, coal-black hair and vibrant violet-blue eyes that had attracted Patrick Wainwright II, who married her after a whirlwind courtship; a year later, they had welcomed their first child.

Amanda rested a hand on Giles's light stubble. "You are definitely your father's son. You always know what to say to make a woman feel good."

Giles kissed her forehead. "You have to know by now that I never lie." He threaded their fingers together and led her through the foyer and into the expansive living-dining area.

She pointed to the dining area table set for two. "You cooked?"

He seated his mother on a love seat and dropped down next to her. "Surely you jest," he said, smiling. His many attempts to put together a palatable meal had resulted in either over- or undercooked dishes that always ended up in the garbage. In the end, he preferred eating in or ordering from his favorite restaurants or gourmet shops.

"I ordered from Felidia. It should be here in about twenty minutes."

Amanda gave Giles a long stare. "Why did you order in? You know I love eating there because the place reminds me of a little ristorante Pat and I discovered when we were in Bologna."

"I decided we'd eat in because I need to talk to you about something."

"Please don't tell me you're going to rejoin the military."

Giles dropped an arm over his mother's shoulders and hugged her. "No. What I want to tell you shouldn't be disclosed in public."

Amanda's eyelids fluttered as the natural color drained from her face. She rested a hand over the pearls. "Please don't tell me something that's going to hurt my heart."

He shook his head. "It's something you claim you've been wishing for. You now have a granddaughter."

Giles knew he had shocked his mother when her hands trembled, but then she quickly recovered and cried tears of joy. Waiting until she was calmer, he told her everything he'd disclosed to Jordan. He left out the fact that he wanted his cousin to conduct a background check into the lives of his daughter's mother *and* adoptive mother.

Amanda sniffled as she opened her handbag and took out several tissues. "What are you going to do?" she asked, after blowing her nose.

"I'm going to take the legal route to claim my daughter."

"You claim you have visitation, so when can we expect to meet her?"

Giles recalled the designated holidays outlined in the codicil. "It probably won't be until Thanksgiving."

A crestfallen expression crossed Amanda's face. "That's more than two months from now."

"I know, Mom. I'm hoping to convince Mya to bring her before then."

"Who else knows about this?"

"Just you and Jordan," he admitted.

Amanda rested her head on her son's shoulder. "I'd rather not say anything to Pat right now, because he's probably going to go ballistic and go after this poor girl who had no idea what her sister was planning."

Giles pressed a kiss to his mother's hair. "You're right." There was nothing his father liked better than a legal brouhaha. "Then this will remain between you, me and Jordan for now." The chiming of the building's intercom reverberated through the apartment. "That's probably our dinner."

He answered the intercom. The doorman announced a delivery from Felidia. "Please send them up."

Two hours later, Giles escorted his mother to the street, waited for her to get into a taxi and stood on the curb watching as it disappeared from his line of vision.

It was as if he could exhale for the first time in more than twenty-four hours. Talking to his mother, and her decision not to tell her husband temporarily assuaged his angst over attempting to explain the circumstances of him becoming a father.

Giles shook his head to rid his thoughts of the possible scenarios Patrick could employ to make Lily a Wainwright, because he intended to use his own methods to get what he wanted. If he was able to get a judge to rule in his favor to grant him joint custody, then he would happily comply with the law to share his daughter with Mya.

The sidewalks were teeming with locals and tourists in sweaters and lightweight jackets to ward off the early autumn chill. Giles, not wanting to return to his apartment, walked along Second Avenue to Forty-Second Street, stopping at intervals to do some window-shopping before reversing direction and heading back uptown. The walk had been the antidote to release some of his anxiety about reuniting with Mya and hopefully agreeing to what was best for Lily.

The night doorman stood under the building's canopy. "Have a good evening, Mr. Wainwright."

Giles nodded and smiled. "You do the same, Raoul."

During the elevator ride to his floor, Giles mentally mapped out what he had to accomplish before returning to Wickham Falls. He knew it was time for him to give Jocelyn more responsibility if he was going to be away for any appreciable length of time. And that meant she would have to accompany him during his next trip to the Bahamas.

Mya sat on the porch, bouncing Lily on her lap. Giles had called to inform her he was in Wickham Falls and for her to expect him to arrive at her house before one that afternoon.

It had been three weeks since their initial meeting, and she had resigned herself to accept him as Lily's father. If Sammie hadn't wanted her daughter to have a relationship with her father, then she never would've added the codicil.

She had gotten up earlier that morning to put up several loads of laundry, give Lily breakfast and followed with a bath. After dressing her, she spent fifteen minutes reciting nursery rhymes. Mya knew Lily was more than familiar with many of the words and would be able to repeat them once she began talking.

Her daughter had become quite a chatterbox when she babbled about things Mya pretended to understand, while their favorite games were patty-cake and ring around the rosy. Now that Lily was standing up while holding on, Mya would gently pull her down to the floor when she sang the line "they all fall down" in "Ring Around the Rosie."

Mya went completely still when she registered the sound of an approaching car. The vehicle maneuvering up the driveway wasn't a town car but an SUV with New York plates. And as it came closer, she noticed a car seat.

Mya held her breath when Giles got out and waved to her. He looked nothing like the well-dressed man who had questioned her late sister's decision not to grant him custody of their daughter. Relaxed jeans, a sweatshirt with a fading USMC logo and running shoes had replaced the business attire.

She rose stiffly, as if pulled up by a taut overhead wire, and waited for his approach. He hadn't shaved and the stubble afforded him an even more masculine quality.

At first, she had asked herself why her sister had put up with him, but seeing him like this, Mya realized Giles Wainwright was not a man most women could ignore at first glance. Piercing blue eyes and balanced features made for an arresting face. He was tall, several inches above six feet, broad-shouldered and appeared in peak physical condition.

Giles slowly made his way up the porch steps, stopping only a few feet from her.

"Hello again."

An unconscious smile parted Mya's lips. "Welcome back. How long do you plan to stay?"

Giles met her eyes. "I don't know. It's open-ended, so I checked into an extended stay hotel."

Her smile faded. "What do you mean by open-ended?"

"I may have to go to New York for a few days for meetings, but once they're concluded I'll be back.

Her jaw dropped. "Oh I see."

"Hopefully you do, because it's going to take a while for Lily to get used to seeing me, so I'm prepared to take as much time as necessary to bond with *my daughter*."

His reference to Lily being his daughter was not lost on Mya. Biologically the baby was his daughter, but legally Lily was hers. "I'm not opposed to you bonding with *my* daughter," she countered, smiling. "And if there is anything I can do to speed up the process, then please let me know."

She knew she had shocked him with the offer when he gave her a long, penetrating stare. It was apparent he hadn't expected her to be that cooperative. His gaze shifted to Lily.

"May I hold her?"

"Hold out your arms and see if she'll come to you."

Giles extended his arms, and much to his surprise Lily leaned forward and held out her arms for him to take her. He smiled at the little girl looking up at him. "She looks different from when I last saw her." Her hair was longer and there was a hint of more teeth coming through her upper gums.

Mya leaned against the porch column and crossed

her arms under her breasts. "I'm able to see her change even though I'm with her all the time. Right now she's teething, so she's drooling on everything." As if on cue, Lily picked up her bib and gnawed on it.

Giles shifted his attention from Lily to Mya. He marveled that a woman without a hint of makeup and wearing faded jeans and a white T-shirt and socks could appear so incredibly sensual.

"How old is she now?"

"She turned eight months two days ago."

He quickly did the math. "Her birthday is February 5?"

"Yes."

"Our birthdays are four days apart. Mine is February first."

"That's quite a coincidence." Mya turned and opened the storm door at the same time Lily let out a piercing scream. "That's her way of telling me she wants to be changed. In fact, it's time for her afternoon nap."

Giles followed Mya inside the house and sniffed the air. "Something smells good."

Mya glanced at him over her shoulder. "I'm making pot roast. You're more than welcome to stay for dinner."

He stared at the denim fabric hugging her hips and smothered a groan. Giles knew it wasn't going to be easy to completely ignore the woman with whom he would spend time whenever he came to see Lily. Everything about her turned him on: her face, body, hair, softly modulated voice with a hint of a drawl and then there was the way she stared at him. It was as if she knew what he was thinking or going to say before he spoke.

Jordan had come up with nothing—not even a parking ticket—in Samantha and Mya's background for him to use as leverage to bolster his case if and when he decided to sue her. The only alternative was to watch for signs of neglect, and watching Mya closely was definitely going to become a delightful distraction.

"I'd like that very much. Do you cook every day?"

"Yes, because I have to prepare meals for Lily."

Giles slipped out of his running shoes, left them on the thick straw mat near the door and followed Mya through the living room and up a flight of stairs to the second story. "You don't buy baby food from the supermarket?"

"No. I've heard stories about jars of baby food being recalled because of foreign objects, so I decided it's safer and healthier to prepare her food myself. I'll cook carrots, beets, spinach or sweet potatoes and then purée them to a consistency where she can swallow without choking."

"That's a lot of work."

"She's worth it." Mya stood at the entrance to the nursery. "Do you want to change her?"

Giles didn't mind holding a baby but usually drew the line when it came to changing diapers. The few times he'd changed his nephews it was apparent he had been too slow when they urinated on him. "I'll watch you do it."

Her eyebrows flickered a little. "You've never changed a baby?"

"Only boys. My brother has two sons." Giles handed her Lily.

"The fact that they're not anatomically the same shouldn't make a difference. You are familiar with the female body, aren't you?"

Giles narrowed his eyes. "That's not funny. I re-member you warning me about being facetious," he added when she gave him a Cheshire cat grin.

She scrunched up her nose. "I do remember saying something like that."

Giles had to smile. His daughter's mother was a beautiful sexy tease. How different she was from their first encounter where he could feel her hostility. This was a Mya he could readily get used to.

"Everything you'll need to change her is in the drawers of the changing table." She opened and closed each drawer. "Here are diapers, wipes, lotion and plas-tic bags for the soiled diapers."

He stood at the changing table positioned at the foot of the crib and watched as Mya removed Lily's bib and onesie. She quickly and expertly changed the wet dia-per and disposed of it in a plastic bag. "Where do you put the plastic bag?"

"There's a garbage can in the mudroom."

Giles studied the exquisite furnishings in the nurs-ery. It was apparent Mya had spared no expense when it came to decorating the space. Green and pink were the perfect contrast for the white crib, dresser and chest of drawers. The colors were repeated in the rug stamped with letters of the alphabet with corresponding im-ages of animals. A solid white rocking chair and foot-stool had covered cushions in varying shades of pink and red roses.

"Is she sleeping throughout the night?"

Mya nodded. "Now she is."

"What time do you put her to bed?"

"Eight."

He angled his head. "That should give you a few hours for yourself before you turn in for the night."

"A few," she said cryptically. Mya handed Lily back to Giles. "You can hold her while I throw away the diaper and bring up a bottle."

Giles smiled as Lily stared up at him with curious, round, clear blue eyes with dark blue centers. "Hello, princess. I'm your daddy and now that I'm here we're going to get to see a lot of each other. I have lots of plans we can do together once you're older. I'm going to teach you to swim, ice-skate and, when the time comes, how to drive. You like sports?" he asked, continuing his monologue with the little girl. "Well, if you're a Wainwright, then you'll definitely be into sports. And if you come to live with me in New York, then you're going to have to decide whether mya like the Yankees or the Mets. Those are baseball teams. You don't have to choose when it comes to football because your cousin Brandt played for the NFL. That means we always cheer for one of the New York teams. Rooting for the Rangers rather than the Islanders is a better pick since you'll be living in Manhattan. Let's see, what's left? Oh! I forgot about basketball. Your daddy is partial to the Knicks, although I also like the Nets.

"Then there's your family. Your birth certificate may list you as Lawson, but I don't want you to ever forget that you are a Wainwright. You'll probably be a little overwhelmed when everyone will want a piece of you, but not to worry because Daddy will make certain to take care of his princess. And when you're older and you want to live with me in New York, I'll make it happen. There's a wonderful school blocks from Central Park where several generations of Wainwrights were educated."

"Don't, Giles."

He turned to find Mya standing in the doorway to the nursery. "Don't what?"

"Don't promise her things that may not become a reality. I know she doesn't understand what you're telling her. And I forgot to tell you that Sammie's will states that Lily should be raised here."

Giles clenched his teeth in frustration. It was apparent Mya wasn't that ready to compromise, that she was going to hold to Samantha's mandate that Lily grow up in a town where the residents appeared reluctant to accept it was now the twenty-first century.

"Do you realize how manipulative your sister was? That she's controlling three lives from the grave?"

Mya reacted as if he had struck her across the face. "Maybe she had a reason for setting up the conditions for how she wanted her daughter to be raised."

"What reason could that be?" Giles spat out, angrily.

"I don't know, because I wasn't aware that my sister was seeing someone until after she'd become pregnant. And even then she refused to tell me your name."

"I think we need to talk."

"What about?"

"About my relationship with your sister."

"You are so right about that," Mya said.

Giles handed Lily to Mya and stalked out of the room. If Samantha hadn't revealed the name of her baby's father, then he had to assume she had never spoken to Mya about him or their on-again, off-again liaison.

He knew he could never move forward in his quest

to claim his daughter if he withheld the truth about the woman who had remained an enigma even before she disappeared from his life.

Chapter Four

Mya found Giles in the family room. He stood with his back to the French doors. "Are you going to stand while we talk?" she asked.

He took several steps and pointed to the love seat. "You first."

She sat and he folded his tall frame down on a chair opposite her. "Where and how did you meet my sister?"

Stretching out long legs, Giles stared at his sock-covered feet. "Samantha was the flight attendant assigned to first class on my flight from the Bahamas to the States. I had a connecting flight in Miami, but all planes were grounded because of severe thunderstorms. I decided to check into a hotel rather than spend hours in the airport waiting for the weather to clear. Samantha and several crew members were checking into the same hotel because they weren't scheduled to fly out again until the following day. She invited me to have drinks with her, and we agreed to meet in the hotel lounge."

"Are you saying that Sammie picked you up?"

Giles shook his head. "No, she didn't. We'd passed the time during the flight from Nassau to Miami chatting about movies, so when she suggested we have drinks, I accepted because I'd found her pretty and outgoing. She told me her parents were dead and that she was an only child. When I mentioned her Southern drawl, she said she'd grown up in a small town in what I'd assumed was Virginia."

Mya bit her lower lip to still its trembling. She wondered how many other men had Sammie told the same lie. "Why do you think she lied to you?"

Giles lifted broad shoulders under his sweatshirt. "I don't know."

"What else did she tell you?"

"She said she hated growing up in a small town and that's why she decided to become a flight attendant. And when I asked her what she wanted for her future, she claimed she hadn't figured that out. When the topic of marriage and children came up, we both agreed we definitely weren't ready for either." Giles paused, seemingly deep in thought. "After seeing her a couple of times, whenever she had a layover in New York I could detect restlessness in her. As if she was always looking for something or someone. And when I mentioned it to her, she played it off, saying she always felt more comfortable in the air than on the ground."

Mya had to agree with Giles when he talked about Sammie being restless. "That someone she was looking for was her birth mother." She told him about Samantha's mother getting into a taxi with her week-old baby and when she got out, she hadn't bothered to take the infant with her. "There were times when I suspected Sammie never really appreciated what our adoptive parents did for us. She'd complain about feeling incomplete because she'd been abandoned."

"I suppose her feeling that way wouldn't permit her to engage in a committed relationship."

Mya stared at Giles. "You wanted a commitment from her?"

He blinked slowly. "I wanted more than her calling me every couple of months to tell me she was in town and wanted to see me."

Mya frowned. "So you just wanted to see her for sex?"

"No! There were times when we were together and never made love. I'd always ask her when I would see her again because she knew her flight schedule well in advance, and her answer was 'I don't know.' We dated off and on for a little more than a year, and then it ended. One month passed and then another and after the third month, I knew it was over."

"Had you argued about something that made her angry?"

"We may have had some minor disagreements but it never escalated to an argument. Come to think of it, I did notice she would become sullen whenever I talked about my family."

"That's because you grew up with your biological mother and father and she didn't."

He sat straight. "So she punishes me by having my child and using her as a pawn so I'll never be able to legally claim her as a Wainwright."

A shiver of annoyance snaked its way up Mya's spine. She wasn't about to let Giles attack her dead sister. "Maybe because you are a Wainwright Sammie feared you would use your family's name and money to take Lily away from her because you'd told her you weren't ready for marriage and fatherhood. In other words you'd take the baby but not the mother."

"I'm not going to lie and say I was in love with your sister, but I'll say it again that if I'd known she was carrying my baby, I definitely would've provided for them."

Mya threw up a hand. "Do you hear yourself, Giles? You talk as if money will solve everything. Sammie didn't need money because our parents made certain we would be financially secure before they passed away. They left us this house and their furniture-manufacturing company, which we sold because neither of us wanted to get involved in running a business. Sammie had two life insurance policies, and as the beneficiary I invested most of the monies in tax-free bonds for Lily's college education and whatever else she'll need to start life on her own."

Giles ran a hand over his face. "None of this makes sense."

Mya closed her eyes when she recalled the times when they recited their prayers before going to bed, and Sammie's prayer was always the same. She wanted to find her real mother. Those were the times when Mya resented the Lawsons for telling Sammie she was adopted. It would've been so easy for them to say she was their biological daughter because of the physical resemblance. But living in a small town where it was difficult to hide anything made that virtually impossible.

She opened her eyes. "It doesn't make sense because you have what Sammie wanted most in life. My sister used to spend hours on the computer pouring over sites dedicated to people searching for their relatives. She told me whenever she had a layover in the Midwest she would search through local birth and death records for a woman who'd given birth to an infant girl around the time she was born. Sammie couldn't know where she was going because she didn't know where she had come from."

"Where did her mother abandon her?"

"It was in New Lebanon. It's a city southwest of Dayton, Ohio."

"What about you, Mya? You've never searched for your birth mother?" Giles asked.

"No. Because whoever she is, I know if she'd been able to take care of me she wouldn't have left me in the hospital. When people ask me about my race, I always tell them I'm African-American. And if they asked whether I'm mixed race, my comeback is, isn't everyone? All they have to do is take the ancestry DNA test to find their true ethnicity."

Giles laughed. "That is so true."

Mya realized it was the first time she'd heard Giles laugh. The sound was low and soothing. "Sammie did take a DNA test and it said she had ancestors who were European Jewish, Russian and Scandinavian. She focused on the Scandinavians because they'd settled in the Midwest."

Giles angled his head and smiled. "I guess that makes Lily quite an ethnic gumbo."

He sobered. "I'm glad you told me about Samantha. I think I understand her a little better now."

"Are you still upset that she didn't tell you about Lily?"

"Whether I'm upset is irrelevant. What's done is done. What you and I have to do is come to an agreement as to what is best for Lily. You have a jump on being a mother while I have to learn that being a father is a lot more than offering financial support. I will not make any decisions concerning Lily unless I discuss it with you. I did tell my mother that she has a granddaughter, so she's anxious to meet her."

"What about your father?" Mya asked.

"He still doesn't know, and Mom and I won't tell him until you're ready to come to New York."

"What if we aim for Thanksgiving?" Mya knew it was one of the holidays Sammie had designated for visitation, yet after talking with Giles she was willing to be flexible as long as he didn't threaten or put pressure on her about Lily's future.

"That'll work. That gives us at least six weeks to get used to being a family."

Mya wanted to ask Giles about his relationship with his father when she recalled his statement about fatherhood: *I have to learn that being a father is a lot more than offering financial support.*

Had his father not been a positive role model? Had he just provided financial support while relinquishing the responsibility of child rearing to his wife? She'd heard the expression *more money, more problems.* Did his father's wealth did not translate into knowing or doing what was best for his progeny?

Mya pushed to her feet. "Where are my manners? I forgot to ask you if you wanted lunch."

Giles rose in one fluid motion. "Thank you for offer-

ing, but I had a buffet breakfast before I left the hotel."
He glanced at his watch. "It's time I go and check in
with my office." He winked at her. "By the way, what
time is dinner?"

"Six."

"I'll see you later, Mya."

Mya nodded. "Okay."

She watched as he slipped into his shoes, walked out
of the house and closed the self-locking door. Giles's
arrival had altered her writing schedule. She had to
tweak a proposal for the next book in her series and
submit it to her editor by the end of the week.

When her sister came back to Wickham Falls with
the news that she was staying until she delivered her
baby, Mya knew her well-ordered life would never be
the same. Before Sammie's return, all she had to concern herself with was refining her lectures notes; reading and grading papers and penning novels in her spare
time. And now when she had adjusted to being a full-
time mother and part-time writer, she would now have
to change again. This time she would have to adapt to
sharing Lily with Giles.

Fortified with a cup of fresh pineapple and a cup
of green tea, Mya raced up the staircase and into the
office to see how much she could accomplish before
Lily woke up.

Giles noticed the blinking light on the hotel phone;
there were only three people who had the number for
the hotel: his mother, Jordan and Jocelyn. He'd sent
Jordan a text with the number to avoid Mya overhearing their conversations if the call came through his

cell. He smiled. Jordan had left a message for him to call him back.

"Hey, brand-new Daddy. Are you getting any sleep?" he asked Jordan.

"Barely. My boy really has a set of lungs. He's hungry all of the time and I've told Aziza to give him a bottle in between breast feedings."

"What did she say?"

"I can't repeat it on an open line. She says she wants to breastfeed him until he starts cutting teeth. Not to change the subject, but what's going on down there with Mya?"

"So far it's all good," Giles admitted. "She seems to have softened her stance about coming to New York with me."

"When is she coming?"

"She mentioned Thanksgiving. Hopefully she'll change her mind and we'll come sooner. I found out that she doesn't need money, so that's an argument I can't use as a basis for joint custody." He told Jordan about Mya's parents leaving her and her sister the house and business. "The baby is getting bigger and more delightful than when I first saw her."

"So you like being a daddy?"

Giles smiled. "I'm getting used to it. What I really want to be is a hands-on father. I want to be there for her piano and dance recitals. I want to become involved during parent-teacher conferences and—"

"Enough, G," Jordan said, interrupting him. "I know you resent your father not being there for you because he put WDG ahead of his family obligations. Think about it, Giles. The company is a python. It constricts and then swallows you inch by inch until you can't get out. Don't be like Patrick. Take time to enjoy your family before it's too late."

"I will." He paused. "And thanks for the pep talk."

Jordan laughed. "There's no need to thank me. You've helped me get my act together more times than I can count. Now, the next time we talk, I want you to tell me that you and your baby's mother have become one happy little family."

"We'll see," Giles said noncommittedly. "Give Aziza my love and kiss Maxwell for me."

"Will do," Jordan said.

After ending the call, Giles thought about his cousin's reference to one happy little family. That had become a reality for Jordan when he married Brandt's attorney. They were now the proud parents of a little boy. He knew Jordan wasn't just blowing smoke when he talked about taking time to enjoy being part of a family. Jordan and his law partner agreed he would take a six-week paternity leave. Six weeks.

And that's how long Giles planned to stay in Wickham Falls, and hopefully when he left to return to New York it would be with Mya and Lily.

Leaning back in the desk chair, he studied a framed print of a beach scene. The suite was a cookie-cutter replica of many others he'd checked into. While some suites were more luxurious and opulent, the overall physical design was the same. He compared the furnishings with those in the villas on the islands owned by WDG International. With the assistance of his broker, WDG, Inc., sold several properties to the wealthy looking to live permanently on their private island, while several others were designated as vacation properties.

Reaching for the television remote, he turned on the television and began channel surfing. Viewing what he sometimes referred to as mindless TV had become the distraction to temporarily take his mind off his work. Occasionally he would get out of bed in the middle of the night to boot up his computer to input ideas for a new project, aware that he had become his father.

Patrick Wainwright II rarely shared the evening meal with his family. He left home at dawn to go into the office and occasionally returned home after everyone had retired for bed. The running family joke was when had Pat found the time to get his wife pregnant—not once or twice, but three times?

In the past, Giles never would've stayed out of his office for more than a week. Now it would be six weeks. And he was prepared to stay in Wickham Falls even longer if he was able to convince Mya that it was in his daughter's best interest to connect with her other family.

Legally, Lily was Mya's daughter, while biologically she was his. And that made her their daughter and a family.

Holding Lily against his heart and feeling the warmth of her little body had elicited an unconscious craving to protect her against everything seen and unseen.

Giles stood on the porch, peering through the glass on the storm door. He rang the bell and within seconds Mya came into view carrying Lily on her hip. Smiling, she unlocked and opened the door.

"You're early."

He kissed her cheek. "I thought I'd come by and see if I can help with something."

His admiring gaze swept over her face, lingering on her mouth, before slowly moving down to a loose-fitting light blue blouse and navy leggings. A pair of blue ankle socks covered her feet. The first time he'd come to the house, he'd noticed Mya did not wear shoes indoors. It was obvious she was a neat freak because everything was in its place and the floors were spotless.

"Should I take off my shoes?"

"Please. Only because Lily's crawling and she puts everything she finds on the floor in her mouth. I should've warned you that jeans and sweats are the norm around here, because Lily will sometimes spit up her food or milk."

Bending slightly, he took off his slip-ons, leaving them on the mat beside her running shoes. "I'll know for the next time." He'd exchanged his jeans and sweat-shirt for a dress shirt and slacks.

"Did you come to help me cook?" Mya asked.

Giles stood straight. "I can't cook. I came to baby-sit." He reached for Lily who extended her arms for him to take her. He pressed his mouth to her hair. "Hi, princess."

Mya stared at him as if he'd spoken a foreign language. "How do you eat?"

"I order in or I eat out."

"You're kidding me, aren't you?"

"No, I'm not. I never learned to cook. I can make coffee and toast, but not much beyond that."

Mya shook her head and rolled her eyes upward. "That's pitiful."

"What's pitiful?"

"What if you can't order in or go out? Do you subsist on toast and coffee?"

Giles winked at her. "I always have peanut butter on hand."

She smiled. "You're hopeless. Come with me to the kitchen. I have to finish making Lily's dinner."

"Should I close and lock the door?"

"You can if you want."

"Do you always leave the inner door open?"

Mya nodded. "Most times I do. Of course I close and lock it at night. Why do you ask?"

"I don't like that you live here by yourself, while your closest neighborhood is across the road."

"I always keep the storm door locked. And my closest neighbor happens to be a deputy sheriff. He'll occasionally come over to check on me and Lily."

Giles sat on a stool at the cooking island and settled Lily on his lap. "I only asked because a woman living alone can become a target for someone looking to take advantage of her." His protective instincts had surfaced, and he did not want to think of something happening to Mya or Lily.

"There's no need to worry about us," Mya said.

"I have to worry about you and Lily." What Giles didn't say was that he now regarded both of them as family, and to him family was everything.

Mya washed her hands in one of the stainless steel sinks and then dried them on a towel from a stack on the quartz countertop. "I have a security system that's wired directly to the sheriff's office, and whenever someone rings the doorbell I see their image on my cell phone. Lastly, I have a licensed handgun and shotgun in the house, and I know how to use both."

"Damn!" he whispered under his breath. "You're a regular Annie Oakley."

"Please watch your mouth," Mya chided. "Lily may be too young to talk, but she does have ears. And d-a-m-n," she said, spelling out the word, "sounds too much like dada."

"Sorry about that. I suppose I don't spend enough time around children."

"Don't forget that you have a daughter and my pet peeve is a girl with a potty mouth."

"You don't curse?"

"I try not to. It comes from my upbringing. My Southern Baptist mama would have a fit if any of us used bad language."

Giles glanced around the ultramodern, all-white kitchen with bleached pine cabinetry and antique heart-of-pine flooring.

"Your home is exquisite inside and out."

"Thank you. I loved growing up here. It was somewhat of a culture shock when I moved to Chicago to attend college. I'd rented a one-bedroom apartment and I always felt as if the walls were closing in on me."

"You didn't like Chicago?"

"Please don't get me wrong. I loved the city, but I wasn't used to apartment living."

Giles digested this information. It was apparent Mya would be opposed to living in New York City, despite him owning a spacious two-bedroom condominium with incredible views of the East River and the many bridges linking Manhattan with other boroughs.

"How long did you live there?"

"Seven years. I stayed long enough to earn an undergraduate, graduate and post-graduates degrees."

Giles whistled, the sound causing Lily to look up at him. "That's a lot of learning."

"It was necessary because I wanted to teach college-level courses." Her head popped up and she gave him a direct stare. "Are you an architect?"

"No. I'm an engineer. I've familiarized myself with different architectural designs since becoming a developer."

"You build in New York?"

"No. I build in the Bahamas."

Her hands stilled. "You must spend a lot of time there because you're quite tanned." She went back to slicing a beet. "I hope you're using sunblock."

Lines fanned out around his eyes when he smiled. "I didn't know you cared," he teased. "And you sound like my mother."

Her smile matched his. "That's because mothers know best." She placed the carrot and beets in a blender. "How long have you been doing business in the Bahamas?"

"Four years."

Giles told her about leaving the military to join his family's real estate company. He set up the international division after he convinced the board to extend the monies he needed to purchase three undeveloped private islands. He subsequently hired an architect to design villas and worked with an engineer to build desalination processing systems to convert ocean water for human consumption. The sale of the islands yielded a three-hundred-percent profit for the company, and he was given the green light to purchase more uninhabited islands. He now headed the division to expand their holdings to build vacation resorts on private islands throughout the Caribbean.

Mya gave him an incredulous stare. "How many more have you bought?"

"We now own twelve. But only half have been developed."

"Are there that many islands up for sale?"

"The Caribbean Sea has an archipelago of about seven hundred islands and at least twenty-five hundred cays."

"That's amazing. I never could've imagined there would be that many."

He smiled. "What's amazing is there's an extensive list of millionaires and billionaires waiting to write checks so they can own an island."

"What specs should I look for if I wanted to buy an island?" Mya asked Giles.

"Acreage, and if it's an island with a beach. Some buyers want one that is turnkey or if it has income potential. Another important factor is access. They want to know if it has an airstrip or the capability for a fly-in."

"What's the price range, from high to low, for these rich folks' playgrounds?"

He smiled. For some owners, it was a private playground. "An island of about seven hundred acres will cost about sixty-two million. A smaller one measuring two acres will go for a quarter of a mil."

"Going, going, gone," Mya intoned, grinning. "I'll take the one with two acres."

"That's two acres with nothing on it. It'll probably set you back several million to make it habitable."

She affected a sad face. "Sorry, but I'm forced to withdraw my bid due to lack of funds."

Giles caught Lily's hand when she reached for his face. "Whoa, princess. Not the eye."

"You have to be careful with her because she likes pulling hair and gouging eyes. I try to keep her fingernails cut to minimize the damage."

"Maybe she's training for the baby WWE."

"That's not nice, Giles."

"What's not nice is her trying to put my eye out." He pretended to bite on the tiny hand as he watched Mya press a button on the blender. Within seconds, the beets and carrots took on a pinkish shade. She continued blending until the vegetables were converted into hot soup. She poured it into a small bowl to let it cool.

"That's remarkable. You just made hot soup in a blender."

"Vitamix isn't your ordinary blender. It doubles as a blender and food processor. I use it to make baby food, soups, smoothies, and frozen desserts." Mya opened a drawer under the cooking island and took out a bib. "You can put her in the high chair so I can feed her."

Giles took the bib from Mya and tied it around Lily's neck. "I'll feed her. I have to learn some time," he added when she shot him a questioning look. He placed Lily in the chair and carried it over to the breakfast bar.

"I'll finish putting dinner together while you feed your princess."

"Does it bother you that I call her princess?" he asked Mya.

She made a sucking sound with her tongue and teeth. "Of course not. Not when her mother is the queen."

It took him several seconds to understand her retort. He wasn't certain whether she was teasing him, and if she was then he wasn't offended. He preferred the teasing Mya to the one who occasionally radiated hostility. He understood her apprehension that he would attempt to challenge her right to his daughter, and Giles knew it would take time before she would trust him enough not to disrupt her life or Lily's. "If you are a queen, then what does that make me?"

"A king." She held up a hand when he opened his mouth. "Our monarchy will differ from most because as king and queen we will rule as equals."

"That sounds fair to me."

"So you're willing to learn to cook?"

"Oh…" Giles swallowed an expletive. "Do I have to?"

"Yes. I'll not have you filling Lily up on processed foods because you can't put together a healthy meal. Do you want your daughter plagued with high blood pressure and elevated cholesterol levels before she's enrolled in school?"

"Damn, woman," he said sotto voce. "You really know how to pile on the guilt."

"What did I tell you about cussin'? Do I have to put out a swear jar and charge you five dollars for every time you cuss?"

"I thought it was cursing, not cussin'."

"You're in the South, so down here it's cussin'."

He executed a mock bow. "Point taken, Miss Sweet Potato Queen."

Mya stared at him and then doubled over in laughter. His laughter joined hers and seconds later Lily let out a cackle and waved her hands above her head.

Even before their laughter faded Giles was filled with an overwhelming emotion shaking him to the core. He, Mya and Lily had become a family in every sense of the word. He was a father, Mya a mother and Lily was their daughter.

Chapter Five

Mya glanced over at Giles as he attempted to feed Lily. Although the vegetable soup had cooled enough for it not to burn her mouth, Lily continue to fret.

"Why is she crying?" he questioned when her whimpers became a loud wail.

"You're not feeding her fast enough."

"You're kidding?"

"No, I'm not."

"But...but won't she choke?"

Mya set down the potato ricer. "It's puréed, Giles." She walked over and took the spoon from him. "Let me show you." She made quick work of feeding the baby, who hummed and rocked back and forth with each mouthful. "It's like eating ice cream. You taste and then swallow."

Giles's dark eyebrows slanted in a frown. "I can't believe you make it look so easy."

"That's because I know what she wants. Do you want to try feeding her dessert?"

He nodded. "I can't give up now."

Mya retrieved a jar of a peach-and-pear mix from the refrigerator and gave it to Giles. She gave him a reassuring pat on the back. "Give yourself a couple of days and you'll be a pro."

She went back to ricing potatoes, adding cream, salt, pepper and garlic butter, then whisked the potatoes until they were smooth and fluffy. She'd made them as a side dish for the fork-tender pot roast. The slow cooker, Dutch oven and pressure cooker were her favorite kitchen appliances, and she alternated utilizing all three when preparing one-pot meals.

"Hooray! We're finished!" Giles clapped his hands while Lily joined him, putting her tiny hands together.

Mya blew them a kiss. "I told you you'd get the hang of it."

Giles proudly pushed out his chest. "What now?"

"Wet a paper towel and wipe her face. She always drinks water after her meals. Please get the playpen from the family room and put her in it. I'll get her sippy cup for you."

Mya filled a cup from the fridge in-door water dispenser and handed it to Giles. She knew it would take a while for him to become familiar with the routine she had established to meet her own and Lily's needs. There were mealtimes, bed, nap and playtimes. In between, she set aside time for grocery shopping, laundry, housecleaning and preparing meals.

Time had become a precious commodity and she jealously guarded the little she had for herself.

Giles placed Lily on the floor, watching as she crawled over to a stool and attempted to pull herself up by holding on to the legs. He moved quickly when the stool tipped precariously, catching it before it toppled over. Now he knew why Mya told him to put Lily in the playpen. He put her back in the high chair, retrieved the playpen and placed it between the kitchen and dining area. Lily took several sips from the cup before tossing it aside and redirected her attention to gnaw on the gel-filled teething ring, as she babbled what sounded like *mumum*.

Giles walked over to Mya and rested a hand at her waist. "I don't know how you do it."

She tilted her chin, staring up at him, and he suddenly found himself drowning in pools of green and gold. His eyes moved slowly over her high cheekbones. He smiled when she lowered her eyes, and charming him with her demure expression.

"Do what?"

"Take care of Lily, cook and keep the house clean."

"I'm no different from other mothers, whether they stay-at-home or work outside the house. We do what we have to do to keep from being overwhelmed."

Giles splayed his fingers over her back. "Don't you know some young woman looking to make some extra money, willing to come in and help clean the house?"

"I really don't need anyone to help me clean the house. There's only me and Lily, so aside from dusting, vacuuming and cleaning the bed and bathrooms, there's not much to do. I get a lot done when Lily's sleeping."

"What's going to happen when she doesn't sleep as much?"

"By the time she's five, I'll enroll her in kindergarten."

"Do you plan to go back teaching once she's in school?"

"If I do, then it has to be locally. I'll apply for a position at the high school. All of the schools in the Johnson County school district occupy the same campus, which makes it convenient for teachers and staff whose children are enrolled there."

He leaned closer and inhaled the lingering scent of Mya's perfume. Giles felt her go stiff and then relax against his hand. "So you have it all figured out as to Lily's future."

"No, I don't. If you want to eat, then you're going to have to let me go. I need to take the pot roast out of the slow cooker. Thank you," Mya whispered when he dropped his hand.

Giles wanted to tell her that if he had a choice between eating and touching her, he would've chosen the latter. He felt more comfortable and relaxed around Mya than he had with any other woman he'd met or known. At first, he'd contributed it to her connection to Lily but after spending time with her, he realized it was the woman herself.

There were so many things he admired about her but it was her sense of loyalty that had won him over. She had willingly sacrificed her career to care for her terminally ill sister and raise her niece. And she had become the perfect mother when she put Lily's needs above her own.

Jordan had revealed that his investigators had not

come up with anything in regard to a man or men in her life. There was no record of her having been married or divorced. And he wondered if she'd been involved with a man before she resigned her position at the college to become her sister's caretaker and Lily's adoptive mother.

Giles thought of Mya as a superwoman as she quickly, with no wasted effort, put dinner on the table. Along with the pot roast, carrots au jus, garlic mashed potatoes, an escarole salad with orange and grapefruit sections and red onions tossed with red wine vinegar, she also included corn bread and pitchers of chilled water and sweet tea.

"Oh my goodness," he crooned after swallowing a forkful of potatoes seasoned with a subtle hint of garlic and rosemary. "These potatoes are to die for." He raised his glass of tea. "I'm ready to enroll in cooking school."

Mya smiled. "When do you want to start?"

"What about tomorrow?"

"Okay. If you come early enough, I'll show how to prepare a traditional Southern breakfast with grits, sausage or bacon, with eggs and biscuits."

"What about lunch?"

"Lunch will be dinner leftovers. We'll vary it with pulled beef sliders. I've put away some of the mash potatoes and gravy for Lily's lunch."

Giles glanced over at Lily in the playpen biting on a rubber duck as he took a sip of sweet tea. Mya told him she preferred agave to sugar to sweeten the beverage. "What do you plan for dinner?"

"Chicken with a brown rice pilaf."

"Who taught you to cook?"

"I'm proud to say it was my mother. Mama earned a reputation as being one of the best cooks in the county. Whenever there was a church potluck dinner or PTA fund-raiser, her pies and cakes were the first to go. I used to come home after school and sit in the kitchen to do homework so I could watch her cook. The year I celebrated my twelfth birthday, she allowed me to assist her—but only on the weekends. Mama refused to let anything come before our schoolwork. She wanted me and Sammie to have careers—something she regretfully gave up after she married my father. She'd gone to college to become a math teacher but wound up keeping the books for Daddy's company after the longtime bookkeeper retired."

Giles listened, transfixed when Mya revealed how much her mother resented spending hours in an office above the factory floor tapping computer keys and writing checks. After twenty years in a childless marriage, she convinced her husband to adopt a child. Graham Lawson finally gave in and they adopted Mya.

"Before my adoption was finalized, Mama had trained a high school graduate to replace her, and at the age of forty-five, she finally become a mother. Then they adopted Sammie and years later, Mama told me that she'd felt complete for the first time in her life. By the time Mama was finally an empty nester, her perfect world crumbled when Daddy called her to say he was working late, but when he didn't come home, she called the foreman and asked him to go by the factory to check on him. They found him slumped over his desk. An autopsy concluded that he'd died from a massive heart attack."

Mya's eyelids fluttered. "Mama kept saying she had nothing to live for, while I tried to reassure that she still had her girls. Less than a year after Daddy passed, Mama died in her sleep. The doctor claimed it was heart failure, but I knew she'd died of a broken heart. She was an incredible mother and I'm certain if she was still alive she would be a spectacular grandmother."

Giles pushed back his chair and rounded the table when Mya's eyes filled with tears. He eased her up and pulled her into his arms. Everyone she loved was gone: mother, father and sister. He buried his face in her hair. "Your sister and parents are gone, but you still have a family. You have Lily."

She nodded. "I know that." Mya lifted her chin and met his eyes; her eyes were shimmering pools of green-and-gold tears.

"I promise to stay in this relationship for as long as it takes for Lily to grow up and walk across the stage at whatever college she chooses to accept her degree."

"Please don't make promises you're not certain you'll be able to keep."

Giles's hands moved up and cradled her face. "I never make a promise I can't keep."

Her hands covered his. "What if you meet a woman, fall in love and want to—"

Giles placed a thumb over her mouth, stopping her words. "Don't say it, Mya. Lily doesn't need a step-mother when she has you."

"You've lost your mind if you believe I'm going to agree to a twenty-year relationship with you just so we can raise Lily together."

His lips twisted into a cynical sneer. "What's the matter, Mama? Are you hiding a secret lover?"

A noticeable flush suffused her face with his gibe. "If I had a lover, I definitely would've married him within days of discovering you were Lily's father, because you showed your hand when you threatened to sue me for custody. And marrying the son of a local family court judge would've definitely stacked the cards in my favor."

"You were engaged?"

The seconds ticked as Giles held his breath and waited for Mya's response. How, he chided himself, had he been so self-absorbed that he hadn't considered perhaps there had been a man in Maya's life? After all she was the total package: looks, brains and poise—everything a most men would want in his woman. And he was no exception.

Mya lowered her eyes. "No. I was seeing someone for a while, but we broke up when I had to take care of Sammie."

"Why did you break it off?"

"I wasn't the one who ended it. He didn't believe me when I told him that my sister was ill. Even before that, we were seeing less and less of each other. A few times he'd go off on a waitress who'd mix up his order, or he'd exhibit uncontrollable road rage because he'd believed another driver had cut him off, and when I tried to tell him that he needed to seek counseling to manage his anger he'd accuse me of not having his back. After a while, I realized I didn't want to deal with his explosive temper and told him it was over. Four months later, he called to tell me he was in counseling and wanted to see me again. We went out a few times, but that's after Sammie returned to the Falls to tell me she was pregnant. When I told him about Sammie, he accused me of using her as an excuse to see other men. He hung up and I never heard from him again."

"Where does he live?"

"Charleston."

Giles brushed his mouth over Mya's slightly parted lips. "He's far enough away so you don't have to run into him. And if he bothers you, then he'll have to deal with me, and that's something I don't think he'd want to do."

She blinked slowly. "What would you do?"

"You don't want to know."

"I don't like violence, Giles."

"I don't, either," he retorted, "but I'm certainly not going to cut and run if he bothers you."

"Now you sound like a former marine."

"Wrong, baby. Once a marine, always a marine. One of these days I'll tell why I enlisted the Corps instead of going to work for the family business."

Lily let out a loud shriek and Giles and Mya turned to find her standing up while holding onto the mesh netting covering the sides of the playpen. "Mumum," she repeated over and over as she jumped up and down on the thick padding.

"What is she saying?" Giles asked Mya.

She shook her head. "I don't know. Usually when she wants me to give her something, she'll open and close one hand and say it. She's probably trying to say *me*."

"When is she going to start talking?"

"That all depends on the child. Some kids talk early and others wait until they're almost two and then speak in complete sentences. Lily is a chatterbox, and I'm sure that when she begins, she'll never stop."

"How about walking?"

"Now that's she pulling up and holding on, I'm willing to predict she'll be walking by herself by the time she's ten months." Mya glanced at the clock on the microwave. "It's almost time for her bath. I usually sit in the rocking chair and read to her before putting her in the crib."

Giles stared, complete surprise on his face. "You read to an eight-month-old?"

"Don't look so shocked. Haven't you heard about pregnant women reading or playing classical music for their unborn child?"

"No."

"Well, there are studies that prove that these babies usually are more alert and display more creativity than those who don't receive the same stimulation."

"What do you read to her?"

"Nursery rhymes and Dr. Seuss. It's the repetition that will make it easy for her to recognize certain words."

Giles angled his head and smiled. "That's why you're the teacher and I deal with putting up buildings while focusing on quarterly earnings and profit margins."

"Well, Mr. Hotshot Businessman, it's time I clear the table and clean up the kitchen. You can hang out with Lily until I take her upstairs for her bath."

Giles sat on a stool in the bathroom watching as Lily sat in the bathtub splashing water. Mya knelt on a fluffy mat and drew a washcloth over Lily's face and hair. She claimed it was only a sponge bath and the warm water helped Lily to relax. Once the baby was dressed for bed, Mya cradled Lily in her arms and rocked back and forth while reading *Goodnight Moon*.

He suddenly realized there was much more to parenting than writing checks to the orthodontist or tuition for private schools and colleges. It went beyond providing clothes, food and shelter. It was about nurturing and making a child feel loved. And it was the love that was priceless. He'd led men and women into combat and found that easier than being a father. His heart turned over when he saw Mya kiss Lily's head before placing her on her back in the crib.

She checked the locks on the windows and switched on a baby monitor and then placed a finger over her mouth and motioned for him to follow her. Mya flipped the wall light switch, and the night-lights plugged into several outlets provided enough illumination to move around the room without bumping into objects.

"She's down for the night."

Reaching for Mya's hand, Giles cradled it gently. "It's amazing how calm she was when you were reading to her."

"I think she likes the sound of my voice."

Giles wanted to tell Mya that her voice had a wonderful, soothing quality that he never tired of listening to. He silently applauded Samantha for choosing Mya to raise her child. He knew if he'd known of the pregnancy and his former lover had agreed to list him as the father on the birth certificate, he would've asked his mother to help him raise his daughter.

However, there were things a woman in her sixties wouldn't be able to do for an infant that a thirty-something woman could accomplish with ease. Amanda had raised three children with little or no input from her husband, and Giles knew it wouldn't be fair to ask his mother to take on the responsibility of raising her granddaughter.

They descended the staircase together. "I'm going to be on my way so you can have some time for yourself."

Mya laughed softly. "A man can work from sun to sun, but a mother's work is never done."

He squeezed her fingers. "I'm a witness to that." Mya walked him to the door where he retrieved his shoes. "What time do you want me to come tomorrow morning?"

"Eight o'clock is good. By that time I've fed and bathed Lily."

"Do you want me to bring anything?"

She smiled. "No, thank you. I have everything I need."

Giles knew he was making small talk because he didn't want to leave Mya—not yet. He wanted to end the evening sitting on the porch and enjoying the silence. It was something he'd found himself doing whenever he returned to his condo. He'd sit in the dark, staring out the window at the buildings across the river. That had become his time to get in touch with himself, to be still and listen to the beating of his own heart, while asking why he had survived when so many he'd known hadn't.

It was also when he questioned his purpose in life. He knew there was more than buying and selling private islands to those to whom price was no impediment. And it was when he realized he didn't see his mother, brother and sister often enough. That he spent too many hours in the office or in the air. His main concern was buying and selling land, while conferring with his Bahamian real estate broker Kurt De-Grom to work another deal. Lily had changed his life and his priorities. His daughter was now first and foremost in his life.

Resting his hands on Mya's shoulders, he leaned down and brushed a light kiss on her cheek. "Good night, my lady."

Her teeth shone whitely when she smiled. "Good night."

Mya closed and locked the door behind Giles before he drove away. She exhaled slowly as she made her way into the kitchen. It felt as if she could draw a normal breath for the first time since she opened the door earlier that morning to Giles's ring. Being around him made her feel as if his larger-than-life presence sucked up all of the oxygen in the room.

She'd always believed she had a monopoly on confidence, but interacting with Giles had her doubting herself, although he hadn't exhibited any of the hostility from their first encounter. It was as if she was waiting for the proverbial other shoe to drop. Whatever she had shared with Giles was still too new for her to lower her guard and trust him enough to let him into *her* life.

Mya knew how important it was for a girl to grow up with a father because Graham Lawson had become her father in every sense of the word. Whenever he came home, he'd called out for his girls. She and Sammie would race and jump into his arms while he spun them around and around until they pleaded with him to stop. Once they grew too tall and heavy and he more frail with age, they were resigned to a group hug.

She missed her parents but missed Sammie even more, because they were inseparable when growing up.

Their mother had given each girl her own bedroom, yet night after night, Sammie would come into Mya's room and crawl into bed with her. She claimed she was afraid to sleep alone because she was afraid of the dark. But even after Veronica installed night-lights in her younger daughter's bedroom, Sammie continued to come into Mya's room.

Sleeping together ended after Veronica offered them the opportunity to decorate their rooms because they were becoming teenagers. Along with the new furniture, each room had its own television, audio components and worktables for their computers and printers.

Sleeping separately signaled a change in Sammie, who had begun to spend most of her free time online searching for her mother.

Mya thought it eerie that her niece would share the same fate as her biological mother. As Veronica had chosen and loved her, Mya would make certain to let Lily know she had made the choice to love and raise her as her own.

Mya knew she should be in her office writing instead of sitting in the kitchen ruminating about the past as she recalled a course she had taught covering the works of D. H. Lawrence. There was something about Giles that reminded her of the characters in Lawrence's novella *The Fox*, where she compared herself and Lily to the author's Jill Banford and Nellie March, two females who live alone, while Giles was Henry Grenfield, a young man who comes to stay with them. Although Henry's presence was more psychological than physical, in the end the lives of the two females would never be the same.

Is that what's going to happen to us? Mya thought. She prayed that she had made the right decision to not only invite him into her home, but also allow him to share Lily's life as well as her own.

Chapter Six

It had taken two weeks, and the doubts Mya had about Giles proved unfounded when he seemed genuinely interested in not disrupting her life as he bonded with Lily. He was a quick study when it came to changing, bathing, dressing and feeding her, yet balked and complained that cooking involved too many steps and he didn't have the patience for measuring countless ingredients. When she reminded him that he was an engineer and had to utilize math, he said he had no interest in learning the differences between thyme, cilantro, parsley or dill. To him, they all were green leaves that did not taste the same. Mya knew it was useless to try to convince him and did not mention it again.

She had put Lily in her crib for her nap when she found Giles waiting for her in the hallway outside the nursery. He had taken her advice to wear jeans and

T-shirts because he liked rolling around on the floor with Lily whenever he pretended he was a cat or dog, barking, meowing, sniffing or nibbling on her toes.

"Is something wrong?" she asked, averting her eyes from the laser-blue orbs that suddenly made her feel as if he was undressing her. It was the first time that she felt physically uncomfortable with him. She come to look for his chaste kisses when he greeted her in the morning and before leaving at night because she felt there wasn't anything remotely sexual in his motives.

"If you don't mind my asking, I'd like to know where you disappear to when Lily takes her afternoon naps."

She took his hand. She knew he was curious when she declined to join him on the porch or in the family room. "Come with me and I'll show you." Mya led him down the hall to her office. Pushing open the door, she stepped aside to let him peer in. "This is where I write."

Giles entered the room Mya had set up as a home office. Floor-to-ceiling shelves spanning an entire wall were tightly packed with books. An L-shaped workstation positioned under one window held an all-in-one computer. Framed photographs of Samantha and Mya at various ages and with their parents crowded an oak drop-leaf table. Rays of afternoon sunlight reflected off the pale green walls and dark jade carpet.

His gaze lingered on a window seat large enough for two people to lay side by side. The fabric on a love seat matched the pink-and-white floral window-seat cushions. The office had everything one would find in a break room: watercooler, portable refrigerator, a single-cup coffee maker, radio and a wall-mounted flat screen television.

He noticed a stack of pages with red-penciled proof-reader notations. "Are you an aspiring writer?"

"Not any longer."

"You're published?"

Mya laughed when he gave her a look mirroring disbelief. The woman with whom he found himself more entranced each passing day continued to astound him. There was nothing about Mya with which he found fault. Even when he'd explained he honestly had no interest in learning how to cook, she did not press him. A lifting of her shoulders communicated *suit yourself*.

"Yes."

"What do you write?"

Mya dropped his hand and selected a paperback from several on a lower shelf, handing it to him. "New adult. This is my latest novel. It will go on sale next week."

He read the back cover of the novel. It was part of an exciting new series featuring a team of twentysomething cyberspace cold-case crime solvers. "Congratulations! That's a mouthful of alliteration," he said, smiling. "How did you come up with the plot?"

"I grew up reading books from my mother's childhood, and her personal favorite was Nancy Drew. I was still in grad school when I overheard several forensic science and prelaw students discussing a mock cold case their professor had assigned the class. I recalled details of their conversation whenever I watched the Investigation Discovery channel for episodes of *Disappeared*, *Snapped*, or *True Crime*. After a while, I'd filled several notebooks with what I'd gleaned from those shows.

"I'd planned to write a novel once I retired, so in my head, the project had become my plan B. Once I joined the faculty at the University of Charleston, plan

B kept nagging at me. I'd come home every night and write and before I knew it, I'd completed a novel. I created my team of cold-case crime solvers with five protagonists, three guys and two girls, who bond in a chat room but never meet in person. Once they become a crime-fighting team, they interact with one another by video conferencing, Skyping or with Face-Time. There's some subtle flirting between one guy and girl despite both being in committed relationships. I've gotten tons of email asking me to have them meet in person, but I'd like to keep their sexual tension going for a few more books."

"You must have an incredible imagination."

"It comes from being an avid reader. As a kid, I'd read any and everything. I'd sit at the breakfast table and read the cereal boxes. I read to Lily because I want her to grow up with her asking me to buy her a book rather than the latest video game."

Giles silently applauded Mya for introducing Lily to books before she could walk or talk. "How many books have you published?"

"Six. I recently submitted a proposal for the next two titles in the series." Mya told him how she'd arbitrarily selected the name of a literary agent from the internet and mailed off a letter outlining her proposed series. It took nearly five months before she got a reply with a request for Mya send her the completed manuscript. She continued to write, finishing two more novels, when she finally received a call from her agent informing her that an editor from an independent New York publisher wanted to publish her series.

Giles continue to stare at the cover. "If you're a *USA Today* bestselling author, why are you using a pseudonym?" It listed her as Hera Cooper. It was definitely the reason Jordan's investigators hadn't discovered she was also a published author.

"I'd thought it best that my students didn't know their professor was moonlighting as a writer."

"Why Hera Cooper?"

"Cooper was my mother's maiden name and Hera was the supreme Greek goddess of marriage and childbirth and had a special interest in protecting married women. She was also Zeus's wife and sister, but that's another story."

"That is creepy."

"There was a lot of creepy stuff going on in Roman and Greek mythology."

Giles dropped a kiss on her curls. "One of these days I want you to give me a crash course on mythology. I never could get the names of the gods straight. I'm ashamed to admit English wasn't one of my best subjects, and that's why I took every elective math and science course available to boost my GPA."

"Where did you go to college?"

"MIT."

"Impressive!"

Giles buried his face in her fragrant hair. He liked seeing Mya with a cascade of curls framing her face. "The University of Chicago is right up there with MIT."

"Yeah, right."

Hugging Mya and kissing her good-morning and good-night seemed as natural to him as breathing. It just happened involuntarily. He pulled back and turned to face her. "You're beautiful and brilliant." He noticed the flush darkening Mya's face with the compliment. "Do you have any idea how incredible you are?"

She lowered her eyes. "I'm far from being incredible."

"Self-deprecating, too?" he added with a wide grin. "The day the book debuts, we'll have to go out and celebrate. The problem is there aren't too many fancy eating establishments around here."

Mya chuckled. "Ruthie's is as fancy as we get here in the Falls. It's an all-you-can-eat, buffet-style family restaurant."

Giles curved an arm around her waist. "I'd like to take you to someplace more upscale with tablecloths, a waitstaff and an extensive wine list."

"We'd have to go to Charleston if you really want fine dining. One of my favorites is The Block Restaurant and Wine Cellar. But if you want exceptional Italian food, then Paterno's at the Park is the place to eat. My other favorite is The Chop House, which has earned a reputation for serving some of the best aged steaks in the state."

"Choose the one you want and I'll call and make reservations."

Mya rested her head on his shoulder. "Have you forgotten we have a baby and no sitter?"

Giles groaned aloud. "I forgot about Lily. I suppose we'll have to wait until we get to New York where my mother will babysit her while we go out or..."

"Or what?" Mya asked.

"What if we don't wait until Thanksgiving to go New York?"

"What are you talking about?"

"Why don't we—you, me and Lily—go to New York now? We can introduce her to my immediate family before the remaining hoard of Wainwrights gather for

Thanksgiving. We can also celebrate the release of your book at the same time. Perhaps you'd even want to drop in and see your editor."

"I did enough celebrating with the release of my first title when I drank four glasses of champagne and woke up the next day with a dry mouth and pounding headache. Sammie sent me a gift of a week's vacation at an all-inclusive resort in the Dominican Republic. She surprised me when she showed up on the second day. We hung out on the beach during the day and danced all night until we dropped from exhaustion."

There was silence for a moment, and then Mya spoke again. "That was one of the happiest times in our lives. It was as if we hadn't a care in the world. There are times when I still don't believe she's gone. I miss her just that much." Going on tiptoe, she buried her face in the hollow of Giles's throat. "Forgive me for being such a Debbie Downer.

"It's okay, baby. I miss her, too."

Giles's hands circled her waist, molding their bodies together. He tried to ignore the crush of her full breasts and failed when the flesh between his thighs stirred to life. He'd told himself that Mya was off-limits because he had slept with her sister, but the silent voice in his head reminded him they were sisters in name only.

Suddenly Giles felt as if he was on an emotional roller coaster, because if anyone would have hinted more than a year before that he would be a father he would've said they were crazy. He'd told Samantha that he wasn't ready to have children, but now that Lily was here he had to ensure his daughter's future, and that meant a relationship with the child's mother.

He had committed to stay connected to a woman for

the next twenty years so they could raise their daughter together, a woman who hadn't given him the slightest indication she wanted anything more than friendship. And at this point in his life he wasn't certain whether he wanted more than friendship from Mya. And if he did, then it would have to be because of her and not because she's was Lily's mother.

"There are times when I think I hear her voice even though I know it's just my imagination," Mya whispered. "I realize now that I should've gone away—anywhere for a while after the funeral, but then I had to think about Lily. I'd thought about taking her to Disney World or on a cruise, but I couldn't pull myself out of a funk to make travel arrangements."

"That's because you're still grieving."

"You're probably right."

"I know I'm right," Giles said. "What about now, Mya? Do you still want to get away?"

Easing back, she smiled. "I do if the offer to go to New York before Thanksgiving is still open?"

Giles cradled her face in his hands. "Of course."

"I'm going to ask my neighbor to pick up my mail and keep an eye on the house, and then make and freeze enough food for Lily."

"You don't have to make anything for Lily. I'll call my mother and have her buy the blender."

"Are we going to stay at your place while we're there?"

"No. You and Lily will stay with my parents, because they have a room that's set up as a nursery. Whenever my brother brings his kids over, he doesn't have to lug around a portable crib or playpen."

"How old are your nephews?"

"Three and eighteen months. I'm going to have to watch them around Lily because they are really rough-and-tumble."

"I wouldn't worry too much about our hair-pulling, eye-gouging feisty little girl. I'm sure she'll be able to hold her own against her rough-and-tumble boy cousins."

"No shit!" Giles clapped a hand over his mouth. "Sorry about that."

Mya held out her hand. "Pay up."

"I said I was sorry."

She glared at him. "And I said pay up."

Mya waited for him to reach into a pocket of his jeans and take out a monogrammed money clip. He thumbed through the bills. "My lowest bill is a ten."

"Hand it over because you know you're going to cuss again." She took the bill from his fingers and slipped it into the pocket of her jeans. "Do you cuss at work?"

Giles shook his head. "No. At least not where my assistant can hear me."

"Is it because she's a woman?"

"Yes."

"Is she pretty?"

"I'd say she is. What's up with the inquisition?"

"Just curious."

He angled his head. "Curious about what?" Giles ran a finger down the length of her nose. "You know what they say about curiosity."

"Yeah, I know. It killed the cat."

"And to satisfy your curiosity, gorgeous, there's nothing going on between me and my assistant. I took her with me the last time I flew down to the Bahamas to introduce her to the broker and when I spoke to Kurt the other day, he admitted he's smitten with Jocelyn and plans on stealing her from me."

"What did you say to him about that?"

Giles chuckled. "I told him to go for it because if Jocelyn decides to move to the Bahamas, then I would bypass him and deal directly with her, cutting him out of his commission."

"That's sounds a little cutthroat."

"All gloves are off when someone messes with my employee." Giles told Mya that he had hired and fired a number of assistants until he found everything he wanted and needed in an admin with Jocelyn Lewis. "I'll take you to the office so you can meet her."

"How long do you plan to stay in New York?"

"That's up to you, sweets. I'm electronically connected to my office, so I can be reached anywhere."

"I'd like to be here for Halloween."

"What's up with Halloween?"

"The whole town turns out to celebrate the holiday. There're games, a photo gallery where parents can pose with their children, face-painting for the kids and tailgate parties for the adults. Once the sun sets, there are hayrides and bonfires with people taking turns reading ghost stories. This year, there will also be a costume party in the church basement. The current mayor and town council have continued the tradition of Halloween as a town celebration that began more than twenty years ago to control teens who were vandalizing properties and terrorizing townsfolks."

"If we come back on the thirtieth, then that will give us about five days to hang out in the Big Apple."

Mya's smile was dazzling. "Can you stay here with Lily while I walk across the road to talk to my neighbor?"

Giles kissed her forehead. "Of course."

"I'll begin packing after I come back. I'd planned to go grocery shopping tomorrow, but that can wait until we return."

"Meanwhile I'll call and reserve a flight for tomorrow afternoon."

"Are you certain you'll be able to get a reservation?"

"Quite certain, sweets. We're going to take the company jet."

"Why do you call me that?" Mya asked.

"Sweets?"

"Yes."

Giles winked at her. "That's because you are sweet. Would you prefer I call you darling or my love?"

Mya blushed again. "Sweets will do—for now."

"So are you saying there's the possibility of you becoming my darling or my love?"

"No comment," she said, smiling. Mya returned his wink. "Later, Daddy."

Lines fanned out around Giles's eyes when he smiled. "Later, Mama."

Mya buckled Lily into her car seat on the sleek modern jet before fastening her own. She was on her way to New York with her daughter and the man who, in spite of her busy schedule, intruded into her thoughts during the day *and* at night.

She'd found Giles to be gentle, generous, patient and even-tempered—the complete opposite of the man with whom she had been involved. And if she had had any reservations as to whether he would be a good father, those doubts were quickly dashed when he had become a hands-on father in every sense of the word. Mya wasn't certain whether he was overcompensating because she suspected it hadn't been that way with him and his father.

"Tell me about your family," she said to Giles when he'd turned the white leather seat to face her. Mya wanted to know what to expect before she met the Wainwrights.

He met her eyes. "There's not much to tell. I have an older married brother with two kids and a younger sister. My father heads the legal department for the Wainwright Developers Group, known to insiders as the WDG. Dad, whom everyone calls Pat, is Patrick II and my brother is Patrick III. Patrick works with Dad in the legal department."

"What about your mother and sister?"

"My mother is Amanda. Even though she's lived in New York for forty years, she still talks like a Bostonian. She majored in art history in college and was hired by the Metropolitan Museum as a cataloguer. She put her career on hold after she married and started a family."

"Did she ever go back to the museum?"

"No, but she's still involved in the art world. She works every other weekend at a Second Avenue gallery. My sister Skye just got engaged to her longtime boyfriend a couple of months ago. My mother's freaking out because this summer, Skye gave up her position as a high school guidance counselor to move to Seattle to live with her fiancé."

"A lot of engaged couples live together to save money."

"Skye doesn't have to save money. She has a trust fund."

Mya didn't have to have the IQ of a rocket scientist to know the Wainwrights weren't pleased with Skye's choice in a fiancé. "What does he do?"

Giles frowned. "What doesn't he do? He's had a food truck business that failed. He was in partnership with some of his friends who had a moving business that also went under. Skye claims he's willing to try anything to find his niche. I try not to get involved in her life, but I did tell her his singular calling is getting his hands on her money. Sometimes my sister may let her heart overrule her head, but not her money."

"What did she do?"

"The last time I spoke to her, she said the love of her life was no longer as affectionate as he used to be because she told him she had put herself on a strict budget because she wasn't working."

"It sounds as if lover boy wants her to bankroll his next entrepreneurial venture."

"Bingo! Give that lady a cigar," Giles teased. "It's not nice, but we're all taking bets that she'll be back before the end of the year."

The pilot's voice came through the cabin instructing the crew to prepare the cabin for takeoff. Mya stared out the oval window as the jet taxied down a private runway before it picked up enough speed for a smooth liftoff. All of the furnishings in the aircraft reflected opulence: butter-soft white leather seating for eighteen, teak tables and moldings, flat screen televisions and a fully functional galley kitchen and bathroom.

She glanced over at Lily who'd fallen asleep almost immediately. It was early afternoon and her nap time.

The aircraft climbed, Mya's ears popping with the pressure, and then leveled off to cruising speed.

The five-hundred-mile flight from Charleston to New York on a commercial carrier would take at least four hours, including a connecting flight, and more than eight hours by car, but their flight on the private jet was estimated to take only ninety minutes. They'd decided to forego lunch because Amanda had planned for an early dinner.

Mya's gaze shifted back to Giles, who smiled when their eyes met. His hair was longer than when she first saw him in the lawyer's office. The ends were curling slightly, reminding her of Lily's shiny black waves. Her gaze lingered on his strong mouth. "You promised to tell me why you joined the Marine Corps."

His smile vanished, replaced by an expression of stone. "I did it to spite my mother." Mya wasn't certain if he could hear her audible exhalation. "I'd dated a couple of girls while in college, but none of the relationships were what I'd think of as serious. Meanwhile unbeknownst to me, my mother was colluding with the mother of a young woman who went to high school with me to set us up. A week after graduation, Mom invited the family and some of her friends with kids who'd gone to my high school over for an informal get-together. I'd remembered Miranda as a nice, quiet girl but she wasn't someone I'd date. Everyone was posing with me for the photographer Mom had hired for the event. Two months later, I get a call from one of my cousins that he saw my photograph alongside Miranda's in the engagement section of the *New York Times*."

"Were you two dating?"

"I told you I had no interest in her. When I con- fronted my mother, she said she'd hoped that Miranda and I would fall in love and eventually marry and she may have also communicated that to Miranda's mother, who'd taken it to the next level. When I demanded they print a retraction, Mom pleaded with me to go along with it for a few months, and then pretend to break it off. What she didn't want to do was embarrass Mi- randa's family.

"Meanwhile people were calling and congratulating me on my engagement. I tolerated it for a week before walking into a recruitment office and telling the re- cruiter if he was looking for a few good men, then I was his man. I moved out and checked into a hotel until it was time for me to go to Parris Island, South Carolina for basic training. I'd attained the rank of captain by the time I was deployed to Afghanistan. Meanwhile I hadn't spoken to or communicated with my mother in more than six years. Not knowing whether I'd come back, I called to tell her I was being deployed and I don't remember what she said because she was crying so hard that I lost it. I told her I loved her and then hung up. That's the memory of my mother that continued to haunt me until I returned from my first tour."

Mya hadn't realized she'd bitten her lip until she felt a throbbing pain. "Did you see her when you got back?"

Giles smiled. "Yes. We had a tearful reunion. She claims I'd left a boy and returned a man. I'd put on a lot of muscle and was in peak physical condition. I signed on for a second deployment and after losing several members of my team, I decided to resign my commission. Transitioning to life as a civilian was very difficult for me."

"PTSD?"

He nodded. "It took six months and a kick in the behind from a cousin for me to seek counseling. Once I felt I was in control of my life, I purchased a condo and went to work for WDG."

Reaching over, Mya grasped his hand. "You're one of the lucky ones, Giles. There are a number of veterans from Wickham Falls who've been diagnosed with combat-related post-traumatic stress disorder. More than half the boys who graduated high school with me enlisted in the military because they couldn't find employment now that most of the mines have closed. There was a time when boys graduated or left school to work the mines like their fathers, grandfathers and even great-grandfathers."

Giles threaded his fingers through Mya's. "Do they come back?"

"A few do. Sawyer Middleton and I were in the same graduating class. He enlisted in the army, became a software engineer, made tons of money and then came back last year to head the high school's technology department. He's now married to one of the teachers at the middle school. And there's my neighbor, the deputy sheriff, who also served as a military police officer before coming back to go into law enforcement."

"Now those are what I call success stories." Giles gave her a long, penetrating stare. "You came from Wickham Falls and you did all right."

"That's because my parents were business owners who employed at least two dozen men and women. When it came time for me to go off to college, all my father had to do was write a check. And once I graduated, I didn't have any student debt staring me in the face. I wasn't as lucky as I was blessed that I was adopted into a family that didn't have to count pennies to make ends meet.

"Many of the folks that live in the Falls are the invisible ones that live at or below the poverty line. Twice a year, the church holds a fund-raiser to help families in need. Someone may request a used car so they can get to work, or a single mother with children will ask for monies to fix a leaky roof or repair her hot-water heater. Last Christmas, an anonymous donor gave the church enough toys, clothes and shoes to fill a tractor trailer."

"That's nice."

Her eyebrows lifted a fraction. "That's more than nice, Giles. I'm going to become a donor this year because I intend to purchase at least two hundred children's books for grades one through six."

Giles sat forward. "I'll match your donation."

Her jaw dropped. "Really?"

"Really," he teased. "Let me know what else you want to donate and I'll cover it."

"You don't have to do that."

"Yes, I do if I'm going to live here."

Mya sat back, pulling her hands from his loose grip. "So you've resigned yourself to living in the Falls."

"Do I have a choice if I want to be with my daughter? And becoming an absentee father is not an option."

"No, you don't have a choice," she countered. "It's what Sammie wanted."

Mya watched a hardness settle into Giles's features as he slumped in his chair and glared at her under lowered brows. Mya had stopped questioning her sister's motives where it concerned Lily, but it was apparent Giles hadn't.

She wanted to tell him to suck it up and accept what he couldn't control, otherwise the resentment would fester like an infection. If he could forgive his mother for trying to set him up with a woman he didn't want to marry, then it was time he forgave Sammie and concentrated on making certain his daughter knew she was loved.

Chapter Seven

Giles switched Lily from one arm to the other as he rang the bell to the town house that once was his childhood home. A buzzing sound answered his ring and he shouldered the door open, holding it for Mya to enter the vestibule. The instant he saw the antique table and two straight-backed pull-up chairs, he was reminded that Mya would be the first woman he would bring home to meet his parents. There were a few women that had been his plus-one for various fund-raisers where social decorum dictated he make introductions but nothing beyond that.

"You can leave the bags by the table," he directed the driver who had unloaded their luggage from the trunk of the limo. Reaching into his shirt pocket, he slipped the man a bill.

"Thank you, Mr. Wainwright."

The door closed behind the driver at the same time the one at the opposite end of the hallway opened. Amanda placed both hands over her mouth, walking toward them as if in a trance.

The tears filling her eyes overflowed and ran down the backs of her hands. "Oh my heavens," she whispered through her fingers. She extended her arms. "May I hold her?"

Giles placed Lily in her grandmother's outstretched arms. "She's heavier than she looks."

Amanda's expression spoke volumes. It was obvious she'd instantly fallen in love with her granddaughter. "She's so precious!" She took a step and kissed Giles's cheek. "Thank you for bringing her." She beckoned to Mya. "Come here, darling, and give me a kiss."

Mya approached Giles's mother and pressed her cheek to the older woman's. "Thank you for opening your home to us."

A tender smile parted Amanda's lips. "You are family. So my home is always open to you. Please come in and relax before we sit down to eat. You picked the perfect time to visit New York because we're having an Indian summer and it's warm enough for us to eat in the backyard. Speaking of food," she continued without pausing to take a breath, "Giles told me that you make your own baby food, so I got the blender you need."

"Thank you, Mrs. Wainwright."

Amanda wagged a finger. "None of that Mrs. Wainwright around here. Please call me Mom or Amanda." She wrinkled her delicate nose. "Personally I prefer Mom."

Mya nodded. "Then Mom it is."

Giles rested a hand at Mya's waist. "Go on in, sweets. I'll bring the bags."

He picked up Lily's diaper bag, grasped the handles to Mya's rolling Pullman and followed his mother and Mya down the carpeted hallway to his parents' street-level apartment.

His father purchased the three-story town house when he was still a bachelor. He renovated the entire structure, adding an elevator, and eventually rented the second- and third-story apartments. There had been a time when the entire building was filled with Wainwrights, when the younger Patrick occupied the third floor and Giles the second. They'd joked about moving out without ever leaving home.

He had just walked into the entryway when his father appeared. "Hi, Dad. I didn't expect to see you here."

"When Amanda told me about the baby, I decided anything I didn't finish at the office could wait until another day."

Giles left the Pullman next to a table with an assortment of African- and Asian-inspired paperweights. Pat talking about leaving work on his desk was a practice he should've adopted when his children were younger. Giles had lost count of the number of times his mother waited for her husband to come home and share dinner with the family, until she finally gave up and fed her children before it was time for them to retire for bed.

"So it takes another grandbaby to pull you away from your office."

Pat smiled, the gesture softening his features. Giles had to admit work was probably what had kept his father motivated. At sixty-six, his blond hair had silvered and there were few more lines around his large, intense blue eyes, while spending hours sitting at a desk hadn't taken its toll on his tall, slim physique.

Pat's pale eyebrows lifted. "Something like that. I'd like to talk to you before I officially meet your baby's mother."

Giles went completely still. There was something in the older man's voice he interpreted as censure. "What do you want to talk about?"

"Are you going to marry her?"

"Why would you ask me that?"

"Because Wainwright men don't get women pregnant and not marry them."

Giles struggled to control his temper. At thirty-six, he did not need his father to remind him of how he should live his life. "Have you forgotten that Jordan's father didn't marry his birth mother?" Edward Wainwright, Patrick's cousin, was engaged when he had an affair, an affair that resulted in a child he and his wife secretly adopted and raised as their own.

"I'm not talking about Edward," Pat countered.

"Well, he's the only Wainwright that I can recall who didn't marry his baby mama."

"I'm talking about you, Giles. Your mother tells me you have a child and when I asked if you had or were going to marry the baby's mother, she said no."

"That's because I can't marry her."

"And why the hell not?"

"Because she died, Dad! Mya is not Lily's biological mother. She's her aunt and adoptive mother." Realization suddenly dawned when Giles saw his father's stunned expression. "You thought I'd slept with Mya and got her pregnant?"

"I guess your mother didn't tell me the whole story."

Giles forced a smile. "I guess she didn't." He paused. "Now, are you ready for me to introduce you to my daughter's mother?"

Pat dropped an arm over his son's shoulders. "Lead on."

Giles and his father hadn't always seen eye to eye on a number of things, but rather than go toe to toe with him as his older brother had, Giles would walk away until cooler tempers prevailed. And what he failed to understand was why Patrick would choose to work under their father when the two argued constantly.

They found Mya in the den with Amanda bouncing Lily on her knee. He registered Pat's intake of breath when Mya rose to stand. The action was as graceful and regal as the queen she professed to be.

When Giles had arrived at her house earlier that morning for the ride to the airport, he had been temporarily stunned by her transformation. Missing was the bare face, jeans and T-shirt and socks; they were replaced with a light cover of makeup highlighting her luminous eyes and lush mouth, and a black wool gabardine pantsuit, black-pinstriped silk blouse and matching kitten heels. She had brushed her hair until there was no hint of a curl and pinned it into a chignon on the nape of her neck.

Seeing her like that had jolted him into an awareness that she had been a career woman before giving it up to become a full-time, stay-at-home mother.

Lily was laughing and squealing at the same time. Mya had changed her and given her a bottle during the ride from the airport to Manhattan, and after spending time with his daughter, Giles was now attuned to her moods. She fretted when he didn't feed her fast enough, cried and squirmed when she needed to be changed and loved crawling around on the floor with him. She was much calmer with Mya when she sang or read to her, and whenever they were together in the rocker, it took only minutes for her to fall asleep.

Mya smiled at the tall, slender blond man striding toward her, arms extended. She noticed the only things the older man and Giles shared were height and eye color. A warm glow flowed through her when he hugged her and then kissed her cheek.

"Welcome to the family."

She smiled up at Giles's father. "Thank you, Mr. Wainwright. I'm Mya."

He kissed her other cheek. "Around here, I'm Grandpa." He eased back, his eyes moving slowly over her face. "My granddaughter has a beautiful mother."

Mya wanted to tell him she wasn't Lily's biological mother, but decided to hold her tongue and leave it up to Giles to explain their connection. "Thank you."

"Don't thank me, Mya. Thank the two people who gave you your exquisite looks."

Her smile faded. *I would if I knew who they were*, she thought. "This is Lily, your granddaughter."

Pat stared down at the baby who'd stopped laughing long enough to look up at him. "It's unbelievable." He was unable to disguise the awe in his voice. "She's the spitting image of Skye when she was a baby."

Amanda pressed her mouth to the back of Lily's head. "Speaking of Skye. I called her to tell her about Lily and she says she'll be here tomorrow to meet her niece."

A slight frown appeared between Pat's eyes. "So, that's why she asked me to buy a ticket for her to come home. I thought she'd gotten enough of that leech sucking her dry and had come to her senses and decided to leave him."

"Please, Pat. Let's not talk about that now," Amanda said softly.

Mya was grateful Amanda wanted to change the topic because the last thing she wanted was to become a witness to what had become a source of contention for the Wainwrights. It was never a good thing when parents or family members did not approve of their children's choice in a partner.

A young woman in a gray uniform and white shoes walked into the den. "Mrs. Wainwright. Dinner is ready."

Giles approached Mya and took her hand. "I'll show you where we can wash up."

She waited until they were behind the door of a bathroom off the den, then asked Giles, "Did you tell your father about us?"

He blinked slowly. "He's knows you're not Lily's birth mother, but not much beyond that. He did ask when I was going to marry you, because Wainwright men don't get women pregnant and not marry them."

Mya felt her heart stop and then start up again. "What did you say?"

"I told him that I hadn't gotten you pregnant, so that lets me off the hook about having to marry you."

She exhaled an inaudible sigh. "That's good."

His eyes grew wider. "What's good? Me not having to marry you, or you not wanting to marry me?"

Mya turned on the faucet and then tapped the soap

dispenser. What did he expect her to say? That she could never conceive of marrying him? Or that she would consider marrying him but only if she found herself in love?

"It's not about me marrying you, because I haven't given it a thought one way or the other." She hadn't thought of it because something kept her from completely trusting him. She was certain he loved his daughter, yet she couldn't rid her mind that if he proposed marriage his ulterior motive would be to try and convince her to allow him to share legal custody of Lily.

Giles took a step, pressing his chest to her back. "You wouldn't do it because of Lily?" he whispered in her ear.

Mya closed her eyes as the heat from his body seeped into her hers, bringing with it an awareness of the man who had become so much a part of her day-to-day existence. She woke anticipating his arrival and felt a profound loss whenever he took his leave at the end of the day.

Giles had unexpectedly come into her life, and like the blistering summer heat that did not abate even after the sun had set, everything about him lingered: the firm touch of his mouth on hers when he greeted her, the muscled hardness of his body whenever he leaned into her, the brilliant blue eyes that seemed to know what she was thinking when she'd struggled in vain not to be caught up in the spell of longing whenever she was reminded of how long it had been since a man had made love to her.

There were nights when she woke in a panic from an erotic dream that made her press her face into the pillow to muffle the screams of pleasure as she experienced long-denied orgasms.

"No. There's no way I'm going to allow Lily to become a pawn in a relationship I'd have with any man."

"I'm not any man, Mya. I'm your daughter's father."

She nodded. "I know that. But I'd only marry you if I was in love with you."

Giles pressed a kiss alongside the column of her neck. "So you would consider me as a potential husband."

"Only if I was in love with you," she repeated.

He caressed her waist. "What do I have to do to make you fall in love with me?"

Mya rinsed her hands and then reached for a guest towel from a stack in a ceramic tray. "Just be you," she said cryptically. She dried her hands, dropped the towel in a wastebasket, then turned to see confusion freezing his features. "What's the matter?"

"What do you mean by that?"

She winked at him. "You're a very bright guy. So figure it out."

Giles caught her around the waist. "That's not fair."

"What's not fair?"

"You teasing me."

Mya stared up at him under lowered lashes. "All I'm saying is don't change, Giles. I've gotten to like you a lot. But you flip the script, then it's not going to go so well with us."

Giles's expression hardened. "Please don't compare me to your ex-boyfriend."

"I'm not. Malcolm is who he is, and you are who you are."

"Does this mean I can kiss you? Really kiss you?" he whispered as his head came down.

His mouth covered her before she could form an answer, her lips parting under the tender onslaught that left her shaking from head to toe. This kiss was different from the others because it was as if he was staking his claim. In that instant, she had forgotten all of the men who had ever kissed her as she returned Giles's kiss with a hunger that belied her outward appearance. Her hands came up and cradled his strong jaw as she tried to get even closer.

Then, without warning, it ended. Mya did not want to believe she was cloistered in a bathroom in Giles's parents' home allowing him to kiss her with wild abandon. And she also felt uncomfortable because it was the first time Giles had acted on his lustful stares. Maybe it was because he was more confident in New York being with his family, while she viewed herself as the outsider despite the elder Wainwrights welcoming her with warmth and open arms.

"Please open the door, Giles."

He released her and pushed open the door. "Wait for me."

Mya nodded. She noticed he was breathing as heavily as she, which meant they both were affected by the kiss.

She waited for him to wash and dry his hands, then followed him along a narrow hallway leading to the rear of the house. Mya smothered a gasp when he opened a door to a backyard garden with trees, bushes with late-blooming fall flowers, a man-made waterfall and tiny white string lights entwined with ivy within the framework of a pergola. A table with seating for four was covered with hemstitched linens, crystal stemware, china and brass candelabras. Pat seated Amanda after she placed Lily in a high chair between his chair and his wife's.

Giles pulled out a chair, seating Mya before he claimed his own next to her. "Don't look so worried," he whispered in her ear. "My mother has more than enough experience raising her children and now occasionally babysitting her grandkids."

Mya forced a smile. She wasn't aware her concern for Lily had shown on her face. She realized there would come a time when she would have to let go of her daughter, but knew it wasn't going to be easy.

Amanda smiled across the table. "Mya, I hope you and Giles will let Lily stay with me while you two take some time for yourselves while you're here, and I want to spend as much time with her before you go back to West Virginia."

"Of course," Mya said reluctantly, when Giles nudged her foot with his under the table.

"What about when you go into the gallery?" Pat asked Amanda.

"Not to worry, darling," Amanda crooned. "I'm taking off for as long as Giles and Mya are here. By the way, when are you going back?"

Mya shared a look with Giles. "We plan to stay until at least the thirtieth."

"Bummer," the older woman said between clenched teeth. "I was hoping you'd stay for Halloween because I always take pictures of the kids in their costumes. Last year, both of Patrick's boys were dressed like pumpkins."

"Maybe next year," Giles said, "that is if it's okay with Mya."

Mya nodded. "We'll definitely think about it."

"Is that a promise?" Amanda asked.

"Of course," he replied.

"We'll be back again for Thanksgiving," Mya added.

"What about Christmas?"

Mya smiled. "We'll be here for Christmas."

She was actually looking forward to celebrating Christmas in New York City. It had always been her wish to eat roasted chestnuts from street vendors while strolling along Fifth Avenue to check out the gaily decorated department store windows. She also planned to have Giles take a photo of her and Lily in front of the Christmas tree at Rockefeller Center.

Amanda pressed her palms together. "You have to spend the Christmas week and New Year's with us. Christmas is when the entire family gets together for what becomes somewhat of a never-ending party. The New Year's Eve ball is always a fund-raiser. The family underwrites the cost of the food, drinks and entertainment for folks with deep pockets to donate to the year's designated charity."

Mya sat straight. "Who selects the charity?"

Giles rested a hand over Mya's. "Those who sit on the Wainwright board of directors, who all happen to be family members. This year, they selected the World Vision's water project for Kenya. We've committed to match whatever we raise for the evening."

Suddenly she saw his family in a whole new light. They were using their wealth to help make the world better for those less fortunate.

Mya's attention shifted to several waiters pushing carts with covered dishes onto the patio. She smiled as Lily babbled incessantly while patting the high chair tray. Amanda had asked whether Lily was lactose intolerant because she'd planned to blend macaroni and cheese for the baby. She confided to the child's grandmother that Lily was a joy to feed because the baby wasn't a picky eater.

"Do you eat like this every time you get together?" Mya asked Giles quietly as waiters set out the food. The table was covered with cold and hot dishes ranging from sushi, tuna tartare, daikon and carrot, lobster and crab salads to pasta with a variety of sauces and grilled glazed pork spareribs, Cornish game hens and eggplant.

"Yes." Giles picked up and held the platter of sushi for Mya. "Mom says she likes to be eclectic when it comes to planning a dinner. In other words, a little something for everyone."

"Does your mother cook?"

"Yes. In fact, she's an incredible cook—like her granddaughter's mother." Giles punctuated the compliment when he kissed her hair. "She ordered in tonight because she wanted to get the house ready for us."

His disclosure caught Mya slightly off guard. "I thought you were going to stay in your apartment."

"Not tonight. Tomorrow you can decide what you want to do."

She gave him a sidelong glance. "What's on our agenda?"

He lifted his shoulders. "Not much. I'll probably pop into the office to check in with Jocelyn, and after that, I'm all yours." Giles paused. "Maybe I'll call my cousin Jordan and see if we can stop by and see his new baby."

"I'm going to call my editor and if she has the time, we can share lunch before we go back."

"Are you guys talking about doing something together?" Amanda asked. "Because Pat and I don't mind babysitting if you want to have some alone time."

Mya shook her head. "I…I don't want to impose on—"

"Don't say it," Amanda warned, interrupting her. "It's not as if you asked us to look after her. We're offering. And once Skye gets here I'm willing to bet you won't get to see your daughter again until it's time for you to leave."

Giles draped his free arm over the back of Mya's chair. "Just make certain you don't spoil her so much that she'll be off schedule and not want to sleep at night."

Amanda glared at him. "I did raise three children, so I believe that qualifies me to look after my grand-babies."

Mya rested a hand on Giles's shoulder. "Let it go," she whispered. She didn't want Giles to get into it with his mother about Lily. She planned to give Amanda a detailed schedule for the baby's nap and mealtimes.

"Don't argue with your woman, son, because you'll only lose."

Amanda glared at her husband. "Stay out of their business, Pat."

"I'm not getting into their business, Mandy. I'm just trying to give him some sage advice."

"Advice they probably don't need," Amanda retorted.

Giles picked up a sushi roll with a pair of chopsticks. "Dad's right. I've learned not to get into it with Mya because I usually end up losing."

Mya's eyebrows lifted, questioning. "Usually?" she teased. "You always lose."

Pat grimaced. "Oh-kay," he drawled. "It's time to drop that topic."

Mya agreed when she said, "How often do you dine alfresco?"

"As often as I can," Amanda said. "Once all of the kids were gone, Pat and I talked about selling this place because it's much too big for two people."

"Do you use the entire building?"

"Not anymore. Once Patrick and Giles left, we rented the second- and third-story apartments to doctors, because New York Hospital is within walking distance. But I didn't like being a landlord, so when their leases were up, we decided to use the entire building for out-of-town friends and family. My brother and sisters have thirteen children and at least sixteen grandchildren among them. Whenever they come down from Boston, it's like summer camp with babies underfoot and kids running up and down the stairs."

Giles smiled. "Don't let Mom fool you. She loves it when the house is filled to capacity."

Amanda nodded. "He's right. When Pat and I were first married, we'd planned on having six children."

"What made you change your mind?" Giles asked his mother.

"I didn't realize how much work went into child rearing. I grew up with a nanny, so I never saw my mother frazzled or overwhelmed. And because I missed that close contact with her, I decided early on that I'd be a hands-on mother. I had your brother and you came along eighteen months later, and now when I look back, I know I was experiencing some postpartum depression. That's when I decided to wait at least five years before getting pregnant again. I felt my family was complete because I had my sons and a daughter."

"And now we have two grandsons and a granddaughter," Pat said in a low, composed voice.

Mya managed to conceal a smile when she pretended interest in the food on her plate as Amanda recalled some of the tricks her sons had played on her. They would hide in one of the many closets in the town house and wait for her to search the entire building to find them.

Amanda wiped away traces of mac and cheese from Lily's chubby cheeks. "I was almost at my wit's end when I decided to turn the tables on them. One day when they left for school, I had a workman come in and change the doorknobs on all of the closets. When they realized they needed a key to open them, it put an end to their disappearing acts. So if Lily is anything like her father, then she's going to be quite a challenge."

Mya nodded. "Thanks for the advance warning."

"I wasn't that bad," Giles said, in defense of himself.

"Not bad, just mischievous," Amanda countered. "Even though I love being a mother, it still doesn't compare to being a grandmother. You'll see, Mya, once Lily's married and has children."

"That's not going to be for a while," Mya said.

"That's where you're wrong because they grow up so fast that you'll wonder where the time went. I preach that to my son Patrick and thankfully he's taken my advice and spends a lot of his free time with his boys."

"That's something I didn't do with my kids," Pat admitted. He met Mya's eyes. "I let work consume me and by the time I left the office, my children were in bed. It was the same in the morning. I was up and out before they sat down to breakfast. I know I can't make it up with my children, but I promised Mandy that it's going to be different with the grandkids."

I have to learn that being a father is a lot more than offering financial support. Now Mya knew what Giles meant. Although his father had financially supported his family, it was the emotional support he had withheld.

"None of us grow up knowing how to parent," Mya said in a quiet voice. "We learn on the job. I've read a lot of books on child rearing, and there's no definitive blueprint for becoming the perfect mom or dad. Lily has her own little personality and there may come a time when we're going to be at odds with each other and I'm going to have to accept that. It's different with girls than boys because of hormones. Once we were teenagers, my sister and I weren't very nice to our mother or each other, but that didn't mean we didn't love one another. My mother admitted she went through the same thing with her own mother, so she waited for us to come to our senses."

Giles set down his fork. "Even though I'm a newbie when it comes to being a parent, I have no doubt Mya is going to make me a better father."

"Don't be a fool and let her get away from you," Pat said to his son.

"Patrick!" Amanda admonished. "Why are you interfering?"

"I am not interfering. I'm just stating a fact." Pat pointed at Giles. "If you let Mya get away—"

"Enough, Dad," Giles said, cutting him off. "Mya and I will be together for a long time."

"How long is long?" Pat questioned.

"Patrick Harrison Wainwright!" Amanda said, her voice rising in annoyance. "Mind your business!"

"Stop it, Dad. Mya and I want the best for Lily, and we will do everything within our power to make certain she knows she's loved and protected."

Mya felt like an interloper when she felt tension in Giles as he engaged in a stare down with his father. She wondered if the older Wainwright felt his son had been irresponsible when he'd gotten a woman pregnant, or resentful that Lily wasn't a Wainwright.

Pat's comments cast a pall over the remainder of dinner as everyone, except Lily, appeared interested in eating what was on their plates rather than engage in further conversation. Mya was certain everyone was relieved when the table was cleared and no one opted for coffee and dessert.

Giles pushed back his chair. "I'm going for a walk. Do you want to come with me?"

Mya turned to look at Giles. "What about Lily?"

"She's going to be all right, sweets. Remember my mother raised three kids, so she's certified to take care of an eight-month-old."

I'm going to have to learn to let go and not become a helicopter mom, Mya thought. The last thing she wanted to become was overbearing and smothering where her daughter's love would turn into resentment.

"Okay. Can you wait for me to go inside and change?"

Giles assisted her up. "Of course."

Chapter Eight

Giles experienced the peace that had evaded him for years as he held Mya's hand when they strolled along Second Avenue. She had changed into a pair of jeans, pullover sweater and running shoes.

"I'm sorry about my father," he said after a comfortable silence.

"Don't apologize, Giles. Your father said what he wanted."

He glanced at her delicate profile. "And what's that?"

"He wants us together and I'm willing to bet that he also wants Lily to become a Wainwright."

"You're probably right about his granddaughter becoming a Wainwright. Dad views being a Wainwright as akin to American royalty. My great-grandfather came to this country broke as a convict. Like so many other immigrants during the turn of the century, he and his new bride shared a railroad flat on the Lower East Side with several other families. Patrick took odd jobs, while my great-grandmother took in wash to pay their share of the rent. Patrick managed to get a position as a building superintendent for several buildings on Houston Street, which allowed him to move into an apartment rent-free. Meanwhile his wife had become quite an accomplished seamstress and would occasionally sew for people in show business. They had three sons and a daughter, who died from diphtheria before her fifth birthday.

"James and Harrison knew their only path out of poverty was education. They graduated high school and enrolled in City College for a tuition-free college education. James became a teacher, while Harrison went into law. Meanwhile, Wyatt, the middle son took the opposite path of his brothers. He dropped out of school in the tenth grade and hired himself out as a bagman for a local thug running an illegal numbers operation. The police never suspected Wyatt because he looked much younger than sixteen. He made certain to stay off the streets during school hours to evade the truant officers, and after a while, he made more in a week than his law-abiding siblings because he had a gift for playing and hitting the numbers. His father gave him an ultimatum—go back to school and get a high school diploma or move out."

"Did he move out or go back to school?"

"Yes. He went back to school. I'm telling you this because I want you to know that the Wainwrights haven't always been legit."

Mya leaned into him. "Don't forget so-called robber barons used dubious means to become very wealthy men."

Giles told Mya that his great-uncle had amassed a

small fortune and, with the assistance of his gangster mentor, bought a run-down tenement and renovated it. He moved into one of the apartments and rented the others to his criminal friends who used them for everything from bookmaking to fencing stolen goods. However, Wyatt drew the line when it came to drugs and prostitution. He was sweet on a young black girl who lived in the neighborhood but nothing came of it because interracial relationships were taboo at the time.

"Once he bought his second building, Wyatt decided it was time to leave his criminal past behind. He got one of his criminal cronies to buy him out and he hired Harrison to set up a corporation for his real estate business. Wyatt had become quite adept at buying abandoned properties, renovating them and selling them at a huge profit. He was flipping properties decades before it became popular. After he'd amassed enough money, he decided to build instead of renovate. He'd become the successful Wainwright son while the other two had to depend on others for their salaries. Wyatt made peace with his father and invited his brothers to join him when he set up the Wainwright Developers Group. Wyatt had yet to celebrate his fortieth birthday when he became a real estate mogul and a multimillionaire. Although he's semi-retired, Wyatt hasn't come that far from the streetwise, baby-faced gangster to family patriarch. He still has a gun in his desk drawer.

"There are times when my father forgets where the Wainwrights came from because he grew up privileged. We all attended private schools, traveled abroad during school holidays and were expected to marry women with impeccable pedigrees. That was okay for my parents and their siblings, but my generation has,

as you say, flipped the script because we marry whoever the hell we want."

Mya giggled softly. "Y'all have gone rogue."

Giles gave her fingers a gentle squeeze. "It feels
good to throw off the shackles of a tradition that money
must marry money."

There came another period of silence before Mya
spoke again. "Is your father upset that Lily is not a
Wainwright?"

"That's only part of it. My father may not have been
there for many of the milestones in our childhood but
there was something he relentlessly preached to me
and my brother and that was making certain not to get
a woman pregnant if we had no intention of marrying
her. He said never to rely on a woman to prevent contra-
ception because there was no way of knowing whether
she was taking an oral conceptive or had an IUD. He
said that the one thing we could be certain of was using
our own condoms. His suspicions came from several
of his college buddies who became fathers before they
were ready when their girlfriends claimed they were
on the pill, or they'd used the girl's condoms."

"Do you resent becoming a father before you were
ready?"

Giles stopped in the middle of the sidewalk and
cradled Mya's face between his palms. "No. I never
would've met you if she hadn't been born."

Her hands circled his strong wrists. "This is not
about me."

"Isn't it, sweets? It's all about you *and* Lily. You two
are a package deal. I can't have one without the other."

Mya's eyes narrowed. "What do you want, Giles?"

He smiled and attractive lines fanned around his eyes. "I want you and I want Lily in my life."

"We are in your life," she argued softly. "Didn't you say we're a family?"

"Yes, but not in the legal sense. I want you to marry me."

A nervous laugh escaped Mya. "You want me to marry you so you'll have some legal claim on me and my daughter."

"Wrong, Mya. I want to marry you because you're the missing piece in my life. I'm no choirboy when it comes to women. I've slept with women I liked and some I didn't like because I needed a physical release, and I'm not very proud of that. Whenever I'm around you, I feel something I've never felt with any other woman and please don't tell me it's because of Lily because right now she doesn't figure into the equation.

"When I went into combat, I didn't know that if I survived whether I'd ever be the same. I did survive but lived in my own personal hell and was racked with guilt because I did survive when other men under my command didn't. Facing death forced me to acknowledge my own mortality and to live each day as if it was my last. I've never been in love with a woman, but if what I'm beginning to feel for you is love, then dammit, I'm willing to embrace it."

Going on tiptoe, Mya brushed a light kiss over his mouth. "Why don't we take it slow and see where it leads."

"Is that a yes?"

She shook her head. "It's not a yes but a maybe. And because I'm an old-fashioned Southern girl, then

I expect you to court me before you ask for my hand in marriage."

Giles flashed a smile, exhibiting a mouth filled with perfectly aligned white teeth. "How long do I have to court you, Miss Mountain State Queen?"

"At least six months of courtship."

He quickly did the calculations in his head. "We met for the first time in September, so next February or March seems appropriate for us to announce our engagement."

"You can't talk about an engagement when I haven't said whether I'll marry you."

"Will you at least consider marrying me?"

Mya paused before giving Giles an answer. She knew she was falling for him—hard—and she had sought to test Giles to uncover whether he wanted her as a wife because he loved her and not because she was Lily's mother. She couldn't dismiss the nagging suspicion that she had become the conduit through which he would eventually claim his daughter legally.

She nodded. "Right now I can say truthfully that I will consider it. And if I say yes, then I don't want a short engagement."

"How long do you want the engagement to be?"

"At least a year." Dating for six months and marrying a year later would allow Mya more than enough time to know if she could trust Giles completely.

"That means we'll marry sometime the following spring."

She nodded. "Do you expect me to sign a prenuptial agreement?"

Giles released her face as his hands curled into tight fists. "Hell no! What made you ask that?"

She withdrew from him without moving when she saw rage lurking in the blue orbs and the skin drawn tight over his cheekbones. "Just checking. I don't want you to think I'm marrying you for your money."

"And I don't want you to think I want to marry you because of Lily."

Mya slipped her arm through his. "Now that we've settled that, we don't have to bring it up again."

She knew Giles was still bothered by her query because a muscle flicked angrily at his jaw. He was probably so used to women falling all over themselves to get his attention because of his name, looks and money that no doubt he believed she was no exception. And no matter how much she liked him, Mya wasn't going to allow her heart to rule her head.

There was a time when she disliked him intensely when they first met, but that was then. Now she enjoyed his company. And she never tired of watching him interact with Lily. At first, she'd believed he was drawn to the little girl because of vanity—that Lily reminded him of his sister—but after a while Mya knew his affection for the child was genuine. He had assumed the responsibility of reading to her before putting her in the crib for her nap. The few times Mya had looked in on them, she found Lily curled up on his chest asleep while he cradled her in his large hands. She had wanted to chastise him for holding her but held her tongue when she backed out of the room. That was when she had to remind herself he shared DNA with the baby and she didn't. That a judge had ruled that she was legally

Lily's mother, while Giles would have to navigate the legal system to claim his daughter.

They continued walking and stopped in front of a sports bar where the doors were open and patrons were yelling at the top of their lungs. "I used to hang out here whenever I came home from college," Giles said.

She noticed his eyes were fixed on one of the many screens. "Do you want to go in?" He looked at her, seemingly shocked by her suggestion.

"You don't mind?"

Mya tugged at his arm. "Of course not. After a few beers, I'll probably scream with the others."

"I didn't know you liked baseball."

"I got into it when I lived in Chicago."

"White Sox or Cubs?"

Her smile was dazzling. "Cubbies, of course."

Giles managed to shoulder his way inside, pulling her behind through the crowd standing three deep at the bar. He managed to find a table for two in a corner near the kitchen and signaled the waiter for two beers.

"Is it always crowded like this?" she shouted to be heard over the babble of voices.

"Yes. But there's more people than usual because it's the first game of the World Series."

Even though she wasn't an avid sports fan, Mya enjoyed the camaraderie of getting together with friends and colleagues to watch an occasional game. And cheering for a particular team allowed her to get swept up in the excitement going on around her.

She had asked Giles to give her time to consider his proposal because she was still grieving the loss of her sister. And it would also take time to accept the reality that she would eventually sleep with the same man as her niece's mother.

After the second beer, she found herself caught up in the hysteria that swept through the sports bar like a lighted fuse. She watched Giles when he recognized someone from his past. There were a lot of rough hugs and back slaps before he introduced her as his girl-friend.

It was close to ten when they returned to the house, and Mya discovered she was slightly tipsy from down-ing two beers. "I'm under the influence," she whis-pered to Giles as he unlocked the front door.

"From two beers?"

"Yes."

"Either you are a cheap drunk or you don't get out enough."

Her lips parted in a lopsided grin. "Both," she slurred.

"Why don't you go upstairs and turn in while I check on Lily?"

"We'll check together." There wasn't a day since Sammie came home with the baby that Mya hadn't checked on Lily before turning in for the night.

They found Amanda and Pat sitting together in the den watching an all-news channel. Pat had his arm around his wife while she rested her head on his shoul-der. Despite Amanda having to raise her children alone even though she had a husband, she had stayed with him. Was it because, Mya mused, she did not believe in divorce? Or did she fear not having a man in her life? Or was it because she loved him and accepted his shortcomings?

Giles placed a finger over his mouth when he led her in the direction of the nursery.

The nursery was set up in an alcove off the master bedroom where Pat or Amanda had easy access in the event one of their grandchildren required their immediate attention. Lily was sleeping soundly on her back in one of the two cribs. Her tiny rosebud mouth twitched as if she wanted to smile at something that had amused her. Mya's loving gaze lingered on the long dark lashes resting on rosy pink cheeks and the coal-black hair grazing her rounded forehead.

She leaned against Giles's body when he put an arm around her waist. Turning her head, she kissed his neck below his ear at the same time his fingers tightened against her ribs. They stood watching the sleeping child, and then as if on cue, they walked out of the room.

"Baby's in bed, and now it's time for Mama to turn in before she falls on her face," he said softly.

Mya giggled. "I told you that I'm not much of a drinker."

Bending slightly, Giles scooped her up in his arms. "You didn't lie about that."

She buried her face against the column of his strong neck. "I never lie." Giles carried her up the back staircase and into the second-floor bedroom Amanda had assigned her. He placed her on the bed and lay beside her.

"Do you need help getting undressed?"

Mya gave him a crooked smile. "I don't think so. I'm just going to lie here for a few minutes, and then I'm going to get up and take a shower."

Giles shifted until they lay facing each other. "What

if I hang around to make certain you don't slip in the bathroom?"

"Sorry, handsome, but no thanks. If you think you're going to get a peek at my goodies before it's time, then you're deluding yourself."

Giles flashed an irresistibly devastating grin. "Please don't tell me you're going to make me wait until our wedding night before I can sneak a peek."

"Yes."

He affected a frown. "That's cruel and unusual punishment."

"No, it's not. Remember what I told you about courting me."

"What about a sniff?"

Before Mya could reply, Giles sprang up, shifted her effortlessly until she lay on her back and planted his face between her thighs. "No!" she screamed before laughing hysterically. She laughed even harder when he made growling noises like rutting bull.

"Don't make another sound," he warned, grinning, "or my folks will think something happened to you.

Mya waited for him to inch his way up her body, while supporting his weight on his forearms. Her body shook as her laughter turned to giggles. "You're incorrigible."

Giles kissed her chin. "No, I'm not. It's just when I see something I want, I go all in."

She sobered and met his eyes. Mya knew she had to stop denying what she so obviously wanted and needed. She'd told Giles that she wanted to wait for their wedding night to make love, yet knew realistically she didn't want to wait that long. "I've changed my mind," she said in a quiet voice. "I'm not going to make you wait until we're married for us to make love. It's just that I don't want our relationship to be based on sex like yours and Sammie's."

"That's the only thing we shared because she didn't want anything else."

"Don't forget Lily," Mya reminded him. She gave him a long, penetrating stare. "You don't like it, do you, when I mention Sammie's name?"

"Why would you say that?"

"Because you get a little frown between your eyes whenever I talk about her."

"I didn't realize that," he admitted. "Maybe it's because whenever you mention her name, I'm reminded that she was your sister."

Mya nodded. "But I am *not* my sister. Sammie was complex and almost impossible to figure out but I'd learned to accept and love her in spite of her peculiar idiosyncrasies."

"It would be a sad world if we all looked alike and thought alike."

"You're so right, love. Now let me get up so I can get ready for bed."

"Where's my night-night kiss?"

Her lips found their way to his, shivering slightly as the contact sent currents of desire racing through her. Giles returned the kiss, increasing the pressure until her lips parted; his tongue searched the recesses of her mouth until she moaned as if in pain. Her tongue touched and dueled with his and ignited a fire that threatened to consume her mind and body.

"Giles," she moaned, the sound coming from somewhere she didn't know existed.

"I know, baby," he whispered against her trembling

lips. He rolled off her body and stood at the side of the bed, staring at her heaving breasts. "Good night, my sweet."

Mya stared up at the ceiling and heard rather than saw him leave the bedroom as he closed the door behind him. Groaning, she turned over on her belly and pounded the mattress. Giles had only kissed her and now she was like a cat in heat. She had changed her mind about them making love because she knew she could not hold off not allowing Giles to make love to her until they were engaged, because she wanted him to want her for herself as if he'd never met Sammie or fathered Lily.

And it wasn't for the first time that she blamed herself for not having as much as experience with the opposite sex as her sister. She'd dated a few boys in high school, but none reached the point where they were intimate. It was in her second year in college that she had her first serious relationship with an adjunct lecturer from a nearby college. He was older, divorced and responsible for awakening her dormant sexuality. They slept together for two years until he secured another position out of the state. It was another three years before she dated again. But it lasted less than four months before she called it quits.

After she returned to Wickham Falls and was appointed to teach at the college, she finally accepted Malcom Tate's invitation to have dinner with him. She had been reluctant because they worked together. She enjoyed his company because he was closer to her age and they had a lot in common. The exception was temperament. She was composed while he was volatile and that did not bode well for a future together.

Mya closed her eyes and willed her mind blank. So much had happened in the past year that she needed a daily journal to record the events: she'd become an aunt, buried her sister and become a mother, and now she had committed to share her life and future with her daughter's father. The million-dollar question was: what's next? She wasn't in love with Giles but with time she knew she would come to love him.

She opened her eyes and slipped off the bed. She had to get up and shower before falling asleep in her clothes.

Mya woke the same time as she did every morning. Her internal clock indicated it was time for her to get up. She completed her ablution in record time because she wanted to be up and dressed before Lily woke.

She made her way down the staircase to the wing of the house with the master bedroom. The door was closed. When Giles mentioned that his parents had installed a nursery in their home, she did not think it would be within their bedroom. Mya knew she would have to wait to see Lily.

Her sock-covered feet were silent on the gleaming parquet floor when she walked down a wide hallway and peered into exquisitely furnished rooms. Paintings, wall hangings and fragile vases validated Giles's claim that his mother had earned a degree in art history. The spaces were reminiscent of rooms in museums with priceless objets d'art. She lingered outside one room with tables and curio cabinets filled with obelisks and sculptures and carvings of Egyptian cats, jackals and crocodiles. She walked down a hallway with framed prints of impressionists, cubists and modern artists and turned into a large gourmet kitchen.

Mya swallowed a gasp of surprise when she saw Pat and Giles sitting together in a breakfast nook. She did not know why, but she hadn't expected them to be up so early. It was only 5:45 a.m. Giles wore a white T-shirt and jeans, while his father was dressed for work. She could not pull her eyes away from Giles's muscular upper body. His clothes had concealed a man in his prime and in peak conditioning.

"Good morning," Mya said cheerfully.

Giles jumped up. Apparently she had startled him. "Good morning." He approached her as she entered the kitchen. He cupped the back of her head and brushed a kiss over her parted lips.

Easing back, she nodded to Pat. "Good morning, Grandpa."

Pat lifted his cup of coffee in acknowledgment. "Good morning. You're quite the early bird."

"I get up early to take care of Lily."

"You don't have to do that with Mandy hovering over her like a mother hen." He patted the bench seat next to him. "Come sit down. Giles, please make her a cup of coffee. I was talking to Giles about Mandy and I taking Lily to the Bronx Zoo today, and he said I'd have to ask you. I plan to go into the office this morning for a couple of hours, then come back and pick up Mandy and the baby. We keep a stroller, car seat and a baby carrier on hand, so transporting her shouldn't be a problem. Mandy says she's going to make her food and store it in a bag that will keep it warm, along with bottles of milk and water."

"If you want my permission, then you have it." Taking Lily to the zoo was a way for them to bond with her. "What do you have planned for tomorrow?"

Pat flashed a sheepish grin. "We were talking about possibly driving up to Boston to introduce Lily to Mandy's brother and sisters. I have a feeling she wants to show her off," he said under his breath. "Skye's scheduled to arrive today, so we'll wait and see if she wants to come with us."

"If you go to Boston, Dad, then that's not going to be a day trip," Giles said as he walked to the breakfast nook carrying a mug of steaming hot coffee. He set the mug on the table. "Coffee with a splash of milk and one sugar for the pretty lady."

"That's what I told your mother. But she says if we hire a driver, then we can do it in a day."

Mya stared at the liquid in the mug. Lily had become somewhat of a novelty to the Wainwrights and she realized they wanted to spend as much time with her before she went back to Wickham Falls. She ignored the anxiety tightening the muscles in her stomach when she thought of not seeing her baby for more than twenty-four hours.

"You can keep her overnight if you want."

Pat's face lit up like the rays of the rising sun. "Bless you, my child."

Giles sat down next to Mya and combed his fingers through her unbound hair. "What do you want to do today?"

She shivered slightly from his light touch when his finger traced the outline of her ear. "Other than a little shopping, I'm open to whatever you want."

"I'd like to take you into the office to meet Jocelyn. After that, you can shop until you drop."

"Who's shopping?" Amanda asked. Bending slightly, she placed Lily on the floor and the little girl crawled over to Mya.

"I am." Mya scooped Lily off the floor. Amanda had given Lily a bath, combed her hair and secured a lock of hair atop her head with a narrow white ribbon. "Good morning. Your grandma made you look so pretty with that ribbon in your hair."

Amanda smiled. "You don't know how long I've waited to put a ribbon in a little girl's hair."

Giles stood up and kissed his mother. "Something tells me you're partial to girls."

Pinpoints of color suffused her fair complexion. "That's not true. I love my sons as much as I love my daughter, but it's different when it comes to dressing little girls."

Giles kissed her again. "Just teasing. Do you want coffee?"

"Yes, please." Amanda sat down next to her husband. "Do you want to eat breakfast here or do you plan to grab something at the office?"

"If it won't be any trouble, I'd like to eat here."

Amanda patted the shoulder of his crisp white shirt. "Of course it's not any trouble."

Mya waited until Giles brought his mother's coffee before handing off Lily to him. "I'm going to help your mother fix breakfast."

Amanda appeared surprised by her offer when she said, "You really don't have to help me."

"But I want to. I'm not used to sitting around doing absolutely nothing."

"That's because you don't know how to relax," Giles interjected.

"That's because mothers aren't allowed to relax," Amanda countered. She took a sip of coffee and stared at Mya over the rim. "Because you've pierced Lily's ears, I have a set of earrings I'd like to give you for her. And once she turns sixteen, she'll inherit the pearls and matching earrings my grandmother gave me for my sixteenth birthday."

Mya was slightly taken aback with the generous offer. She'd noticed the magnificent strand of South Sea pearls and matching studs Amanda wore the night before. "Don't you want to give the pearls to your daughter?"

Amanda slowly shook her head. "There's a little wicked tale attached to the baubles. My grandfather died suddenly, leaving my young and attractive grandmother a very eligible widow. After a respectable period of mourning, men came calling on her. She went out with some and rejected a number of others. What she suspected was that most were after her money. So she decided to test them. In other words, put your money where your mouth is. She told each of them that her birthday was coming up and she wanted jewelry as a gift. Some gave her earrings and others broaches. There was one gentleman in particular who'd asked her father what was her favorite jewel. He told him pearls. And not the ordinary cultured pearls but the golden South Sea variety.

"The potential suitor paid someone to sail to Tahiti and bring him back enough thirteen millimeter pearls for a necklace and earrings. It took nearly four months but when he presented my grandmother with the pearls, she decided he was the one. They were married a year later and she gave him six children—all boys. I was her only granddaughter, so I inherited all of her jewelry. I've put aside some for Skye, and the rest I was saving for my granddaughter."

Mya knew Amanda loved talking about her family and there was no doubt she had many, many more stories to tell. "Lily's a very lucky little girl."

"After breakfast, we'll go through the jewelry and you can pick out what else you want for Lily."

Pat cleared his throat. "I hope you save some for Patrick because he and Bethany may change their minds and have another baby. And it could be a girl."

Amanda shook her head. "That's not happening because Bethany told me she's done having children. I didn't press her about it, so I'm assuming she's either having or had a procedure so she wouldn't get pregnant again."

Sitting in the kitchen and talking was something Mya missed with her family. Her father would come home and vent about his workmen or customers who changed their minds after he'd designed a table or a headboard. Then it was her mother who updated everyone with news from home about a relative who'd been caught cheating on his wife or a wife cheating on her husband. Mya never thought of it as malicious gossip but idle chatter because there wasn't anything else to talk about. Occasionally they would discuss politics and the fact the country was going to hell in a handbasket as it had over the past two hundred years. What Graham and Veronica sought to do was shield their daughters from local gossip, but as they got older what they heard from their classmates they never repeated to their parents. Their peers whispered about girls who'd slept with every boy on the football team, and several underage girls who'd sought to hide their relationships with older men, and then there were the boys and girls who were gay—rather than come out they waited until graduation to leave Wickham Falls to escape the taunts and harassment to live openly with a same-sex partner.

And nothing had changed when Sammie came back to the Falls to live and people began noticing that she was putting on weight. Once her condition was evident, folks wanted to know who the father was. Both she and Sammie were mute because her sister wasn't the first single mother in Wickham Falls and she definitely would not be the last.

Mya joined Amanda at the cooking island as they selected the items needed to make breakfast for their men.

Chapter Nine

Mya stared at the emerald-cut ruby ring surrounded by a double halo of flawless blue-white diamonds set in twenty-four carat gold on her left hand. Amanda had insisted she wear it because the blood-red stone was the perfect match for her golden skin tones.

"I can't take it."

"You can and you will," Amanda insisted. "That ring belonged to my mother but she hardly ever wore it because she didn't like red. And the gold made her pale skin look washed-out."

"It's magnificent."

Amanda smiled. "I agree." She pressed her palms together. "Now let's see what else is in this so-called treasure trove I can give away."

Mya was in awe when Amanda handed her a pair of diamond earrings for Lily. They totaled a carat, set in platinum and the accompanying appraisal certified they were flawless.

"I think Lily and I are good for now," she said when Amanda selected a diamond bracelet. "Why don't you wait until she's older when she can really appreciate the sentimentality. Then she can say Grandma gave me this ring for my tenth birthday or this necklace for my high school graduation."

Amanda nodded. "You're right."

Mya hugged the older woman. "I'll always remember today because of the ring."

"So will I, because it is the day I got my second daughter." She pulled back. "I get on Pat about interfering in his kids business only because I don't want him to make the same mistake I did when I tried matching Giles up with my best friend's daughter. He punished me in the most severe way possible when he disappeared for years. No one in the family knew where he was, and there was a point when I didn't know whether he was dead or alive. I had no idea he'd joined the military until he called to let me know he was being deployed. It was that day I swore I would never meddle in my children's lives again. Pat and I are not happy with the man Skye has chosen to live with, but I refused to say anything to her. When she's had enough, she'll leave him. There is one thing I know about the Wainwrights. They are survivors."

Amanda was right. Sammie had died so that Lily would survive. And not only was Lily a survivor but Mya knew she was also a survivor. She watched Amanda lock the box and return it to a wall safe behind a framed Rembrandt reproduction.

"Art students would love your home."

"You're probably right. I had a photographer approach me with an offer to photograph the house for a slick architectural magazine but I turned him down. Some of the pieces are originals and many are copies, and I don't want to invite thieves who use the most devious ways to break into someone's property. It was only after I became an empty nester that I decided to turn the house into somewhat of a museum. Whenever the grandkids come over, I simply close the doors to the rooms with the art. I've catalogued and have every piece appraised, and I've indicated in my will who gets what. I will not have my children fighting one another over material items."

Mya wanted to tell Lily's grandmother that she and Sammie hadn't had that problem. Their parents had divided everything they owned evenly. Amanda was candid when she said there had been a time when she'd had a live-in housekeeper, but now she valued her privacy, and the housekeeper only came in two days a week and whenever she hosted a get-together.

Mya nearly doubled over in laughter when she saw Lily crawling along the carpeted hallway to get away from Giles, who was on all fours crawling after her. Piercing screams rent the air as Giles pounced on Lily and pretended to gobble her up. Pressing her back against the wall, Mya moved past them and took the staircase to her bedroom.

Mya emerged from the en suite bath after brushing her teeth to find Giles sitting on a chair bouncing Lily on his knees. "You better be careful juggling her like that before she barfs on you."

Giles lifted several strands from Lily's moist forehead. "That's all right. My princess can do anything she wants." He glanced up, his gaze lingering on her hand. "Where did you get that ring?"

She held out her hand, fingers outstretched. "Your mother gave it to me. She said it belonged to your grandmother."

Giles dropped a kiss on the back of her hand. "It's beautiful."

"I agree."

"She also gave me a pair of diamond earrings for Lily, but she won't be able to wear them until she's older."

"Mom loves giving gifts. You'll discover that when we come back for Christmas."

Mya knelt near the chair, her eyes meeting Giles's. "Are you going to miss not living in New York?"

Giles pressed his forehead to Mya's. "What I'd miss is not being with you and Lily. I could live anywhere as long as we're together. Dad and I had a very candid talk earlier this morning about what it means to be a father. His father was a workaholic and Dad followed in his footsteps. I hadn't realized how much I resented my father not being around for dinner until I shared this morning's breakfast with you and Lily. Night after night, I'd watch my mother hold back tears when she stared at the empty chair at the opposite end of the table waiting for my father because he was always running very late. One night, Patrick had had enough when he raised his voice to Mom and told her that she was deluding herself if she expected her husband to share dinner with his family. That must have been a wake-up call for her because she never waited for him again."

"Lily and I will not eat with you whenever you leave on business."

"Not if you travel with me. I'd like you to apply for a passport for Lily, so when we fly down to the Bahamas, she can come with us."

Mya stared at him, momentarily shocked with his offer of wanting her to accompany him on a business trip. However, a silent voice nagged at her that he'd offered because he didn't want to be away from Lily. If not, then he could've suggested they leave the baby with his parents until their return.

"How long do you normally stay?" she asked when she recovered her voice.

"It can be two days to more than a week. Meanwhile, you and Lily can have the run of the resort."

"Does it belong to WDG?"

Giles rubbed their noses together. "Yes. You're now unofficially a Wainwright because you just called Wainwright Developers Group WDG."

She smiled. "That's because I've heard you refer to the company as WDG, and it's also stamped on the sides of the jet."

"You don't miss much, do you?"

"Nope."

Giles glanced at his watch. "I'm going to my place to get dressed, and when I come back, we'll leave to go shopping"

"Do you live far from here?"

"No. I'm about twenty blocks away and closer to the river. I'll take you there before we come back tonight."

"When is your sister coming in?"

"Her flight is scheduled to touch down around one this afternoon. Dad has already arranged for a car to pick her up. She'll be jet-lagged for a few days, then watch out. If you think Lily's a squealer, then you have to hear Skye. It's ear-shattering."

Mya extended her arms. "Give me the little squealer. I'll be dressed and ready by the time you come back."

Mya stood in the private elevator with Giles as the car rose swiftly to where WDG occupied the entire top floor in the Third Avenue office building. Giles had informed her that although WDG owned the building, the company leased office space to other businesses on the other twenty-six floors, and space on every floor of the high-rise structure was filled to capacity.

His attire harked back to the time when she'd first encountered him in Preston McAvoy's conference room. The dark gray suit, white dress shirt, royal blue silk tie and black wingtips reminded her he was a businessman who bought and sold multimillion-dollar properties with the stroke of a pen. She eschewed entertaining negative thoughts, yet she couldn't rid her head of the fact that Giles would become disenchanted living in Wickham Falls, that if they married he would somehow concoct a scheme where they would have to live in New York.

"You look very nice."

Mya inclined her head. "Thank you."

She had packed several outfits she had deemed business attire. When many instructors and professors favored jeans and running shoes, she had opted for pantsuits and conservative dresses. Today, she had selected a black lightweight wool sheath dress with a matching hip-length jacket. Sheer black nylons and a pair of leather-and-suede booties were in keeping with the favored ubiquitous New York City black. The elevator opened to doors with the company's name etched in silver across the glass.

Resting his hand at the small of Mya's back, Giles swiped a key card and when the light changed from red to green, he pushed it open. The receptionist sitting behind a mahogany counter smiled at him. The screen on the wall behind her displayed the time, temperatures and headlines of countries from around the world.

"Welcome back, Giles."

He returned her smile. "Thank you, Linda." Giles escorted Mya up three stairs to an expansive space covered in pale gray carpeting spanning rows of glassed-in offices with the names and titles of the occupants.

"Nice views."

He nodded. "I agree, but occupying a space enclosed by glass has its advantages and disadvantages. There're times when I find myself staring out the window daydreaming." Giles nodded and greeted employees he rarely saw because he didn't spend much time in his office. His fingers tightened on Mya's waist. "My office is at the end of the hall."

"Where are your father's and brother's offices?"

"They're in what everyone refers to as the West Wing. Legal, accounting and cyber security are thought of as the heart of the company, while all of the other departments are its lifeblood."

"How many people do you employ?" Mya asked.

"The last count was thirty-eight. We have a number of real estate agents based in upstate New York, Massachusetts, Connecticut, New Jersey and as far south as D.C. They come into the office the second Friday in the month for a general meeting, while the board meets the first Monday of each month."

"Do they expect you to attend those meetings?"

"I just got special dispensation from my uncle Edward to participate using videoconferencing because of Lily. It's a perk all Wainwrights are afforded whenever there's a new baby."

"I suppose it pays to be a Wainwright around here."

Giles pulled her closer to his side. "You've got that right." He wanted to tell Mya that doors would open and Lily given full discretionary privilege if she was Lily Wainwright rather than Lily Lawson.

He opened the door and was met with a bright smile from Jocelyn sitting in an alcove outside his private office. "Hello, boss. Thanks for holding it down," Giles said teasingly."

Jocelyn's smile got even wider. "I had the world's best teacher."

Giles turned to Mya. "Mya, I'd like you to meet Jocelyn Lewis, the third woman in my with life whom I cannot live without. Jocelyn, Mya Lawson."

Jocelyn extended her hand and Mya took it. "It's a pleasure. Giles told me about you and your precious daughter." She pointed to the ruby on Mya's left hand. "Your ring is beautiful."

The skin around Mya's eyes crinkled in a smile. "Thank you." She patted Giles's shoulder. "And thank you for keeping my man sane. He says you're invaluable." Jocelyn lowered her eyes with the compliment.

Giles could've kissed Mya at that moment. He liked the comment about him being her man. "Are there any updates since our last email?"

"No. But I'm expecting a call from Kurt this afternoon about the Pederson deal. As soon as I hear anything, I'll update you."

"Thanks, Jocelyn. I'm going to see my father before we leave. You know how to reach me."

"She is very pretty," Mya said once they were far enough away so Jocelyn couldn't overhear them. Jocelyn's demeanor indicated she was older than Mya, but she felt envious of the woman's flawless complexion. Her chemically straightened hair, parted off-center, ended at her jawline, and there was a subtle hint of color on her full mouth while the only allowance she made for eye makeup was mascara.

"Jealous, sweets?" Giles teased.

"Should I be?"

"Never. Remember, I'm committed to you until Lily graduates college."

"What happens after that?"

Giles stopped, nearly causing Mya to lose her balance. He pulled her over into an area with a low table cradling a large fern growing in a painted glazed pot. "What do you mean by what happens after that?"

"Will we still be together?"

His brows lowered in a scowl. "What do you think?"

Mya stomped her foot. "Why are you answering my question with a question?"

"Because you're not making sense, Mya. What do I have to do or say to convince you that I'm just not in this for Lily? Even if you decide not to marry me I'll buy a house in Wickham Falls and come to see Lily everyday so she can grow up knowing that I'm her father."

Mya felt a fleeting panic grip her until she found it hard to breathe. She didn't want to lose Giles, because she needed him, needed him for more than a physical craving that grew stronger with each passing day. She needed him to love her and to restore her faith in men; after dating Malcolm, she still harbored a fear that she would become involved with another Jekyll and Hyde.

She found Giles even-tempered and soft-spoken, yet she sensed he could be unrelenting and uncompromising.

His expression changed, softening when he saw indecision in her eyes. "You've reminded me that you're not your sister, and I have to remind you again that I'm not your ex-boyfriend. What you see is what you get."

A trembling smile flitted across her lips. "You just read my mind."

"Let's hope you can't read mine because it would be rated triple X right about now." His eyes made love to her face before they moved lower over her chest. "Damn, woman. Do you know that you're sexy as hell?" he whispered in her ear.

Mya swatted at him. "Shame on you," she chastised, "talking dirty in the middle of a hallway where anyone can come by and hear you."

"There's a company policy about gossiping. One infraction and you're canned."

"That's a little severe."

"Spreading gossip is not only malicious but a form of bullying, and around here, that's grounds for an immediate dismissal. Come with me, baby. I want to introduce you to my brother."

Mya felt more in control when she followed Giles into an office next to his father's. The blond head popped up when the occupant realized he wasn't alone.

Patrick Wainwright stood up and winked at her.

"So you're the woman who has my brother stuttering every time he mentions your name." He rounded the desk. "Come and give me a hug."

The resemblance between Giles and Patrick was remarkable enough for them to be twins. The only difference was the color of their hair. Patrick was fair and gorgeous and Giles dark and dangerous. Mya found herself in Patrick's arms as he lowered his head and kissed her cheek.

"It's nice meeting you, Patrick."

He pulled back, holding her at arm's length. "I must admit my little brother has exquisite taste in women."

"Stop flirting with my woman or I'll tell your wife."

Patrick cut his eyes at Giles. "Nice try. You know my wife wouldn't believe anything negative you'd say about me." He lifted Mya's left hand. "Is that what I think it is?"

Mya smiled. "Yes. It's your mother's ring."

"Does this mean you and my brother are engaged?

She shook her head. "No." Even though she was vacillating about whether she wanted to marry Giles, deep down inside it was something she wanted more than any else thing in the world. She had always grown up believing she would fall in love, marry and have children. She wanted a family of her own and to share all of the wonderful things her parents had given her.

The few times she and Sammie argued it was when Mya accused her of being selfish and ungrateful because their adoptive parents had given them what their biological parents hadn't been able to. She tried to make her sister see the flip side of their lives where they could've grown up living in squalor where hunger was commonplace instead of a rarity. They'd known kids they'd gone to school with who, if it hadn't been for free lunch or food stamps, they would have been malnourished.

Patrick kissed her on both cheeks. "Dad told me about Lily and I can't wait to meet her. I know my boys will happy to know there's another cousin they can play with. It's going to be a while before Jordan's little boy will be underfoot."

"You know Lily is the only princess among these young princes," Giles bragged.

"No shit," Patrick drawled. "We'll have to wait and see what Brandt and Ciara have."

"Ciara's pregnant?" Giles asked his brother.

"I don't know, but the last time I spoke to Brandt, he said they were going to get a jump on starting a family because he wants a football team."

Giles grunted. "There's no way Ciara's going to agree to having eleven kids."

"By the way, how many kids do you guys plan to have? I mean if you do decide to marry," Patrick blurted out.

Mya shared a look with Giles. They'd talked about marriage but not about whether they would have children together. Suddenly she felt as if she'd been put on the spot because she was wearing Amanda's ring. Patrick had assumed she and Giles would eventually marry, and wondered how many more Wainwrights would come to the same conclusion. "We'll probably have another two," she said after a noticeable pause.

"Why stop at three?" Patrick questioned. "Why not round it out and have four?"

Giles dropped an arm over Mya's shoulders. "Mya

and I would like to wait until Lily's walking and talking before we go back to changing diapers."

"I hear you, my brother." The phone on Patrick's desk rang. "I'm going to have to take that call. It's nice meeting you, Mya. If the family doesn't get to meet you and Lily before you guys go back to West Virginia, then it's Thanksgiving for certain."

Mya noticed Pat's office was empty when they retraced their steps to the elevator. "I hope folks don't assume we're engaged because I'm wearing your mother's ring," she said once they stepped into the car.

Giles crossed his arms over his chest. "People will always draw their own conclusions. Once we're officially engaged I'll buy you a ring."

She held out her hand. "What's wrong with this ring?"

"Nothing. I just believe a woman should have her own ring."

"If my birthstone was a ruby rather than a pearl, I would definitely consider a ruby."

"When's your birthday?"

"June 12."

"The month for weddings and graduations." He reached for her hand when the doors opened. If they married on her birthday, then he would have no excuse for forgetting their wedding anniversary. "Are you ready to go shopping now?"

Mya smiled. "Of course."

"Do you know where you want to shop?"

"Yes. I researched online and discovered a few shops on Madison Avenue that carry the labels I like."

"I hope I don't come to regret this," Giles mumbled under his breath.

"I heard that, sport."

"I wanted you to, sweets. Are you the type of woman that has to try on a dozen dresses and then decides to buy the first one she tried on?"

Mya rolled her eyes at him. "I'm not even going to dignify that with an answer."

Giles waved his hand and whistled sharply between his teeth to flag down a taxi. The driver came to a screeching stop at the curb. Giles opened the rear door and allowed Mya to enter, then slid onto the seat next to her. He gave the driver their destination and the driver took off as if he was racing in the Indy 500.

Mya huddled closer to Giles. "I hope we'll get there in one piece."

He buried his face in her hair. "New York City taxi drivers are notorious for weaving in and out of traffic."

She closed her eyes. "Let me know when we're there."

Mya found a boutique that carried the designs she favored. Several salesladies fussed over Giles as he sat in a comfortable chair in the seating area and was given green tea and sliced fruit while he watched a wall-mounted flat screen television.

It was too early for cruise wear, but the salesperson said they still had some items in stock from the beginning of the year. She wanted a few outfits for when she went to the Bahamas with Giles. Mya preferred shopping in specialty shops because of the individual service and there weren't endless racks of the same mass-produced dresses and blouses.

It took more than an hour for her to try on dresses, jackets, slacks, blouses, shorts and several swimsuits.

When the assistant helping asked if she wanted her boyfriend to see her in anything, Mya told her no, because she wanted to surprise him. She wasn't certain whether Thanksgiving and Christmas were semiformal events for the Wainwrights so she chose several dresses that she deemed appropriate. Mya thought about asking to see formal wear for the New Year's Eve fund-raiser, and then changed her mind. She decided to wait until they came back for Thanksgiving to shop for a dress. It would signal the beginning of holiday shopping and she knew she would be able to select something appropriate for the event.

"I suppose that's it," she said to the assistant who'd help her into and out of garments.

The woman smiled. "I'll take these up front while you get dressed."

When Mya emerged from the dressing room, she found Giles at the register as the cashier rang up her purchases. He pushed her hand away when she handed him her credit card. "Put *that* away," he ordered between clenched teeth. He took it from her fingers and slipped it into his shirt pocket when she hesitated. "I'll give it back later."

He turned back to the cashier, offering her a friendly smile. "Could you please have someone deliver these to my apartment?"

The clerk glanced at the card he'd given her. "Of course, Mr. Wainwright. Is it all right if we deliver it tomorrow because deliveries for today are already out on the van?"

"Of course." He plucked a business card off the counter and jotted his name and address on the back.

The woman glanced at the address. "It should arrive before noon."

"No problem. Let the driver know he can leave it with concierge." He signed the receipt and returned the card to a case in his jacket's breast pocket. "Let's go, sweets. I don't know about you but I'm hungry enough to eat half a cow." He whistled for a taxi that sped by without stopping. "I'm going to order something and have it delivered to the apartment. What do you feel like eating?"

Reaching into her hobo bag, Mya took out a pair of sunglasses to shade her eyes against the glaring autumn sun. "Half a cow," she said, deadpan.

He splayed his hand over her hips. "You could use a little more meat in this area."

"I have enough, thank you." She wrapped her arm around his waist under his suit jacket. "Thank you for paying for my clothes."

Giles frowned. "There's no need to thank me, Mya. Whenever we're together, I don't want you to go into your wallet for anything. And I repeat—*anything*."

"Oh, that's how it's going to be?"

"No. That's how it is."

Mya decided it was futile to verbally spar with Giles. Most times it accomplished nothing so she mentally accepted his mandate that he would pay for whatever she needed when they were together. After all, it was his money and he could spend it however he wished.

Chapter Ten

Mya sat on the balcony outside Giles's bedroom staring out at water views while enjoying the most delicious chicken piccata with a side dish of broccoli in garlic and oil she had ever eaten. And throwing caution to the wind, she had accepted a glass of rosé to accompany the meal. She had shed her dress, jacket, nylons and booties in exchange for one of Giles's long-sleeved shirts.

She closed her eyes for several seconds and turned her face up to the warm sun. "This is wonderful." She opened her eyes to find him watching her. "How often do you sit out here and have your meals?"

His lids came down, concealing his innermost thoughts from her. "Not enough. Whenever I sit here, it is usually to clear my head." A faraway expression swept over his features. "This is what I call my therapy place. When I first bought this condo, I would sit out here for hours until nature forced me to get up. At that time I was in a very dark place."

She recalled him admitting to experiencing post-traumatic stress disorder. "What about now?" she asked in a quiet voice.

He blinked as if coming out of a trance. "I'm good. Very good." Giles pointed to her half-empty wineglass. "Do you want more wine?"

She placed her hand over the top of the glass. "Please no. I'm surprised I'm having it when I'd gone down for the count after two beers."

"I do happen to have a bed where you can sleep it off," he teased.

Mya glanced over at the king-size bed with a massive dark gray quilted headboard. "I just might take you up on your offer." She patted her belly over the shirt. "Right now I'm as full as a tick on a dog's back."

Throwing back his head, Giles laughed. "I'm going to have to get used to your regional expressions."

"Like, if the creek don't rise, or she was madder than a wet hen."

"Exactly."

"Once you spend some time in the Falls, you'll become familiar with all of the expressions. I…" Her words trailed off when Giles's cell phone chimed.

He picked it up and read the text message. "My sister decided not to come. She says she'll see you and Lily at Thanksgiving."

"Is something wrong?"

Giles shook his head. "I don't know. Half the time I wonder what she's going through with that clown. I hope and pray he's not abusing her because it won't go well for him. My father is a laid-back dude, but don't

mess with his little girl because he can more dangerous than Uncle Wyatt."

"Do you think she would put up with a man abusing her?"

"Skye is a throwback to a flower child. She believes
in peace and live-and-let-live. She feels guilty that she
was born into money when there're so many people that
are hungry and homeless. When I suggested she donate
her trust fund to charity, she said she's wary of chari-
ties because the money will usually pay for administrative salaries rather than for the earmarked need."

"Why doesn't she set up her own charity? That's
what Sawyer Middleton did when he donated almost
a million dollars to update the technology lab at the
school. Not only does he head the charity, but he's also
responsible for overseeing the project. If she's a guidance counselor, then she can set up a counseling center for kids with emotional issues. And if she's really
ambitious, she can add a tutoring component and hire
teachers looking to supplement their income to help
students needing extra help with their schoolwork. I'd
be willing to volunteer to help kids struggling with
English."

Giles leaned back in his chair and pressed a fist to
his mouth. "I think you've got something there. I'll
be certain to mention it to Skye. She'd fit right in living in Wickham Falls because she's so unpretentious."

"There you go," Mya drawled. She pushed off the
chair. "I'm going to accept your offer to take a nap before we go back to your folks' place."

"Leave the dishes. I'll put everything away."

She walked off the balcony and into the bedroom.
Pulling back the white silk comforter, she slipped

under a sheet and lightweight blanket. "Are you going to join me?" she asked Giles when he entered the room balancing plates along his forearm.

"Later."

Giles wanted to ask Mya if she had lost her mind inviting him to share the bed with her. Did she trust him that much not to try to make love to her? Then he had to remember she would be the first woman to sleep there, because every woman he'd slept with since returning to civilian life had been in a hotel. It was as if the condo was his sacred sanctuary and he didn't want to defile it by having sex with different women. And sex was what it had been. He had never allowed himself to feel anything other than hormones calling out to one another for a physical release.

Giles didn't need a therapist to tell him he would've continued to live his life by his leave: spending hours in his office, traveling to the Caribbean and waiting for women to call him, if it hadn't been for Mya and Lily. He had made it a practice never to call a woman but waited for them to call him.

He put away the food and stacked the dishwasher. Spending time with Mya had enhanced his domestic skills. She'd shown him how to load and operate the dishwasher, washing machine and dryer. The last bastion for him to scale was learning to cook. Although he had balked, Giles knew eventually he would have to make an attempt.

He returned to the bedroom, slipped off a pair of walking shorts, leaving on his boxer briefs, and got into bed with Mya. Her back was turned to him. "Are you still awake?"

"Yes. I'm not as sleepy as I am relaxed."

He kissed the nape of her neck. "Good." A pregnant silence ensued, and he felt her suddenly go stiff. "What's the matter, sweets?"

"I was just thinking about Sammie sleeping here with you."

"She never slept here with me." Mya turned to face him, and he told her about the suite at a Chelsea boutique hotel where he conducted his affairs. "I pay for the suite every month even if I didn't use it. Something wouldn't allow me to bring a woman here."

Mya rested a hand on his cheek. "Until now."

He smiled. "Yes. Until now." Giles pulled on a curl that escaped the pins in the chignon. "There are times when I need you to be patient with me if I become somewhat overbearing. I suppose it comes from giving orders and expecting them to be followed without question."

Her fingernail grazed an emerging beard. "Did you enjoy the military?"

"I did because it was strictly controlled, regimented, and I needed discipline at twenty-one." Giles met her large, slightly slanting, catlike gray-and-green eyes. "I'd grown up believing as a kid of privilege I could do whatever I wanted and the hell with everything else. I went to a private school where infractions at a public school would've resulted in a suspension or expulsion, but because our parents were doling out the big bucks for tuition or bestowing substantial endowments, we got away with things that would've been questionable by law enforcement. Like a lot of teenagers, we drank, smoked weed, had sex with girls willing to give it up, and a few kids ended up in rehab because they got hooked on crack or heroin.

"I was an above-average student and was accepted by several top universities but in the end, I chose MIT. I continued to drink and smoke weed, but I'd become discriminating when it came to sleeping around because I knew I wasn't ready to deal with an unplanned pregnancy. My senior year signaled a change when I stopped hanging out as much and stopped drinking and smoking altogether. I managed to graduate with honors and Wyatt, who was at the time WDG's de facto CEO, asked me to join the engineering department."

"What did you tell him?"

"'Ask me again in three months and I'll give you my answer.' I was burned-out and needed that time to recharge. That's when my mother decided that her youngest son needed a steady girlfriend."

"Is that when your mother tried to set you up with Miranda?"

Giles nodded.

"But you were so young to think about settling down with a wife."

"I know that and you know that, but people in particular social classes are always looking for their children to make a proper match, much like an arranged marriage in some cultures. Once I discovered the subterfuge, I enlisted in the branch of the military with the toughest basic training. I met the initial requirements for officer eligibility and worked and studied harder than I ever had in my life to graduate Officer Candidate School. It was when I was mentally, physically and morally at my best."

Mya cradled his face. "You've come a long way from

that weed-smoking, skirt-chasing and binge-drinking boy to a man Lily will grow up to be proud of."

"And I swear if I find some pimply faced, pothead cretin sniffing around my daughter, I'll snap his head off and roll it down the street like a bowling ball."

Mya's laugh was low, throaty. "Why do men always talk about hurting a boy if they come around their daughter?"

"That's because we know what we've done to some man's daughter."

"It's called karma and payback."

Resting an arm over her waist, Giles pulled Mya closer until her breasts were flattened against his chest. "Karma is a very nasty girl."

"That she is."

Those were the last words she mumbled before Giles registered her breathy snoring. He had done something with Mya he had never done with another human being and that was to bare his soul. His parents never knew of his drinking and drug use either because he'd become so adept at concealing his destructive behavior or they were in denial, unable to believe their so-called model son was less than perfect.

"I love you."

Giles knew Mya couldn't hear him, yet he felt compelled to say what lay in his heart. He loved everything about her: her loyalty to her sister, willingness to sacrifice her career to take care of her sister's child and her feistiness when she refused to back down when he challenged her.

He was aware of her reluctance to share her life and future with a stranger and he was willing to wait however long it would take to convince her he wanted her as his wife with or without Lily. Mya had accepted the responsibility of raising his child with or without him, while offering him an alternative to a lifestyle where he had become so self-absorbed that his only focus was doing what made him happy.

Wickham Falls would not top his list of places to live and retire; however, he found himself looking forward to living in the Louisiana low-country style house with a woman and child that had him planning for their futures.

Giles's breathing deepened, and after a while he joined Mya in the comforting embrace of Morpheus.

Mya held Lily to her chest as she paced back and forth on the sidewalk while she waited for Pat to retrieve his car from the indoor garage. A freezer chest with jars of baby food and bottles of milk and water, a carry-on with Lily's diapers and clothes, a portable crib and a car seat sat on the curb.

"You are becoming quite the traveler," she crooned. "First you visited the Bronx Zoo and now you're going to Boston." Lily cooed and patted Mya's face with her small chubby hands. "You have tons of cousins so I want you to be on your best behavior when they meet you. We can't have them thinking you have no home training." She went completely still when she detected the familiar scent of Giles's aftershave and the warmth from his body as he came up behind her. His moist breath feathered over her ear. "I was just giving your daughter a pep talk about behaving."

He laughed softly. "She's my daughter when she misbehaves and your daughter whenever she's a good girl?"

Mya smiled. "You said it and I didn't."

"Isn't that what you implied, Mama?"

"Not in the least, Daddy."

Giles rested a hand on Mya's shoulder and he leaned over to blow Lily an air kiss who pulled at her hand-knitted hat in an attempt to pull it off. He gently brushed her hand aside. "Don't, princess. Once you get into the car, I'll take your hat off."

Mya reached up and adjusted Lily's hat. "We're going to have a problem once winter arrives because she doesn't like wearing hats or socks."

"That's because she's a free spirit."

"You won't think she's that much of a free spirit when she comes home from college in bare feet, one side of her head shaved and a boyfriend with a braided beard trailing behind her. And the first words out of her mouth will be, 'But, Daddy, I love him!'"

"And Daddy will throw him in a Dumpster where he belongs."

Tilting her chin, Mya scrunched up her nose. "Why so violent?"

"I'm not going to let anyone mess over my baby girl. Here comes Dad."

A black Lexus SUV maneuvered up along the curb and came to a complete stop as the hatch opened. Mya continued to hold Lily as Giles stored everything in the cargo area and then placed the car seat on the second row of seats. He returned to take Lily from her arms.

Mya gave her a kiss and then turned and walked back into the house. She didn't know why but she felt as if she was losing her baby, even though she had a responsibility to let Lily know she had a large extended family. What Mya feared was that as Lily grew older, she might eventually lose her to the Wainwrights.

Amanda, carrying several bags, found her sitting on a chair in the entryway. She was dressed for traveling: cropped khakis, pullover sweatshirt, running shoes and a cap bearing a Yankees logo.

"We're going to take good care of your baby."

Rising to her feet, Mya flashed a smile she didn't feel. "I know you will."

"I'll call Giles to let him know we've arrived safely."

She hugged her future mother-in-law. "Safe travels, Mom."

"Thank you, darling."

Mya was standing in the same spot when Giles returned and closed the door.

"What's the matter, sweets?"

"Nothing."

Giles didn't believe Mya. She looked as if she was struggling not to cry. His fingers curved under her chin. "She'll be back tomorrow."

Mya nodded. "I suppose I'll have to get used to sharing her."

"Remember, you're sharing her with her family."

"I know that."

"If you know that, then why the long face?"

"I really don't want to share her, Giles. When Sammie put her in my arms and made me swear an oath to love and take care of her baby, I interpreted that to mean she wanted me and not you, Amanda or Pat to be responsible for her. Now this is the second time that I've allowed someone else to assume that responsibility, and if you think I'm being selfish, then just say it."

Giles searched her upturned face, his heart turning

over when her eyes filled. "You're not selfish, Mya. You're just being a mom. You've been with Lily every day of her life, and when you wake up, you look for her and it's the same at night when you get her ready for bed. But today is different because someone else will put her to bed and do all of the things for her you would normally do. Her grandparents taking her away for a day or two is preparing you for a time when Lily will leave for a much longer period of time. Maybe it will be sleepaway camp or an out-of-state college."

"I can't even think that far ahead."

"Neither can I, but we both know it's going to come. You've been rehearsing for your role as Mommy for eight months, while I just got the part as Daddy, so it's going to take us time before we really master our starring roles in this production based on parenting. Characters may come onto the stage for a brief moment before disappearing and others may become major supporting characters that remain on the stage until the final curtain comes down. We are the protagonists and my parents and the rest of the Wainwrights are the major supporting characters. They're not going to leave the stage, Mya. They're going to become a part of Lily's very existence because that's what Samantha wanted when she added the codicil. She wanted Lily to know who her biological father was and connect with his family because that's what she'd wanted for herself."

Mya rested her head on his shoulder. "Thanks for the pep talk. You're going to be an incredible father."

He buried his face in her curls. Giles wanted to tell Mya that he wanted to a good father and an incredible husband. "Now that we don't have to concern ourselves with a babysitter, I'd like to make good on my promise to take you out to dinner to celebrate the release of your latest book."

"Where are we going?"

"I have a few places in mind."

"Should I wear something nice?"

Pulling back, Giles smiled. "Yes." He still hadn't decided where he would take her but he wanted to make the night a special one.

"I bought an outfit yesterday that may be appropriate. But…"

"But what?"

"I need shoes and accessories."

Shaking his head, Giles rolled his eyes upward. "More shopping?"

"I don't need you to come with me."

"Do you know where you're going?"

She laughed softly. "I'm not going to get lost, Giles. I've downloaded a maps app on my cell and if I want to find a particular store, then I'll just Google it."

"I suppose you'll do okay in the big city."

"Just okay? Remember I lived in Chicago for nearly seven years."

Giles wanted to tell Mya that even though Chicago was a big city, it still wasn't New York City with its five boroughs and countless neighborhoods. "While you're shopping, I'm going to visit a cousin. I'm going to give you the keycard to my apartment and leave instructions with the doormen to let you into the building. Meanwhile, I'm going to call a few places to see if we can get a reservation for tonight."

"Maybe I'll stop and get a mani-pedi." She ran her fingers through her hair, frowning when she rubbed the curls between her thumb and forefinger. "And if I have time, I'll try to get my ends trimmed."

"I'll give you my charge card in case you run out of money."

"You gave me back my card and I have enough of an available balance to cover what I need to buy."

"I want you to take it anyway and buy whatever you want. In fact, keep it. I'll call the company and have them overnight me another one."

"You may come to regret that decision."

Giles winked at her. "I don't think so, sweets."

Mya returned his wink with one of her own. "Do I have a spending limit?"

"There is no spending limit."

Her expression changed, amusement crumbling like an accordion. "You're kidding?"

"No, I'm not." One of the many perks of having a Black Card was no spending limit. He knew it would take Mya time to adjust to the changes in her life once they were married. She would not have to concern herself with standing in line at airport terminals to take a commercial flight because a single phone call would give her direct access to a private jet. She would no longer stick to a budget when it came to managing household expenses, and if she wanted a new car, she wouldn't have to negotiate with the dealer for discounts on optional features.

"Okay."

His eyebrows lifted questioningly. "Just okay?"

"Yes. I can't think of anything else to say."

Threading their fingers together, Giles brought his hand to his mouth and brushed light kisses over her knuckles. "Have fun shopping."

Her smile began with a slight parting of her lips before moving up to her eyes, and Giles felt as if he was staring into a misty gray pond with delicately floating water lilies. "Thank you."

He kissed the back of her hand again. "There's no need to thank me because there isn't anything I wouldn't do to make you happy."

"I am happy, Giles. Happy that you're Lily's father and happy that you're in both of our lives."

She eased her hand from his loose grip, turned on her heel and headed for her bedroom. Inviting her to come to New York with him signaled a change in Mya. She appeared less tense, with the exception of agonizing over not having Lily with her 24/7.

When he'd introduced her to his friend in the sports bar, the word girlfriend had come out unbidden, and despite her wanting to wait until next spring to announce their engagement, he had begun to think of her as his bride-to-be. When she had asked him to court her, Giles knew the tradition of a man dating a woman for a specific period of time before proposing marriage had come from her traditional mother's Southern upbringing.

Giles regarded Mya as a small-town girl with big-city sensibilities. She could navigate a city with a population of millions, but it was her small town roots that surfaced when she preferred spending hours cooking to eating at a restaurant. She said grace before every meal, kept the tradition of making Sunday dinners the most important meal of the week, and whenever she sat at her computer, it was to pen her novels and not post messages to her friends on various social media groups.

Giles did not want to fool himself into believing that

relocating from New York to Wickham Falls would be without angst. He would miss going into his office, interacting with WDG employees and sitting in on meetings with department heads and the board of directors. He wouldn't be able to pick up the phone and make dinner plans with his mother or join Brandt or Jordan at baseball and basketball games. The only constant would be the flights to the Bahamas, and the upside to that was the probability of Mya and Lily accompanying him.

His life had become a series of highs and lows. He'd graduated college with a degree in engineering but within months, he'd turned his back on his family when he'd enlisted in the Marine Corps. He'd taken to military life like a duck to water when graduating as an officer and rising to the rank of captain. But after facing and cheating death twice, he wasn't ready to challenge it again when he resigned his commission and returned to life as a civilian, unaware it would become the darkest period of his young life. And in reconciling with his mother, facing his post-wartime demons and joining WDG, he'd become the phoenix rising from the ashes to soar and come into his own as the head of the company's international division.

Giles smiled as he exhaled an audible breath. His life was good and he predicted it would become even better once he, Mya and Lily became a legal family.

Chapter Eleven

Jordan Wainwright opened the door and pulled Giles into a rough embrace. "I'm glad you came over because right about now I need some serious male bonding."

Giles studied his cousin. The brilliant attorney looked different. His dark hair was close-cropped and instead of being clean-shaven, he now sported a short beard. Giles noticed there were dark circles under Jordan's large hazel eyes. He'd earned a reputation as a champion for those less fortunate, and many of the residents who recognized him on sight had dubbed him the Sheriff of Harlem.

"You now have your son to bond with."

Jordan blew out a breath. "I love my boy to death but all he does is cry, pee, eat and sleep. Then he wakes up only to repeat the cycle."

Giles smiled. "That's what babies do. And as a new

dad, you have to sleep when they sleep or you'll end up falling on your face."

Jordan led the way into the maisonette. He and his wife divided their time between their Manhattan duplex facing Central Park and a house in Westchester County. "Do you want anything to eat or drink?"

"Why? Did you cook?"

Jordan flashed a wide grin. "I'm learning. Zee told me if I'm going to hang around the house for six weeks, then I should learn to put a meal on the table."

"How's it going?"

"I made chicken with dumplings last night. She gave me an A, so if you want to sample leftovers, I'll heat up some for you."

"No, thanks. I'm good." Mya and his mother had prepared a buffet-type breakfast.

"Sit down and take a load off your feet," Jordan said as they walked into the living room. "Zee's upstairs feeding Max."

Giles sat on a butter-soft leather chair. He'd always liked Jordan's apartment because of its proximity to the park where he had an up-close-and-personal view of the changing seasons. However, for Giles it had one drawback: the noise of traffic along Fifth Avenue. His condo, high above street noise and the pollution from nonstop vehicles along the FDR Drive, was his sanctuary, a place where he decided who came and went.

Mya had been the first woman, other than his female relatives, he had invited in. And she was the only woman to share his bed

Jordan stretched out long legs and crossed his feet at the ankles. "Sleep has become a premium around here. By the way, do you sleep when your daughter sleeps?"

"Not really. Whenever Lily takes her afternoon nap, I usually hang out on the porch reading or relax in the family room watching television." Giles didn't tell Jordan it was a time Mya jealously guarded whenever she retreated to her office to write.

"What about at night?"

"I don't sleep over."

A slight frown creased Jordan's forehead. "I thought you and the baby's mother were getting closer."

"We are." Giles candidly told Jordan everything that had transpired since he left New York to move into the extended stay hotel so he could see Lily every day. "I've gotten her to agree to consider announcing our engagement sometime next year, but even that is tenuous. She wants us to date before we take what we have to another level."

Smiling, Jordan tented his fingers. "In other words, you're not sleeping together."

"We did share a bed but nothing happened. Our relationship is different from boy meets girl, boy likes girl, and then they fast-track their relationship from platonic to intimate. Right now, Mya and I are still in the platonic stage."

Jordan angled his head. "I'm going to ask you a question, and you don't have to answer it if you don't want. Are you in love with her?"

"Yes," Giles replied without hesitation. It was the easiest question he'd ever had to answer. "I've never been in love before so what I'm feeling for her has to be love. I say that because she's the first woman I've known whom I want to see every day. I like that she can be serious and teasing at the same time. I love her strength, intelligence and her devotion to Lily. And I admire the sacrifice she's made to give up her career to raise her niece."

Jordan chuckled under his breath. "She sounds quite remarkable."

"She is. And on top of that, she's gorgeous and sexy.

Jordan sobered. "When you called me, I thought you were going to bring your daughter so we could meet her."

"I would have if she wasn't on her way to Boston to meet her grandma's people."

"Are they flying up?"

"No. Mom and Dad decided to drive."

Jordan went completely still. "Your father took time away from the office to go on a road trip?" Giles nodded. "But he never takes off. Only when he's sick. Which my father says isn't often."

Giles had to agree with his cousin. Jordan's father, Edward, was now CEO, and there was an ongoing joke throughout the office that Pat was looking to replace Edward once he announced his retirement. Giles knew his father did not want to take over the reins as head of the company. He loved heading the legal department. Pat was single-focused, a workaholic, a perfectionist and a control freak. Patrick told him that their father tended to micromanage everyone and everything in the legal department, and that's why Giles knew he could never work for his father.

"Dad took one look at Lily and it was like he'd become a different man. And because he isn't a first-time grandfather, I'm willing to bet having a granddaughter is the reason for the change. I remember my mother mentioning that he took off for two weeks when she had Skye, compared to leaving the office to drop Mom off at the hospital once she went into labor with me and Patrick and then going back to the office. Once she came home with his sons, he hired a nanny to help her out because he claimed his work was piling up and he didn't want to fall behind."

"Are you saying my uncle has a soft spot for girls?"

"What else can it be?" Giles saw movement out of the side of his eye and stood up when he saw Aziza descending the staircase cradling her son in her arms. "Hey, beautiful."

"Don't talk the talk if you can't walk the walk, playa," she teased.

Giles winked at his cousin's wife. "My playa certification expired once I discovered I had a daughter."

"When Jordan told me you were dropping by, I thought you were bringing your daughter and her mother."

Aziza Fleming-Wainwright sat on the love seat next to her husband and then placed the infant in his arms. The new mother wore a white man-tailored shirt over a pair of black leggings and had styled her shoulder-length dark hair into a loose ponytail. When Jordan had introduced Aziza as his fiancée, Giles hadn't been able to resist staring at the tall, brown-skinned, slender woman with large, round dark eyes in a doll-like face with a hint of a dimpled chin. And when she'd smiled at him, he'd been completely enthralled with her.

Aziza's connection with the Wainwrights began years before she met Jordan. Their cousin Brandt had been and still was her client whenever she reviewed his NFL contracts and now his business projects. Jordan confided that he'd had to work hard to convince

Aziza to marry him because she had been burned by a disastrous first marriage.

"She's on her way to Boston because my mother wants to show her off to her relatives."

Jordan chuckled. "Aunt Mandy must be over the moon now that she has a granddaughter."

Giles nodded, smiling. "You're right about that." He told Jordan and Aziza they probably wouldn't get to meet Lily and Mya until Thanksgiving. "We'll be back again for Christmas and stay until after the New Year."

"You guys are welcome to spend a couple of nights with us," Aziza said.

"I'll definitely run it past Mya." Giles was certain Mya would probably want to hang out with Jordan and Aziza because they all were around the same age. "Who are the designated babysitters for New Year's Eve?" he asked Jordan.

"My sisters Chanel, Stephanie and Keisha have volunteered to monitor the childcare center."

A suite in the Wainwright family mansion had been transformed into a permanent nursery with cribs, youth and bunk beds. Another area had been set aside as a playroom rivaling those at some fast-food restaurants.

Soft grunting from Maxwell garnered everyone's attention. The infant had inherited his father's swarthy complexion and his mother's features. Sparse dark hair covered a perfectly rounded little head.

Jordan wrinkled his nose. "I think somebody needs to be changed."

Aziza reached for her son. "I'll do it."

Waiting until Aziza took the baby upstairs, Giles asked Jordan, "You don't change diapers?"

Jordan rubbed a hand over his bearded jaw. "Not if I don't have to." His hand stilled. "You change diapers?"

Giles nodded. "I've been certified as a Mister Mom. I've learned to diaper, feed and bathe Lily."

"There's no doubt you've earned your Daddy certification. I took off six weeks to help Zee around the house. We still use the cleaning service, but there's laundry and cooking. Now that I no longer have a live-in housekeeper I've learned to operate the washer and dryer and fold clothes. Instead of going to the supermarket, we now order online and have the groceries delivered." Shaking his head, Jordan blew out a breath. "I can't even begin to imagine what a single mother has to go through caring for her new baby and keeping her house in order and still remain sane. And those who make it look easy are definitely superwomen."

Giles knew exactly what Jordan was talking about. Before he'd stepped in to help Mya with Lily, she had done it all. "I hear you, cousin."

Crossing his arms over his chest, Jordan gave Giles a prolonged stare. "How are you adjusting to life in the country? Have you traded your luxury SUV for a pickup with a gun rack?"

"That's not funny, man. When I first got there, I was ready to cut and run, but now I can't wait to get back." He held up a hand. "Don't get me wrong, Jordan. I love New York but I think of Wickham Falls like finding an oasis in the desert. It's where I'm able to feel at peace with myself and everything around me."

"Maybe it has something to do with your new family."

"Maybe," he conceded. "Or maybe it goes beyond Mya and Lily. There are times when it's so quiet I can hear crickets in the daytime. Wickham Falls looks like a picture postcard with mountains, forests, waterfalls and white-water rapids. Once Lily's older, I'm going to teach her to swim in a lake rather than in a pool. I want to take her fly-fishing and white-water rafting. And because we live in a rural area, I'll also teach her to handle a rifle and a handgun. And of course whenever we come to New York I'll take her to most of the sporting events."

"So it looks as if you have your future all mapped out."

"Not really. Those are just some of the things on my wish list. I…" His words trailed off when his cell phone vibrated in the back pocket of his jeans. Rising slightly, he retrieved the phone and answered the call. It was a store calling to ask if his charge card was missing or stolen. "No, the card isn't stolen. I gave the card to Miss Lawson for her use. Thanks for calling." Giles ended the call. "Sorry about that. I gave Mya my charge card and a store clerk thought she'd stolen it."

"What you need to do is apply for one in her name."

"I've already done that." He'd called the credit card company earlier that morning and requested an additional card for an authorized user. Giles glanced at his watch. He stood up. "I have to head out now because I have a three o'clock appointment with my barber."

Jordan pushed to his feet. "I know you have your itinerary planned out in advance while you're here, so I guess we'll see you guys for Thanksgiving."

"You bet." Giles's parents were hosting Thanksgiving, while Jordan's parents had assumed the responsibility of planning Christmas. He hugged Jordan again before taking his leave. "Kiss Aziza and that beautiful boy for me. I'll see you guys next month."

Giles left the maisonette, walking east to Lexington Avenue where he hailed a cab to take him downtown. He'd called a former high school classmate who recently opened an intimate restaurant with a piano bar on a quiet block between First and Second Avenue and within walking distance of his Sixty-Second Street apartment. He knew Mya was in a funk because it was the first time since Lily came home from the hospital that she hadn't been there with and for her, and Giles hoped eating out and listening to music for several hours would help to lift her dark mood.

If Mya entertained doubts as to whether Giles would approve of her outfit, they vanished completely when she walked into the living room to find him waiting for her. He stared at her as if she was a stranger as he slowly rose to his feet. She held her hands out at her sides.

"I hope I'm not overdressed."

Giles blinked once. "Oh my... I... I don't," he stuttered, seemingly unable to get the words out. He cleared his throat. "You are beyond perfection."

She'd chosen to wear a sleeveless, high-necked, mid-calf, ruby-red, lace sheath dress with an attached black underslip. Black silk-covered, four-inch stilettos and an evening clutch completed her elegant look. A stylist had trimmed the ends of her curly hair just above her shoulders; each time she turned her head, the loose gold-streaked curls moved as if they'd taken on a life of their own.

He headed toward her, and Mya recognized lust

shimmering in the depths of his electric-blue eyes at the same time a shudder of awareness eddied through her. At that moment, she felt an intense physical awareness that was frightening and palpable.

Giles leaned into her. "You smell and look good enough to eat."

Mya was helpless to stop the swath of heat that began in her face before slowly moving to her chest and even lower. She knew it had been a long time since she'd made love with a man, yet she did not know if she wanted that man to be Lily's father. Not before she sorted out if what she was beginning to feel for him was love or simply a need that reminded her she was a woman who'd denied her femininity for far too long.

"I think we'd better leave now before we're late," she lied smoothly. Mya knew if they lingered, then she would beg Giles to strip her naked, take her into the bedroom and make love to her.

Giles picked up his jacket off a chair and slipped his arms into the sleeves, and then handed Mya her black cashmere shawl. He waited for her to wrap it around her shoulders before reaching for her hand and leading her out of the apartment and down the hall to the elevator.

She averted her eyes as he continued to stare at her during the ride to the lobby. It was the first time since meeting Giles that she wasn't as comfortable and confident with him, and she attributed her uneasiness to the realization that her pretense of keeping him at a distance was nothing more than a smoke screen for her true feelings: she was in love with Giles Wainwright.

Although she had stopped thinking of him as her sister's lover, Mya was still attempting to sort out if

Giles wanted her for herself and not just because she was Lily's mother. And whenever she thought about Sammie adding the codicil to the will, she wondered if her sister wanted her and Giles together because she probably knew how much family meant to him. Mya had witnessed for herself that the bond between the Wainwrights was strong and invincible. They'd embraced her as if she had given birth to Lily, and before Giles's sister postponed her travel plans, Skye had been ready to drop everything to fly across the country to meet her niece.

It was as if her life had come full circle: she had been adopted by a couple who had given her everything a child could want or need, and now years later, she had adopted a baby and she and Lily were now a part of a large family who would give her daughter everything she could want or need.

"What are you thinking about?" Giles asked, once the car stopped at the lobby.

"Lily."

"What about her?"

"How blessed she is to have a big family."

Giles tucked Mya's hand into the bend of his elbow as they exited the elevator car. "Her blessings came from Sammie sacrificing her life to give birth to a healthy baby, and the second from having you as her mother."

"You're saying that because you're biased."

"No, I'm not. Seeing you with Lily has allowed me to see women and mothers in particular in a whole new light.

"Even though my mother grew up with nannies and live-in help, she didn't want the same for her children because she claimed she saw her nanny more than her mother. I remember her and Dad arguing constantly about having a resident cook and live-in housekeeper. In the end, Mom compromised when she allowed for a cleaning service to come in twice a week to clean the townhouse. She claimed she felt uncomfortable with having strangers living in her home with her children."

"I agree with her," Mya said. "Our house isn't *that* big that I can't maintain it." Although the house where she'd grown up was larger than many of the homes in Wickham Falls, it wasn't ostentatious. When her father hired an architect to design the house, he'd planned on having at least four children. The plans included two full baths, a half bath, five bedrooms that included the master bedroom on the main level with easy access to the veranda.

Graham had insisted on woodburning fireplaces and window seats in every bedroom, and a fireplace in the living room. The architect had divided the downstairs space into three zones: the front for two formal rooms for entertaining and dining, to the rear was the family room and kitchen with an eating area off the outside porch, and the third was the main-floor master bedroom suite.

Then there was the flower garden because Graham knew how much his bride-to-be loved tending her rose garden. He'd hired a landscape architect to create a garden on the one-acre property with flowers, trees, ornamental grasses and aromatic herbs. Every Saturday morning after breakfast, Veronica could be found in her garden, weeding and pruning her collection of hybrid roses. Now a landscaping crew came every week beginning in the spring to mow the grass and maintain the garden until early November when the flower beds were covered to protect them from wildlife foraging for food during the winter months.

Giles smiled when Mya said *our house*. It was apparent she had begun to think of them sharing a future where they would eventually live under one roof. "Our house is perfect for a couple with at least two or three kids. I'd like Lily to have a brother or sister before she turns two."

She shot him a questioning glance. "Please don't tell me you're planning for the next baby even before Lily begins walking."

Giles nodded to the doorman as he escorted Mya across the marble floor to the street. "I'm going to turn thirty-seven in February, and I don't want to find myself out of breath running after a toddler when I'm forty-five."

"There are a lot of men who have kids in their forties and fifties."

"I'll be fifty-five when Lily's eighteen and by that time, I will have earned membership in the silver fox club. And I don't want my six-year-old embarrassed when his friends ask if I'm his grandfather."

"How many kids do you plan to have? And have you selected the woman who will agree to bear your children?"

Giles stopped in midstride, nearly causing Mya to trip and fall. He caught her, holding onto her arm to steady her. "Did you think I was thinking of someone other than you?

She blinked slowly, reminding him of an owl. "I don't know what to think, Giles. I can't understand why you continue to make plans for us without talking to me first."

Giles felt properly reprimanded. He knew Mya was right because he hadn't had to think of anyone else but himself until now. He was single-focused when it came to securing Lily's future and he figured Mya would just go along with whatever he proposed. Unknowingly he had become his father, micromanaging Mya's life and expecting her to agree with his decisions.

He cradled her face between his hands. "I'm sorry, sweets. I've spent so many years doing what I want that it's going to take some time for me include others in my decision-making."

Mya's eyes clung to his. "You can make all of the decisions you want when you're at your office, but at home you're going to have to discuss things with me before we can compromise on anything that impacts our future."

"Yes, boss."

She lowered her eyes. "I'm not your boss."

"You think not," Giles teased. He pressed a kiss on her fragrant curls. "Let's go before we lose our table."

They continued to the corner and waited for the light to change. "I'm sorry, Giles."

Giles registered raw emotion in Mya's apology. "What are you sorry about?"

"I didn't mean to bite your head off, but I don't want you to forget that we're not even engaged and meanwhile you're talking about having more children. I'd believed I would raise Lily as a single mother. That I could be mother and father, but now I know I was deluding myself when I recall my own childhood. As a child, I loved coming home from school to find my mother in the kitchen preparing the evening meal. But the highlight of the night was when my father arrived because he'd open the door and yell in a perfect Ricky Ricardo imitation, 'Honeys, I'm home.' I thought he was just greeting my mother but he kept calling for his honeys. After a while, I knew he wanted me and Sammie, too. Then all of us would have a family hug and Daddy would say how much he loved his girls. That hug said more than words. It meant we were a family and nothing or no one could break that bond. That's what I want for you, me and Lily."

"And that's what we'll have. A bond that will last all of our lives." An expression of triumph and satisfaction showed in Giles's eyes.

Chapter Twelve

Mya, holding onto Giles's hand, slowly made her way down a flight of stairs to Dewey's Hideaway, a below-street-level restaurant. She didn't know what to expect but it definitely wasn't the grotto-like eating establishment with the only illumination coming from a wood-burning fireplace, a backlit indoor waterfall, dimmed recessed lights and the candles on nearly two dozen tables positioned close together to maximize space. Most of the tables were filled with diners, as the soft sound of the pianist playing show tunes competed with conversations and the distinctive rattling of serving pieces and plates.

"How did you find this place?" she whispered to Giles when she saw the hostess coming in their direction.

"A friend owns it." Giles smiled at the young woman

with neatly braided hair. "I have a reservation for two. The name is Giles Wainwright."

Picking up two menus, she lowered her eyes, then stared up at him through eyelash extensions. "Please come this way."

Mya didn't miss the flirtatious glance the woman directed at Giles. She seated them at a table not far from where a gleaming black concert piano sat on a raised platform. The hostess removed the Reserved sign from the table and walked away with an exaggerated roll of generous hips.

"How often do you come here?" Mya asked, as she folded her shawl over the back of her chair.

"Not often enough," answered a deep baritone.

Her head popped up while Giles came to his feet. She stared at a tall black man with a black bandana covering his head, chef's jacket and black pinstriped pants with Dewey's Hideaway and D. Dewey, Executive Chef stitched on the tunic over his heart. Giles and Dewey thumped each other's back in greeting. Mya found herself smiling when the two men began talking at once.

"I didn't want to believe it when my sister told me G. Wainwright made a reservation for two."

Giles pumped Dewey's hand. "Who did you think it was?"

"Your brother Patrick. When he calls to make a reservation, he identifies himself as P. Wainwright. He and his wife eat here at least once a month. She likes our mac and cheese with truffle oil." He winked at Mya. "Aren't you going to introduce me to your beautiful lady?"

Cupping Mya's elbow, Giles helped her come to her

feet. "Darling, this is Darryl Dewey, proprietor, chef and all-around good guy. Dewey, Ms. Mya Lawson."

Mya extended her hand to the handsome man with a complexion reminiscent of whipped chocolate mousse. The skin around his dark eyes crinkled in a perpetual smile. "It's a pleasure meeting you, Dewey."

Dewey kissed the back of her hand. "No, Mya. It's my pleasure to meet you." His eyes lingered on her left hand. "I don't know if your fiancé told you, but we go way back as far as the first grade."

"No, he didn't, but I'm certain he's going to fill me in," she replied. It was apparent Dewey thought the ring was an engagement ring.

"You guys can order on or off menu." He pounded Giles's shoulder. "I have to get back to the kitchen because we're down one chef tonight. I have your number, so I'll be in touch."

Mya sat down again. "Please don't tell me you two spent more time in the principal's office than you did in the classroom?"

Giles shifted his chair until they were seated side by side. "Wrong, sweets. Although we were best friends, we were also very competitive when it came to grades. When we graduated, Dewey's GPA beat me by one-tenth of one percent. He enrolled in New York University as a business major and, after graduating, went into investment banking. Dewey said although he made tons of money he hated it because his real passion was cooking. One day, he walked away from his six-figure salary and applied to the Culinary Institute of America to become a chef. He bought this place two years ago and now he's living out his dream."

Mya placed her hand over Giles's. "Are you living out your dream?"

A mysterious smile tilted the corners of his mouth. "I am. Before I met you, my sole focus was on work, and the harder I worked, the more I was able to convince myself that I didn't need or want anyone to share my life." He pressed his forehead to hers. "Meeting you has proven me wrong. Not only do I want you but I also need you."

Mya closed her eyes, too stunned to cry. Men had told they needed her, but they were glibly spoken words they believed she wanted to hear. She felt his hand shake slightly under hers and in that instant she was aware of the power she wielded over Giles. That he'd shown her vulnerability for the first time.

"I need you, too." Her voice was barely a whisper. "I need you to love and protect me and our daughter. When you go away on business, I'll be counting down the days until you return. And I want every subsequent homecoming to be as special as the first one. I know you want more children, but I want to wait and give Lily time to experience being an only child. I also need to warn you that I can be stubborn when—"

"Enough, Mya," Giles admonished softly. "You don't have to try and convince me that you're not perfect because no one is."

"Not even you?" she teased.

"Above all, not me." Cradling her jaw, he brushed a kiss over her mouth. "And I'll try and make certain every homecoming is more special than the one before it. We'll talk about you, me and Lily when we get home."

She nodded. "Speaking of home, I'd like to suggest

you give up your hotels and move in with your *fiancée* and daughter so we can begin living as a family. I'll fix up one of the bedrooms for you."

Giles pulled back, his features deceptively composed. "Are you serious?"

A slight smile softened her lips. "Very serious. You no longer need your love shack and you can stop polluting the environment driving between your hotel and Wickham Falls."

"Consider it done." Giles shifted his chair to sit opposite her, while resisting the urge to pump his fist. It was obvious Mya was willing to consider sharing her life and future with him. He did not tell her that he hadn't renewed the Chelsea hotel suite reservation for the month of October. Once he discovered he'd become a father, he realized he couldn't continue to have sex with arbitrary women to slake his sexual frustration. It had become a wake-up call that not only had his life changed, but he had to change.

Some of the guys with whom he'd attended college had planned to marry their girlfriends and start a family. They found it odd that he never mentioned having a special woman or marriage. At the time, giving up his bachelor status had not been an option. He had not wanted to be responsible for anyone but himself. However, fate had a way of altering his well-ordered lifestyle when he unknowingly became a father. Even the best-laid plans were known to go awry.

The spell that Mya had unknowingly woven wrapped him in a cocoon of peace. The newfound joy was shattered when a waiter came to take their drink order.

It was as if any and every other woman Giles had

dated ceased to exist as he shared nearly ninety minutes of eating, talking and listening to live music. The four-course meal began with a toast to her latest novel and followed with a salad of bitter chicories paired with crisp lardoons, toasted pine nuts and crumbled feta tossed with red wine vinegar and extra-virgin olive oil; the salad was followed with an appetizer of baked clams and entrées of marinated grilled skirt steak and shrimp scampi with side dishes of macaroni and cheese and linguine with garlic and oil. Their waiter had suggested sparkling white peach sangria as a cocktail, which had become an excellent complement for the expertly prepared dishes.

"Are you under the influence?" Giles asked Mya after she'd drained her wineglass. He noticed she did not take a sip of the wine concoction until after she'd finished the first two courses.

She smiled and the flame from the flickering votive cast flattering shadows over her delicate features and highlighted her hazel eyes with a golden glow. "Surprisingly, no. Maybe it's because I ate first." She touched the napkin to the corners of her mouth. "I see why your sister-in-law orders the mac and cheese. It's insanely delicious."

Giles wanted to tell Mya that she was insanely beautiful in red. Her palomino-gold skin reminded him of liquid gold, and his mother had chosen wisely when she gave Mya the ruby and diamond ring. As a young boy, he would watch his mother go through the jewelry she had inherited from her grandmother and meticulously select what she wanted to wear for a luncheon with her friends or a formal event with her husband. He remembered his elderly grandmother telling him that while some women in her social circle collected wealthy husbands, she preferred priceless jewels. He wondered if Mya would continue the tradition of giving the ring to their granddaughter.

Giles shook his head. He did not want to think of Lily marrying and making him a grandfather. At least not for a long time. He wanted to watch her grow up from infant to toddler, to young girl and teenager and finally a woman. He wanted to be there to cheer her successes and comfort her during disappointments. An unconscious smile crinkled the skin around his eyes. And more important, he wanted to be the role model for the man she would eventually chose as her husband and partner for life.

"What are you smiling about?" Mya questioned.

"I was just thinking about Lily making us grand-parents."

"Bite your tongue, Giles. She's still in diapers, meanwhile you have her having babies."

He sobered. "You know it's probably going to happen one of these days."

"I know, but there's still so much I want to do with her before she's a woman."

Reaching across the table, Giles held Mya's hand. "And you will." He winked at her. "Are you ready for coffee and dessert?

"I don't think so. I am stuffed. The next time we come back to New York, we have to eat here again. Tell your friend that he's a gastronomical genius."

Releasing her hand, Giles signaled the waiter for the check. "I'll definitely let Dewey know you give him an A." He settled the bill, leaving a generous gratuity, and escorted Mya out of the restaurant.

She moved closer to his side. "It's really getting cold. Wearing lace in late October without a coat isn't very bright."

He looped an arm around her waist, sharing his body's heat. "It's chilly because we're not far from the East River." Her dress reminded Giles of the song "The Lady in Red." Raising his right hand, he whistled for a passing taxi.

"I think I can make it back to your place before turning into an icicle."

Giles opened the rear door to the cab when it maneuvered up to the curb. "We're not going back to my place. I figured we'd spend the night at my parents' house. I don't want you staying there alone and I want us to be there when Mom and Dad bring Lily back. My father always gets up early and is usually on the road before sunrise."

He did not tell Mya that if they did spend the night in his condo, he did not trust himself not to try to make love to her. And more important, he did not have any condoms on hand and he didn't know if Mya was using birth control.

Mya huddled close to him in the back seat. "I called my editor and was told she's in Europe for a book fair."

Giles buried his face in her hair. "Maybe you'll get to see her when we spend the week here between Christmas and New Year's."

"I doubt that. Publishing usually goes on hiatus that week. I'll probably hook up with her sometime next spring."

Meeting her editor in person was not a priority for Mya. Having Giles live with her was. She'd told him that she wasn't raised to shack up with a man and now she was going against what she'd been taught once she invited Giles to move in with her and Lily. Living together would offer her a glimpse into the life she would share with a man who'd roared into her life like a tornado that had touched down to sweep up everything in its path. Her emotions were strewn everywhere and once the twister was gone, she was left craving his touch, his kiss and wanting to know how it would feel to have him inside her.

"Speaking of spring," Giles said after a pregnant silence, "I know I'm fast-forwarding almost two years, but do you want a spring or summer wedding?"

"I'd like a late-spring wedding. It can get quite hot and uncomfortable in the summer."

He went still, and then his head popped up as he met her eyes. "You want to get married in Wickham Falls?"

"Of course."

"Is there a venue large enough to accommodate our family and friends?"

Mya nodded. "We can hold the ceremony and reception in a hotel off the turnpike or interstate."

"Would it bother you if I hire a wedding planner?"

She gave him an incredulous look. "Of course not. Did you think I would object?"

"I don't know. You've ragged me enough about not checking with you when making decisions that affect both of us."

Mya lowered her eyes. "You would remind me of that."

"Only because I don't want you to think I'm trying to run your life. I'd like to hire Signature Brides. Even though they're based in New York, I'm certain they would like to add another Wainwright wedding to their long list of high-profile weddings. They were responsible for coordinating my cousin Jordan's wedding and now they're involved in planning Brandt's destination wedding."

"You can hire them. All I want to do is show up and enjoy our special day."

"Would you like to become a June bride?"

She smiled. "Yes."

Giles retrieved his cell phone from the breast pocket of his suit jacket and tapped the calendar icon. "Your birthday falls on a Sunday. Would you like to share your anniversary with your birthday?"

She buried her face against his neck. "Of course not. It will give me an excuse to celebrate not once, but twice."

"And I don't have an excuse that I forgot our anniversary."

Mya laughed softly. "Something tells me that you don't forget much."

"Not when it comes to you."

Mya stared through the glass of the French doors. She'd returned to Wickham Falls in time to join in the town's Halloween festivities, while counting down the days when she, Giles, and Lily would return to New York for Thanksgiving However, the weather had conspired against them.

The house would've been as quiet as a tomb if not for the tapping of frozen rain against the roof and windows. She was mesmerized by the ice coating the branches of trees and a carpet of white turning the landscape into a Christmas card winter scene.

But it was still four weeks from Christmas, and the plan to go to New York to share Thanksgiving with the Wainwrights had been cancelled because of ice and snow storms ravaging the East Coast from North Carolina to Maine. Flights were grounded and states of emergency had been declared by governors in all of the affected states.

She felt the warmth from Giles's body as he stood behind her. There were times when she marveled that he could enter a room so silently that she would look up and finding him standing there. He had moved into the house and into the master bedroom. To those who saw them together, they were a normal couple with a child, but behind closed doors, they shared everything but a bed.

His arms circled her waist as he pressed his chest to her back. "You're not writing today?"

Mya closed her eyes and rested the back of her head against his shoulder. "I don't feel like writing."

"Do you have writer's block?"

"No. I revised my schedule because I thought we were going to New York this weekend."

"I was looking forward to it, too. So it looks as if we'll have our own Thanksgiving here."

Turning in his embrace, Mya went on tiptoe and brushed a kiss over his parted lips. "I have so much to be grateful for. I never could've imagined being this contented. And you're responsible for that."

Giles affected a half smile. "Only because I love you."

"Not as much as I love you."

He eased back, staring at her as if she had spoken a foreign language. "What did you say?"

Mya knew she'd shocked him, because it was the first time she'd admitted what lay in her heart. "I love you, Giles Harrison Wainwright, and right now I want you to take me to bed so I can show you how much I love you."

Giles blinked once. "I don't have any condoms with me."

"You don't need condoms, darling. I'm on the pill."

Giles knew Mya could feel the runaway beating of his heart against her breasts. He and Mya had been living together for nearly a month, and during that time, he had been reluctant to seduce her in an attempt to get her to agree to sleep with him. He hadn't thought of himself as an overly patient man but somehow she'd proven him wrong when he decided to wait—wait as long as it would take for her to come to him of her own free will.

Bending slightly, he swept her up in his arms and, taking long, determined strides, headed for the rear of the house and the master bedroom. Giles placed her on the king-size bed and lay beside her. He threaded their fingers together. "Are you certain you're ready for this?"

"Yes."

Moving over her while sitting back on his heels, Giles's hands searched under the hem of her T-shirt, massaging the tight flesh over her ribs before moving up to cover her breasts. Her breathing deepened as he slowly and methodically undressed her, and then himself. There was enough light coming through the windows to make out her eyes. Her steady gaze bore into his as he lowered his head and kissed her mouth.

Giles wanted Mya because he found her sexy, sexier than any woman he had ever met. That he wanted her because he knew he couldn't have Lily without her. And that she unknowingly had cast a spell over him, bewitching him with her poise and beauty. She challenged as well as seduced him, and instinctively he knew he could grow old with her.

She extended her arms and he went into her embrace. Placing his hands under her thighs, he parted her knees with his and eased his erection inside her. She gasped once, and then moaned and writhed in an ancient rhythm that needed no prompting or tutoring.

The impact of their lovemaking matched and surpassed the ferocity of the ice storm lashing the countryside with its fury as Mya ascended to heights of passion she had never experienced before. She sought to possess Giles as he did the same with her. Her sighs from experiencing multiple orgasms had not faded completely when Giles reversed their positions. Burying her face against the column of his strong neck, she kissed him under his ear at the same time he growled deep in his throat and caught the tender flesh at the base of her throat between his teeth, leaving a visible imprint of his claim. She savored the lingering pulsing of his hardness inside her.

Her fist pounded the pillow beneath his head. "Why did you wait so long?"

Giles frowned up at her. "Wait for what?"

"To make love to me."

"I can't believe you'd say that," he drawled. "If you'd given me the slightest hint that you wanted me to make love to you, I would've had you on your back a long time ago."

She smiled. "I suppose that means we'll just have to make up for lost time."

Giles winked at her. "You've got that right, sweets."

Two weeks before they were scheduled to fly to New York for the Christmas week Mya felt as if her fairytale world had suddenly imploded.

The fear and uneasiness she'd managed to push to the recesses of her mind had suddenly had resurfaced. The man with whom she had fallen love, made love with every chance they got, and looked forward to sharing her daughter and their future with had deceived her.

She had just put Lily down for her nap and walked into her office only to overhear Giles on his cell. The door was slight ajar and she heard Giles talking to someone. Her step faltered when she heard him mention Lily's name. Her heart stopped, and then started up again when he said, "Her name should be listed as Lily Hope Lawson-Wainwright. Yes, Wainwright."

Mya didn't wait to hear anymore. She made her way down the staircase to the kitchen at the same time she tried to slow the runaway beating of her heart. What she'd suspected all along had become a reality. Giles had wined and dined, wooed, courted and proposed marriage because it was the only way he could claim his daughter. She glared at him when he walked into the kitchen.

"Hi, sweets. I thought you'd be upstairs writing."

"I don't feel very much like writing. Not after overhearing your conversation."

An expression of confusion settled into his handsome features. "What are you talking about?"

"Lily Hope Lawson-Wainwright," she spat out. "How dare you go behind my back and –"

"Stop it, Mya!" Giles said, interrupting her. "It's not what you think."

"It's not what I think but what I overheard."

"Why were you eavesdropping?"

Mya's temper flared. "Eavesdropping? In my own home?"

He managed to appear contrite. "Maybe I used the wrong word."

"You're damn right you did." Giles moved closer at the same time she slipped off the stool, putting more distance between them. "Don't touch me." She held up a hand. "And please don't say anything because right about now I'm ready to lose it."

A muscle twitched in Giles's jaw. "Suit yourself." Turning on his heel he walked out of the kitchen.

Mya closed her eyes, willing the tears welling up behind her lids not to fall. How could she have been so blind? The silent voice had nagged at her not to trust Giles, but unfortunately she had ignored it when time and again Giles made decisions without first consulting her. She was not his employee or soldiers under command where he issued orders and expected them to be followed without question. It had been a while since she had to remind Giles that legally he had no claim on Lily, and it was apparent that he had forgotten that fact.

Chapter Thirteen

"I can't believe we had to wait until New Year's Eve to meet you for the first time."

Mya smiled at Giles's cousin's wife. She never would've guess that Aziza Fleming-Wainwright was the mother of a three-month-old. A black off-the-shoulder gown clung to the curves of her tall, slender body. "I don't know, but every time Giles and I plan to come to New York it's as if the weather conspires against us. First, an ice storm for Thanksgiving and then a blizzard with nearly two feet of snow for Christmas."

Temperatures in the northeast had gone from below freezing to mid-fifties and within days mounds of snow had begun to melt.

What she did not say was her relationship with Giles had gone from frosty to icy. They had become polite strangers living under the same roof, while Lily continued to thrive. She was walking, holding on to objects to keep her balance and had begun calling Giles 'Da-da.'

When Mya arrived earlier that afternoon she'd found the suites in the four-story, gray-stone mansion spanning a half block on Fifth Avenue filled with several generations of Wainwrights, and she hadn't seen Lily once Amanda discovered her granddaughter was in the nursery with the other young children.

There was a soft knock on the door before it opened and a young woman wearing a black backless gown with a full skirt swept into the room. Her chemically straightened hair was styled in a loose, curling ponytail. Mya knew without introductions that she was Ciara Dennison, Brandt's fiancée. During their first visit to New York Giles had pulled up several family photographs on his computer and given her an overview of each person. Mya had teased him about the two, very pretty African-American women definitely adding a bit of color to the overwhelming number of Wainwright blonds.

The diamond ring on Ciara's left hand caught the light when she held out her arms to Mya. "All of the guys were whispering about how beautiful you are, and I just had to come and see if they were blowing smoke," she said with a wide grin. "Girlfriend, you are stun-ning!" She drew out the word in two distinct syllables. "I'm Ciara."

Mya pressed her cheek to Ciara's. "And I'm Mya."

Aziza rested her hands at her waist. "I'm certain when people hear your names, they probably think of the two female singers."

Mya laughed. "I'd starve to death if I had to sing for a living."

Ciara patted her hair. "I'd probably do a little better than you because I can carry a tune."

Her clear brown eyes sparkled like newly minted pennies. "It looks as if we sister-girls are batting a thousand when it comes to scooping up these fine-ass Wainwright men."

"I second that," Aziza drawled.

Mya had to agree with the attorney and psychiatric nurse. Even if their men weren't Wainwrights, Jordan, Brandt and Giles were the heroes women fantasized about when reading romance novels. "Excuse me, but I have to see Giles about something." Lifting the skirt of her chocolate-brown strapless gown, she walked out of the suite.

Turning on her heel, she made her way down the wide carpeted hallway to the curving staircase leading to the great hall. The mansion was decorated for the season: live pine boughs lined the fireplace mantel as a fire blazed behind a decorative screen. Lighted electric candles were in every window, and the gaily decorated, twelve-foot Norwegian spruce towered under the brightly lit chandelier suspended from a twenty-foot ceiling. Many of the more fragile glass ornaments on the tree were purported to be at least two hundred years old.

The ball was in full swing with formally dressed men and women eating and drinking, and many couples were dancing to a live band. Someone tapped her shoulder, and she turned to find a young man with brilliant green eyes in a deeply tanned face smiling at her. "May I have this dance?"

Mya returned his smile. "Of course."

"Who are you here with, beautiful?" he whispered in her ear as he spun her around the marble floor.

"Giles Wainwright."

"It's just my luck you would be connected to the folks hosting this shindig."

The song ended and Mya barely had time to catch her breath when she found herself dancing with another man. This one held her too tight as he couldn't pull his eyes away from her chest. When she pleaded thirst, he led her to the bar and waited until she asked the bartender for a club soda with a twist of lime.

"How about another dance?"

"Dude, how about finding another woman to dance with." Mya turned to find Giles glaring at the man. "Move along," he added when her dance partner hesitated and then walked away.

"What's the matter with you?" Mya asked between clenched teeth. "Have you gone and lost your mind?"

The coldness in Giles's eyes reminded her of chipped ice. "You have the audacity to ask me what's wrong when I'm forced to watch you disrespect me when you flirt with every man salivating over your chest."

"Disrespect! You have a nerve to talk to me about—"

Giles's fingers curled around her upper arm. "Come with me. We don't need to air our problems in front of everyone."

"Problems? I don't have a problem. You're the one with the problem," she said as they wove their way through the throng and out of the ballroom. Mya followed Giles to an area near the elevator. She was too angry to acknowledge he looked magnificent in formalwear.

Holding onto her shoulders, Giles gave her a death-stare. "What the hell was that back there?"

"Nothing!" she spat out. "A couple of men asked me to dance and I saw nothing wrong with dancing with them. Now if you're going to go off every time I talk to a man, then I don't think we should be together."

"What do you mean that I'm the one with the problem?"

"You have a problem being truthful, and I'm angry with myself because I allowed you to lure me into a trap where you can get legal custody of Lily and change her name by marrying me."

"If you hadn't shut me out I would've told you about my conversation with my cousin. I was talking to Jordan about setting up a trust fund for our daughter."

Mya blinked as if coming out of a trance. "She doesn't need a trust fund because I've set aside monies for her future."

"Why is it always what you want for Lily, Mya? Can't you just this once include me in the equation. Lily's not only your daughter but *our* daughter. I know I can get ahead of myself when it comes to planning her future, but from now on I again promise to talk to you first before making *any* decision about her."

Mya smile mirrored relief. Giles wasn't planning to change Lily's name. "And I'll be certain to remind you of that in case you forget."

"You can do anything you want to me, but promise me you won't shut me out again."

"I'll think about it."

"While you're thinking about it I need to do this." Giles lowered his head and brushed a light kiss over her mouth.

She bit down on her lip as she fought back tears. "I'm sorry, babe, for not trusting you." She took a step and curved her arms around his inside his tuxedo jacket. "Can you forgive me?"

Giles cradled her chin, his eyes making love to her. "Of course I forgive you. But can you forgive me for going Neanderthal on you?"

"Yes. Now kiss me again before we go back."

Giles needed no further urging when he lifted Mya off her feet and kissed her with all the passion he could summon for the woman who'd stolen his heart. "What do you say we go upstairs and have a quickie before everyone rings in the New Year?"

Mya shook her head. "Don't you ever get enough?"

Throwing back his head, Giles laughed loudly. Before their heated confrontation, they had made love nearly every night. "As long as I can get it up, I'll never get enough."

Mya looped her arms through his. "Let's go back before folks come looking for us." Midnight would signal a new year where she could look forward to marrying a man who had promised to love and protect her and their daughter all the days of their lives.

Eighteen months had sped by quickly and Mya would celebrate not only her birthday but also her wedding day. She'd chosen Giles's sister Skye to be her maid of honor and Aziza and an obviously pregnant Ciara as her attendants. Giles had selected Jordan as his best man and Brandt and his brother Patrick as his groomsmen.

Mya had asked her future father-in-law to give her away and he appeared visibly overcome with emotion when he nodded mutely. The weather had cooperated. Bright sunshine and afternoon temperatures were perfect for a garden wedding.

She touched the diamond necklace Giles had given her for a wedding present following the rehearsal dinner.

The owners of Signature Brides had arrived two days ago to make certain the tent was scheduled to be up for the ceremony and coordinate with the hotel's banquet manager for the reception. There had been a steady stream of Wainwrights checking into the hotel over the past three days. Some of the men were talking about returning in the fall to go hunting. A few of her colleagues from college were also in attendance.

She adjusted the flowing skirt of her gown with white lace appliqued flowers and a trailing train. A pale pink belt with silk roses matched the underslip. In lieu of a veil, she had selected to wear pink and white rosebuds in the chignon on the nape of her neck.

The string quartet played a Mozart concerto as Skye, Aziza and Ciara processed down the white carpet with their partners. The entire assembly under the tent rose to their feet with the familiar strains of the "Wedding March."

Mya and Pat shared a smile before she turned her attention to the man waiting to make her his wife. She was smiling from ear to ear when he winked at her. She counted the steps that would take her to his side. He reached for her hand even before the judge asked, "Who gives this woman in marriage?"

"I do," Patrick announced loudly, as a ripple of laughter came from those under the tent.

Mya did not remember repeating her vows or when

Giles placed a wedding band on her finger. However, she did recall his long and passionate kiss when the judge told him he could kiss his wife.

When they turned to face those who'd come to witness their nuptials, Mya smiled at Lily who squirmed to escape Amanda's hold. "Daddy!" she screamed, extending her arms for Giles to take her.

Not only was she walking but she was also talking. A photographer and videographer captured the image of Giles holding his daughter while he curved an arm around his wife's waist. He had given Mya the necklace for a wedding gift, while she'd handed him a gaily wrapped box with a copy of Lily's birth certificate with a note that it was time to amend the certificate so their daughter could legally become Lily Hope Wainwright.

When Giles had walked into the lawyer's office what now seemed eons ago, he never knew how his life would change. It was better than he could have ever imagined. He'd claimed his baby and a woman whose love promised forever.

* * * * *

MILLS & BOON®

A sneak peek at next month's titles...

In stores from 11th January 2018:

- **The Spanish Millionaire's Runaway Bride** – Susan Meier *and* **No Ordinary Fortune** – Judy Duarte
- **Stranded with Her Greek Tycoon** – Kandy Shepherd *and* **An Engagement for Two** – Marie Ferrarella

In stores from 25th January 2018:

- **Reunited with Her Italian Billionaire** – Nina Singh *and* **A Bride for Liam Brand** – Joanna Sims
- **Falling for His Convenient Queen** – Therese Beharrie *and* **A Soldier in Conard County** – Rachel Lee

MILLS & BOON®

Coming next month

THE SPANISH MILLIONAIRE'S
RUNAWAY BRIDE
Susan Meier

She laughed again. "I can't even figure out how to explain running from my wedding. It's not as if I was such a great prize myself."

"You are a great prize." The words came out soft and filled with regret that her dad had skewed the way she saw herself.

She stopped at her door, but she didn't use her key card to open it. She glanced at Riccardo, her pale pink face illuminated by the light beside her door. "I'm a twenty-five-year-old woman who doesn't know who she is."

"You have to know you're beautiful."

She caught his gaze. Her long black lashes blinked over sad blue eyes. "Physical things fade."

"You're pretty in here," he countered, touching her chest just above the soft swell of her breasts. "When you're sixty, eighty, a hundred, you'll still be compassionate."

She shook her head. "You don't know that. We just met. Aside from the fact that I ran from my wedding and my dad's a bit of a control freak, you don't know much of anything about me."

Silence hung between them as they stared into each other's eyes. The warmth in her big blue orbs touched his heart, but the lift of her lips sparked a small fire in his belly. Everything male inside him awoke. The urge to kiss her tumbled through him.

He should have turned, walked the few steps to his own room and gone inside. Gotten away from her. Instead, he stayed right where he was.

Continue reading
**THE SPANISH MILLIONARE'S
RUNAWAY BRIDE**
Susan Meier

Available next month
www.millsandboon.co.uk

LET'S TALK
Romance

For exclusive extracts, competitions
and special offers, find us online: